Evans Bell

Memoir of General John Briggs

Evans Bell

Memoir of General John Briggs

ISBN/EAN: 9783337400484

Printed in Europe, USA, Canada, Australia, Japan

Cover: Foto ©Raphael Reischuk / pixelio.de

More available books at **www.hansebooks.com**

MEMOIR

OF

GENERAL JOHN BRIGGS,

OF THE MADRAS ARMY;

WITH COMMENTS ON

SOME OF HIS WORDS AND WORK.

BY

MAJOR EVANS BELL,

AUTHOR OF "RETROSPECTS AND PROSPECTS OF INDIAN POLICY", "THE OXUS AND THE INDUS",
ETC.

LONDON:
CHATTO AND WINDUS, PICCADILLY.

1885.

PREFACE.

My grateful acknowledgments are due to Mrs. De Morgan for the letters from General Briggs to her late distinguished husband, and to the Right Honble. M. E. Grant Duff, for his sanction to my publishing his father's letters. To all the surviving members of General Briggs's family I owe some words of regret and apology for the long delay that has attended the publication of this work, arising chiefly, I must explain,—while I am not free from self-reproach,—to the embarrassment of an over-supply of materials. The autobiographical papers alone, if printed as they stood, would have made at least six volumes such as this is. Whatever force and value there may be in Chapter VII, which expresses my firm convictions, and for which I am fully responsible, must be attributed to my friend Colonel R. D. Osborn, who has made the condition of the Indian peasantry, as affected by British administration of the Land Revenue, a special study. To him my warmest thanks are due for allowing me to present that Chapter almost entirely in his own words.

CONTENTS.

CHAPTER IX.
1831–1832.

CHAPTER X.
1832.

CHAPTER XI.
1832.

CHAPTER XII.

SOME WORDS AND WORK

OF

GENERAL JOHN BRIGGS.

CHAPTER I.

JOHN BRIGGS entered the 15th Madras Native Infantry as Lieutenant on the 10th of July 1801, before he had attained the age of sixteen, and died in his ninetieth year on the 27th of April 1875. During the first eighteen years of the century he saw some active service, and subsequently won distinction in several important administrative and political offices under the Government of India. It cannot, however, be said that his name has ever filled a large space, or figured very conspicuously in the annals of the Indian Empire. He left India, never to return, in 1835. During the last thirty-nine years of his life he had no official employment. His professional career was not, as we shall see, uniformly serene and unruffled, and if anyone should please to pronounce it to have been a failure, he will not, from one point of view, be altogether in the wrong. Notwithstanding his services, both in the military and civil departments, General Briggs, by a series of fatalities, public and personal, never became entitled to append any distinctive letters to his name, except those of F.R.S. He had no decoration but the war medal. Previously to 1838, when he attained the rank of Major-General, and when his succession to the "off-reckonings" had led to his permanent residence at home, the honours of the Bath were rarely accorded to officers of the Company's Service. The Star of India had not yet risen. That "light" of the official "Heaven" had not yet come to be "our guide". Although the

B

activity of his mind, and the strong interest he took in
public affairs, and in literary matters connected with the
East, were continuously proved, even up to the last year
of his life, by numerous published writings, and by the
prominent part he took in many political movements, the
General's later labours were given rather to national
and Imperial objects, than to such as might have been
directly conducive to the purposes of men in power, to
what are called the interests of "the Services", or to his
own immediate profit. Far from conciliating the President of the Board of Control or the Directors of the East
India Company, when he had settled himself in England,
he was for several years a leader of ineffectual opposition
in the Court of Proprietors. He was not, in short, remarkably successful, in the self-regarding sense, either as a
public functionary, or as the founder of a private fortune
and a brilliant reputation.

And yet he was undoubtedly a man of a more original
and rare type than most of his fellows whose merits have
been told to the world by outward marks of distinction.
That very political foresight which makes his acts and
testimony more worthy of recollection, will account in a
great measure for the extreme confidence in his own
views, and impatience of being impeded, which led to an
occasional want of harmony with his colleagues and
official superiors. He had all the defects of his qualities,
and suffered loss accordingly. An able administrator and
thorough man of business, he was not so enamoured of
his mystery, not so proud of his practical achievements,
as to be blind to the inherent limitations and drawbacks
of British rule in India. Largely endowed with tolerance and sympathy for the alien tribes over whom he
was placed in a position of command, he acquired an
insight into their opinions, feelings and temper, that gave
a prophetic strain to some of his utterances. But a
prophet hath not honour among his own people ; and those
who occupy the highest seats in the administration of
India naturally prefer hearing of its "unspeakable bless-
ings" to being reminded of its drawbacks and limitations.
A very natural conviction of his own invaluable qualifi-.

cations—similar to that of the traditional cobbler that "there is nothing like leather"—possesses almost every member of almost every profession. One of the craft, who is known to be free from this conviction, is very likely to considered in the light of a traitor in the camp, and to be regarded with scanty favour. And this, I believe, with but little deduction to be made for avoidable faults and errors, is the true explanation of General Briggs's want of material success ; of his having failed to secure a full appreciation and recognition of his merits by the public authorities of his time. In the race of life and action he was not left behind by better men,—it was rather that he saw the goal too clearly from the starting point, went too straight at it, and ran too far ahead, got, perhaps, on the wrong side of the post, was jostled by his competitors, and lost the prize for want of a moment's guidance, not from want of endurance or speed.

For what he was, and for what he did, for what he saw and for what he foresaw, the work and the words of General John Briggs deserve to be remembered. He stood between the old and the new schools of Indian statesmanship. His labours extended over three great periods of British rule in India,—that in which supreme power was attained ; that in which supremacy was asserted and enforced ; and the more critical period, still in progress, in which we are striving to find a basis of permanent policy on which the Imperial structure may safely rest. During the first period he took his part in conquest, diplomacy and settlement. In the second, he controlled and organised a Kingdom, and placed on record those political doctrines, not yet officially accepted, by which alone British domination can be reconciled with Indian self-respect and local self-government. Briggs did thoroughly well a description of work that has, perhaps, never been done so well since, that will certainly never again be done so well. He never overdid it,—he never overrated it. In the third period he consistently maintained the principles by which his official career had been animated, against the advocates, for a time irresistible, of the annexation policy ; he predicted the widely spread disaffection, especially among the Native troops, that was to arise from that policy; he lived to see his predictions disastrously fulfilled, and the policy he had denounced abandoned and disowned.

If the plan of constituting an Indian Empire on the principles of tutelary federation and reform, which he saw more clearly and propounded more distinctly than any one of his contemporaries, should become, through these pages, better known, more generally accepted and associated as it ought to be with my venerable friend's name, my object will have been fully attained.

Within his life-time and recollection five generations of General Briggs's family had occupied places in the Indian Army and Civil Service,—his father, himself and his brothers, his nephews, his grandchildren and his great-grandchildren. By the time that the patronage of Leadenhall Street, heavily stricken in 1853 by open competition replacing Haileybury nominations to the Civil Service, ended in 1858 with the political extinction of the East India Company, the descendants and collateral relatives of General Briggs—the Lysaghts, the Ludlows, the Wilberforce Birds, the Watkins, Nicolays and Humes—had become one of those wide-spreading Anglo-Indian trees, which, with their roots in the Court of Directors and their topmost branches in the Supreme Council, flourished and fructified both in the East and at home.

John Briggs came of a sturdy stock. In the days when his great-uncle Stephen, and his grandfather Gilbert, left Scotland and came South with the scanty proceeds of a small estate, opportunely yet hastily sold, young men whose father had, like theirs, "disappeared" soon after the battle of Culloden, might have good reason to find the air of their native district decidedly unwholesome. In those days there was no halo of romance—not, at least, in the eyes of the Whig majority—around the name and personality of the Young Pretender. Many years elapsed before it became safe to speak of " the '45 ", except in an undertone, and in well-selected company. More years passed before the genius of Burns and Sir Walter Scott removed the stains of supposed coarseness and savagery from Scottish annals, and rendered the admiration of Highland character and Highland scenery permissible among people of good taste, and even in good society. There was, however, little temptation to speak of " the '45"; little or no controversy between Jacobite and Hanoverian, at Southampton, where the brothers settled, and where Stephen Briggs very soon acquired a considerable income and great repute as a medical practitioner.

Both brothers married early in life, and Gilbert died young, leaving three children, James (father of General John Briggs), Stephen and Elizabeth, scantily provided for, who were adopted and brought up by their uncle Stephen,who was prospering in his profession,and occupied a handsome house in the Polygon. Elizabeth was married in 1772 to Edmund Ludlow, a person of some consideration in the town of Southampton, though, according to the family tradition, distinguished for nothing but his skill as an amateur violin-player. By his wife, who died in 1803, he had two sons, Edmund and John. The former of these had six sons, four of whom entered the Indian Army. One of them, John, who died with the rank of Major-General, at a very advanced age, on the 30th of November 1882, ought to be remembered with honour for having caused, by a persuasive method that induced conviction and willing acquiescence, the prohibition of widow-burning in its last stronghold among the Princes of Rajpootana.*

John, the second son of the elder Edmund Ludlow, also served in the Bengal Army; was in the expedition to Egypt, under Sir David Baird, in 1801 ; distinguished himself in the war with Nepaul; was made a C.B., and died in 1822, Colonel and Brigadier in command at Meerut, from the consequences of exposure and fatigue, during the campaigns of 1818 and 1819 against the Pindarries. His son, John Malcolm Ludlow,—now Chief

* *Widow Burning*, by H. J. Bushby (Longmans), 1855.

Registrar of Friendly Societies, and well known for the interest and active part he has taken in the co-operative movement,—has made contributions to Indian history and politics that deserve the attention of all who wish to appreciate those matters in their ethical and legal aspects,* and will throw much light on the past, when the ultimate and retrospective survey of our Indian Empire comes to be taken by future historians.

The wife of Uncle Stephen Briggs was a Miss Pasley, by whom he had three children,—Thomas, afterwards Admiral Sir Thomas Briggs, K.C.B.; Mrs. Blackburn, wife of Chief-Justice Blackburn, of the Court of King's Bench in Ireland ; and Mrs. Venour.

Margaret Pasley, younger sister of Mrs. Stephen Briggs, married George Malcolm, of Burnfoot, Dumfriesshire. One of their sons became Admiral Sir Pulteney Malcolm, and another was General Sir John Malcolm, distinguished as an Indian soldier and administrator, as an Oriental diplomatist, and as a writer on Eastern history and Indian politics. From October 1827 to December 1830 he was Governor of Bombay, and died in 1833. Thus Admiral Sir Thomas Briggs, first-cousin of General John Briggs, stood in the same relationship to Sir John Malcolm. It will be seen further on that Briggs and Sir John Malcolm were thrown very much together in public duties ; and although there was only a connection by marriage, and not even by affinity between them, Briggs was always called "cousin" by Sir John Malcolm, and treated by him with constant and cordial affection.

The elder Stephen Briggs, great-uncle of the General, brought up his nephew James, the General's father, to his own profession, and got him an appointment in the medical service of the Madras Presidency, where he rose to the rank of Physician-General.

Dr. James Briggs was twice married, first in 1784 to Martha, daughter of Mr. John Bryan Pybus, of the Madras Civil Service, and widow of Major Arthur Lysaght,

---

* *British India, its Races and its History* (Macmillan and Co., 1858) ; *The War in Oude;* and *Thoughts on the Policy of the Crown towards India* (Ridgway, 1859).

brother of the first Lord Lisle. Admiral Arthur Lysaght,
—born 1782, died 1859—was half-brother to General
John Briggs.

By his first wife Dr. James Briggs had two sons, of
whom the General was the elder, born on the 18th of
September 1785. His younger brother, Stephen, born
in 1787, entered the Navy in 1799, saw much service in
the West Indies; and in 1821 fitted out a corvette, and
helped his old companion-in-arms, Lord Cochrane,—afterwards Earl of Dundonald,—in the Chilian war of liber-
ation. On his marriage with Louisa, daughter of Admiral
Hamilton, who is said to have "brought him some
property near Shrewsbury", he settled there, and died a
Post-Captain, leaving one daughter, who married her
second-cousin, Mr. Venour, a barrister, by whom she had
several children.

Mr. John Bryan Pybus, the General's maternal grandfather, was in the Madras Civil Service, and retired
about 1786, after having been a Member of Council. He
had three daughters,—the eldest, Martha, was the wife
of Dr. James Briggs; the second, Anne, of General Sir
Robert Fletcher; and the youngest, Catherine Amelia,
born after her father's return to England, was married in
1800 to the Rev. Sydney Smith, afterwards Canon of
St. Paul's, renowned as a wit, and as one of the first
Edinburgh Reviewers. Their daughter, Saba, wife of
Sir Henry Holland, Bart., the eminent physician, was
thus first-cousin to General Briggs.

On his return to England, Mr. John Bryan Pybus
founded a bank in Bond Street, in partnership with Sir
John Call, Bart., which subsequently became the house
of Martin Call & Co., and is now represented by the firm
of Martin & Co., in Lombard Street.

Besides his three daughters, Mr. Pybus had two sons,
both of whom were educated at Harrow, and subsequently
performed what was then styled "the grand tour",
visiting the principal capital cities of Europe. John, the
elder, became a partner in the bank. The younger,
Charles Small Pybus, was M.P. for Dover for many years.
He was made a Lord of the Admiralty by William Pitt

in 1791, and a Lord of the Treasury in 1797, but lost his seat at the general election of 1802, and died in 1803.

" By his second wife, Miss Honor Dodson", says General Briggs, in some autobiographical papers from which I shall occasionally quote, "my father had two daughters and nine sons, of whom both the daughters and one son died in childhood. His remaining eight sons all entered the public service in India, and five of them have died in that country."

" After the loss of his first wife, my father came on furlough to England with his two sons in 1789. We embarked at Madras in the ship *General Goddard*, which was wrecked off the Needles, Isle of Wight, but the passengers and crew were saved. I was only four years of age, and have, of course, a very faint recollection of what happened.

" My father remained in England till the month of May 1794, when he returned to India in the same ship as the new Governor of Madras, Lord Hobart, afterwards Earl of Buckinghamshire, in whose family he resided till he obtained the appointment of Physician-General to the expedition, under Major-General James Stewart, for the capture of the island of Ceylon from the Dutch. There my father became acquainted with Miss Honor Dodson, who became his second wife. During his former residence in England I and my brother Stephen were placed at the school kept by Dr. Winter in Ormond Street, preparatory for some of the large public seminaries. We were left under the guardianship of our uncle, John Pybus, and I was shortly after placed as an Oppidan at Eton, while Stephen was sent to the school at Salt Hill, kept by Dr. Caleb Cotton.

" I was then only nine years old, but on examination I was placed in the fourth form, and before I left, in 1799, when nearly fourteen, I was in the upper remove of the fifth. I am sorry to say that I benefited little by my public school education. Perhaps it was my own fault. I know I was very often flogged.

" My father returned home once more on leave in 1799, with his second wife and an infant son. He had been obliged to leave India on account of having burst a blood-vessel in the lungs, and he went, almost immediately after his arrival, to Clifton, where he placed himself under the care of the celebrated Dr. Beddoes.

" I am afraid I must confess that, both in the case of my brother and myself, there was the ancient and proverbial want of sympathy and affection between us and our step-mother, of whom, I must moreover explain, we saw very little. In the spring of 1799 we were removed from Eton, and Stephen was sent to a

Naval Academy, and at the end of the year was shipped on board a frigate.

"I obtained my appointment as Cadet for the Madras establishment in the latter end of 1800, and in order to brush up my French, my father placed me in London in a French boarding-house, where little else was spoken. I was always, however, a welcome guest at the house of my uncle, John Pybus, till it was time for me to embark for India. My passage was taken on board the *Charlton*, the same ship on which the Commander-in-Chief, General James Stewart, was to embark, and the time was fixed for our departure in the last week of January 1801. My father accompanied me to Portsmouth, where he introduced me to his friend the Commander-in-Chief, under whom he had served in the capture of Ceylon, and to the Captain of the ship.

"We were to have sailed in a few days, but strong westerly winds set in so persistently that, tired of the delay, my father left me to the care of Captain Cumberlege, of our ship the *Charlton*. The Portsmouth roads were now full of shipping, and here we were detained for two months. My father had provided for my being boarded in the ship while in harbour, and I received his instructions, as well as the Captain's, never to sleep ashore. I now found myself fairly launched on the stream of life as my own master at the early age of fifteen, with all the world before me through which I was to make my way. My moral habits and principles had been acquired amid the several branches of my mother's family, with whom I and my brother Stephen regularly spent our holidays, where we had examples of the strictest integrity, and where any loose sentiment inadvertently expressed was sure to meet with instant reproof.

"The tedium of a ship at anchor soon became very wearisome. There were several Cadets on board considerably senior to me, two of whom had already been to India as midshipmen, but had now changed their profession. It was natural that I should court their acquaintance, and look up to them as companions of great knowledge and experience. Having been supplied by my father with a few pounds in case the ship should be detained at any part on the voyage, I was enabled to accompany some of my fellow-passengers ashore occasionally, but I always returned aboard to sleep. I was, however, tempted to become one of a party to visit Gosport, where I had become acquainted with a friend of my father's. We were to dine together, and afterwards go to the play. I soon suffered from the evil consequences of disregarding my father's injunctions not to sleep out of the ship. Absence for the whole night necessarily formed part of our scheme. At dinner I had been induced to drink more wine than I was used to, and further potations were pressed upon me later in

the evening. I saw nothing of the play. I became so unfit to
take care of myself that, after leaving the ferry-boat from Gosport
to Portsmouth, on our return from the theatre, I lost all sense and
recollection, until at noon next day I found myself in a comfortable
bed in a strange place. On ringing the bell a respectable lady
entered, and asked me how I felt, and what I required. With
shame I confessed I did not know where I was, but she soon
informed me that I had been brought into the Blue Posts Inn, by
some other gentlemen, in a state of insensibility and put to bed.
Although suffering much with a racking headache, I arose at once,
bathed my head with cold water, and proceeded to dress. It was
now I discovered that the little money I had in my pocket, and a
gold watch, formerly belonging to my mother, were missing. I
rang again and mentioned the circumstance to the chamber-maid,
who said, to my great relief, that both money and watch were
quite safe in the hands of the landlady. They were honestly
restored to me, and after paying my bill, and something more than
was charged for my entertainment, I returned to the ship, which I
did not quit again till I landed in India. This little incident had
the effect of cautioning me against excess at table, and rendered
me through life habitually sober.

" The wind proved fair on the 1st April, and on that day the
fleet of merchantmen for all parts, amounting to more than one
hundred sail, left Spithead under convoy of the Channel fleet,
which saw us safe out of the narrow seas, when each vessel left
for its destination. In a few days our East India fleet was going
well together, consisting of twenty or thirty fine vessels, under
convoy of two line-of-battle ships and a frigate, which escorted us
as far as the Canary Islands.

" Our Captain, Cumberlege, was not only an accomplished gentleman, but an experienced seaman and skilful navigator, as was
subsequently proved. From the Commander-in-Chief I experienced
great kindness. He introduced me to his secretary, Captain
Campbell, and made me over to his special care, advice, and protection. This gallant officer was subsequently killed at the head
of his regiment on the capture of the Mauritius in 1812. We had
a favourable and pleasant passage, without any dissensions among
us, although there were about thirty young men for the Civil
Service and the Army on board. As was the custom in those days,
there was a great deal of drinking, but my first lesson against
intemperance was not thrown away upon me. I was destined,
however, to receive another on the habit of smoking. I shared a
cabin with a brother Cadet, who had occasional smoking parties
there, which to me were very disagreeable. I endeavoured to
overcome this feeling, and to appear sociable by taking a pipe
myself. Of course, my chum and his friends encouraged me, and

I was led on from one to two or more pipes; but I suffered so much that night and during the following three days, that I never gave in to the habit again through life.

"I have already alluded to the Captain of our vessel, who, as I have stated, was a skilful navigator, as the following instances proved. When we reached the latitude of Ceylon, at the entrance to the Bay of Bengal, on the 16th of July, we had seen no land from the day of our departure on the 1st of April. The ships for Bombay had parted from us some time before, while those for Madras and Calcutta kept together. The Senior Captain, or Commodore, was bound for the latter port, but had never touched at Madras. Owing to the length of time which had elapsed since we left England, he was unwilling to trust to the correctness of his longitude, and accordingly, as he approached the Coromandel shore, he made a signal for the fleet to heave-to during the night. Our Captain, who was familiar with the coast, and who had more confidence in his reckoning than the Commodore, made signal to speak to him. The two reckonings did not quite agree, but our Captain of the *Charlton* offered to lead the fleet during the night, and stated confidently that he should strike soundings off the east coast of Ceylon about midnight at one hundred fathoms. As the conversation was carried on through a trumpet, we all heard what passed. The *Charlton*, according to permission, went ahead, and sure enough, as the bell struck at midnight, the lead was hove, and ground was reached at a little beyond a hundred fathoms. The announcement was made by signal to the whole fleet astern, and was received with three cheers from the passengers, who were then assured by the experienced Captain that, if the same wind lasted six-and-thirty hours, we should see the Madras flag-staff at daylight on the 20th July. This also came true, and seemed to us, as I believe it was, a splendid example of nautical skill. I had plenty of leisure on board to read and improve myself, but I turned my attention principally to understanding the duties of the ship. I learned the name and special use of every sail, rope, and spar. I studied the mode by which the ship was navigated, the particular effects produced by the rudder, and the object of each trimming of the sails; and I took advantage of the knowledge of one of the Cadets, who had been twice to India as a midshipman with our Captain, and who assisted him in the daily settlement of the latitude and longitude, to learn how to take observations, so that whenever I had an opportunity on subsequent voyages—and they were many—I kept up my nautical knowledge and practice, especially the use of the sextant, which was most useful to me afterwards in several surveys on land that I was enabled thereby to undertake. Our approach to Madras had been announced ten days previously by the arrival of one of the ships of our large fleet, a very fast sailer, which had parted company off the island of Mauritius, and as the date of each Cadet's commission was regulated by his arrival in India, the Government resolved that the whole number of 170 of the season of 1800 for Madras should bear their commissions from the 10th July 1801.

" I was most affectionately received by the brother-in-law of my father's second wife, and, as soon as practicable, obeyed orders to proceed with others to join the Cadet Company at Chingleput, about thirty-six miles from the Presidency town.

" The Commandant of the Cadet Company, though only a Captain, was an old and distinguished officer, selected to superintend that establishment on account of the admirable qualities he possessed of firmness, kindness, generosity, discretion of character, and good sense. In fact, he was one out of a thousand, who united these qualifications for his situation. He was assisted by two or three junior officers and a number of steady sergeants. There were at this time altogether about two hundred Cadets at Chingleput, all quartered within the fort, and employed, as soon as they were fit to perform them, in all the duties of the garrison. The guards were mounted on the parade ground daily, after the ordinary drill. The Cadets were provided with military clothing and accoutrements on their arrival. The Commandant and officers attended at the mess dinner, the expense of which was deducted from the pay to which the Cadets were entitled. After the arrival of all the Cadets of the season they were appointed to regiments, their standing in which was regulated according to the seniority of the East India Directors who had nominated them. The Cadet Company was told off in squads, to each of which was attached a Sergeant-Instructor, but the officers and the Commandant entered into all details, and an Orderly hour was appointed for receiving daily the reports of officers and authorised applications from the Cadets. Besides mere military instructions, every Cadet was required to receive at his quarters, for a specific time, a Moonshee, or Native instructor in the Hindustani language ; and no Cadet was allowed to leave the establishment without having acquired some knowledge of the colloquial dialect. It may well be supposed that the duties of these learned men among a number of high-spirited youngsters were not always agreeable ; but as they were well paid, they were induced to submit to a good deal of horse-play and practical joking. One of these Moonshees, who conscientiously refused to quit a Cadet's quarters during the hour assigned for a lesson, was driven out of the house by a mischievous trick that might have cost him his life. The young Cadet, finding he could not prevail on the tutor to quit his cane-bottomed chair, quietly emptied a powder-flask under it, carrying a train thence to the door. He then lighted the train. The unfortunate Moonshee was dreadfully scorched; his clothes which, as usual, were of light muslin, and loose, were set on fire; and though, fortunately, he escaped with his life, he was for some time under the surgeon's hands. It may be imagined that this frolic did not pass unpunished. The Cadet was kept for some days in the guard, prevented from holding conversation with his comrades, or of messing with them, and subsequently kept on duty on alternate days for some time, and was also sentenced to pay a fine out of his pay as some compensation to his Native instructor. The culprit afterwards turned out a steady, gentlemanly officer, and passed through a long military career with credit.

"The Commandant's mode of breaking the Cadets from being late on parade was one not unusually practised in well-disciplined regiments. He himself seldom appeared on parade for four or five minutes after the time announced in orders, but he inculcated on all the Cadets as a rule to be a few minutes before the hour. 'This rule', he said, 'should be observed on all occasions of ordinary duties,—Seniors a few minutes after time, and juniors a few minutes before time.' When, however, a Cadet came after time, he was required, before falling into his place, to come up to the senior officer on parade and report his arrival. On such occasions the Commandant directed him to stand where he was, and exhibited him as a lingerer to the whole Cadet Company during exercise. If this occurred more than once, when the guards were paraded with all the requisite ceremony, the defaulter was attached to one of them and performed an extra tour of duty for this second instance of negligence, which seldom occurred again. Our dear Commandant felt it his duty to study the character of every young man in the Cadet Company, and he noted down every incident which brought it out. He was well acquainted with my father, and took an interest in me from the date of my arrival. He quartered me with a son of the General Officer commanding the division, a Westminster boy of my own age, between whom and myself arose an intimate friendship. We paid a Sergeant for extra drill at our own quarters, and devoted as much time as we could spare to our Native instructor of languages; and as we had both been born in India, and had spoken the Hindustani tongue as children, we very soon fell into the correct pronunciation, and were favourably reported on. My chum's father paid an official visit to the Cadet Company on his inspection tour of the division. Advantage was taken of this occasion to promote some of the old and new Cadets to the non-commissioned ranks, and among others my chum was raised to the grade of Corporal, while I remained in the ranks. This made no difference in our friendship. It gave rise to no jealousy on my part, as I looked on the circumstance as a natural compliment to my friend's father; nor did my chum assume any superiority on his accession to this dignity.

"An occurrence took place shortly after which brought me to the special notice of the Commandant. One night, while I was sentry over the front of his house, one of those fearful tropical storms of thunder, lightning, and heavy rain occurred. I might have taken shelter under the open verandah, but my ignorance of military practice and a strict sense of duty induced me to continue walking up and down on the gravel-walk in front, where I had been posted to protect the house. The slamming of the Venetian shutters and open doors attracted the Commandant's attention, and he got out of bed to shut them. During this operation he caught sight of his sentry walking up and down, in the midst of the storm, in front of the house, and by means of the vivid flashes of lightning he discovered who it was. He said nothing, but left me to my fate. On the following morning I received a message, through his Orderly, to request my attendance at breakfast after relief of guards. I was received with kindness; and during the breakfast, which was usually well attended, he asked me if I was on duty over his house the previous night during the storm. I replied in the affirmative. He said, 'Why did not you take shelter in the verandah?' I replied that I was posted in front of the house to take care of it, and I thought it my duty to remain there, in spite of the storm, till I was relieved. He said, with a smile, 'You are a very young soldier, but destined to be an officer, and not to have much more sentry duty; and my object in not calling on you to come in was to let you feel how unpleasant it is to be soaked in the rain on a stormy night, and to explain to you now that the duty of an officer is to save his men as much as possible from such exposure, and never to keep them out in bad weather unnecessarily. You did more than your duty; but let this be a lesson to you, that whenever you can do so, preserve the health and study the comfort of those under your command. They will then be all the more ready for occasions when duty requires them to submit to hardships and hunger.' Shortly after this I was promoted to be an Ensign, and having passed as an officer fit to join a Company, I was posted to the 15th Native Infantry Regiment, and joined it as sixteenth Lieutenant, there being still six vacancies in that grade, and all the ten Ensigns being deficient. This state of things was due to the casualties in the late Mysore War, and to the additional number of troops required to occupy the provinces conquered from Tippoo and added to our former possessions.

"My first station was in the territory then lately acquired from the Nizam, entitled the Ceded Districts, and such was the state of disorder existing when it fell into our hands, that it became necessary to distribute two or three battalions, by single companies, to occupy the posts from which certain turbulent chiefs had been forcibly expelled, or where others who had fled threatened to recover what they deemed their just rights. When I joined the corps, there were only the Commandant and Adjutant with a few men at headquarters, occupying the tolerably strong fort of Cumbum. Two companies, consisting of nearly two hundred men and their officers, had been detached as a treasure escort to the headquarters of the division; and as they were detained there, and employed in another very arduous duty, it seems the right place to advert to it, though I myself was no sharer in the danger or the honour connected with the event. I have stated that the Madras Ceded Districts in 1801 were in a very disturbed state, which I mention as connected with the event which brought our two companies into notice. These districts were tolerably well peopled, but they had for the greater part of the previous century been subject to the incursions of the Mahrattas, and each village was protected by a wall with round bastions or towers to keep off Cavalry, and had not unfrequently a fortified building or cavalier, for it could hardly be called a castle, which not only commanded the whole village, but a certain portion of the township beyond it. At the period I now speak of, the village of Turnicul was inhabited by an indigenous tribe, of whom at that time Europeans knew nothing. They had succeeded in the south of India in resisting the fate of the Hindu Governments and Chieftainships which had fallen before the sword of the Mohammedans, while these aborigines held their own under each successive sovereign as feudatories paying a certain variable tribute for lands they had held from time immemorial, in consideration of protecting the country from robbers. The Government of the Ceded Districts had been entrusted to a highly distinguished military officer, who for some years had been employed in different parts of the South in Civil administration. He was aware that under the former Government it had been a common custom to exact from all Chiefs at the head of agricultural communities like the one in question—who were not strong enough to resist—as heavy a tribute annually as could be obtained, and this was effected by putting up the Government revenues to competition, and farming them to the highest bidder. In this way a great part of the Chiefships had been out-bidden and destroyed; and, unfortunately, in his anxiety to secure a large revenue for Government, the same measure was applied by the English officer in the case of the estate of the Chief of Turnicul, who had always hitherto been influential and strong enough to resist this oppressive practice under the Native administration. He found it impossible to come up to the figure bid by one of the Brahmins who had followed the European Magistrate's camp, and in a fit of despair, rather than relinquish his estate peaceably, he drew his sword in open Court, cut the throat of the successful competitor, and retired, with the numerous followers who accompanied him, into his fortified village.

"Deeming it requisite to make a prompt and signal example of such conduct, the military power was called in to demand the surrender of the murderer. For this purpose a force was organised, consisting of a Regiment of Native Cavalry with its two galloper guns (6-pounders), a Native battalion of Infantry, and the two companies of my own Regiment which had brought the treasure to headquarters. The village into which the Chief had retired was like those before described. His followers were simply armed with spears, swords, and matchlocks. From the description of the place, it was thought that the gates might easily be blown open by light guns in case of the Chief not surrendering, and in the event of his attempting to escape, a body of Cavalry might be sent to overtake and cut off himself and followers. The General Officer of the division from which the force for this service was derived was himself a Cavalry Officer, and he nominated one of his own Staff (also a Cavalry Officer) to command the expedition. The distance from headquarters was about forty miles. The detachment left in the afternoon, and in order to lose no time, marched continuously till near daylight, when the object of attack was still a few miles off. The Cavalry, with the guns, pushed on, and the Chief refusing to surrender, one of the guns was run up to the gate in order to blow it open. This gate was covered by a traverse wall of stone, and defended by a loop-holed parapet above. It was blocked up with stones on the inside, and there was a difficulty in working the gun within the protecting traverse wall. The enemy reserved their fire till the gun was discharged, when they plied their matchlocks with such success that the loss sustained by the Cavalry induced them to leave the gun in position and retire, covering it, however, by the fire of the other guns, to prevent its being taken by the enemy. The Cavalry Commandant now sent word back to the Infantry to hasten on; but the sturdy old Major who led them sent word back that he would come up without hurry, as quickly as his men could after a fatiguing march of fourteen hours. On their joining, the Infantry were directed to bring away the gun at the gate, which the enemy had spiked in the meantime, by letting one of the garrison over the walls by a rope. It was now seen that the detachment was wholly unprepared to undertake the capture of the place, and on its being represented to the headquarters of the division, the gallant veteran General commanding organised a reinforcement of a Regiment of Dragoons, a Regiment of European Infantry, another battalion of Sepoys, and all the field Artillery (6-pounders) at his disposal. The General himself, though considerably past his grand climacteric, headed the Dragoons, and made the march of forty miles at one stretch.

On reaching his ground, he was met by the Commander of the late attack, and without dismounting, he closely reconnoitred the place, regardless of the frequent shots with which he was assailed. After breakfast he wrote out his orders for an attack on the following day. He had taken the precaution to bring scaling ladders, but they proved too short. An attempt was then made to force an entrance through a sally-port on the side opposite the main gate. This, too, was found impracticable, the narrow gate being also solidly built up on the inside. In this attack the Commandant of one of the Sepoy Regiments was killed, and many officers and men fell before the troops were recalled. A third attack took place a few days after with scaling ladders of greater length, which had been constructed in camp for the purpose, but the assailants only now discovered that there was no rampart behind the curtains, while the storming parties were assailed from the bastions which enfiladed their ranks with missiles of all available descriptions. Every man of the storming parties who ascended the ladders and showed his head above the walls, was instantly shoved back at the point of a spear from within, while a smart fire from the flanking bastions was poured upon the assailants, aided by the discharge of large stones. After considerable loss, the storming parties were recalled, but the two Companies of my Regiment, which had been sent round on the opposite side to make a false attack, in order to divert the fire of the enemy from the real ones, were forgotten, and they remained at their post till they had expended their ammunition, and lost in killed and wounded exactly half of their number. On this occasion, several gallant officers and men of the force were sacrificed to no purpose, and the General found it necessary to confine his operations for the time to a close investment of the place, and to wait the arrival of a regular battering train with an adequate number of Engineer and Artillery Officers.

" Meanwhile, the garrison were informed that all that was required of them was that they should deliver up their Chief. They replied that ' he was their master, their father, and the Head of their Clan, and that they were ready to die for him'. Before the heavy ordnance had shattered their walls they were invited to send out their families; to which they answered, 'they were useful in discharging stones, and in other ways repelling assaults, and could not be separated from their homes'. A few hours, however, convinced them that they had no longer any chance against British power. By one o'clock on the first day the battering guns opened, a practicable breach was effected, and the storming party, led by the Europeans, rushed to the assault. Instead of meeting with resistance, they found the weapons of the garrison piled up at the foot of the breach, while the latter stood in a mass, unarmed, to await their doom. After the heavy loss sustained, connected

C

with the circumstance that led to the defence, no quarter was given, and not a soul was spared within the place, while those who managed to fly outside the fort were destroyed by the Cavalry. Thus terminated this ill-conducted undertaking.

"I had not been many weeks with my Regiment before I was ordered, with my Company, to join a detachment consisting of two Companies of Infantry under the same Captain who had commanded our two Companies at the Siege of Turnicul, accompanied by a troop of Cavalry, for the purpose of scouring the country in the endeavour to capture another of the turbulent Chiefs who refused to submit to the conditions required by our Government. We were accompanied by the Civil Authority, at whose requisition we were put in motion, and to whom our Commanding Officer looked for information and instructions. Our expedition, which was no further successful than in expelling the enemy from the Company's territory for the present, lasted about three months. During this time we had no mess, but dined with each other by turns; and when not actually in motion we generally sat down at night to play at cards. At this I was not skilful, and was consequently unsuccessful, and in the course of a week or two I lost more than I could conveniently pay, and I declined joining the next party. I was terribly bantered for my want of enterprise; but as I was determined not to become further involved, I adhered to my resolution, which I found absolutely necessary for my peace of mind; for as it was, I was compelled to borrow money of my own servant in order to give my dinner when my turn came round; and I could barely discharge my debts of honour out of my pay before the detachment returned to head-quarters. Thus, before I had left my father's house two years, and before I was seventeen years old, I had been effectually cured of three fatal propensities, that of drinking and gambling, besides that of smoking tobacco—habits which once acquired are not easily abandoned—and of the disastrous effects of which I have had frequent proofs in my earliest and in my latest observation and experience. On my return to the Regiment, my Company was detached to an outpost in a small Fort or Castle, the late residence of one of the turbulent Chiefs with which the country abounded. The garrison was commanded by Captain de Morgan, who had married a sister of my father's second wife. He left it, on leave, shortly after I joined, and I, at the age of sixteen and six months, was left as Governor of an important post. Fortunately, I had an experienced Native Officer of the old school as my second in command, and there being no other European in the garrison, I soon added to my knowledge of the Hindustani language, which all the Native Officers and most of the men spoke. At the same time I was fortunate in obtaining the services of a learned Mohammedan accustomed to teach Persian to his countrymen in his Native city. I was thus left to prosecute my studies in the most favourable manner during the greater part of two years, when my Company was relieved, and I rejoined the head-quarters of my Regiment at Hyderabad in 1803. I had made such good use of my time, that I was called on to translate into Persian the Duke of Wellington's official despatch after the battle of Assaye, for which I obtained a most flattering compliment from a very eminent scholar, who went so far as to predict that if I persevered I should become one of the best interpreters in the army. During this year I accompanied my Company on other service, and was employed as Persian and Hindustani Interpreter, and returned to head-quarters in August 1804.

"In consequence of the breaking out of the Mahratta war of 1802 and 1803, it was thought expedient to recruit additional Native troops to provide for casualties in the field The operations of the Madras and Bombay Armies extended as far north as the Nerbudda; while those of the Bengal Army spread over Central India, the regions of Agra and Delhi, and even to the banks of the Sutlej, on the frontier of the Punjaub. The state of affairs induced the Government of Madras to increase the number of Infantry Regiments, in the course of which the Adjutant of my Corps was promoted, and the Commander-in-Chief appointed me to that office. Scarcely had this change occurred, when it was discovered that by an official mistake the Officer who had been promoted in orders to the rank of Captain, was really unaffected by the augmentation. He therefore resumed the Adjutancy from me. At the same time the Government directed the formation of five 'Extra Battalions' to be drilled and kept ready, and to be dealt with, during or after the war, according to circumstances.

"A list of five officers was made out as Commandants, to whom the choice of their Adjutants was left. There were to be only these two European officers to each extra Battalion, with an Assistant-Surgeon. Among the Commandants was my old friend Captain Armstrong of the Cadet Company, and it was a subject of great gratification to me that he selected me as his Staff-Officer to assist in raising a new Corps. Native Commissioned and Non-Commissioned Officers were supplied from the Army at large. Our station was Trichinopoly, two hundred miles south of Madras, and about four hundred from Hyderabad, where my own Corps was stationed. I had scarcely been three years with my Regiment, but I had for a great part of the time been in the field, and for more than a year, as already mentioned, in the command of a small fort with my own Company.

"My Commandant was so thoroughly master of his business that my time was fully and well occupied. In the morning I rose

at day-light, and was soon on parade, superintending the drill of
the recruits, under the eye of my excellent and indefatigable Commandant.   At nine I returned to breakfast, and at ten attended
at the Major's Quarters with the regimental orderly book, and a
morning report, which exhibited the actual condition of the Corps,
the number of men on duty, those on the sick-list, those enlisted
during the preceding day, those who were absent on leave, or
without leave, and those present for duty.   All this information
was collected from the reports of each Company, framed by the
Native Officers, the whole being collected and formed into the
general morning report of the Regiment.   I returned to my
quarters at twelve, and was attended by a Persian Moonshee till
one o'clock, when I took a hasty tiffin alone, and from two till four
I was engaged in examining and enlisting recruits preparatory to
taking them before the Commandant, who then regularly accompanied me to the afternoon drill, which terminated at sunset.
Bed-time was very welcome after a late dinner and a little conversation with the Commandant and the Doctor.   We got on, fortunately for us three, perfectly well together.

"Such was the life I led till my Commandant was promoted
and removed to another Corps, and his place was supplied by the
same Officer under whom I served in the Ceded Districts at the
small outpost.   This event occurred in May 1805.   The routine of
duty was now familiar to me, and the health of the new Commandant did not allow of his taking the same active part in the
advancement of the new Corps as his predecessor.   The Corps
now consisted of about six hundred men, of whom more than half
were fit to join any Regiment.   In July, orders were received to
break up the Battalion and to distribute the men, according to
orders, to different Corps of the Line.   I was directed to take
charge of the Battalion, and march it to Madras, a distance of two
hundred miles, while the Commandant proceeded to join his own
Regiment in another direction.   Thus at nineteen years of age I
commanded a Battalion on the march.   On my arrival at Madras
I had to deliver over their quotas to several Regiments whose
Officers were there to receive them; each man with all his papers
complete, and his pay paid up to date.   I was now left with one
hundred and twenty men for my own Corps, then stationed at
Hyderabad, nearly 400 miles from Madras.

"In the month of November 1805 I brought into Secunderabad,
the military cantonment of Hyderabad, my large batch of recruits
in good condition, and without having lost a man on the road by
death or desertion.   I got great credit for it, and I think I deserved
it.   The men, though of a different language and nation, the
Tamul, from the Telugu Sepoys of which my Corps had chiefly
consisted, had taken my fancy completely, and I believe they had

become attached to me. I was, however, chiefly indebted to the good influence of the Native Officers.

"I had not been many weeks at Hyderabad when the Adjutancy of the 1st Battalion of my Regiment fell vacant, and I was appointed to it. This circumstance removed me not only from my recruits, but also from the 2nd Battalion, in which I had hitherto served, and in which I knew all the men, and was known by them. The mutiny which broke out at Vellore in the next year was the first effort made by the discontented Mohammedans to effect the destruction of our power in the South, where, during the sovereignty in Mysore of Hyder and Tippoo, they had enjoyed a sort of social supremacy, and opportunities for an honourable career, that were closed to them under our Government. As in the late mutiny of 1857, the origin of the outbreak was a mere pretext, without any substantial grievance in the alleged interference with rules of caste and religion. Undoubtedly the wording of the orders by the Commander-in-Chief at Madras, in which certain alterations and innovations in dress and toilette on parade were prescribed, afforded a handle to the disaffected, but this could have been, and would have been, modified if a calm representation had been made; but the conspirators really rejoiced at the opportunity, and turned it to their purpose. Unfortunately, as it turned out, the Governor, Lord William Bentinck, was himself a soldier, and took a great interest in the smartness and efficiency of the Madras Sepoys. Unfortunately also, the Adjutant-General of the Army, the chief adviser in such matters of the Commander-in-Chief, who was, of course, a Queen's Officer, had served a very short time in a Native Corps before being placed on Staff duty, conducted entirely by English agency. The Deputy Adjutant-General and the Quarter-master-General had only served regimentally with European troops. These gentlemen, taking their cue from their superiors, found out that there was a complete want of uniformity in the interior economy of regiments, particularly with regard to the details of dress, and under the Commander-in-Chief's orders they produced a code of regulations for general observance throughout the Madras army. One most offensive and imprudent point in this new code was the introduction of a stiff white stock, and also of a new head-dress closely resembling that worn by English soldiers, which, under the name of 'topee' or hat, is held and noted by all Natives as the distinctive mark of a European Christian.

"There was, moreover, a very offensive clause in the code, penned in the following words; and as if to mark it out as most peremptory and essential, it was picked out for translation into Hindustani, not well understood by any Madras Sepoys except the Mohammedans, and copies of it were distributed in each company.

"'A Native soldier shall not mark his face to denote his caste, or wear ear-rings when dressed in his uniform; and at all parades and upon all duties, every Sepoy of the Battalion shall be clean shaved upon the chin. It is directed, also, that uniformity shall, as far as it is practicable, be preserved in regard to the quantity and shape of the hair on the upper lip.'

"The Commander-in-Chief himself was struck with this clause, and desired the attendance of both the Adjutant and Quartermaster General, and of the Deputy Adjutant-General, to consult regarding it. The Commander-in-Chief was expressly assured that it only specified what was the actual practice in well-regulated Regiments. The Deputy Adjutant-General declared that he could not recollect having ever seen a Native soldier on duty with the caste-mark on his forehead, or with large rings in his ears; and that if any man had appeared so bedecked he would have been turned off parade and punished. The Commander-in-Chief was unjustly censured, after the mutiny at Vellore, as being the author of these innovations; but he very justly asked in a letter he wrote at a subsequent period, when dangerous dissatisfaction had become apparent:—'As a stranger, and in the hands of the principal Staff Officers of the Honourable Company's army, how could I oppose to their experience my single sentiment, and direct the overthrow of what I was told was an established custom?'

"The Deputy Adjutant-General had a sort of mania for dress. A Captain of my own Regiment, just about that time, appeared in the Adjutant-General's Office to report his arrival at headquarters on leave of absence. The Deputy Adjutant-General observed that there was a button too little on his coat. Not much liking the sharp accents of the Staff Officer, who, after all, was only of his own regimental rank, my brother officer replied that if it was anyone's fault it was the tailor's, and that no mortal man could keep up to time with the new regulations for dress. The unfortunate Captain, who had just travelled four hundred miles to see some friends recently arrived from Europe, received a peremptory order the next day from the Commander-in-Chief—of course at the instance of the Adjutant-General's Office—to rejoin his regiment forthwith, and to quit the Presidency in four-and-twenty hours. Nor was he, to my knowledge, the only commissioned victim to this martinet's mania.

" When these new regulations reached Hyderabad, I had been removed from my own old Battalion, as before stated, and had become Adjutant of the other, with the men of which I was less familiar. I, however, took the best means in my power to ascertain what was the general feeling of the Sepoys. One of my most trusted informants was a lad, who had been for more than two years my personal attendant as a recruit boy under age; and another was a

Native officer of the old-school, who had served under Sir Eyre Coote and Lord Cornwallis. The first had been the most faithful and affectionate of servants, always remarkable for his gentle and respectful demeanour. During my absence he had been regularly enrolled in my old Company, and from him I expected the honest truth. I was not deceived. At that time the new head-dress, or 'turban', as it was called, was the chief cause of discontent. After asking him how he was getting on, and what was the news, he answered cheerfully as usual; but when I spoke of the new turban his eyes flashed fire; his mien was entirely changed, and he replied, 'Sir, it is of no use calling it a turban; it is a European soldier's hat; and neither I nor any man in the Regiment will wear it. We would sooner die.' I felt that if I, whom he loved affectionately, had attempted to enforce its adoption, he would have been the first to rise in mutiny. I then requested a visit from the Native officer with whom I had served in the 2nd Battalion. But how different was his behaviour. Having described my interview with my young friend, he smiled, and said, 'The boy, like the rest of the Regiment, has run mad. There is nothing really objectionable in the new turban. The fact is, there is a deep-laid Mussulman plot, in which the population of Hyderabad are mixed up, to make use of these new orders as a plea for a general row. I wore the turban yesterday throughout the day in the barracks, and no one officer or private ventured to say a word against it, though many looked askance at it. But take my advice —break up this force, and send the Battalions to different stations, where there is a European Regiment; and you may then place on our heads any English *utensil* you think becoming.' I translate his words with as much propriety as possible. 'I have served the Company,' he continued, 'from the age of fifteen till now, when I am fifty-four, and I never yet heard of a Government order being discussed or disobeyed. That is a new custom you had better not allow.'

"I immediately communicated my two interviews to my own Commandant, as well as to the Colonel of the Regiment; but they both of them treated it lightly. After a day or two, the officer commanding the Force, on inspecting the pattern-men of each company of our Battalion, pointed to a fine young Hindustani, the trim of whose whiskers and moustaches pleased him, and almost touching his face with a somewhat muddy stick he held in his hand, desired that the whiskers of the whole corps should, as far as possible, be brought to that shape. The poor lad did not understand English, but was evidently alarmed and offended, though no one but myself seemed to observe it. Undoubtedly, in consequence of the interpretation he put upon the speech and gesture of the Brigadier, twenty-four of the finest young men of the Light Company, including himself, deserted on that very night. The same feeling of apprehension, fostered by the evil-minded, as to some attack on the rules of caste or on the notions of personal self-respect connected with beards and whiskers, soon pervaded the whole force.   So strange and suspicious was the sudden change in the manner and aspect of the six Battalions of Sepoys in the Hyderabad Force, that many · officers slept with loaded pistols under their pillows, a fact which became known to the men.   At length the news of the Vellore mutiny arrived, and was hailed without much disguise by all Native ranks of the force, well or ill-disposed, as an opportune token of the general feeling against the new regulations.   Soon after this the news arrived of the terrible retribution taken upon the mutineers at Vellore.   The offensive orders were rescinded, and the issue of the new turbans discontinued.   The withdrawal of the new code acted like oil on the troubled waters, and in a few weeks all was forgiven and forgotten.   Among us, at Hyderabad, no overt breach of discipline had as yet taken place to prevent the English officers from maintaining their authority.   Nevertheless, I know that the Mohammedans of both Battalions of my own Regiment were deeply implicated in hostile intrigues in the city of Hyderabad, and at their instigation a murmur was now got up against the leathern · stocks, covered with white calico, which had been worn without complaint for some time.   This grievance was not openly brought forward, and the rumour of discontent was treated with indifference by the highest military authorities.   The feeling, however, broke out in our Regiment on one occasion, and, but for the promptness with which it was quelled, might have revived the dangerous disaffection which had so lately been suppressed.   On the occasion of a regimental parade of both Battalions, nearly 2,400 strong, a corporal punishment by sentence of court-martial was about to be inflicted. The culprit was of the 2nd Battalion, and, according to the usual custom, all the Native officers were called to the front to hear the charge and sentence read, and to witness the punishment, the European officers, with the exception of the two Commandants and the two Adjutants, remaining with their Battalions in line. While the charge and sentence were being read, Captain Limond, the Captain of Grenadiers of the 2nd Battalion, brought forward the right hand man of his Company, and reported to the Commanding Officer that he had detected him in attempting to set the example of taking off his stock and throwing it on the ground, which he observed nearly all the men of the 1st Battalion had already done.   I immediately cast my eyes in that direction, and perceived on the ground in front of my own Corps a good sprinkling of white stocks.   I immediately called the attention of my own Commandant, Major A. H. Macdowell, to what was only too apparent. He, however, declared he saw nothing of the sort, and that it was only my fancy. I felt no time should be lost, and, without waiting for orders, galloped towards the centre of the Battalion, and called out to the men to pick up their stocks. Not one of them stirred. I saw the few European officers present had gallantly checked the movement by each one stepping in front of his own Company, and threatening with instant punishment any man who dared to take off his stock after this fair warning. The Captain of Grenadiers of the 2nd Battalion had rather over-esti-mated the extent of the mischief, in which nothing like a majority of the men had yet joined. I pushed my horse close up to the centre of one of the centre companies, and singling out half-a-dozen men who had clearly acted in concert, I made use of the flat of my sword right and left among them, wounding one man slightly on the side of the head, though I did not intend it, while I used some strong language in their vernacular which I knew would impress them with a belief in my determined purpose. In an instant more than a hundred young Sepoys had picked up their stocks, and replaced them on their necks, and the remainder, seeing the game was up, followed suit. My Commandant, Major McDowell, never made any official report of this incident, received my account of it very coldly and ungraciously, and somehow or other his relations with me were never on a cordial footing after that day. Some years afterwards, as will appear, a serious rupture took place between us.

"When the 2nd Battalion on that day had been marched off the parade ground by companies, led by their respective Native officers, the European officers, as usual, went home. The Grena-dier Company, of which the right hand man had been confined, in order that further inquiry might establish how far he was guilty in throwing off his stock, refused to quit their arms till the pri-soner was released. The Native officers endeavoured in vain to dismiss them, and to make them lodge their arms. In a few minutes men from the other companies crowded round the Grenadiers, while a few Sepoys, who were personally attached to the Captain, ran up to the mess-house, where he was about to dine, and told him what was going on. Limond was not the man to hesitate. He mounted his horse, accepting my offer to accompany him, and we rode down full gallop to the spot where his men were assembled. He asked the senior Native officer why the Company was not dismissed. The state of the case was explained to him. The Captain drew his sword, the men standing with ordered arms, and addressed them as follows :—'You have heard the matter ex-plained to me, so that I can quite understand it. You all know me pretty well by this time, and you know that I never give an order that I don't mean to have executed, and to see executed.

Your comrade was put in the guard by my orders; he will be tried and found guilty or not guilty, according to the evidence. Your duty is obedience, and I know mine. Now then,—one at a time,—the first man who refuses to obey shall have this sword through his body.'

" He then went straight up to the right hand man, and ordered him, by name, to shoulder arms, which the man instantly did. He then addressed the second and third, with equally prompt effect. He now felt that the spell was broken, and gave the word, ' Grenadiers, shoulder arms.'. The word of command was instantly effectual; the Company was marched to its barracks, and the arms lodged as usual.

"These two incidents, which occurred under my own eyes on one day, show the effect of stern discipline, and prove that the English officers had not in those days lost their personal influence over the Sepoys.

"In a day or two after these critical occurrences there was a general parade of the Force, consisting of two Regiments of Native Cavalry, one Company of European and one of Native Artillery, H.M.'s 33rd Foot, and six Battalions of Native Infantry. Three Mussulman officers, one from each Battalion of my Regiment, and one from another, were called to the front, and being tried and convicted by a drum-head court-martial of holding seditious correspondence with certain fanatics in the city of Hyderabad, they were marched off the parade in irons, under an escort composed partly of European soldiers and partly of Sepoys. They were sent away to Masulipatam that night, and thence transported to one of the islands of the Eastern Archipelago.

" Such is an episode of the volcanic period of 1806, of which the chief eruption took place at Vellore. On investigation, it was clearly proved that the original plot at Vellore was got up by some of the family of Tippoo, who were there detained as State prisoners, —almost as prisoners at large, for they were only required to confine themselves within certain prescribed limits, and had almost too handsome a provision for their comfort and dignity. A Mohammedan feeling of hostility towards the British Government was not then unnatural. Since the fall of Seringapatam in 1799, seven years only had elapsed. Not only was the Mussulman kingdom of Mysore subverted, and the Hindoo Raj restored, but several other Mussulman chieftains had been degraded, and many families of rank of that faith placed in reduced and humble circumstances. Among the Sovereign Princes who had suffered was the Nawab of the Carnatic, our oldest ally, who had been compelled to transfer his authority and his country to the British Government, retaining a stipulated portion of the revenue with an empty title. Many petty Nawabs of the Ceded Districts, acquired from the Nizam in 1801, had lost their service jaghires and all hope of honourable employ, and their families and followers remained unprovided for. Even at the present day, though more than half a century has passed, much discontent prevails among the Mussulman population of the Madras provinces, whether in or out of the Army, in consequence of these unpleasant reminiscences."

CHAPTER II.

As my object in this book is to give an account of the opinions and acts of General Briggs, in connection with Imperial policy and executive administration in India,—opinions and acts that were emphatically his own, and often widely divergent from official commonplace,—I shall not devote so much space to his earlier career, when he held a subordinate place, as to the period when he acted more distinctly on his own initiative, and spoke with some of the authority of experience and position.

Moreover, the military operations and diplomatic transactions in which Briggs was engaged in the first fifteen or sixteen years of his service in the East, have been frequently made the subject of published reports or narratives by those who took the leading part in them, or have been told in their biographies. The interest in them has died away, and in several instances we are now able clearly to recognise how much their objects and their results were miscalculated and overrated at the time. There would, for example, be no good in my telling at full length the story of the second mission of Sir John Malcolm to Persia in 1808-9, and of its cross-purposes and collision with the rival embassy of Sir Harford Jones. That story has not been left half told. Sir Harford Jones has told it in his way,* and Sir John Malcolm in his. Suffice it to say that Sir John, according to Sir Harford, was only an Envoy from Lord Minto, Governor-General of India. Sir Harford, according to Sir John, was a poacher on the Oriental preserves of the Honourable Company. But Sir Harford Jones, being duly accredited

* He afterwards took the name of Brydges,—*Sir H. J. Brydges, Transactions of Missions in Persia*, 2 vols., 1834.

by the Foreign Office and the King of Great Britain and Ireland, managed to get received at Teheran, while the Shah requested Sir John Malcolm to go to Shiraz, and negotiate with one of the Persian Princes, a request which was indignantly declined. The whole affair on both sides was a thing of sound and fury, signifying nothing. There was undoubtedly gross mismanagement in the want of concert between the Foreign Office and the India Office. But the difference between the two Envoys, their aims and the means at their disposal, was very small. And even if they had made up their differences and combined their efforts, they would have gained no advantage, and saved no expense, for Great Britain, or for India. As it was, the Envoy from Calcutta did nothing; the Envoy from London, Sir Harford Jones, did some very absurd and costly business. In March 1809, he concluded a Treaty by which Great Britain was to pay an annual subsidy of £100,000 to the Shah, and to supply him with 16,000 muskets and 20 field-pieces, on condition that he would assist us in repelling any attempt on the part of the French to invade India through Persian territory—a military operation about as practicable as an invasion of Russia through Siberia.

That was the scare of the day—a French invasion of India by way of the Persian Gulf—a scare quite as reasonable, however, as that of later date—far more costly in blood and treasure, and, unhappily, not yet extinct—regarding a Russian invasion of India through Afghanistan. The arms and munitions of war, and the annual subsidy—not continued for many years—granted to Persia in 1809, and all our meddlings with Persia, friendly and hostile, down to the war of 1856, have not cost a fifth part of the resources wasted by Lord Palmerston and Lord Auckland's restoration of a "legitimate" king, devoted to our interests, in 1839, and by Lord Salisbury's "created object" and "scientific frontier" of 1879. India was made to pay more than forty millions sterling for those two bloody and bootless invasions of a free and unoffending State. The crazes and scares of the officials attached to our own Foreign and Colonial Offices, our

Envoys, Consuls, Governors, and Under-Secretaries—
though they have done pretty well with their Kaffir
Wars, their Zulu War, their Abyssinian and Egyptian
expeditions—have not, somehow or other, been as expensive, for the last three generations or so, as those of our
Indian experts.

Sir Harford Jones's gifts in goods and in cash cannot
have cost a tithe of the expense that would have attended
Sir John Malcolm's brilliant plan—the plan which, when
driven from Persia by his cold reception, he pressed on
Lord Minto at Calcutta, and which, after a good deal of
vacillation, was finally rejected. This was for a combined naval and military expedition to the Gulf, and the
occupation of the island of Karrack, where Sir John
Malcolm was to be established as " lord of a fortified isle
and arbiter of the destinies of Persia and Arabia."*

Briggs had enjoyed very good health ever since his
arrival in India down to the cold weather of 1806, when,
during the march of his Regiment from Hyderabad to
the Mysore country, he was attacked with acute inflam-
mation of the liver. Being for the time quite incapacitated for his duty as Adjutant, he accepted a general but
cordial invitation, obtained a short leave of absence, and
instead of proceeding with his corps to Bangalore, turned
aside to pay a visit to Sir John Malcolm, then Resident
at Mysore. The Residency, a very fine house, built at
the Maharajah's expense, with a fine garden and park,
was at Yelwall, commonly called the French Rocks, a
few miles from the town of Mysore. The General says
in his autobiographical papers :—

" Nothing could have been more kind, I may say affectionate,
than my reception. As I got a little stronger, I was enabled to
make myself useful by translating a considerable portion of a
Persian work from the original, which assisted Sir John, eventually,
in writing his History of Persia, published some few years afterwards. My health, however, did not return, and I was ordered by
my medical attendant to sea for change of air. During my residence at Mysore, I had the good fortune to become acquainted

* Kaye's *Life of Sir John Malcolm* (Smith, Elder & Co., 1856), vol. i,
p. 422.

with Colonel Mark Wilks, the distinguished historian of the South of India. He kindly invited me to accompany him to Madras, whence I embarked on board the East India Company's ship *Preston*, commanded by my old friend Captain Cumberlege, in the month of November 1807, for Calcutta. I am bound to acknowledge my gratitude to the Captain, who most generously gave me a passage free of expense, and treated me with the utmost degree of kindness. I brought with me letters from Colonel Malcolm and others to friends in Calcutta. Among them was one to Mr. (afterwards Sir) Henry Ellis, of the Bengal Civil Service, with whom I resided, and contracted an intimate friendship which ceased only with his life. I had not completed the full period of my leave of absence when one morning he advised me to get well quickly, and to return to Madras at once, where, he said, I was certain of being employed on the Staff. He assigned no other reason, excepting that he felt sure that an appointment was actually awaiting my arrival. He was at that time an Assistant in the Secret and Political Department, and though I had been his guest for the last two months, he could not conscientiously let me behind the scenes, and inform me of Lord Minto's Persian policy, or the exact reasons for urging my immediate departure. I accordingly embarked on board the *Venus* merchantman, and after a tedious passage reached Madras in the end of March. On my arrival I was sent for by the Commander-in-Chief, and was congratulated on my appointment as one of the attachés to the Persian mission under Colonel John Malcolm."

After several delays, and a long voyage from Bombay in company with his cousin, Dr. George Briggs, who was appointed physician to the Embassy, the young *attaché* arrived at Bushire, on board the Honourable Company's corvette the *Benares*. In their passage up the Persian Gulf they encountered H.M.'s frigate *Chiffonne*, carrying back to Calcutta Colonel Malcolm, after his unsatisfactory reception and stoppage on his way to Teheran. The envoy was accompanied by Mr. Henry Ellis, who, having been appointed senior *attaché*, had left Calcutta a few days after Briggs and joined the envoy by land at Bombay. Malcolm was there bent on his fruitless endeavour to lead Lord Minto into the capture of Karrack, and a " spirited" treatment of Persia.

"During our stay at Bushire", says Briggs, "the Persian authorities made our position very unpleasant, not by positive acts of hostility, but by incivility and petty

annoyances, to such a degree that Captain Pasley, who
was in charge, thought it expedient to remove the mission,
in order to prevent some occurrence that might thoroughly
compromise either himself or the Persian Governor, and
lead to a rupture and to war.   After communicating with
our Consul and Commercial Resident at Bussora, Mr.
Manisty, as to the accommodation that could be procured,
and as to the advisability of such a movement, we proceeded to that city, and encamped within Turkish territory."

As it was impossible to disavow Sir Harford Jones's
royal credentials, it was debated for some time in the
Calcutta Council Chamber whether an Indian mission
should be sent at all, and Briggs was recalled from
Bussora, *viâ* Bushire, to Bombay.   Lord Minto finally
decided—although the force for the occupation of Karrack
was for some time actually assembled at Bombay,—not to
place Malcolm in a position "to menace Arabia and Persia,
and to baffle the designs of Napoleon and the Czar."*
Sir Harford Jones's treaty could not be repudiated, and
he was, moreover, firmly established at Teheran as Envoy
from His Britannic Majesty.   But for the exquisite
reason that "the Company's Government must not be
lowered in the eyes of the Shah", Malcolm was promoted
to the rank of Brigadier General, and reappointed Envoy
to Persia from the Indian Government in January 1810.
He started once more from Bombay, taking with him a
somewhat imposing escort of Madras Native Horse
Artillery, with six guns—intended as a present for the
Persian King—a dozen of the 17th Light Dragoons, a
troop of the Madras Body Guard, and forty Bombay
Sepoys.   The detachment of Horse Artillery was under
the command of Lieutenant Henry Lindsay, an officer of
gigantic stature, afterwards General Sir Henry Lindsay
Bethune, who for many years commanded the Persian
army.   Among Malcolm's well-chosen staff were his
kinsmen, Captain Charles Pasley and Dr. George Briggs,
Lieutenant Josiah Stewart, afterwards Colonel and Resident at Hyderabad, and John Briggs, in whom, as

* Kaye's *Life of Sir John Malcolm*, vol. i, p. 443.

Malcolm's biographer says, were "then discernible the germs of the ripe scholar and warm-hearted philanthropist who still" (in 1856, at the age of seventy-three) "discusses questions of Indian policy or Indian philosophy, with all the ardour of a boy."[*]

Briggs and a portion of the staff proceeded from Bombay in advance of the Envoy and his party. The warlike episode of their voyage may be related in the words of the autobiography.

"Just before our embarkation an expedition under Colonel Lionel Smith, consisting of the 65th Foot, the flank companies of the 47th, and the Bombay Native Marine Battalion, with a proportion of Artillery, had sailed for the Gulf, under convoy of H.M. ships *Chiffonne* and *Caroline*, and was lying in Muscat Harbour, when our vessel arrived at that port. We availed ourselves of this opportunity of active service by accompanying the expedition to the piratical town of Ras al Khyma, which was the first object of attack. Captain Pasley, Dr. Jukes, and myself volunteered our services, and we landed as extra Aide-de-Camps to Colonel Lionel Smith. The expedition was prepared for the attack on the following day. The Marine Battalion, under Captain Egan, had for its share in the day's work to turn the enemy's right flank, after landing from the boats, and to take a series of batteries along the coast which protected the town; while the main body, including all the Europeans, under Colonel Lionel Smith himself, proceeded about a mile further down the coast to dislodge the enemy by our attack on his other flank. I could not but admire our Commander's coolness.

"On the line of boats coming within musket range the enemy began to fire. The officers and men on our side became impatient, and several got up preparing to fire also; the Colonel, in whose boat I was, stood up and called out to the landing party to sit down, and to pass the word along the line of boats; at the same time directing the officers, who were distinguished from the men by the long red and white feather in their caps, to take them out. Not a shot was fired by the troops, but occasionally, as a good chance presented itself, a discharge took place from the carronades which were in the launches of the two frigates. The infantry landed, nearly up to their waists in water, formed as regularly as on parade, and as they got into order each company advanced according to the instructions they had previously received, and soon drove the enemy out of their field works. By this time Colonel Lionel Smith had landed, but before ordering a movement

[*] Kaye's *Life of Sir John Malcolm*, vol. i, p. 511.

in advance against the town, he had to wait about half-an-hour for all the guns at his disposal to be put on shore. Unfortunately, the heavy guns, intended for battering the fortifications, had been lost in a brig which went down at sea with all hands, including all the European Artillerymen and their two officers. The Colonel, in a most flattering manner, placed me in charge of the four field-pieces which were manned by Infantry soldiers. The town was very soon taken. Some strong, flat-roofed houses held out against the advance of the Europeans of the right attack, and, among others, Captain Dansey of the 65th Foot was killed. The Arabs, considering they only had matchlocks, defended themselves well behind cover, but they made no attempt to charge or stand a charge. By about 2 P.M. all the fighting men were driven out of the town, and the piratical fleet of sixty or seventy vessels was burnt by means of fire-balls. The town and its outskirts were strewed with killed and wounded Arabs, but our loss was not heavy. Captain Dansey was the only English officer killed, and our wounded were not numerous. Having made an example of the town and its piratical inhabitants, and effected all that was intended, the troops re-embarked the same evening. The following day our party waited on the Colonel commanding the Force on board his frigate, when he thanked us warmly for our services. We were each of us mentioned in his despatches to the Government of Bombay."

As soon as their travelling arrangements could be completed after their arrival at Bushire, Briggs and his party, under instructions given before they sailed from Bombay, proceeded from Bushire to Shiraz, where they awaited the arrival of the Anglo-Indian Envoy Extraordinary. " Here", says Briggs, " we remained, receiving and returning visits among the Persian nobility of the Prince's Court, which afforded me an opportunity of becoming better acquainted with the people, and of improving myself in the vernacular language ; so that before I quitted the country, and had travelled over the greater part of Western Persia, north and south, I could distinguish the local dialects so thoroughly that I could at once discover from what province any stranger addressing me came, with as much facility as anyone in England can distinguish the Scotch dialect or the Irish brogue."

Colonel Malcolm appointed Briggs Quartermaster-

General and baggage master, which gave him charge of
several hundred mules, no wheeled conveyance being of
any use on the roads they traversed. The King had
sent a high nobleman of his Court to act as Mihmāndār
or host, to see that supplies were amply furnished at
every halting-place; and also a story-teller or impro-
visatore to beguile the tedium of the way by relating
those tales with which he was wont to entertain his
Royal master. "Being one of the few", says Briggs,
"together with Henry Ellis and Dr. Jukes, who had sufficient knowledge of Persian to enjoy these tales, it was
our privilege to ride close to the Envoy, and observe all
the dramatic changes of voice and action of the narrator,
whose charming stories, well remembered, were subsequently given to the world as the Persian Tales, by Sir
John Malcolm."

The Shah not being then at Teheran, the capital, the
cavalcade proceeded by a route which enabled them to
visit the ruins of Persepolis and the city of Ispahan.
They halted also at the cities of Kāshān and Kūm,
"the latter distinguished for the splendid domes of its
mosques. Between the citizens of these two ancient
cities there is an immemorial jealousy, and the country
people admit that there is a distinction to be drawn, not,
however, of a very flattering nature even for the city to
which a preference is given; for thus runs the Persian
adage: 'A dog of Kāshān is better than a grandee of
Kūm, but a dog is better than a man of Kāshān.'"

"It was with some difficulty, and very much to the admiration
of our Persian companions, that the guns we were conveying as a
present to the King reached their destination without injury. The
roads, if they could be called roads at all, were fearfully bad.
Young Lindsay, commanding our little troop of Artillery, who
became afterwards distinguished in action against the Russians,
and in defeating a formidable body of rebels under one of the
King's sons, surprised the Persians on more than one occasion by
the dashing manner in which he got over the broken ground. No
obstacle seemed to prevent his finding or making a way for his
battery; and where the path was obstructed by crowded horsemen
he dashed through them, shouting out—for he had soon learned so

much Persian—' Clear the way, clear the road for the guns !'   It happened on one occasion that the Mihmāndār and his suite were an obstacle, but the young Commandant, disregardful of his Lordship's dignity, forced his way through, calling out, ' By your leave, my Lord, the road belongs to the guns.'   The noble Mihmāndār took it with the wonderful politeness characteristic of Persians, and seemed much amused.   Whenever he afterwards encountered the giant Artilleryman, with or without his battery, he used to salute him with comic deference, and say, ' You are quite right, Captain Lindsay, the road belongs to the guns.'

"Nothing of importance occurred on our journey towards the King's camp at Sultania, before entering which, or making any arrangements for waiting on his Majesty, there were some long interviews, and what may be called negotiations, between General Malcolm and Sir Harford Jones, who was also encamped near the town. There must have been—it was, in fact, visible enough—a good deal of awkwardness and embarrassment in the meeting of the two Envoys.   Sir Harford Jones was not really in a position to fulfil the financial engagements into which he had entered in his Treaty, for every payment was to be made by the Government of India represented by General Malcolm.   The General paid a visit of ceremony to Sir Harford Jones, the day after his arrival.   They had become acquainted when Sir Harford was Consul at Bagdad, some years before, on the return of General Malcolm from Persia, on his first mission in 1800.   They now met under different circumstances, and the King's Ambassador naturally felt that the duty with which General Malcolm was charged reflected on the dignity of the Mission from the Crown.   The General hoped that Sir Harford would not object to be present at his reception by the Shah.   To this Sir Harford did not then make any objection, but when the time arrived, he sent word that he had another engagement, which would prevent his accompanying the General."

All the difficulties of etiquette and the conflicting claims of the two Envoys having been overcome, the day of audience was appointed.   Malcolm was most cordially received by the Shah, with a degree of good humour and familiarity for which he was hardly prepared.   The brilliant young Staff were all in full dress, and his Majesty appeared to be much struck with the varied uniforms of the Horse Artillery, Cavalry, and Infantry, and expressed his admiration at "all these fine youths that you have brought with you, Malcolm".   The escort was paraded, the guns were handed over, and, with an abundance of flowery speeches on both sides, the audience concluded.

" No inquiry", wrote Briggs exultingly at the time in his diary, " was made regarding his Excellency the King's Ambassador. Neither his name nor his mission was mentioned." All the Staff, in fact, were agreed that " although Sir Harford Jones had been enabled to pave his way, and to conciliate the venal persons about the Court with a profusion of presents, he did not gain that personal influence with his Majesty that was exercised by Sir John Malcolm, the first English Envoy to Persia in modern times."

Sir Harford Jones, who, to fortify him for his work, had been created a baronet, had persuaded the Shah to grant him a patent, subsequently confirmed by the King, and duly entered in Heralds' College, entitling him to blazon in his arms an effigy of his own design representing the crown of Persia on a cushion. A similar patent for Sir John Malcolm would clearly have been, at this juncture, unacceptable and objectionable. But the Indian Envoy induced the Shah, who was delighted with the idea, to institute the new Order of the Lion and the Sun, of which Sir John Malcolm was the first Knight. Sir Harford Jones was beaten at all points, and the Governor-General's dignity was vindicated.

From Sultania the mission proceeded, in July 1810, to Tabreez, where a large camp of exercise had been formed under the command of the heir apparent, Prince Abbas Mirza, who was much delighted with the manœuvres of General Malcolm's escort of Horse Artillery and Dragoons. At Tabreez General Malcolm received despatches from the Governor-General, transmitted through Constantinople to England, where they had received the sanction of the Home Government, which ordered his return to India by the Bagdad route. From Bussora General Malcolm, with Mr. Henry Ellis, his first Assistant, and the Dragoons, embarked for Bombay. Briggs was left in charge of the mission and the Native soldiers of the escort, with orders to return to India as shipping could be found. They landed at Bombay early in 1811, and Briggs was detained there some weeks, winding up the accounts of one of the most fruitless missions that

ever was despatched to a foreign country. It was utterly
unproductive of good to India, to Persia, or to Great
Britain. He proceeded to Madras in H.M. ship *Minden*,
and arrived there in April. Two important events in
his life—his next appointment to the Staff, and his marriage—may now be related in his own words.

" On reaching Madras, I received a cordial and pressing invitation to occupy a room in his house from the Governor of the
Naval Hospital, who was married to a sister of my step-mother,
whose younger sister, Miss Jane Dodson, was living with them.
My health required that I should remain on the sea-coast for some
time, and I obtained a medical certificate to that effect. I had
not been long at the Presidency when a Captain of my own
Regiment returned from the capture of the Mauritius, and after
residing for about a month with my kind connection of the Naval
Hospital, my brother officer and I took a small house together.
There I passed through the ordeal of a cold water cure, not very
different from that which has of late years become familiar and
famous through the practice of Herr Preissnitz and his disciples.
I was recommended to take active horse exercise at daylight
every morning, and after an hour's ride to take a douche bath in
the form of a dozen large pots of cold water thrown rapidly over
me in succession, and then, after being rapidly rubbed with towels
for half a minute, to lie down, warmly covered, till I was quite
calm and comfortable, before I dressed. This had a decidedly good
effect on my general health, but it produced several large boils,
which, although unpleasant and painful at the time, seemed to
form a necessary incident in my cure. During my stay at the
Presidency, a masked ball was given by the Governor ; and one of
my companions of the Embassy and myself went in the character
of Persian travellers, in very handsome dresses we had brought
from that country. As soon as we entered the crowded assembly
we were accosted by the Persian Secretary to Government, and
another gentleman on the Headquarters Staff, who was an accomplished Oriental scholar. They were evidently very anxious to
display their knowledge of the Court and diplomatic language of
Western Asia, and we had little difficulty in understanding the
commonplace and hackneyed phrases of salutation which they
addressed to us. They, however, found it quite impossible to
converse freely, or to make anything out of the flood of colloquial
talk with which we met their polite advances. They were in
much the same situation as a Greek Professor from Oxford would
be if he landed at a port in Greece, and tried to understand the
modern Greek of his hosts. When, after amusing ourselves for a
few minutes with the bewildered efforts of the great Persian

authorities at Madras to understand good Persian, we suddenly spoke to them in good English, the dignified Staff officers were extremely vexed, and they were mightily quizzed by some of the ladies, for they had taken us for genuine Orientals. How this circumstance reached the Governor's ears I do not know, but it was, I know, partly to it that I owed my nomination shortly afterwards to the situation of Persian Interpreter to the Hyderabad Subsidiary Force, an appointment granted without any application on my part.

"I have already mentioned that the wife of my good friend of the Royal Naval Hospital had a sister living with her. I was a frequent visitor at the house after I had left it for a separate residence. I found Miss Jane Dodson so fascinating a companion, that I married her on the 3rd of September 1811."

Their union, which lasted for some years beyond the date of a golden wedding, was in every sense and in every respect a happy one. Miss Jane Dodson, nearly twenty years younger than her sister Honor, her husband's step-mother, was the youngest of the nine daughters and eleven children of Mr. John Dodson, of the London Custom House, whose father, James Dodson, was an early F.R.S., and author of the *Mathematical Canon*. Another sister was married to Colonel De Morgan of the Madras Army, and thus Briggs became uncle by marriage to Augustus De Morgan, the eminent mathematician,* with whom eventually he contracted a warm friendship.

* Born 1806; died 1871.

CHAPTER III.

CAPTAIN BRIGGS remained during the greater part of the years 1812 and 1813 as Persian Interpreter to the Officer commanding the Hyderabad Subsidiary Force at the cantonment of Jaulna. During this period he had completed the translation of most of the minor histories of Ferishta, and had made much progress in revising the principal portion of that author's works from the old versions of Colonel Jonathan Scott and of Colonel Dow, by comparison with several manuscript copies, supplying the requisite notes, identifying and correcting names of places by means of the best maps, verified in many instances by his own topographical observations. During his residence at Jaulna he made his first appearance in print. The amount of Persian interpreting that was required being very limited, the Commandant seems to have employed his Interpreter, nothing loth to have plenty to do, in the field carriage and intelligence department. And thus, he writes,—

" I was brought in communication very frequently with that singular race, divided into many clans, of itinerant dealers in grain and salt, the Brinjarries, who live entirely in the open air, perpetually on the move, and who make it their business to convey goods and cattle, sometimes on their own account, or as carriers for others, from one part of India to another, purchasing in the cheapest and selling in the dearest markets. In the campaigns of 1803-4-5, under General Arthur Wellesley (afterwards the Great Duke), he had in his service very often as many as 80,000 bullocks furnished by these carriers, so that he commanded ample supplies at all times, while the enemy was often distressed. No description of this people had yet been published, so I wrote a short essay on the subject, the materials being gathered entirely from my conversations with them, and inquiries as to their traditions and customs, which appeared in the *Transactions* of the Bombay Literary Society. This was my first attempt to appear before the public as an author, since which time I have been a great intruder."

In 1815 he was appointed Junior Assistant to the Resident at Poona, the Honourable Mountstuart Elphinstone, whose acquaintance he had made in 1811, when passing through Poona from Bombay, on his way to Jaulna. Bajee Rao, destined to be the last of the Peishwas, was then on the throne, and a very full sketch of his career and of the Mahratta Confederation during its period of dissension and decay, is included in General Briggs's papers, a few extracts from which will make the picture sufficiently distinct.

"At the death of the Peishwa Madhoo Rao Narrain in 1796, the whole of the great Mahratta Chiefs, the Bhonsla of Nagpore, Scindia, Holkar, and the Jagheerdars of the Deccan ,appeared at Poona for the last time as vassals of the Empire. The power and influence of the Minister, Nana Furnavees, the last of Mahratta statesmen, was insufficient to control this tumultuous assembly, and scenes of intrigue and violence ensued. Nana Furnavees and his colleagues did all they could to obtain the assent of the Chiefs and nobles to the adoption of an heir by the widow of Madhoo Rao. But the claims of Bajee Rao, the son of the proscribed Rugonath Rao, were too strong to be set aside. His handsome face and figure, together with his reputed accomplishments, won the hearts of the great feudatories, and he was supported both by the British Government and by the military power of Scindia. He had not, however, been long in power before he betrayed his treacherous and cruel nature. Although for two generations at least Scindia and Holkar, always rivals for influence, had ruled almost independently over millions of subjects, each being able to bring from fifty to sixty thousand men into the field, they were nominally and ceremonially vassals of the Peishwa. While Dowlut Rao Scindia, having lately succeeded his uncle, was yet encamped within twenty or thirty miles of Poona, his rival in Hindustan, Wittojee Rao Holkar, was taking the part of some feudatory Chiefs in the Deccan, who had unsettled claims against their acknowledged lord, the Peishwa. Bajee Rao sent a well-organised force against Wittojee Holkar, who was defeated and brought a prisoner to Poona. Bajee Rao had him trampled to death by an elephant, on a charge of rebellion, and looked on with undisguised satisfaction from a balcony while the execution took place. Wittojee's brother, the celebrated Jeswunt Rao Holkar, immediately vowed vengeance against the Peishwa and Scindia, and, after many vicissitudes and adventures, in the course of two years, marched upon Poona with a well-appointed army of horse, foot, and artillery, drilled by European officers, most of them English. By very skilful manœuvres he arrived before the city of Poona, with all his forces in good condition, and, on the 25th of October 1802, found the combined armies of the Peishwa and Scindia drawn up to oppose him. A furious battle ensued, in which Holkar obtained a decisive victory. During the engagement the limits of the British Residency were marked out by small union-jack flags, which ensured respect from the combatants on both sides, and complete immunity from plunder or molestation. Scindia retreated Northwards, and Bajee Rao fled to the Western coast, where, embarking in an English vessel, he, like his father before him, threw himself on the protection of the British Government. Mr. Elphinstone was then at Poona as Assistant to the Resident, Colonel Barry Close, and accompanied him to pay his respects to the conqueror. I recollect well Mr. Elphinstone's description of the reception they met with. They found Jeswunt Rao Holkar in a common bell-tent, sitting on an ordinary peasant's bedstead covered by a small cotton carpet. His right arm, which had been severely wounded, was bound up. He apologised for the want of accommodation by saying that he was a plain soldier, and accustomed to rough it in the field. He regretted the heavy loss he had sustained in the battle, especially making mention, with many words of respect and sorrow, of the death of Captain Dawes, his English Commandant of Artillery. He assured the Resident that he was quite prepared to meet the wishes of the British Government in every point except that of the restoration of Bajee Rao. Colonel Close replied that the recent events had made such a sudden and unexpected change in the affairs of Poona, that he had received no orders from his own Government, and could not anticipate the instructions he might receive.

"Eventually, the fugitive Peishwa was restored by the British Government, after the conclusion with him of the Treaty of Bassein, which led to the first Mahratta war, and the victories of Sir Arthur Wellesley and Lord Lake.

"From the very day that Bajee Rao returned to Poona he resented the deprivation, under the Treaty of Bassein, of his authority, though it had been little more than nominal, over the great Mahratta Princes; and even while the war was going on, which had broken out in consequence of his restoration, he did all he could, secretly and indirectly, to detach his feudatory Chiefs who were in the field with their quotas co-operating with the British Army, and even seized some of their lands on the plea of their unauthorised absence. General Sir Arthur Wellesley wrote to the Resident, ' The policy of Bajee Rao is to deceive everyone'; and he predicted, with remarkable sagacity, that as soon as the war was over, Bajee Rao would try gradually to absorb all the feudal estates in the Deccan, more particularly of those Chiefs who had shown themselves well disposed to the British Government. He recommended that at the end of the war, we should make such arrangements with the Peishwa and the Southern Chiefs as would place them under our guarantee. If this measure were delayed too long, he said, the Peishwa would resent our interference, would probably enter into some combination with the Northern States, and form a league against us which would bring on another war. This advice, given in 1805, was not acted on, but the necessity of doing something to save the Jaghiredars who had been friendly to us had become very apparent in 1811, and British protection was extended to some of them, very much to the indignation of Bajee Rao.

"The Gaekwar, the Mahratta Chief of Baroda, was also far more under the influence and protection of the Government of Bombay than the Peishwa liked. There had been for some years a disputed balance of accounts between the Gaekwar and the Peishwa, and it was arranged that an envoy or agent on the part of the former should come to Poona and bring the matter to a conclusion. Gungadhur Shastree, a Brahmin, one of the Ministers of the Baroda State, was sent on this mission, under pledges given by the Peishwa to the British Government for his safety and honourable treatment. The Peishwa, whose habits were scandalously immoral, endeavoured to conciliate or to corrupt the envoy by not only inviting him and the ladies of his family to the Palace, but by proposing a matrimonial alliance between his house and that of Gungadhur Shastree. The Shastree had seen and heard so much in and about the Palace that offended his notions of propriety that these overtures were as respectfully as possible, but still strenuously, resisted. This was a slight that the Peishwa could not pardon, but he concealed his furious indignation under forms of courtesy and marked attentions that almost lulled the Shastree's fears and suspicions to sleep. On the eve of his intended departure, no settlement having been made, the Gaekwar's envoy was invited to a great festival at a temple, where he was accompanied by a favourite and confidant of the Peishwa named Trimbukjee Dainglia. On his way home to his lodgings that evening, the envoy's palanquin was arrested by a dense crowd ; a scuffle took place, and Gungadhur Shastree was then and there stabbed to death. Suspicion immediately fell on the Peishwa's messenger, Trimbukjee Dainglia, and conclusive evidence was soon obtained that he was the assassin. After much negotiation, the Resident, Mr. Elphinstone, firmly insisting on the point that Gungadhur Shastree was at Poona under a safeguard from our Government, obtained the custody of Trimbukjee Dainglia as a prisoner, and sent him off to Bombay. Trimbukjee made his escape on the road, reappeared in the Deccan, and began to raise troops and levy contributions, unquestionably in collusion with Bajee Rao, who denied all knowledge of his proceedings. The Resident, acting under the orders of the Governor-General, peremptorily demanded the apprehension of Trimbukjee. The Peishwa pretended to issue orders to that effect, but was treacherously entering into communications with all the Mahratta Chiefs, taking measures to increase his army, and to put the numerous forts in good order and mount guns on their ramparts.

" It was in that year, 1816, that I became a member of the Poona Resident's family, and the events which subsequently occurred, within my own observation and knowledge, necessarily form part of the history of my life.

"Mr. Elphinstone had ceased to visit the Peishwa in person, confining his communications to receiving visits from his Highness's Ministers. On these occasions he always required some of his Assistants to be present, and to minute after the conference, as near as each could remember, the very words which had been used. At length, one day—it was in April 1817—the Peishwa sent a message by his Minister that he desired to see Mr. Elphinstone, to confer on State affairs. Bajee Rao was an accomplished hypocrite. No one who knew him ever trusted him, though for many years he succeeded in deceiving almost everyone on a first acquaintance. His language was fluent, and even eloquent; his arguments so specious that it was not easy to refute them. On the arrival of Mr. Elphinstone and suite the Peishwa was found sitting in a small private apartment, from which, after the usual compliments, he dismissed the attendants, and said, ' I have requested this meeting, Mr. Elphinstone, to endeavour to disabuse your mind of some injurious impressions you seem to have formed as to my feelings and intentions towards your Government. Remember, that I have been connected with you from my childhood. Let me go back to the time when a cabal united against my father, now in heaven, on the death of his nephew, who was assassinated by his own guards in his palace; and when he, the next heir, came forward to claim his rights, you are aware how he was persecuted, and driven by the rebellious nobles out of his country. At this crisis there were the great chiefs, Holkar and Scindia and Gaekwar, to whom it would have been natural for him to apply for aid against his own subjects, but he passed them by, and placed himself under the protection of the British Government, and made a treaty with it. Scarcely had I reached the age of manhood when an accident left the Musnud again vacant, and my enemies desired to deprive me of my claim of succession. Your Government interfered, and I eventually obtained my rights. But my opponents were too strong, and, having marched an army to Poona, defeated my troops. I fled, not to seek assistance from my countrymen, but from the English at Bombay, and by your armies I was restored to my capital and my throne. How can you believe that, with all this load of obligation to your Government, I should ever have a design to make war against it? My whole body, from my head to my feet, has been nourished by the salt of the English. Look at the situation, however, from another point of view. I am not so ignorant of the history of British power in this country as not to know that whosoever has engaged in war with it has been defeated, and his sovereignty has passed away. In former times, when Hyder Ally, aided by the French, made war against the English, he could gain no ground; and it is said that on his death-bed he urged his son, Tippoo Sultan, to keep at peace, and to cultivate the friendship of the English. He was too proud and too confident. In two great wars, although assisted by the French, Tippoo was beaten, his territories divided, and at last he was destroyed. Since my re-establishment at Poona, have I not wit-nessed the defeat of those regular troops of infantry and artillery, trained under ¡European officers for the great Mahratta chiefs, Holkar and Scindia, who carried everything before them in Hin-dustan, but who, when they ventured to oppose the English, were beaten time after time with heavy losses, and eventually reduced to make peace at great sacrifices of territory and treasure? In my case, however, I ask, where are the regular troops? where are my infantry or my guns to cope with your armies? Yet, I am sus-pected of desiring to engage in war against my best friends.'

"During the whole of this speech, which was delivered in his native tongue, Mahrattee, the Peishwa was perfectly cool, nor did he exhibit any symptoms either of agitation or resentment. Mr. Elphinstone replied in the most polite manner in Hindustani, the language in which the Peishwa usually conversed with the Resident: 'All that your Highness has stated with regard to the connection of your family and yourself with my Government is perfectly true, and I am glad that your Highness apparently appre-ciates the many advantages you have derived from that connection. What your Highness has stated with respect to the absence of regular infantry and artillery against a disciplined European army is also correct; but the Mahrattas have not always relied upon such troops.'

"This was a hint to Bajee Rao, which Mr. Elphinstone did not think it advisable to make more explicit, that we had full information that there was a strong military party not only at Poona, but at Nagpore and in the camps of Scindia and Holkar, who strongly advised the discharge of all European commanders and drill instructors, the discontinuance of all attempts to rival the British Government in regular battalions and trains of artillery, and a return to the old Mahratta system of predatory tactics with ·large bodies of horse. I return to Mr. Elphinstone's little speech in reply to the Peishwa.

"'The evidence of warlike preparations in your Highness's territories is not wanting. It is notorious that all your Jaghiredars have been recruiting so as to fill up their quotas for field service. Your cavalry and infantry have been increased in number and constantly exercised. The forts have been put in repair and fully garrisoned. Guns have been brought into the City, and also the teams of bullocks for moving them with an army. These are warlike preparations; but against whom can they be directed except against the British Government? If not, it behoved your Highness, according to the Treaty, to communicate with the British Government on the subject. There was, however, one point in your Highness's address to which you did not allude, namely, that of your late communications with the Northern Mahratta States — an intercourse which by treaty you were bound to relinquish. Of these communications the Governor-General has received convincing proofs, and if I am not greatly misinformed, two emissaries from Dowlut Rao Scindia reached the neighbourhood of Poona within the last few days, and remained concealed in a village outside the City walls till midnight yesterday, when they were brought to the Palace. And', continued Mr. Elphinstone, ' they left this morning after two hours' stay in the Palace, no doubt with a reply from your Highness, and before daylight they were several miles on their return to Gwalior.' Mr. Elphinstone, however, ended by expressing an earnest hope that, as his Highness so fully appreciated his obligations to the British Government, and also recognised its power, his Highness would not be induced by evil and interested counsellors to depart from that line of conduct which would ensure to him the continued friendship of the British Government.

"The Peishwa replied that Mr. Elphinstone was greatly misinformed on many points to which he had adverted, and that he might rely on it he would never break faith with the British Government. ' As to going to war,' he said, ' the idea is absurd, when it is well known that I have such a horror of the sound of guns, that whenever salutes are fired, they are not allowed to take place till after I have passed the batteries to a considerable distance.'

"Almost immediately after making this curious appeal to his own constitutional timidity, Bajee Rao called for the silver trays of betel-nut and spices, and the perfumes offered to guests as a signal that they may take leave, and presented them with his own hands to Mr. Elphinstone, with most gracious expressions of goodwill and with a smiling countenance. Mr. Elphinstone's good-humoured and unimpassioned style of letting the Peishwa know that all his machinations had been watched and detected, was perfectly admirable. At one of his meetings with Sir John Malcolm, after his deposition, Bajee Rao complained, with deep emotion, that such was the espionage established by Mr. Elphinstone that even the very dishes provided for his Highness's meals were described in detail every day at the Residency.

" The Peishwa usually conversed in Hindustani, which he spoke with great fluency; but I have said that on the present occasion he chose to make use of his mother tongue. He was aware that Mr. Elphinstone understood Mahrattee perfectly, and not a word was lost on him. The practice I had had in translating so much from that language daily for the last year made me also master of all that was said. Notes of this important and remarkable conference were afterwards submitted by each of the members of the Residency who was present, and a full report transmitted to the Governor-General. No sooner was this report perused by the Marquis of Hastings, than he required the Resident to take such precautionary measures as he deemed necessary to defeat the Peishwa's evident designs, preparatory to binding him to our alliance by a new treaty more strictly than before."

The force of British troops at the cantonment near Poona having been considerably reinforced, and disposed so as to overawe the City, Bajee Rao subscribed to terms in the early part of May 1817, whereby he engaged to give up Trimbukjee within a month, and to place three of his principal hill-forts in our hands; and on the 13th of June a treaty was concluded whereby the Mahratta Confederation was dissolved, and the Peishwa renounced not only his supremacy over the Bhonsla of Nagpore, Scindia, Holkar, and the Gaekwar, but all connection and communication with them. Very few months elapsed before it became quite clear that the Peishwa was again bent upon hostile proceedings against the British Government. Numerous attempts were made by his emissaries to corrupt the Sepoys of our Bombay Regiments recruited in the Mahratta provinces.

" It appeared clear that Bajee Rao had made up his mind to embark in an extensive Mahratta confederacy against the English. His proceedings were conducted with the greatest secrecy, but they did not escape the vigilance of the Resident. In order to obtain intelligence of what the latter absolutely knew, and what he proposed doing, the Peishwa was lavish in promises and bribes to all whom he could seduce about the Residency. The Doctor, who was in the habit of passing an hour every day with Mr. Elphinstone reading Greek and Italian, was supposed to be in his confidence, though he was only treated as a common friend. The Peishwa begged that the Doctor might be sent to attend some members of his family; and the kindness that he there received, and the manner in which the Peishwa spoke of his fidelity and attachment to the English, deceived the Doctor till the day when war was declared. In the same manner he gained over the services of the English Commandant of the Contingent, who, to the last hour, professed to believe that the Peishwa would never make war with us. Bajee Rao invited this officer to dine with a large party of English officers at the Palace, kept him there for a few minutes' conversation after the other officers had left, and then sent after him the massive service of silver plate which had been used at the entertainment. This last gentleman received, also, two lakhs of rupees from Bajee Rao to obtain information of Trimbukjee and his proceedings; but it is only just to him to say that he rendered an account of the manner in which he had employed part of it, when afterwards called upon by Mr. Elphinstone to do so, and he then paid the balance into the Treasury.

"I joined Mr. Elphinstone as his third Assistant early in 1816, and left him, to take the field as Sir John Malcolm's Assistant, in July 1817. The other two Assistants at Poona were Francis Whitworth Russell, the third son of Sir Henry Russell, Chief Justice at Calcutta, and Henry Pottinger, afterwards well known as Sir Henry. My acquaintance with the languages induced Mr. Elphinstone at an early period to employ me in making translations of the numerous *akhbars* (news-letters) he was at that time in the habit of receiving from the Native Courts where he had established intelligencers, his own previous acquaintance with the Ministers of India while Resident at Nagpore having made him familiar with their characters and connections. At the time I speak of we had regular postal communications with the several capitals of these chiefs; and as the whole of that department was under our own Postmaster at Poona, it was not difficult in a great degree to depend on their reports, which were occasionally checked by sending a confidential agent along each line, under the plea of paying these intelligencers, to report circumstantially the actual state of affairs. Bajee Rao's foreign communications were made either by means of camel hircarras, or by special foot messengers, whose progress was detected by the small javelins they carried, every Court having them painted differently, to enable them to command any necessary aid they might require on their route. This answered as a sort of livery, but was recognised only by the officials of the several Princes. Similar javelins were used by the messengers of the bankers of the different cities in the Native States, but they were for the most part painted only in one colour. In this way we at Poona obtained instant information of the entry of any of the messengers of foreign Courts that might pass our postal stations, and were enabled to be on the look-out for their arrival, as well as to trace the direction of any despatched by the Peishwa. As it was subsequently ascertained from the public records of the Government that, out of the million and a half sterling of revenue which Bajee Rao received, he laid by half a million annually, he must have had at his disposal in 1816-17 upwards of eight millions of treasure in jewels and in specie, and he was by no means parsimonious in dispensing it to effect any of his purposes. He laid himself out to gain over by bribery every servant of the Residency; but such was Mr. Elphinstone's vigilance that he was aware of those in the Peishwa's pay, and took care to make use of them for his own objects. So complete was our information, that one of the complaints made by Bajee Rao against Mr. Elphinstone to Sir John Malcolm at Maholy, was, that he was so completely watched that the latter 'knew the very dishes that were served at his meals'.

"One night, after a day that had been passed in considerable anxiety, owing to reports of troops brought into the town, I received certain information that the cattle for the guns had been sent for, and had arrived an hour before; that the artillery were drawn up in front of the park; that the streets were full of mounted men; and that the Peishwa was in full durbar discussing with his chiefs the subject of immediate war. I hastened to inform Mr. Elphinstone, whom I found sitting in a large tent, engaged in playing a round game of cards with a party, among whom were several ladies. He saw me enter, and observed my anxiety to speak with him; but he continued his game for half an hour, when, after handing the last lady of the party into her palanquin, he came up to me rubbing his hands, and said, 'Well, what is it?' I told him the news, which he received with great *sang-froid*, and we walked together to the Residency office. There we encountered the European Commandant of the Contingent, above alluded to, and Mr. Elphinstone asked him the latest news from the city. He appeared not to be aware of what was in progress, but observed that the Minister, whom he had just left, had told him that the Peishwa had discharged some of the troops lately entertained, and that all was quiet. Mr. Elphinstone then called on me to state what I had heard, and distinctly told the Commandant that he did not believe a word of his report. The latter

E

said that his information was from the Minister himself, and that
as to the troops in the streets, he did not observe any beyond the
usual patrols, and knew nothing about the arrival of gun-bullocks.
The moment was critical, the Residency was incapable of being
properly defended, especially by the ordinary escort, and the idea
of attacking the Peishwa at once from the cantonment, though
hastily expressed, was subsequently abandoned.   Mr. Elphinstone
resolved to defer doing anything until the morning, and then to
take such precautionary measures as he might deem proper.   I
believe that neither he nor I had much sleep during that anxious
night, which fortunately passed quietly, owing, as was said, to the
opposition to war evinced by some of the Ministers.   Bajee Rao
was physically an arrant coward ; he had always displayed this
weakness, and was not ashamed to avow it.   No steps were therefore taken by either party during the night, but in the morning a
requisition for a reinforcement was made, and two guns accompanied it to the Residency.

" I was not present at the battle of Kirkee, the cantonment near
Poona, on the 5th of November 1817.   I had left the Residency
in September, my friend and patron General Malcolm, now Sir
John, having invited me to join him as one of his personal staff
and Political Assistants.   He then held the double appointment
of Commander of the 3rd division of the Deccan Army, and of
the Governor-General's Agent with the Commander-in-Chief.
With the full approval and the kindest encouragement from Mr.
Elphinstone, I started from Poona very soon after the ratifica-
tion of the Treaty of June had arrived from Lord Hastings's head-
quarters, and when almost everyone, myself included, with the
exception, I think, of Mr. Elphinstone, who was never either too
confident or too communicative, had come to the conclusion that
Bajee Rao would not fight.   But though I was not at the Poona
Residency when the battle of Kirkee took place, I had been compelled to leave behind me hostages to the fortune of that day ; and
in consequence of my close and recent connection, I heard so much
at the time from eye-witnesses, from Mr. Elphinstone and my wife
among others, that I must say a few words about the occurrences
immediately after my departure.   I started in the height of the
monsoon, having to pass over a large tract of country without
anything like a ' made' road, the soil consisting of the black, sapo-
naceous and tenacious earth called cotton soil, which when dry
splits into hard blocks with deep fissures, dangerous to horses' legs,
and when saturated with rain is so soft that beasts of burden sink
up to their knees in it.   It was out of the question that my wife
and family should accompany me at this time of the year, more
especially as there was no small chance of encountering stray
Pindarrees and plunderers, in which case a train of palanquins

would have been a temptation to them, and an encumbrance to us. I travelled, of course, on horseback, with a small escort.

"Bajee Rao remained tolerably quiet until, in the course of the strategic arrangements by which the several Mahratta Powers were to be watched and held in check while the Pindarrees were assailed on all sides, the Subsidiary Force was ordered to the front under General Lionel Smith, leaving only a weak brigade in cantonment at Poona. Mr. Elphinstone, suspecting that a treacherous attack might be made some night without warning, had the small force taken a little further from Poona, across the Mooteemoola river, where it occupied the village of Kirkee, about two miles from the City. The Resident had, also, made application for the reinforcement of an European Regiment from Bombay, and strengthened his own escort at the Residency by an additional company of Sepoys. It was concerted also between the General and Mr. Elphinstone, that in case the former did not hear by every post, he might conclude that the latter had been attacked. On the very day after the arrival of the European Regiment, the Peishwa's Army of at least twenty-five thousand men, chiefly Irregular horse and foot, with ten or twelve guns, issued from the City on the 5th November, when an Aide-de-Camp of His Highness galloped up to the front verandah of the Residency and shouted, 'It is War!' Major Ford, the Officer Commanding the Auxiliary Force, was at that moment at the Residency, and received Mr. Elphinstone's orders at once to range his brigade along-side of the British line. Mr. Elphinstone placed my wife and children, besides two other ladies then at the Residency, in their palanquins, leaving with them his own escort for their protection to the Camp at Kirkee, while he, crossing the river with his suite where there was no regular ford, just escaped being taken prisoner, and joined the troops as they were advancing to meet the enemy. It is right here to mention that Mr. Elphinstone, fourteen years before, had been attached to General Arthur Wellesley's Force in the Assaye and Argaum Campaigns of 1803-4, that he was his Political Secretary and his guest during the whole of that time, and was at his side in every battle and siege of the war; in fact, there was no more experienced officer at the battle of Kirkee than the Resident himself, and it would be hardly too much to say that he took and retained the command throughout that day.

"Our force, consisting of one European Regiment and four Battalions of Sepoys, besides Artillery, did not number quite three thousand men on the field. The battle of Kirkee was fought through the persuasion of Gokla, one of Bajee Rao's best commanders, his over confidence and impatience being founded on the certainty that our Sepoys would come over by companies or battalions as soon as the first shot was fired. The Peishwa's Cavalry, numbering more than 10,000, only made one attempt at a charge, but they were received with a steady fire, and their leader, Moro Dixit, being killed by a cannon ball, they did not renew the attack. Our loss was inconsiderable, nineteen killed and sixty-seven wounded. That of the enemy was much more severe, and several Chiefs of rank fell in the action.

"The enemy plundered and burnt the Residency, directing their destructive efforts especially against Mr. Elphinstone's books, which were believed to include many on alchemy and the occult arts, and to have given him almost magical powers. All the houses, goods and chattels of the Resident's suite were destroyed; also, my own house and valuable library included. My wife and her three children, one in arms, were huddled into a palanquin, saving nothing but the clothes on their backs. So also were two other ladies, the whole party being protected by the Resident's infantry escort in their journey over fields for the most part covered with high grain, on their way to the British lines. Before they reached their destination a party of the enemy's horse arrested their progress. The infantry escort, already loaded, surrounded the palanquins. The husband of one of the ladies, who was not a military man, and was dressed in plain clothes, dismounted and called on the infantry to fire. The steady Native officer who commanded the party knew better. He desired the gentleman to mount his horse and be quiet. 'We are infantry,' said he, ' we don't mind these Cavalry.' This gallant soldier now addressed the party of horse which had surrounded the palanquins, though still about twenty yards off :—' These are only women and children, and you are not come to fight them, I suppose. There is no plunder here for you. We are soldiers and bound to sell our lives for these ladies. Stand off, or it will be worse for you ; we shall not give fire till you are within a spear's length, and then some of your saddles will be emptied.' The troopers laughed at the coolness of the veteran, and having satisfied themselves by the screams of the women and children in the three palanquins who they were, one of them said, 'The Subadar speaks truth, they are only women and children, let them go.' And so they did, and the party arrived safely at Kirkee, after all the fighting was over. Such acts of gallantry and fidelity on the part of our Native soldiers were not uncommon in those days, and were not, I fear, thought so much of, or so well requited, as they ought to have been.

"I received from Mr. Elphinstone a short note written in the field to the following effect :—

"'We have had a battle, and have driven the enemy into the City. Bajee Rao behaved like a gentleman, which I did not expect, by sending me word while the troops were coming out, "It is War". Mrs. Briggs and the children are safe with us in Camp, and well; but I fear your house, like the rest, is burnt, and all your manuscripts are sacrificed.'

" This was, also, too true, I lost all my library, and my valuable journal in Persia of 1808-9-10. My unfinished translation of Ferishta was, fortunately, with a friend in Bombay; and I afterwards recovered two other valuable manuscripts, bought for me by a Native friend in Poona from a plunderer.

" Immediately on hearing of the outbreak of hostilities, General Lionel Smith, with the main body of the Subsidiary Force, then on the Godavery river, returned to Poona without opposition by forced marches, and a second battle was fought, wherein the enemy was even more signally beaten, dispersed and pursued by the British Cavalry and Horse Artillery. My family found shelter in a cowshed, which Mr. Elphinstone had made his head-quarters on the night of the first battle, and in which he had written his despatches. My wife received from my friend Henry Pottinger, then an Assistant like myself,* an entire piece of calico which he had brought from Bombay—whence he arrived the day after the battle —for his own use, and with this material she made up some changes of clothing for herself and the children. Another friend saw that she was regularly supplied with poultry and vegetables, brought in by our foraging parties. Mr. Elphinstone and his Staff accompanied the army in its pursuit of Bajee Rao; but in the midst of his endless and engrossing public business he managed to see that my wife was supplied with every sort of provision and comfort from his own stores, just arrived from Bombay, including plate, crockery and glass, writing out the list with his own hand. At his advice, she took the earliest safe opportunity—as it was supposed to be—of leaving Poona for Madras, where she remained till the war was over with one of her married sisters, having narrowly escaped encountering the enemy's army, which had crossed her route twenty-four hours before she passed over it.

" As a proof that travelling across country was dangerous at this period for Europeans, I may mention that in April 1817 Lieutenant Dacre, of the Madras Artillery, with a small escort, fell in with a body of Pindarrees, and was robbed and murdered. On the 6th of November, the day after the battle of Kirkee, two officers coming from Bombay, Cornets Morrison and Hunter, were plundered and taken prisoners by some of the Peishwa's horsemen, and sent to a hill-fort in the Konkan, whence they were eventually released. A few days later, Captain Vaughan, of my own

---

* Afterwards the Rt. Honble. Sir Henry Pottinger, Bart., G.C.B., Envoy in China, Governor of Madras, etc., etc.

regiment, and his younger brother, just arrived from England, marching without an escort, were seized and taken to Futtehgaon, a place about twenty miles from Poona, and were hanged there. About the same time, Lieutenant Ennis, of the Bombay Engineers, who was surveying, attended by a small guard, was attacked and killed by a party in the service of Trimbukjee Dainglia. In consequence of these outrages, Mr. Elphinstone had it proclaimed, and took care it should be made known in the Peishwa's camp, that if any prisoners were put to death or maltreated, he should retaliate on any prisoners that fell into his hands, whatever their rank or station might be.

" I joined Sir John Malcolm on the Nerbudda in the middle of September 1817, shortly after the united 1st and 3rd Divisions had received their orders to cross the river and to take up a position between the army of Holkar and a strong force belonging to Scindia, near Oujein. Holkar's army was encamped in a strong position at Mahidpoor, constantly sending out parties of Light Cavalry to cut off our supplies and capture our carriage cattle. The British force, under General Sir Thomas Hislop, consisted of one wing of the Madras European Regiment and the flank companies of the Royal Scots, amounting in all to less than 600 bayonets, and seven regiments of Native Infantry, about 3,000 strong ; two batteries of Horse Artillery with six-pounders, one squadron of Dragoons, and three Regiments of Regular Native Cavalry, besides the Mysore Irregular Horse, numbering about 4,000 swords, under their Native Chief, with a European Commandant and Brigade Major to direct their movements. The enemy had fourteen Regiments of Regular Infantry, a train of seventy guns, including many twenty-four and thirty-two pounders, and a body of several thousand well-equipped Cavalry."

General Briggs always condemned the tactical conduct of the battle of Mahidpoor, and contended in an argument of great length that there was a great want of military skill displayed on that occasion. But his controversy with Colonel Valentine Blacker, who was Quartermaster-General of Sir Thomas Hislop's Force, and wrote a military History of the Mahratta War, and the discussion in general on the campaign, can have scarcely any interest now. There was certainly no lack of gallantry or of steady soldiership on that day, on the part either of the English officers and men, or of the Madras Sepoys. Captain Briggs himself acted as an Aide-de-Camp to General Sir John Malcolm, to whom was given the immediate command of two brigades of infantry destined to attack the enemy's left. The whole of this operation was performed with great steadiness, although our Horse Artillery was nearly silenced during the advance, for their six-pounders, though well served, were unequal to the guns of heavy calibre in position before them, and many of our pieces were dismounted or disabled.

"Sir John Malcolm personally led the right brigade under Colonel Robert Scott, against the battery on the enemy's left, receiving a very heavy fire, first of round shot and then two salvoes of grape, the rattle of which against the barrels of our muskets, for that was what most struck my ear at the time, I shall never forget. Our Sepoys advanced most steadily, hardly a shot being fired, except by a very few young hands, till within a few yards of the batteries, when, on receiving the order, they halted to give one volley, and then rushed on to the charge. Holkar's Infantry, ranged closely behind their guns, were unable to act, and very soon broke and fled after receiving our fire at close quarters. Sir Thomas Hislop and his Staff followed quickly after the success of our attack, and we were soon gratified by the appearance of the Deputy Adjutant General, Colonel Leicester Stanhope, afterwards Lord Petersham, galloping from the front, waving his hat over his head, and proclaiming the capture of the batteries on our left; after which the same work was completed all along the enemy's line. Holkar's Artillerymen showed undaunted courage, fighting to the last with their spunge-staffs and swords until bayoneted or cut down.

"The loss of the enemy was estimated at 3,000 men, and one of their principal Chiefs, Roshun Beg, was severely wounded. Young Holkar, quite a child, was in the action on horseback, and fled with the main body of his Cavalry after the capture of the guns. Sixty-three guns of all calibres were taken with their tumbrils and waggons. The loss of the British Army was 778 men killed and wounded, including 38 European and 27 Native officers. Leaving out the 4,000 Mysore Horse, who were very useful in the pursuit, but who only lost 65 men, we numbered only 4,800 of all ranks, so that our loss was about 1 in 7. There were only seven Companies of Europeans, and one squadron of Dragoons besides the Artillery; the remainder, about 4,000, were all Madras Sepoys. On that day the Madras Rifle Corps, numbering only 240 rank and file, lost 135, including ten officers, and the only one who came safely through the battle had his horse shot under him.

"The battle of Mahidpoor was fought on the 21st of December, the day of St. Thomas, the patron-saint's day of our Commander-in-Chief, Sir Thomas Hislop. On Christmas Day he held a levée, and received all the officers of the Force, European and Native. On that occasion, only one officer of the Rifle Corps, Captain Evans, was able to attend, the ten others had all been put *hors de combat*, one killed and nine severely wounded."

Peace having been made with the Government of Holkar, under the Treaty of Mundissore on the 6th of January 1818, and Sir John Malcolm having been detached in January 1818, with his division, in the pursuit of the Peishwa Bajee Rao, Captain John Briggs was left in charge of the office of Governor-General's Agent with the army under Sir Thomas Hislop. In this capacity he was present at the storm of the strong fortress of Talnair on the 27th of February, and at the surrender of the forts of Gaulna and Chandore, opening a communication between the army of Hindustan, under Lord Hastings, and the Deccan, still occupied by the forces and partisans of the Peishwa.

In May, Captain Briggs was ordered to take charge of the cessions and conquests in Khandesh; while another of his friends and comrades on the list of Mr. Elphinstone's Assistants, Captain James Grant,[*] was appointed Political Agent, subsequently termed Resident, with the Rajah of Sattara, just rescued from his palace prison in the Peishwa's custody, and placed in possession of a small sovereignty carved out of the central portion of his ancestors' dominions.

Captain Briggs started at once for his new charge, and just before his departure wrote a letter to Sir John Malcolm, from which the following extract is characteristic of the man and of the spirit in which he worked among the Indian people.

It is dated "Mahidpoor, 19th January 1818".

"Don't forget to let me know about the son of Goolzar Khan Toky of Lassoor. It is a small matter, but I think we ought to ensure friends and local information in Khandesh as fast as possible, after which we shall soon see our way. I will send you all

---

[*] Afterwards Grant Duff, author of the *History of the Mahrattas*, father of the Rt. Honble. Mountstuart Elphinstone Grant Duff, Governor of Madras.

the information I can collect about Holkar's Government after I reach Oujein, to which place my coadjutor, Munseram, accompanies me. I shall give him letters to you and Agnew. He has been immensely useful to me, and deserves everything at our hands. He has received from Bhopal, from Tantia Jogh, and from Ghuffoor Khan the kindest letters, most of which he has shown to me. He is one of the most sensible Natives I have ever met with, always communicative and obliging."

The next letter, written to Sir John Malcolm when on the march to enter on his new duties, will at once give some insight into the problems that had to be considered and solved on the first acquisition of ceded and conquered provinces in India, and will show the cheerful confidence and mastery of details with which Captain Briggs entered on the task allotted to him in the great work of invoking order out of chaos.

" Camp on the river below the Simrole Ghaut,
" 7th February 1818.

" MY DEAR SIR JOHN,—We have this day received a copy of Mr. Adam's to you of the 20th January. I observe the Governor-General is prepared to make an allowance for the advances made on account of the Pergunnahs of Chandore and Nundoorbar for the revenues of the current year. This may be all very proper as a passing measure of conciliation, and by way of acceding to some of the many demands made by Tantia Jogh during the course of the negotiations. But I observe the Governor-General also authorises your holding out hopes that Holkar's Government may keep the hereditary lands about Chandore and at Wabgaum in the Deccan. It may be presumption in me to dissent from what you seem to have recommended, and Lord Hastings has approved; still, I will venture to say in plain terms that if Holkar has one *beegah* of land in which he can have a karkoon, so as to give him a plea for holding communications with the Deccan, there will be more mischief done some of these days than good can accrue just now from the most gracious concession. Our object certainly should be to consolidate the territories of each of the predatory Powers ; to cut them off from any pretext for foreign communication and intrigue; to separate effectually each State from every other ; and to break the neck of that abominable propensity that every true Mahratta has, according to their own saying, ' to get one hand into every one's dish'—to have a claim, however small, in every quarter— without which he would no longer be a true Mahratta. We want no more true Mahrattas. Our interest, and that of every State in

India, is to have a settled government everywhere; but the policy
in which all Indian princes and chieftains have been brought up
will not in the present day lead them, of themselves, to find and
keep their centre of gravity; and it has, therefore, become necessary to the tranquillity of the country for the great preponderating
Power to hold the scales in its own hand, and establish by force
that balance which they are incapable of settling, or of even com-
prehending.   I think Mr. Elphinstone will agree with me as to the
inexpediency of allowing Holkar to hold any lands in the Deccan.
Their annual value is trifling, and might be made over to the
Durbar, but don't let Holkar have the appointment of a cow-keeper
south of the Sindwa Ghaut.   I would say the same of Scindia—
nor should any Peishwa be allowed to make or meddle north of
the river Taptee.   Let us now break for ever what was only nominally broken before, the link of political connection between these
Mahratta Princes generally, and between those in Hindostan and
their old homes.   All persons who can have any personal recollection or sentiment regarding the hereditary estates of Holkar in the
Deccan must now be out of date.   The beautiful Bheema Baee,
now only sixteen, may remember her imprisonment as a child in
the fort of Asseerghur by Scindia; but I doubt if she has any
feelings of affection to the Deccan on that account.   By-the-bye,
talking of this lady, I hear she is most anxious for her debts to
her troops—about a lakh of rupees—being paid, and to retire to
Benares on a pension, giving up her *mehals* (estates) *in toto*.[1]   I
merely mention this to enable you to make the suggestion yourself,
if you think it advisable.   If I am not misinformed, Tantia Jogh
was willing enough to accede to this arrangement, when the battle
of Mahidpoor put an end to all their plans.

" I long to be up and doing in Khandesh, and I am in hopes Sir
Thomas Hislop will take the Governor-General's hint and settle it
himself, leaving the hunting of the Peishwa to younger and more
active people.   All my reports and intelligence will go under his
name to Government; and I confess that I think he would, on the
score of character, gain more in reducing the forts and pacifying
the country with me, than in driving Bajee Rao with light troops,
a business quite out of his line, but in which he would let no one
help him.   Couldn't you follow up Lord Hastings's hint?

" I am, my dear General, with sincere esteem,

" Your very faithful and obliged friend,

" JOHN BRIGGS."

There was much rough work to be done in the Gun-

---

* This lady died in 1858, when her jaghire estate of Koonch was resumed by the Government of India.—Aitchison's *Treaties*, vol. iv, p. 282.

gaturree country and Khandesh before Briggs could set about his task of civil administration. Immediately after the conclusion of the Treaty of Mundissore, the ruling authorities in Holkar's camp had given to Sir Thomas Hislop orders, duly executed and sealed, to the Killadars, or commandants of all the forts in the conquered provinces, explaining the cession of territory, and requiring them to hand over charge of their military posts, with all guns and stores, to the English officers duly authorised to take possession. But in the political uncertainty of the time, obedience to these orders was by no means universal or prompt. Several forts had offered resistance, and as those in Khandesh were known to be held in many instances by bands of mercenary Arabs, claiming large arrears of pay, military operations were clearly necessary before the real work of pacification could be practically commenced. In May 1818 the army of the Deccan was broken up. General Sir Thomas Hislop, on his arrival with the main body of his force at Aurungabad, on his way to resume his ordinary duties as Commander-in-Chief at Madras, delivered over to the charge of Captain Briggs all the forts and dependencies ceded by Holkar and conquered from the Peishwa, north of the river Godavery, as far as the Sātpūra mountains ; and he was directed to consider himself under the direct orders of the Honble. Mountstuart Elphinstone, sole Commissioner for the government of our acquisitions in the Deccan. Ever since Briggs had left Poona to join Sir John Malcolm he had still remained on the establishment of Mr. Elphinstone as one of his Assistants, and had continued to correspond with him. Mr. Elphinstone had, in fact, as he informed Briggs in a most friendly and flattering letter, recommended him to the Governor-General for the almost independent functions that were now entrusted to him.

The country lying between the Godavery and the Sātpūra Hills may be considered as a tract containing about nineteen thousand square miles, comprising Gungaturree, or the valley of the Godavery, a well populated region, and Khandesh, scantily inhabited. The plain of the Godavery was bounded on the west by the Syadri range of mountains, in which were situated twenty-three hill-forts, all occupied, with hostile intent, by garrisons who refused either to obey the orders of transfer issued by their old master Holkar, or to acknowledge the British Government. For the purpose of introducing the new authority and restoring order in these parts, a force, commanded by Lieutenant-Colonel MacDowell,* consisting of half a regiment of European Infantry, two Sepoy battalions, three companies of Pioneers, with five Engineer officers, an efficient Staff, and a small battering train in addition to the field guns,—altogether about 2,500 men —was placed under the political direction of Captain Briggs.

Besides this strong brigade of regular troops, there was an excellent body of Irregular Horse, numbering 1,750 swords, which had been enlisted for the Honourable Company's service out of Holkar's disbanded army, after the battle of Mahidpoor. They had behaved extremely well when accompanying Sir Thomas Hislop in his march from Malwa, and were now to be paid by Captain Briggs, and to form a local force entirely at his disposal, under their own Commandant, Lieutenant Rind, of the Bombay Army, judiciously and considerately selected by Mr. Elphinstone as much on account of his friendship for Briggs as of his remarkable qualifications for such a command.

In entering upon this highly responsible charge, Captain Briggs found himself placed in an extremely delicate position. The situation bristled with difficulties, both in his personal relations with the Commandant of the Force, and in the antagonism which immediately grew up between his functions as protector of the civil population and the tendency of the troops to consider as booty everything portable or convertible on their route.

Briggs had now been seventeen years in the service, and was the second Captain in his Regiment, but the Lieutenant-Colonel commanding the Field Force was his

---

* Afterwards General Sir Andrew Hay MacDowell, K.C.B.

senior by nearly twenty years. The Commandant and the Political Agent had been brother-officers in the same Regiment. When Briggs joined the 15th Madras Native Infantry as Ensign in 1801, MacDowell, whose first commission was dated in 1785, was already a Captain, and had seen much active service. It will be remembered that in 1806 Major MacDowell was in command of the 1st Battalion of the 15th, with Lieutenant Briggs as his Adjutant, when the "white stock" incident occurred, the only outward symptom of the conspiracies at Hyderabad in that year, a pale reflex and reverberation of the Vellore mutiny.[1] Having parted in 1808, on Briggs going to Persia with Sir John Malcolm, they met once more in 1818, and were then associated on public duty, under very different circumstances. The junior was no longer subordinate to the senior. Although the military command was in the hands of Colonel MacDowell, the Khandesh Field Force was placed under the direction of Captain Briggs, and could hardly be moved ten paces to the right or left except at his instance or with his approval. The young Political Agent was the ever present representative of the Governor-General, whose confidence he was supposed to enjoy, and with whom he was in direct communication. He says, in the autobiographical papers :—

"As Commandant and Adjutant of the 1st Battalion of the 15th, MacDowell and I did not get on well together, and I know that he did all in his power to get me removed to the other Battalion; but, very much to his annoyance, instead of my being removed he was. From 1808 we had never met till our positions were now so curiously reversed, but he seemed to have forgotten what had taken place ten years before, and met me with apparent cordiality, avowing his desire to accede to my wishes in everything for the benefit of the Service. It became my duty, as it was my wish, to forget all that had passed in former times. I must do him the justice to say that not only were his military operations conducted with the utmost gallantry, judgment, and skill, but that they were certainly not injuriously affected, as to promptitude or decisiveness, by his personal feelings towards me. Perhaps, however, I may claim some little credit for this, for I had to exer-

* Ante, pp. 24, 25.

cise a good deal of patience and, I may say, tact, to avoid clashing. Our old regimental position soon became known in the camp, and some of his Staff were not slow in keeping the Commandant's mind in a state of irritation. I, however, scrupulously avoided all interference or even suggestion in military details, and abstained from assuming any of the 'political' state so common in those days—pitching my tents almost within his lines, displaying no flag of my own, and submitting for his information all my reports of military movements. He seemed to appreciate this conduct on my part, which I think I may call frank and conciliatory, and himself adopted the plan of abstaining from formal correspondence with me while we were in the neighbourhood of each other, but we carried on business by verbal intercourse and semi-official notes on trivial as well as important matters. This correspondence I still retain in my possession, and it serves me as a guide both as to facts and dates. I believe myself that but for the disputes as to prize property we should have ended the campaign on good terms."

The inclination to plunder has characterised belligerents, by sea and land, in all ages of the world. In the various forms of ransom and booty, the soldiers' lottery, with its bloody blanks and golden prizes, has been recognised always and everywhere; and, however mitigated and regulated, is not, as the annals of 1870 testify, by any means extinct in the third quarter of this enlightened nineteenth century. So long, indeed, as war continues to be one of the most effectual agents in developing the destinies of the world, it is useless to bewail the survival of the destructive and predatory instincts. It is natural enough that those who have to endure the stress and spasm of warfare, who are compelled to stake their limbs and their lives on innumerable and immeasurable hazards, should think themselves entitled, when there is any visible prize before them, to make the losers pay.

The main principles as to what constitutes lawful prize, what persons are liable to lose, and who may keep or share—for example, the Government, or the troops, the main body, or the detachment that actually makes the capture—have been more fully discussed and more definitely settled with reference to naval operations than to warfare on land; and in fact no single prize taken at

sea can be finally appropriated without a formal process
and condemnation in some Court of Admiralty. From
various causes—chiefly, perhaps, because the rights of
neutrals and of the captors' fellow-subjects have so seldom
been involved—a regular adjudication is not an essential
preliminary to the partition of booty taken on land, and
the whole subject of army prize money is in a compara-
tively loose and unsettled state.

In India the perplexities regarding what is lawful
prize have been less remarkable than the summary assumptions, usually granted in favour of the troops.
Political, civil, and military authorities never seem to
have been able to make up their minds whether India is
to be considered and treated as part of the British
Empire or as a foreign country, and whether its inhabitants are subjects of Her Majesty or aliens—citizens or
Helots. All the Indian allied, protected, and tributary
States, whose relations and responsibilities as federal con-
stituents of the Empire ought to be equitably defined,
are arbitrarily controlled by what is called the "Foreign"
Department. Lord Dalhousie, who extinguished and
despoiled so many of them in very cavalier fashion, habitually described them, with an inaccuracy that almost
appears ironical, as "independent" States. Since the
process of annexation has been checked by English
opinion, acting through the Home authorities, Anglo-
Indian officialism has taken to designating the Native
States, indiscriminately, and with equal inaccuracy, as
"feudatory"; while, in some instances, undoubted feudatories of the Native Princes have been quietly detached
from their proper allegiance and turned into tributaries
to our Government. Neither in peace nor in time of
rebellion have our "Foreign" Secretaries or our Councillors been able to make the right distinctions between
Princes connected with the Imperial Power by Treaties,
Chieftains having heritable jurisdiction, mere private
landlords, and political stipendiaries.

There have been some strange and very questionable
cases of plunder claimed and granted as prize to troops
in Indian campaigns, such as the Bhurtpore prize of

1825, when we emptied the treasury and jewel room of the Prince we professed to protect from a cruel usurper; such as the Scinde prize-money—Sir Charles Napier's share of which was upwards of £50,000—derived from confiscating the private valuables, including the ladies' jewels, of the Ameers' families, seized in cold blood, without any storm or siege, in the Palaces of Hyderabad.

There was the quiet misappropriation in 1849 of the jewels and other personalty, worth about £250,000, of our Ally and Ward, the Maharajah Duleep Singh, which, being in charge of his guardian, the British Resident at Lahore, were handed over as prize money to the British troops that had taken part in the Punjaub campaign. This property, together with the person of the Maharajah, had been uninterruptedly in charge of the Resident as head, under Treaty, of the Punjaub Government at Lahore, the capital of the State, which throughout the war had never been besieged, assailed, or, in a military sense, threatened. The war had, from first to last, been carried on under Treaty, and by public proclamation, for the suppression of a mutiny and rebellion against the Maharajah's Government, and with the aid of the Maharajah's councillors and troops.* The Maharajah Duleep Singh's jewels and plate, even if they had fallen into the hands of our army through some military exploit, were not the property of an enemy, but of a friend, held by our Government in trust. I cannot see, and have never had pointed out to me, any military, executive, or legal process, up to the present day, whereby that trust has been dissolved, or our Government exempted or indemnified from having to account for it.

Then there were some singular interpretations and assumptions of customs and precedents relating to plunder and booty, during the operations for suppressing the mutinies and rebellion in India between 1857 and 1859. Without entering on the more debatable appropriations in and about Delhi, Lucknow, and other places where

---

* See *Punjaub Papers*, 1849, pp. 374, 375, 448, 449, 591, 187, 197, 256, 289, 379, 457, 584, 585, 589, 631.

fighting took place, there was, for example, the case of the Kirwee prize-money, the largest haul made by any body of troops in those days, and about which there has been so much litigation. This was really the plunder of the undefended house of private persons charged with rebellion,—not the fort or palace of a Prince or ruling Chieftain, but the house of two brothers of high rank and great wealth, who had probably conspired against the Government, but had certainly taken no part in hostilities, had committed no overt act of rebellion, and had actually surrendered themselves to the General in command, before the troops were anywhere near their place of residence.* It was just as if the British troops had claimed the private property of Lord Lovat or Lord Derwentwater during the rebellion of 1745, and their claim had been admitted.

The Crown, I believe, granted the Kirwee booty to the troops,—a preliminary left out, as could hardly be avoided, when the Maharajah Duleep Singh's jewels were handed over—and therefore it may be presumed there was no illegality; but it is not easy to see any justification for such a grant.

It would have been impossible, it seems to me, for any Attorney-General, Advocate-General, prize agent, or any expert in the law of booty, to have drafted a royal mandate for the condemnation of the Maharajah Duleep Singh's goods. And for that reason, I suppose, they were handed over without any such formality.

But even the Crown draws the line somewhere in the liberality of its grants, particularly when the plunder is not palpably in possession of the troops, and in the case of money in the public funds belonging to the Kirwee brothers and other rebels of 1857, declined to transfer it as booty to the troops. The claim to such a transfer was, however, actually made, and great expectations were entertained of its success !

It is no doubt always a matter of primary and indispensable importance in military operations to keep soldiers in good temper, and some relaxation of discipline

* Malleson's *History of the Indian Mutiny*, vol. iii, p. 199.

is generally overlooked in the progress of a campaign, so long as prompt and implicit obedience can be maintained among them on the march and in action. What they find after a storm or an assault they must generally be allowed to keep ; and a speedy distribution, or the expectation of it, after or before the grant from the Crown, is the best safeguard against indiscriminate and irregular plunder, against each man keeping what he finds for himself, instead of all being thrown into a common stock. But it is the duty of the Commandant to see that nothing is taken but what is lawful prize, a duty generally understood and observed in European warfare, but often overlooked when war is waged by a civilised nation in such outlandish regions as India, China, or Burma, against barbarous races of a different complexion and creed.

The difficulty with which Captain Briggs had to contend on this campaign was the inclination of the troops, from the Commandant downwards, to consider every desirable object they came across to be " Bajee Rao's", and everything that was " Bajee Rao's" to be good prize. At the very outset, on the 8th of April 1818, Colonel MacDowell writes to Captain Briggs :—" With regard to forage, I consider that we are in an enemy's country." By virtue of this inaccurate and very insufficient assumption, all hands began to help themselves, with very little restraint, to whatever they could pick up on the road, or near the halting places. It seemed to be considered quite enough by Colonel MacDowell, if, in his own words, " everything was paid for that was brought to the camp for sale."

Captain Briggs, on the contrary, conceived it to be his first duty to let the inhabitants understand that we did not consider them as enemies, that the Force was not marching in " an enemy's country", but in territory ceded by Holkar to the British Government under a Treaty, or conquered from the Peishwa ; that if the people remained peaceably in their villages, and pursued their ordinary occupations, they would not be wronged or molested in any way; and that all supplies required would be paid for at the market price.

On the second day after entering Khandesh, the 9th April, a small village, surrounded with the usual mud wall of defence, having been entered without any resistance, Colonel MacDowell writes to Briggs :—" I have ordered the place to be immediately occupied by Lieutenant Rule, and have directed him to communicate with me. His first duty, of course, will be to take charge of whatever may appear to be prize property, and send in an account of it."

On the 29th of April the Commandant writes :—" I received information last night that a number of Bajee Rao's sheep are in a jungle within twelve miles of this, and I have sent a guard under a Native officer with orders to bring them in, and in order to prevent mistakes, if there should be any doubt of their being the Peishwa's, to bring in the head-man of the village. There can be no doubt about it."

Briggs had to explain to Colonel MacDowell that not only was there very great doubt whether the sheep were Bajee Rao's, but that there was no doubt at all in his mind that sheep grazing in a jungle twelve miles from the line of march could not, to whomsoever they belonged, become prize property. He had, moreover, to give his very unwelcome opinion that Bajee Rao's treasure or property of any description, wherever found, unless taken in the storm of a town, was State property, and must be carried to the account of our Government. This doctrine, bad enough when applied to grain, sheep, and such commonplace commodities, was peculiarly irritating when made applicable, as occurred very early in the campaign, to a genuine discovery of jewels, coin, and bullion belonging to Bajee Rao. When he had thus placed himself, though ineffectually as it proved, between his old comrades and their prize, Briggs came to be regarded as a sort of traitor in the camp. His incessant occupation, on horseback and at his writing-table, left him little time for social intercourse at the Mess, or in his own tent, with officers of the Force. He saw little of them, except in company with the Commandant, who, though, as afterwards appeared, sharing in the bitter feeling against the

F 2

over-scrupulous Political Agent, allowed no symptom of
that feeling to break out in his conversation, or in the
familiar notes in which their daily correspondence was
carried on.

At a very early period in the campaign of 1818, the
Governor-General had laid down as a general rule that
" property taken in an open town, without resistance, by
the civil authority, and by irregular troops, such as
Sebundy, is not to be considered as prize to the Army".
It was by endeavouring in vain to adhere to this rule,
that Briggs incurred the animosity of too many of his
fellow soldiers, and had to endure some of those injurious
imputations, which, just because they are vague and im-
palpable, may cast a shade over a man's good name for
years without its being possible to call any one to account,
or to obtain a definite statement of their nature.

On one of the last days of April 1818, Briggs had
received an intimation from the Honble. Mountstuart
Elphinstone, his immediate superior, then at Poona, that
a considerable quantity of jewels and plate belonging to
the Peishwa Bajee Rao was in the town of Nassik, and
that steps ought to be taken for securing this property
without delay, before it could be removed and hidden
elsewhere.   The name of the actual custodian, and the
quarter and street in which his house was to be found,
were all given from an informant in the Peishwa's capital,
Poona, whence Mr. Elphinstone wrote.   The letter arrived most opportunely, when the Force was within a
very few miles of Nassik—a town of about 25,000 inhabitants and a place of great sanctity among the Hindus.
Captain Briggs immediately applied to Colonel Mac-
Dowell for a guard of Sepoys under an officer, and a
small party of Pioneers, in case any excavation, as was
very probable, should be required ; and as the occasion
was one of some importance and interest, and the value
of the treasure likely to be very large, he invited Colonel
MacDowell to accompany him, and to assist in the
operation.   The Commandant sent this reply :—

"MY DEAR BRIGGS,—I send one Native officer, two Havildars,
two Naigues, and thirty Privates, as well as a party of Pioneers.

"I fear it will be too late to commence the search to-night. If I can, I shall call on you to-morrow before breakfast.

"Yours very sincerely,

"2nd May, 2 P.M.   A. MacDowell."

Briggs could not delay proceeding to Nassik and commencing the search because the Commandant did not choose to come with the guard, as he could easily have done. Colonel MacDowell's presence was by no means necessary, nor was his assistance required. There was ample time to march to Nassik and get the work done that evening; which meant that there was ample time, in case of half an hour's delay, for notice to be given to the custodian, and for the removal of the treasure to some unknown or inaccessible place. Briggs, therefore, set off at once, the treasure was found in the place indicated, catalogued that night in the presence of his two assistants, his brother, Lieutenant James Briggs, and Captain Davies, and the officer of the guard, packed in a tumbril, and sent off to the encampment of the Force, not as prize, but for safe keeping.

The officers acting as prize-agents to the Force immediately claimed it as lawful booty, although taken by the civil power in an open town, without resistance, chiefly on the plea —of no validity, even had it been accurate— that they had received information as to the treasure quite as soon as the Political Agent, if not sooner; the fact being that they had heard nothing but a general rumour that some of the Peishwa's jewels were in the town, without any clue to the place of deposit. But even if the plea had been accurate it would not have made the property good prize.

A correspondence on the subject ensued, and was continued for some months, every point being ultimately submitted both to the Commissioner and to the Governor-General. Captain Briggs gave his report and his opinion; the Commandant and the prize-agents expressed their views as to their claim on the property, and the question was for some time in suspense. Eventually, it may be added here, the Crown granted the treasure to the troops, —a grant which may have been advisable, as a measure

of military policy, but which seems to me, as it did
to Captain Briggs, to have been based on no legitimate
claim or recognised custom of war. In the meantime,
although nothing was said or hinted against his proceedings publicly or officially, a most offensive report found
circulation in the camp, and into some private correspondence, that the prize-agents were much disappointed with
the amount of the jewels, and that Briggs had taken
possession of them with only his brother as a companion,
although he had promised Colonel MacDowell that he
should be present at the search and during the appropriation. The Colonel's note of the 2nd May shows that
he was not at the time particularly prompt or anxious to
take part in the search, when invited to do so, and the
other strictures on the Political Agent's course of action
were equally without foundation. More correspondence
ensued, and Briggs was disposed to demand a court-
martial either on himself or on one of the prize-agents;
but both the Commissioner and the Commander-in-Chief
decided that no such step was called for, since no one had
made any intelligible charge against the Political Agent,
and the Marquis of Hastings, as Governor-General, finally
disposed of the controversy in these terms, contained in
a despatch dated 20th of June 1819, to the Honble.
Mountstuart Elphinstone :—

"His Excellency cannot omit remarking in this place that he
has perceived with much regret the tone of the observations made
relative to the conduct of Captain Briggs by Brigadier-General
Doveton, Colonel MacDowell, and the Prize Committee in Khandesh. The difference of opinion does not seem to His Excellency
to have been maintained, on the part of the latter-named officers,
with that degree of courtesy and attention towards the other party
that might have been looked for in a fair discussion of the question.
The misconception of the Prize Committee in asserting that the
information given by them of a large amount of treasure in the
town of Nassik led to its seizure by Captain Briggs, is evident
from the circumstances under which that knowledge was obtained
by you, and communicated to Captain Briggs. It is due to that
officer to state that the Governor-General considers the whole of
his procedure to have been unexceptionable, and deems his exertions in securing the treasure to have been highly commendable."

There is really nothing more to be said on this matter, which nevertheless, as may easily be understood, gave rise to much bad feeling among the younger officers in the camp, and caused great exasperation and unmerited pain of mind to Briggs for a long time, more especially as General Sir Andrew MacDowell to the last day of his life never ceased to persist most perversely in saying that " Briggs ought to have waited for him that evening".

The forts of Rajdehr and Trimbuk having been taken and occupied, the most serious operation of the Khandesh campaign, and that which put an end to all serious resistance, was the siege of Malligaum, a very strong fortress with an Arab garrison. It was invested on the 16th of May; an unsuccessful assault was made on the 29th, and it was not taken until the 15th of June, Colonel MacDowell having been reinforced by a detachment from the division of General Sir Lionel Smith, under whose command Briggs had served as a volunteer at Rasul Khyma,* consisting of two more Sepoy battalions, 800 horse, and a strong company of artillery with six heavy battering guns and four mortars. A practicable breach was effected, the enemy's principal magazine was blown up by a shell, and everything was prepared for storming the place, when the Arab garrison surrendered, and were allowed to march out with a promise that they should be shipped, unmolested and with their private property, to their native land.

Briggs was destined to have one more collision with the Prize Agents. It will be remembered that one of the sinister events that preceded and led to the second Mahratta war, was the murder of Gungadhur Shastree by Trimbukjee Dainglia, one of Bajee Rao's favourite counsellors. Trimbukjee having escaped from British custody,† rejoined the Peishwa after the battle of Kirkee, and accompanied him throughout the campaign; but on the surrender of Bajee Rao to Lieutenant (afterwards General Sir John) Low, who treated with him under instructions from Sir John Malcolm, in the middle of June 1818, Trimbukjee Dainglia fled, slenderly attended, to

* *Ante*, pp. 33, 34. † *Ante*, pp. 43, 44.

the neighbourhood of his birthplace in the Gungaturry region, near the town of Trimbuk. Just after the taking of Malligaum, Captain Briggs, following up a clue given by Mr. Elphinstone, despatched a body of cavalry under the command of Captain Swanston, with full instructions, to the village of Aheergaum, where the fugitive's brother-in-law resided, and Trimbukjee Dainglia was cleverly captured with all his baggage and his two wives, after some severe forced marches. At the time of his escape in 1817 a reward of two lakhs of rupees had been publicly offered for his apprehension, but the war having virtually ceased with the surrender of Bajee Rao, Trimbukjee ceased to be a person of such importance as to warrant the offer of so large a gratuity for his capture. The reward of two lakhs of rupees was therefore withdrawn, and the notification of this withdrawal only arrived in camp a week before Captain Swanston's horsemen started on the trail of Trimbukjee. Briggs writes :—

" The Sowars under Swanston's command had behaved so admirably, and I was so gratified at the success of the expedition, that considering the disappointment to which the men were subjected by the withdrawal of the reward, and the unfavourable impression likely to be produced on their minds, I ventured on my own responsibility to make over to Captain Swanston and his 800 Horse all the property taken with Trimbukjee, amounting to 60,000 rupees in gold and silver, jewels to the value of about 5,000 rupees, and four horses. Trimbukjee Dainglia was sent to the fort of Chunar, there to be imprisoned for life.

" The letter from Mr. Elphinstone on the apprehension of Trimbukjee Dainglia was highly flattering, while that from the Governor-General was even more so. The Secretary to Government at Calcutta wrote at once to Mr. Elphinstone as follows :—' The Governor-General in Council has instructed me to express his high satisfaction at the receipt of the intelligence of this important capture, due to the active and judicious conduct of Captain Briggs in immediately despatching Captain Swanston to the town where he had learned that Trimbukjee Dainglia was concealed, as well as to the measures he concerted for arresting him, should he have escaped from Aheergaum. His Excellency in Council feels also that much praise is due to the exertions of Captain Swanston and his party in rapidly marching from Malligaum to the place of Trimbukjee's concealment. For the complete success which attended that extraordinary activity both of these officers are entitled to the applause of the Government, and I am desired to request that you will convey to them the assurance of approbation of the Governor-General in Council and his high sense of their distinguished merits.'

"Some months afterwards an application was made by the Prize Agents of Colonel MacDowell's Force for the property taken with Trimbukjee Dainglia as prize to that detachment, with an exaggerated statement of the amount realised. I replied that ' the seizure of Trimbukjee Dainglia, a proscribed criminal, after the war with Bajee Rao had ceased, appears to me purely an act of civil magistracy, and I am at a loss to conjecture upon what grounds the Prize Committee can found its claim to the private property of such a person, which from his being an outlaw is, in my opinion, rightly confiscated to the State. The means I employed to seize this criminal .were unconnected with the operations of the war. The measure I adopted for rewarding Captain Swanston's body of Irregular Horse for their exertions in the immediate distribution of the property so confiscated was one which I considered just and politic under the peculiar circumstances of the case, and for that step I hold myself responsible to the Government. I shall, however, forward a- copy of your letter and of my reply to the Commissioner, the Honourable Mountstuart Elphinstone.' Mr. Elphinstone replied that he concurred with me in the opinion that the property found with Trimbukjee Dainglia could not be considered as prize to the army. A letter dated 13th December 1818, from the Secretary to the Governor-General, contains the following decision :—' Captain Briggs's view of the case, I am desired to inform you, seems to the Governor-General in Council to be perfectly correct, the property in question not appearing to be on any ground claimable as prize to the army. The distribution of it, which was made among Captain Swanston's detachment, is accordingly confirmed.' "

On the report of the fall of Malligaum, the Governor-General tendered his thanks to Lieut.-Col. MacDowell and Captain Briggs, in a despatch to the Hon. M. S. Elphinstone, dated 14th July 1818, of which this is an extract :—

"The energy and success of our operations in Gungaturry and in Khandesh have been no less distinguished than in other quarters, and the zeal of Captain Briggs and Lieut.-Col. MacDowell and the officers and troops of the small detachment employed in that quarter, by which the whole of the country on both sides of the Godavery has been reduced, and the conquest of Khandesh nearly achieved, demand the warmest expression of the Governor-General's admiration.

" The occupation of Khandesh, which was ceded to the British Government by Holkar, having been connected with the conquest of the Peishwa's possessions in that Province, I am directed to take this opportunity of signifying his Lordship's approbation of the measures pursued by Captain Briggs for that purpose, after the conduct of political affairs had devolved on him in Khandesh on the departure of his Excellency Sir Thomas Hislop.

" The plan of operations proposed by Captain Briggs for the establishment of our authority throughout Khandesh, and the movements by which it was to be supported, are regarded by the Governor-General as being highly judicious. It is his Lordship's hope that the force which has now been allotted to Khandesh, coupled with the reduction of Malligaum and its probable consequences, will enable Captain Briggs to enter on a regular and systematic plan for the subjugation of that part of the Province which still resists our power, and the settlement of the whole.

" The judgment, ability, and prudence displayed by Captain Briggs throughout the late services justifies the most confident expectation of the success of your views under his management."

CHAPTER IV.

ALL military resistance having ceased by the first week of August 1819, Captain Briggs had taken up his quarters at Dhoolia, a considerable town on the road from Bombay to Agra, and then almost the only place worthy the name of a town that was left in Khandesh.

Khandesh, literally the hollow country, is a valley or basiñ, traversed by the river Taptee, and surrounded on three sides by hill ranges; on the north by the Sāt-pūra range; on the south by the hills on which are the fort of Chandore and the pass of Adjunta, near which the battle of Assaye took place; and on the south-west by the expansion of the Syadree or Western Ghauts. On the south-east the boundary is but slightly elevated, gradually sinking to the plain or valley of Berar, in the Nizam's dominions. The hills are not very high, averaging from 1,000 to 1,800 feet, many of their summits being flat tables of basaltic rock, affording tempting sites for hill forts, of which more than twenty were occupied, and had to be emptied, before any measures of civil administration could be undertaken. The inhabitants are principally Mahrattas, including many bold and restless clans, from which the predatory forces of Jeswunt Rao Holkar had been largely recruited. Still more restless and less removed from barbarism were the Bheels, a tribe supposed to have been the aborigines of Guzerat and Meywar. The earliest notice of the race occurs in the Mahabharata. The Bheels are estimated to form one-eighth of the population of the province.

"Khandesh", writes Briggs, "the province I was destined to govern for some years, was one of the six Mohammedan kingdoms of the Deccan, or South of India, which flourished between the fourteenth and sixteenth centuries of our era. The founder of the kingdom, established about A.D. 1370, traced his pedigree through thirty-seven generations to Omar, designated ' Al Farukh', or the fortunate, one of the four companions of Mohammed, and who succeeded as Khalifa in A.D. 636. The Farukhi kings of Khandesh reigned prosperously, sometimes at war, sometimes forming matrimonial alliances, with the kings of Guzerat and Malwa, until these petty states were subverted and incorporated with the Empire about the year 1600 by the Emperor Akbar. Khandesh fell into the hands of the Mahrattas in the middle of the eighteenth century, and was allotted for the support of troops to the charge of Holkar, in the possession of which family it remained until ceded to us in 1818. In a despatch of Mr. Elphinstone to the Court of Directors, after alluding to the Mahratta war of 1817-18, he writes :—' The part in which difficulties were most to be apprehended was Khandesh, at one time the seat of a flourishing kingdom, and one of the most prosperous provinces in India down to the year 1802. In that year it was devastated by Holkar. A famine and a long-continued period of tumult and insurrection ensued. No fewer than 180 distinct bands of plunderers with territorial pretensions had succeeded each other during sixteen years, when this country fell to be occupied by our troops. Immediately before this occupation its miseries had reached the utmost height. Bands of mercenary Arabs had seized the hill fortresses, and levied contributions on all within their reach. The Bheels poured down from the surrounding mountains, and renewed their connection with their brethren in the plains, who, from being the watchmen and police of the country, suddenly became the most formidable of its marauders. Before the decline of Khandesh had been consummated by the rapacious misgovernment of the Peishwa and Holkar, the Bheels of the plain had lived mixed with the Hindu cultivators, and as village watchmen had been the chief protectors of life and property. They now for the most part withdrew into the surrounding hills, whence they made incursions on the low country, and carried off cattle and prisoners, whom they held to ransom. As village police they had held lands on the borders, exempt from assessment, besides being entitled to certain portions of grain from every crop. As the villages were plundered and devastated by Pindarrees and Arabs the Bheels lost all their means of subsistence, and all their interest in the settled occupations of the plain. They fled to the mountains, and reverted to their ancient habits.'

" It was one of my first duties to reclaim this race, and through the agency of the hereditary village and district officers I gained over many of the chiefs in the mountains, granting them stipends on condition of their sending the village Bheels of the plain back to their villages, where I stipulated they should be well received and their lands and share of grain secured to them. Some of those nearest to the mountains stood out for confederate agreements, which I strenuously resisted, insisting on the several chiefs of districts entering into distinct terms with me for each separately. To this end I called in the services of Lieut.-Colonel Jardine, who commanded the detachment stationed at Nandurbar."

The commandant of the small brigade at Nandurbar was supported by a regiment of 500 Horse under Captain Swanston, whose operations in preventing the Bheel chieftains in the Hills from obtaining grain and other necessary articles of subsistence from the plains were chiefly instrumental in bringing them to terms of submission. Mr. Elphinstone describes the principal conditions of the problem and the method adopted for its solution in these words of a despatch already quoted :—

" The expulsion of the Arabs was a natural consequence of the war, and no parties of plundering horse were able to keep the field, but the settlement of the Bheels was a work of more time and difficulty. Those in the Sātpūra Mountains were the most formidable ; as that range, though nowhere, perhaps, more than 1,500 feet high, contains many deep gorges and strong places, and is so unhealthy that no stranger can long remain in it.

" The plan adopted by Captain Briggs, and zealously executed by Lieut.-Colonel Jardine, was to stop the supplies of the Bheels, which were drawn from the plains, to cut off any parties that attempted to plunder, and to make vigorous attacks on the points in the Hills to which the principal Bheels had retired. These measures soon reduced the Bheels to accept the very favourable terms held out to them, the chiefs receiving pensions and allowances for a certain number of men, and binding themselves to restrain the depredations of their people. The same plan was carried out more easily with the Bheels of the Chandore range, and with those of the low country.

" The terms have been occasionally broken by some chiefs, but, on the whole, they have succeeded beyond my most sanguine expectations, and have effectively delivered the province from this species of invasion. The only attacks of the Bheels are now made in small parties of three or four, who rob passengers. These outrages have been resisted by the police, and are stated by Captain Briggs to be greatly on the decline."

Briggs himself says that when any of the Bheel chiefs broke faith by perpetrating or allowing one of the old-fashioned incursions, they were summoned to appear before him to clear themselves of the charge ; " and if ", he continues, " they held aloof, I always found a reward of one or two hundred rupees sufficient to induce the Bheels of another district to bring in the accused, who, if convicted—provided there had been no bloodshed in the case—was astonished by the brief term of imprisonment to which I sentenced him. They knew very well that their fathers and their brethren had been frequently invited under the former government (if so it may be called) to come in and make terms, and on doing so, had not unfrequently been put to death."

Some notion of the intermediate process that had been going on in the two years before the date of Mr. Elphinstone's despatch may be derived from the following two letters from Captain Briggs to Lieut.-Colonel Jardine and to Mr. Gerald Wellesley, the Resident at Indore, capital of the conterminous Holkar State, to which Khandesh had belonged before the war.

The first is to the military Commandant :

" Dhoolia, April 1st, 1819.

" MY DEAR SIR,—I have just received your private letter of the 29th ultimo. The enormities committed by Ramjee and Owchait Naig have placed them in the blackest part of my list of Bheel Chiefs. Some of their outrages appear quite wanton. It is too soon, however, for us to say that the door of repentance is no longer open to them, and if you can catch hold of either of these Chiefs, or any of their principal followers, by fair or foul means, we will treat them more gently than they expect or deserve, and you will add very much to the number of your eminent services in settling this quarter of Khandesh. Ramjee promised to be quiet if we gave him a pension. He got it, and immediately became the rallying point for all the greatest villains in the district. We can have no reliance on any more promises that he, or, indeed, any of them, may make. It will not be till they are convinced they cannot plunder with impunity that we shall have any hold on their fears. And yet I think we have made considerable progress. The legions of robber Bheels in the impenetrable fastnesses of the Sātpūra Hills, whom Mr. Elphinstone, down to a very late period, wanted me to embody into a corps of Sebundees, have been dispersed. The change has been gradual, and is not yet complete, but I firmly believe our plan has solid advantages, and that before you return you will have the consolation of knowing that you have been the principal cause of dispelling a formidable obstruction to good government. If any of these refractory and pertinacious villains are brought in to me, I am determined that they shall settle in the plains on *cowl*,* or be imprisoned. I am determined, and I feel convinced it can be done, to bring the whole mass down here; and if we require 400 or 500 Sebundees, and 200 or 300 Horse to cut off communication between the hills and the villages, the money will be well laid out. I am ready to pension all the Chiefs on reasonable terms. None have yet received more than 2,000 rupees per annum, and Ramjee and others of his class must certainly not get more than I have already agreed to pay, and they to accept. He and his brother were to receive fifty rupees monthly. I am prepared to advance money to the Bheels for cultivation—to give them land on advantageous terms, to provide for them in their *wuttuns*,† but they must and shall quit the Hills first. This is applicable only to those who formerly belonged to villages in the plain, though I should wish to draw them all from the Hills, if it could be done.

"Your precautions to protect Boraree were highly judicious. We must never allow anyone to suffer for supporting us, and not be sparing in rewards where they are well merited. Keep on, my dear Sir, in the same way, and I feel sure you will soon carry out, to the fullest extent of our most sanguine expectations, every object of the command in which you have already been so successful."

" To Gerald Wellesley, Esq., Resident at Indore.

" January 3rd, 1819.

" MY DEAR SIR,—From the proximity of our public situations it is probable that we shall have frequent occasions to correspond, and I have therefore taken this opportunity of introducing myself, and of returning my thanks for your polite attention in forwarding your public and private letters to Mr. Elphinstone, regarding the Bheels, open for my perusal. We had originally intended to have a corps of Hill Rangers here, but on a closer acquaintance with the condition of the Sātpūra Bheels it was considered more advisable to pension the chiefs, and to induce their followers, who had originally been inhabitants of villages in the plain, and had only lately become Hill people, to return to their old homes. I have recommended a place to Mr. Elphinstone which will provide for them, and make them the instruments of our police in Khandesh. My Bheel reports of the 24th September and 19th November, copies of which were forwarded to Sir John Malcolm, who will

* Conditions of pardon.   † Their homes, or original villages.

furnish you with them, will give you an idea of my opinions
regarding the Bheels with whom I have to deal. Those who live
on highroads and passes have an acknowledged and immemorial
claim to a toll on merchandise, and even on travellers proceeding
through their limits; and for this privilege they are bound to
protect them till well beyond their confines. With all the Bheels
in my jurisdiction I have at once admitted this right, and
demanded in return their duty of police and safeguard : but the
customary collections are made by my own karkoons and paid to
the Bheel Chief. This admission on my part extends to all tolls
admitted by Holkar's government in Ahalia Baee's time. Whatever has been usurped since has been relinquished.

"Goomanee Naig of the Sindwa Ghaut has lately conducted himself in a manner which seems to be approaching to downright
rebellion. The mode of punishing him and all Bheels in the
Sātpūra Hills is by pushing up a few Horse to the skirts to
occupy the villages from which they draw their supplies; and
for the infantry to endeavour to surprise, or at any rate to reach
and burn, their huts. As they never have any store of provisions,
this invariably compels them to accept our terms without our
being obliged to attack them or to hunt them down. In this
way, by stopping their supplies, I have compelled all those to
submit who obstinately refused to come in, and continued to
plunder for many months after our settlement with Holkar. I
thought Goomanee Naig had been brought to his senses. If it
should become necessary to take hostile measures against him, I
shall do myself the honour of suggesting what co-operation we
should require from Nimawur.

> "I am, my dear Sir,
> "Your very faithful and obedient servant,
>
> "JOHN BRIGGS."

Nearly all the Bheel Chiefs and their followers fulfilled
their engagements, and became once more an effective
body of police under Captain Briggs's administration.
Bheels were employed to convey all the local post letters,
and even to convey to the treasury the revenue of the
country; for a whole year gang robbery everywhere
ceased to exist. In 1821, however, a military expedition
on a small scale was required to dislodge, both from the
northern and southern ranges of hills, some refugee Bheels
who had not been able to take to the quiet life of cultivators and watchmen in the plain, owing, as they said,
to the utter devastation of their old settlements, and

there being no room for them in other villages. There
was not much resistance, and there were few casualties
among our troops on this occasion, but outrages and
robberies had been committed ; some of the delinquents
were known to have already received for former offences
all the consideration that it was advisable to give them,
while they had violated the conditions under which they
had been previously set free. More than 200 prisoners
were made. In these operations the villagers were active
assistants, under a pledge on the part of Captain Briggs
that the Bheels, if captured and identified, should not
again be released without a long term of imprisonment,
unless they could find some responsible persons to be
security in a large sum for their good conduct. The
Patels of several villages swore the peace against the
Bheel chiefs and their leading partisans ; no security, of
course, was forthcoming, and a large number of these
freebooters were sent for safe custody to the prison of
Tanna, near Bombay. Khandesh now remained quite
tranquil for three years, and two Bheel chiefs who mis-
behaved were delivered up by their neighbours to the
Political Agent.

The Home Government, however, actuated by solici-
tude, which we cannot but admire, for strict adherence
to legal principles and procedure, found fault with the
detention in prison of men against whom no specific
charge had been substantiated by judicial proof, sent out
directions in 1824, after Briggs had left the charge of
Khandesh for the Residency of Sattara, that unless there
was enough evidence for a regular trial, the imprisoned
Bheels should be released. If this punctilious observance
of legal forms had been maintained, Thuggee would never
have been extirpated, but would have flourished to this
day. The orders of the Court of Directors were obeyed ;
the Bheels were released ; they returned to Khandesh ;
they murdered all those whom they suspected of having
aided in their apprehension, and terror was spread
through the province. Under these circumstances Captain, afterwards General, Sir James Outram, at the very
outset of his distinguished and chivalrous career, was

G

sent to pacify Khandesh.   This work he carried out
mainly by the formation and agency of a Bheel corps,
which absorbed within its ranks most of the outlawed
and disaffected men of the tribe—a measure which Briggs
had recommended, but had never been allowed to undertake—and thus most of the credit due for the conciliatory
subjugation and settlement of the Bheels, nearly accomplished by Briggs, has always been placed to the account
of Outram, who finished well a task that had already been
well commenced.

Among the secondary matters of public usefulness
voluntarily undertaken by Briggs during his administration of Khandesh, was the construction of a map of the
country.   He says :—

" Only some imperfect and incorrect maps were in existence,
which had been used by the commanders of our troops in the
former Mahratta war of 1803.   A very few points of longitude
had been determined by celestial observations.   Two Engineer
officers were sent to me in 1818 to complete this desirable object,
but both of them very soon contracted the malignant intermittent
fever so prevalent on the outskirts of the hills, and had to go
away on sick leave, and the Government declined to send others.
I then procured instruments from Bombay, selected by a scientific
friend, and with my own knowledge of surveying, I was enabled
to direct the operations of three young native engineer clerks,
whom I engaged as my assistants.   In the course of two years
I produced a complete map of Khandesh, which, together with
the field books and map of triangulation, I submitted, on my
quitting the country, to the Bombay Government; which, on
ascertaining the value of the work, by sending professional sur-
veyors to verify its correctness, reimbursed me for the trifling
expense that I had incurred.   That map was lithographed in
Bombay, and has been included in the trigonometrical survey of
the Deccan."

The best general description of the measures adopted
by Captain Briggs for pacifying and establishing a regular
government throughout Khandesh, and especially for the
administration of justice, will be found in a letter he
wrote to Sir John Malcolm when he had been at work
for rather more than a year.

" Dhoolia, 17th October 1819.

" MY DEAR SIR JOHN,—I have just received your note, written on the back of Mr. Wellesley's letter to you, acknowledging the receipt of one of mine to you, which I perceive he has had copied, and intends sending to Mr. Gardiner. Now, although this is very flattering to me, particularly as my letter was written in great haste, I hope that it may not be forwarded until I have had an opportunity of expressing myself more fully, and with more reflection, on the subject. I daresay I can compress all I want to say into this letter.

" In the month of August 1818, we all received our instructions from Mr. Elphinstone on the subject of judicial administration. They were very short, and the tenor of them seemed to me at the time to direct that all judicial proceedings should be conducted by Punchayuts; and that the opinions of the Mufti or Shastree should be recorded on the face of them, and unless the punish-ment should be at variance with our customs, their award should in general be adopted; the name of the law book from whence the Shastree or Mufti quoted should also be recorded. I accordingly adopted Punchayuts as juries on all criminal cases, and in this instance, although I mistook Mr. Elphinstone's instructions, he directed me to continue the custom. So much for the origin of criminal courts of Punchayut, the first and only ones, I believe, ever adopted under our Government.

" In entering on this subject, I shall commence with the ordinary Punchayuts in civil cases. These are neither more nor less than courts or juries of arbitration, assembled by authority of the chief civil officer on the spot, and the process is simply this :—

" N. has a demand on B.; he makes out a written statement of his case, and denounces himself as guilty of an offence to the Sircar, if he has misstated anything. B. is called on for a counter-statement, by which the civil officer is generally able to judge if the subject calls for a trial or Punchayut, for it frequently happens that the question has been before decided by Punchayut many years ago at some other place. After being satisfied that the plaintiff has a real cause of complaint, the parties each select two persons, and the Sircar another, making the *Punch* or Court. The parties then enter into a written engagement to agree to the decision of this Court, when the statements of each are made over to the Punchayut, which proceeds to examine witnesses, whose depositions are committed to writing. The Court at length comes to its decision, which is signed by the whole of the members. The award is then given to the party in whose favour the decision has been made, signed by the chief civil officer, and the whole forms a public record. When the amount of the award, if it is money, is paid, or when the plaintiff is cast, the defendant

G 2

party receives a *Farikut-Nāma*, or writ of absolvence from any further demands, etc. In cases where the parties require witnesses from a distance, they are made to give security for the payment of their expenses before they are summoned; and, therefore, on most occasions their depositions, taken before some local authority, and attesting witnesses are considered sufficient by the Court; and in such instance it is rare to find false statements given, unless the witnesses are much interested, when the Court usually require their attendance. Such are the proceedings in civil cases. At these Punchayuts I do not preside. I merely settle the issues, order the investigation, and confirm the award before the parties. It frequently happens that four or five Punchayuts are going on at a time. This system ensures the following great objects of justice: immediate investigation, full and patient hearing, least possible expense, and the award being confirmed by an impartial superior, who is open to complaints against corruption, the only ground of appeal. Justice is thus administered in the most simple and popular mode, according to the forms and customs understood and preferred in the country over which we rule.

" Criminal cases under the late rule were tried solely by the chief magistrate of each talook, and summary punishment followed. Murder cases were only taken by the Soobas, and were often compounded in some way. All criminal cases of importance are conducted by myself or my Assistant, acting as Judge, with a Punchayut as a jury, and the Mufti and Shastree as expounders of the law. I shall, in giving an account of this system—as it is entirely novel in our administration—go into some detail. On any crime being committed in the province, the nearest civil authority, on receiving intimation of it, proceeds with the informant to ascertain the truth, either by taking the depositions of the parties, or, if a murder has been committed, by going to the spot and acting according to the circumstances. If the criminal has not been secured, all particulars are collected as to his name and personal appearance from witnesses, and the proper steps taken for his apprehension. The crime, the time and place, the informant, and the names of witnesses, with their depositions, are sent to me, and all the parties as soon as possible. When the parties arrive, no delay takes place in assembling a criminal Punchayut, which is convened by my orders. The Shastree, the Mufti, and the clerk who records the proceedings, sit on one side of the Bench, the Punchayut on the other. This Court is formed according to no particular law, and bound by no particular form, its object being merely to ascertain the truth. In this Court there is no respect shown to the English maxim, that a prisoner cannot criminate himself. On the contrary, the acknowledgment of the prisoner is considered rather a satisfactory element in the perfect conviction of crime; and, therefore, if the evidence is only collateral, the prisoner is cross-questioned and examined. If two or three prisoners are supposed to be concerned in the same crime, they are each separately examined before the Court. The prisoner has a right to challenge, and is first asked if he consents to be tried by the Court. No preliminary deposition is brought in as evidence unless the party is unable to be produced, when it is admitted, and receives its due weight only. The examinations being concluded, which are on oath, and the prisoner having pleaded in his defence, the Court proceeds to pronounce whether he is guilty or not guilty, and in what degree. The Shastree or Mufti then proclaims the law, which is entered on the face of the proceedings, upon which the Judge passes sentence, entering his reason on the face of the proceedings only when he finds it proper to dissent from the law officers. The law officers in this Court, therefore, you perceive, are not the judges; they are the expounders of the law. The judgment is solely vested in the European officer sitting as Judge. A copy of all the trials is sent off monthly to Mr. Elphinstone, who makes his comments on them and confirms them.

"By this system of judicature I have no causes lying on the file after sufficient evidence is once obtained, though it has happened that adequate evidence of highway robbery has not been procurable for two or three months after the criminals had been secured. Only one robbery within the last ten months has taken place in which the criminals have not been apprehended, and that was committed by some Bheels who made their escape from prison, and have taken refuge in the Adjunta Hills, where they find protection from some of the Nizam's zemindars. I am hatching mischief against them, and shall have them at my feet in a fortnight after I begin. When the jungles become less unhealthy, and my information is complete, and when my maps are ready, I shall form a plan of operations like that against the Satpoora gentlemen, and, in concert with the agent at Aurungabad, occupy the friendly villages. The troops need not pursue them into the hills. They will be starved into terms in a very few weeks. The great secret in Bheel fighting is to know from whence they get their supplies. Attack them, carry off and destroy what stores they have, and occupy their friendly villages to starve them out. All the Hill Bheels are dependent on the plain for food. They are for the most part originally natives of villages on the plains. When they are caught or subdued, I have not tried and hanged them, as used to be done. I have pensioned the chiefs, and distributed their followers into villages where, if they choose, as for the most part they do, they can earn a livelihood. The chiefs I have either allowed to be at large, or have confined them, according to circumstances. Some few of their retainers have been employed as guards in ghauts, so that, although I entirely put down their predatory habits by force, I ensure a good number of friends, even amongst the most powerful of them.   The only one who has turned traitor after being admitted to this indulgence is Dusrut Naig of Pergunna Chopra, who finds protection in Nimawur. Thirteen Bheels who escaped from the prison here have, I hear, found refuge with him, and I learn also that he has now left his village on the plain, and is assembling a band for plunder some-where.   If this be true, Colonel Jardine and I must stop his pro-visions, clap a good round sum on him, and when I have got him, he shall be sent as a prisoner to Malligaum fort, where I have two other incorrigibles of the same character.   On this subject, how-ever, I shall write publicly soon.

" In order that you may further comprehend what we have been about here, I send you a series of questions from that most inde-fatigable of all investigators—our master, Mr. Elphinstone—with my answers.   I hold a *furyād** kutcherry from nine to eleven daily, when all complaints are heard, verbally, or written in Mah-rattee.   A notice to this effect is posted up in every village.

" Believe me, dear Sir John, with great esteem,

" Ever most sincerely yours,

" JOHN BRIGGS."

The continuance of his historical and philological studies and recreations, in the midst of administrative labours, is indicated in the following letter to his old friend and comrade, Captain Grant Duff, then Resident at Sattara.

" Dhoolia, 24th August 1820.

" MY DEAR GRANT,—I only received your letter of the 15th yesterday, and have been the whole of this day employed in endeavouring to fix the date of Malik Amber's death.   He was alive when Ferishta finished his work, and I have somewhere met with an account of his death and the succession of Futteh Khan, during the life-time of Moorteza Nizam Shah.   The latter lies interred under a plain slab at Roza, in the same cemetery with Syed Rajoo Kuttal.   I had a thick folio volume, nearly full, con-taining notes, taken on the spot, of all the dates, carefully worked out, with descriptions of the tombs at Beejapoor, Golconda, Bidar, and Roza, clearing up and confirming all the remarkable events in the Mohammedan history of the Deccan ; but this, and all my

* Complaint.

MSS., which I thought were valuable, were lost in the conflagration of the Sungum.*

"Surely you don't mean by saying that you ' can find no vestige of a Desmookh or Despandia previously to the period of the Tartar Nobles establishing their independence in the Deccan,' that you believe these officers, with purely Hindoo designations, to have been created by the new Mohammedan dynasty. If so, how do you account for the same offices being known and held under the Mysore Government before a Mohammedan ever set his foot in those territories ? And from whence have sprung the Dessayes of Ceylon, which was never conquered by the Indian Mohammedans ? Whenever the Mohammedans introduced reforms they had the vanity to stamp their new regulations with indelible marks of their origin; and the Institutes of Akbar, though his revenue system was due entirely to the labours of Todur Mull, afford a striking example of the propensity to perpetuate the fame of Islam by names and titles. And I believe you are right so far, or rather I believe here is the source of your mistake,—that in the history and old records of the Deccan, you will not find the name of one Hindoo Chief or officer mentioned for more than a century after the rise of Mussulman power. The gradual reappearance of the Hindoo names and offices proves, or strongly hints, that the Mohammedans tried to extinguish them, and could not do it.

"I am glad, as you have not yet got satisfactory proof regarding the Desmookh, that you stand out against the generally received opinion, because these disputes lead to useful investigation. I have set my hands to work, and hope to be able to discover something in these parts, but I despair of delivering over to you a Desmookh of the old Raj precisely circumstanced as the Desmookhs with whom we have lately come in contact. We must recollect that the Mussulman invasion and innovation swept away everything that was a prominent obstruction to its absolute and despotic sway, and levelled to the ground much that had formerly been the highest, while ancient institutions and internal arrangements, which rather aided in the re-establishment of order and in the collection of revenue, were not only tolerated, but sometimes cherished.

"I am happy to find our Mahratta boundaries so nearly agree. I will not quarrel with you for differing a few miles to the right or left in defining Maharashtra. But, recollect, I admit no village into the Mahratta limits whose native tongue is not Mahratta; and I do most stoutly reject all places which have ' pully', ' hully',

---

* The Residency at Poona, near the "Sungum" or confluence of the two rivers, Muta and Mula, burnt and plundered on the day of the battle of Kirkee, 5th November 1817, *ante*, p. 53.

'kotta', 'kot', 'hul', 'kul', 'hal', or 'petta', as terminations or initials;*
while I embrace with parental fondness all the 'gaums', 'nuggurs',
'gurhs', 'kherds', and 'warrees', that may have escaped my boundary line.† There are some few, such as 'oor', 'poor', etc., that are
common to the Mahratta, Telinga and Canara limits. ·

"I am quite vexed at my failure to aid you in determining the
time of Malik Amber's death. I have no knowledge of him
beyond what Ferishta tells us, but he appears to me to have
been the most sensible Mussulman who ever managed revenue
matters. Do you know that I have a theory of my own regarding
the Indian system of finance in general, and that I would go back
for guidance to the good old times of Menu, who required only
one-sixth of the produce for the Raja, and who made land-
ownership permanent, hereditary, and saleable. To draw our
resources on a constantly increasing scale from the land, is very
like digging away the root of a tree to get at its fruit, or tapping
the palm for toddy, and still expecting to have dates. A comfortable peasantry is the basis of an affluent gentry and nobility, and
affluence is the parent of manufactures and trade, which are the
most desirable, the most productive, and the most durable sources
of wealth to a state. Look at the actual picture before us—an
indigent peasantry that cannot afford to purchase anything but
the produce of its own district, whose wives, children, and themselves go all but naked. What can such people contribute to
trade, what have they to do with manufactured goods ? Look at
the gentry, deprived of employment, who cannot afford to cultivate
because the produce will not cover the cost of culture and the
assessment on the land. What have they to do with trade or
manufacture ? Look at the noble, reduced in his income and
power, but not in his pride or in his retinue of needy adventurers,
continuing to run in debt, with no prospect whatever of improving
or keeping up his fortune, or of retaining that importance to
which he was born and to which he is accustomed. How little
can he encourage trade or manufactures. The manufacture of
goods for home consumption soon swells in value, and overflows
into commerce abroad. But where there are no home consumers
there can be no manufacturers. Land is in the same falling predicament on another account. As far as food goes, there will
always be demand in proportion to the population. But the
more costly and profitable raw material—such as cotton, opium,
dyes of all kinds, oils, tobacco, hemp and flax, will only be produced

---

. * These are all Canarese words for "hill", "fort", and "rock", ending
the names of towns and villages.
  † These are Mahrattee terminations, meaning " village", "fort", and ·
"camp".

in proportion to the demand ; and where is the demand to arise among a nation of beggars ?

" Experience has convinced European financiers of the errors of those French economists who, after the Revolution, expected to draw enormous revenues from an enhanced land-tax. Five or six years reduced the nation to ruin, and necessity was one of the principal incitements to carry on an ever-lasting, self-sustaining war to maintain an army, which it was impossible, even if it had been politic, to reduce, in foreign countries. Things have now resumed their original order, or found their level, and French financiers are recovering. But if I don't dismount my hobby, I shall carry myself and you away the Lord knows where.

" Believe me,

" Sincerely yours,

" JOHN BRIGGS."

CHAPTER V.

On the retirement of Captain James Grant Duff from the office of Resident at Sattara in January 1823, Captain Briggs was appointed to succeed him. When the British Government had determined, on account of Bajee Rao's repeated acts of treachery, to make no peace that would restore him to power, the policy was adopted, with a view to conciliate the Mahrattas, of setting up once more the Rajah of Sattara, the representative of Sivajee's dynasty, whose authority had been usurped for several generations by their chief Ministers, the Brahmin Peishwas. Before the Rajah of Sattara had been rescued from his captivity in the Peishwa's camp in the pursuit after the battle of Ashtee, a proclamation had already been issued by Mr Elphinstone to the following effect, as quoted in the autobiographical papers :—

" ' The Rajah of Sattara, who is now a prisoner in Bajee Rao's hands, will be released and placed at the head of an independent Sovereignty of such an extent as may maintain the Rajah and his family in comfort and dignity. With this view the Fort of Sattara has been taken, the Rajah's flag has been set up in it, and his former Ministers have been called into employment. Whatever country is assigned to the Raja will be administered by him, and he will be bound to establish a system of justice and order.'

" At the termination of the war, accordingly, the Rajah was placed on the throne, and a treaty of alliance and friendship was concluded between His Highness and the British Government.

" By this treaty, although the limits of the Rajah's territory are accurately defined, yet several of the estates of the feudatory chieftains, originally granted by his ancestors, prior to the usurpation of the Peishwas, were partly detached beyond the Rajah's boundaries, and surrounded by British territory. When, however, those feudatories elected to remain under the restored Rajah's rule, those estates became properly a portion of the reconstituted kingdom of the Rajah. Such was his view, and such was always mine.

It was owing to the opposite view of this question, taken by the Government of Bombay several years afterwards, that the discussions began which ended in the unfortunate Prince being ignominiously and unjustly deposed, so that he ended his days in exile.

"The Rajah Pertab Singh was twenty-four years of age when he was installed as ruling Rajah of Sattara. Owing to the rigid seclusion in which he had been kept from his birth, under the power of the Peishwa, and his being wholly unused to business, it was determined that his country should, for a time, be under English management. It was thought right not only that the British Government should be satisfied of His Highness's capacity and disposition, but also that means should be taken to disabuse his mind of the exaggerated pretensions to supremacy over all the Mahrattas, encouraged by his mother and other relations. With this view, Captain Grant (afterwards Grant Duff), who was intimately acquainted with the Mahratta customs and languages, was appointed Resident, with full power to conduct the administration under instructions from the Sole Commissioner, Mr. Elphinstone, who furnished a complete code of rules by which the Government was to be conducted ; a civil list, equal to one-fifth of the revenue, being assigned to the Rajah and his family. During the time that I remained at Sattara the Rajah, who had been entrusted with full powers, strictly abided by Mr. Elphinstone's rules, and would permit no deviation from them. Captain Grant Duff had carefully trained the Rajah in public business. He kept a diary in his own hand-writing, and attended to state affairs with great assiduity and interest. He was naturally shrewd, free from most of the ordinary prejudices of his countrymen, and not having been instructed in Brahminical lore, had little respect either for the religious doctrines and ceremonies of the Brahmins, or for their cosmogony and science, 'falsely so called'. He was extremely desirous of educating all the Mahrattas, so that they might be able to break up the Brahmins' monopoly in office; for which purpose he established a school within his Palace, to which he invited the attendance of all the sons of his Mahratta chiefs and high officers. He entertained strict notions of justice and morality, and was incapable of telling a direct falsehood, but was not free from finesse, amounting sometimes to dissimulation, which, considering the school in which he had been brought up, among a host of artful flatterers, selected to be spies over him by the Peishwa, was not to be wondered at.

"In his deportment the Rajah was always dignified and self-possessed, and very particular in the observance of the distinguishing style and forms in the reception of his guests, visitors, and suitors, according to their rank and position. He was polite in his conversation, and though very sensible of any want of courtesy or propriety in others, he never forgot the self-restraint of a Prince and a well-bred gentleman. He was naturally kind and liberal to those about him, and humane to all his servants and subjects. By his frugal and careful management, the Rajah kept free from debt, while he expended large sums in the construction of roads, public buildings, and other useful works, and in the improvement of the country. Captain Grant Duff, before quitting Sattara in 1853, had made over the entire management of public affairs to the Rajah, so that I had little else to do but to make myself acquainted with all that took place, to be always ready to give information and advice to His Highness, but to abstain from interference except when I thought the interest or objects of my own Government required my action, while I, of course, reported regularly everything of importance that occurred."

The General, in his autobiographical papers, goes at very great length into the causes and circumstances of the Rajah's deposition in 1839, which he attributed to a Brahmin conspiracy, stimulated and encouraged by the official ill-will which the Rajah had incurred at Bombay from the pertinacity with which he asserted his Suzerain rights over his feudatory chieftains, and against the inter- ference of our local authorities. But it is too late for a discussion at full length of the complicated Sattara case, for many years dreaded as an infliction and a bore by the majority in the Court of Proprietors and in the House of Commons. It is no longer, unfortunately, a practical question. I shall, therefore, only give such extracts and explanations as may suffice to vindicate the views adopted by General Briggs, by two subsequent Residents at the Rajah's Court, Generals Robertson and Lodwick, and by all the most competent and impartial persons who inves- tigated the charges that were brought against the Rajah.

"Nine years after I had left the Sattara Residency, the Court of Directors, in consequence of repeated letters from the Govern- ment of Bombay praising the Rajah's conduct, passed a resolution in July 1835 that a jewelled sword should be purchased, suitable for presentation to the Rajah, and should be sent to His Highness, accompanied by a letter from the Court, in which it should be declared that 'this mark of distinction is founded not solely on the public spirit evinced by the Rajah in the construction of roads, and the execution of other public works, but on the general and distinguished merits of His Highness's administration, which justly entitle him to applause, as well as on the liberality which he has displayed in disbursing his private funds for public purposes.'

"A letter to that effect was accordingly addressed to the Rajah, and sent with the sword for presentation, through the Government of Bombay. But neither sword nor letter was ever delivered. They were detained in the Chief Secretary's office at Bombay, because the Rajah had already committed himself to a decided opinion regarding the interpretation of those articles in the Treaty relating to his feudatory chieftains, and his jurisdiction over their estates as affected by the boundaries of his principal piece of territory, which was opposed to that of the Bombay Government, and which, more especially as the Rajah appealed to the Court of Directors, was considered at Bombay to be disrespectful and contumacious. But at this time there were no charges against the Rajah. The treasonable plot imputed to him was not thought of till July 1836. Moreover, the Home Government acknowledged the correctness of the Rajah's views regarding his feudatories. In a despatch of the 22nd November 1837, sixteen months after the pretended discovery of the plot, the Court of Directors again take occasion to express the pleasure they feel from the Resident's reports of the Rajah's administration. The Rajah's rights, freely admitted by the Home authorities, were obstinately resisted by the Bombay Government; all his appeals were unheeded; his grievances aggravated by delay, and still more deeply embittered by withholding from him the despatch of the Court of Directors which contained the sanction to his claims. This course of proceeding was, in my humble opinion, a positive breach of treaty on our part.* The disagreeable relations between the Bombay Government and the Rajah were the signal and the starting-point for the machinations of his enemies. And the Rajah had against him the most powerful enemies that any man can have against him in India—the Brahmins. Against the Brahmins, as the tribe to which the Peishwas belonged, this unfortunate Prince, though he could not help employing a great many of them, entertained an invincible prejudice, almost amounting to hatred. During Captain Grant Duff's management of the Sattara State, his principal Native assistant and agent was a Brahmin of great capacity, named Balajee Punt Natoo, whom I knew well, as he had been in the intelligence department under the Poona Residency during the

---

* It is one of many instances on record of the distinct instructions or orders of the Imperial Government being boldly disregarded and baffled by the local authorities in India. The overland mail and the telegraph may have made such acts of official self-will and self-interest more difficult, but they are still a great source of political danger.

last two years of the reign of the Peishwa Bajee Rao.   Having
good claims on the consideration of our Government, he had been
presented with a small jaghire at the end of the war, and was held
in high favour and esteem by all English officers under whom he
had been employed.   As usual in such cases, he brought several
relations and hangers-on of his family into the Sattara service
when he was the Resident's first assistant.   When Captain Grant
Duff, just before his own retirement, placed the Rajah in power,
Balajee Punt Natoo fully expected to have been made Dewan or
Minister, but the Rajah dreaded a second Peishwa supported by
British authority, and had, moreover, an aversion for the man.
Grant Duff would not force or press on the Rajah a Minister
whom he disliked, and Balajee Punt withdrew to Poona, but had
one of his relations in a place at the Residency to tell him all
that passed.   He was a plausible gentleman, and professed to
keep me well informed of all occurrences at the Sattara Court.
He knew very well what was also brought to my notice from
several sources, that the Rajah's weak point was an exaggerated
notion of his own hereditary dignity and consequence, and of his
rightful claims as representative head of the Mahratta Empire in
its brief period of triumph.   He gloried in the titles of 'Maharajah Chuttraputtee' and 'Hindooput',* and always alluded to
the Peishwas, especially the last, Bajee Rao, as unfaithful servants
of his house, who had abused his confidence, and all of whose
acts, their treaties as well as their wars with the Honourable
Company, were unauthorised by the legitimate sovereign, and
therefore politically of no effect.   But these absurd pretensions,
though not matters of indifference to me, and duly reported to
Government, never, I am convinced, went beyond the small circle
of the Rajah's intimate friends and favourite companions.   They
were mere subjects of talk and dreamy speculation, the Rajah
having sufficient good sense and sound knowledge to be fully
aware of the altered circumstances of military and political power
in India.   But when it became known that the Rajah was in
trouble with the Bombay Government, and had incurred the
serious displeasure of our authorities in 1835, Balajee Punt Natoo,
in concert with the Rajah's brother, who was on bad terms with
him, and who was put in his place after the deposition in 1839,
saw his opportunity had come, and commenced the calumnies and
intrigues which ultimately proved successful.

"What was called evidence of the most preposterous and ridi-
culous plans of raising rebellion throughout India, with aid from
Portugal and Russia, was collected, behind his back and without
allowing him, or anyone on his behalf, to see or cross-examine the
witnesses, these inquisitorial proceedings being spread over three

* Lord of the Umbrella and Lord of the Hindoos.

years. The name of his traducer, Balajee Punt Natoo, was concealed throughout the proceedings."

" A mass of fiction, as I verily believe," said Mr. Forbes, one of the Directors in 1840, "consisting of letters not proved to be authentic, of seals and ciphers forged, of oral evidence obtained under every suspicion of undue influence, of partnerships contracted with bankers, and false entries made in their books; every artifice, in short, that the great cunning, great ability, deep personal interest and inveterate hatred of Balajee Punt Natoo and his ignoble instrument, Appa Sahib, could employ, has been directed against this devoted Prince."[*]   But, as I said before, it would be wearisome and useless now to enter on a detailed inquiry into the question of the Rajah's guilt or innocence.   Suffice it to say that four of the Directors of the East India Company, Messrs. H. St. George Tucker, Cotton, Shepherd and Forbes, recorded Minutes of dissent against his deposition; that Mr. Henry Shakespear, a member of the Supreme Council of India, considered that " no charge of a serious nature had been substantiated against the Rajah";[†] that Mr. Forbes declared his belief that all that Prince's misfortunes were caused by a Palace conspiracy, of which, in his words, we were "the dupes" and he was "the victim";[‡] and that many other competent judges at the time expressed opinions equally decided in favour of the Rajah.   And there is at least this presumptive proof of his innocence, that he steadily rejected all compromise, and when a full amnesty was offered him, resolved to sacrifice his throne, to abandon his treasures, to relinquish his home, and to go into exile with his family to a distant part of India, rather than subscribe certain articles which implied a confession of his criminality.   "Guilt", said Mr. St. George Tucker, "would have found it easy to accept the conditions proposed, in order to escape from the threatened penalty.   The consciousness of rectitude must be strong when it impels a man to make a great sacrifice to

---

[*] *Sattara Papers* (569 of 1843), p. 70.   [†] *Ibid.* p. 1260.
[‡] *Ibid.* p. 1258.

a sense of honour, however mistaken."* And in this instance the sacrifice was tremendous, and was made with perfect deliberation and great dignity.

The Rajah Pertaub Singh of Sattara was dethroned and deported to Benares in 1839. He died in 1846, having adopted in the previous year the son of his first cousin, Bala Sahib Bhonsla, the titular Senapati, or Commander-in-Chief. His brother, who was installed in his place under the title of Rajah Shàhjee, died in 1848, having also adopted a son with every due formality. But Lord Dalhousie's career of annexation, sustained by the cordial approval and applause of the Anglo-Indian Civil Service, had commenced. The imputed treason of the elder brother was used, with complete success, as a plea for the extinction of the State on the death of the younger brother. The Government of India, in defiance of the opinion of Sir George Clerk, then Governor of Bombay, rejected both the adopted sons, and took this occasion to forge the machinery of imaginary precedents and sham prerogative by which the rightful heirs of the Rajahs of Jhansi and Nagpore were subsequently disinherited, and those faithful and useful States destroyed.

The beneficent rule of the two successive Rajahs, and the prosperity of their subjects, were not allowed to plead against the policy of annexation. "There can be no doubt", said the Hon. Mr. Willoughby,† one of the Bombay Councillors, in June 1848, "of the excellence of the late Rajah's administration." To the same effect, and in the same Council, wrote the Hon. Lestock Reid.

" Whether it is expedient in this case to admit the adoption and succession to the Sattara musand, is a question for the decision of the highest authorities. In favour of this course are the policy of conciliating the population of what formed the Mahratta Empire ; the advantage of having a perfectly friendly and dependent State in the heart of our districts, whose power and influence can be made use of by us in the maintenance of internal tranquillity ; and probably a conviction that under the mild and excellent

* *Sattara Papers*(569 of 1843), p. 1258
† Afterwards Sir John P. Willoughby, a Director of the East India Company, and a Member of the Secretary of State's Council.

government of the late Rajah, his country flourished in a degree
with which our neighbouring districts cannot well sustain a comparison. I believe it will be universally admitted that the manner
in which both their Highnesses, Pertaub Singh and Shahjee, administered the internal affairs of the Sattara State was such as to
hold them up as models to all Indian Princes."*

Both of these gentlemen, however, voted in favour of
the annexation. But that subject will be more conveniently treated when we come to the period in General
Briggs's life when he took a prominent part in the
discussion ; when he was one of a small minority who
deprecated and opposed by all available means the policy
that then prevailed of territorial aggrandisement and
administrative uniformity in India.

Although the salary allotted to the Resident at
Sattara was exactly the same—2,500 rupees a month—
as that drawn by the Political Agent in Khandesh, Briggs
had gladly accepted the Residency, as a post offering a
healthier climate and somewhat more of society to his
wife and children, and more leisure to himself, after five
years' hard and harassing work, for study and literary
pursuits. At Sattara he completed his translation of
Ferishta's *History of the Rise of Mohammedan Power
in India*, and also his Persian edition of the same historian's works, collated from many manuscripts, which
was printed at Bombay in 1831, perhaps the most beautiful and extended specimen of Persian lithography ever
executed.† It was in this period, also, that he translated the *Siyar-ul-Mutakhirin*, or "Review of the
Moderns", by Ghulam Hussain, the chronicle of the
decay of the Mogul Empire and Mussulman domination
in India, which was published in London by the Oriental
Translation Fund.‡ He had been collecting and digesting
for years the materials for his book on the Land Tax of
India, and great progress was made in this work before
Major Briggs left Sattara, in December 1826.

* *Sattara Papers* (83 of 1849), pp 54, 66.
. † One or two copies may still, I believe, be found at Quaritch's, in
Piccadilly.
‡ 1832, John Murray, Albemarle Street ; and Parbury and Allen,
Leadenhall Street.

H

" I had now been more than twenty-five years continuously in India and Persia, and, besides making many sea voyages, had had my full share of severe and anxious duties and of unhealthy stations. I had suffered considerably and very frequently from illness, especially from a very bad chronic headache, during the previous ten years, and I was strongly recommended to return to England. The Rajah's assiduous attention to the duties of government, and the liberal scale of his expenditure on public objects of general utility, were all that could be desired; but I was much annoyed and embarrassed by those hints and symptoms of the Rajah's overweening notions of his inherent grandeur, and of its inadequate recognition by our Government, of which I have already spoken. Some quiet remonstrances of mine on the subject, in consequence of private information I had received, led to a misunderstanding and a coolness between myself and the Rajah, which I have no doubt I should have dispelled, as well as the exaggerated pretensions, had my health permitted me to stay a little longer at Sattara. But my last days there were passed in sickness and low spirits, and I was not equal to the long interviews that would have been required to bring His Highness to a sense of his errors.

" Those errors, I must add, were by no means unnatural or inexcusable on the Rajah's part, or entirely without grounds in the declarations and action of our Government. Even while the Peishwas ruled, like the Maires du Palais with the Merovingian kings, they paid ceremonial homage to the Rajah, received their own investiture from him, and made no appointment to high office or public act of any consequence without his formal assent under seal. Before the Rajah and his family fell into our hands, on the capture of Sattara by our troops, Mr. Elphinstone ordered the British flag, which was at first hoisted, to be hauled down, and the flag of the Rajah displayed, and by proclamation, and in other forms intended to attract and conciliate the Mahratta chiefs, implied that the claims to federal supremacy of the Rajah of Sattara were more legitimate than those of the usurping Peishwa, whom we denounced and proscribed. There was never, of course, any intention or promise of restoring the extended sovereignty of Sivajee's House, but there was quite enough advantage taken of its old headship for our political purposes at the time to give the Rajah and his personal adherents an uneasy feeling that his full rights had been unduly cut down by the Treaty. The other side of the question was easily argued; and on the side of the Rajah, the pretensions referred to never advanced beyond idle and sentimental talk. It was my duty to report these matters to our Government, and I did so, without attaching to them any extraordinary importance. I never said, nor believed, that the Rajah, who was gifted with much good sense and shrewd powers of calculation, would ever be drawn into a violation of the Treaty, the binding nature of which he well understood, or into any hostile intrigues against the Honourable Company. But in later days, in the proceedings before and after the Rajah's deposition, my despatches were most unfairly used to prejudice the Rajah's cause, and to disparage my efforts on his behalf.

"The Rajah and I parted with every appearance of friendship— I do not think he had any grudge against me. I know I had no ill-will towards him, and I had a great respect for his many excellent qualities as a man and as a ruler. He came to see me off, and on taking leave presented me with the sword he was then wearing, and with a diamond ring of small value, which, according to custom, I had to surrender at Leadenhall Street on my arrival. The sword I was allowed to keep.

"I remained some weeks at Bombay with my wife and family as the guest of the Governor, my old master, Mr. Elphinstone, who took great interest in my literary labours, and whose friendship I retained after his retirement until his death. We embarked in the good ship *Upton Castle*, on the 18th of January 1827, and reached England in June."

CHAPTER VI.

Since his first appearance in print with the treatise on the nomad carriers of India, the Brinjarries, in 1812, Briggs had, beyond the necessary sphere of his official duties, written many papers on social, ethnological, and economic subjects, which were chiefly communicated to the Government of Bombay, and in some cases printed. He had a natural facility in the acquirement of languages, and was fond of associating with well-informed Natives. Thus he obtained rare opportunities of gaining an insight into their manners, habits, and institutions, religious and civil. Before leaving Sattara he had supplied the Bombay Government with a very full account of the peculiar laws and customs of the Hindus of the Deccan—that part relating to the Mahrattas being the most complete—with regard to the surnames of families ; propinquity of relationship and line of descent as affecting marriage and adoption ; and the property and family position of widows. He had also compiled a sort of Mahratta Peerage, in which the origin and pedigree of the principal chieftains were traced, and a description given of their political claims, and the actual condition and tenure of their estates. But the most important of the literary labours to which he referred, in the extract at the end of the last chapter, was the translation of the great historical work of Mohammed Hussain Asterabadi, commonly called by his literary name, Ferishta, in which he had made great progress when appointed Assistant to Mr. Elphinstone at Poona in 1816. He says:—

"I began with the minor dynasties, which had never been rendered into either English or Hindustani. I was very fortunate in coming across a good copy of these parts, as well as the better known histories of the Kings of Golconda, or Hyderabad. I found that those parts of Ferishta which had been published by Dow and

Colonel Jonathan Scott were extremely inaccurate, both of them having translated from a Hindustani version. They were merely narratives founded on Ferishta. The proper names of men and places were fearfully distorted, and often rendered unintelligible. Before proceeding to the field in 1817, I had, fortunately, sent part of my translations to my friend, Mr. William Erskine, at Bombay, and another portion to Mr. (afterwards Sir) Richard Jenkins, then Resident at Nagpore. Meanwhile, as has been related, the Residency at Poona was sacked and burnt, and all my valuable Oriental MSS., together with my Persian Journal and other papers, the produce of great labour, and which neither money nor memory could replace, were destroyed. I may observe that, in spite of the remonstrances of Mr. Elphinstone, no adequate compensation was granted by Government to me and the other sufferers for the loss of our houses and their contents. My occupation in the field for the next two years, and my extensive range of duty in the Government of Khandesh, prevented me from giving much time to these pursuits. During my stay in that province, however, I gained an intimate knowledge of the landed tenures and village institutions, of which I recorded copious notes, utilised subsequently in my work on the Land Tax.

" It was in Khandesh, also, that I obtained from two Pundits, who were intimately acquainted with, modern Mahratta history and politics from about 1760 to 1800, a very detailed narrative of the life of the great Minister, Nana Furnavees, the autobiography of whose early life I afterwards obtained from his widow when I was at Sattara. This document I brought to England, and it will be found among a mass of Mahratta papers preserved in the archives of the Royal Asiatic Society. I translated the autobiography, and it was my intention to have published these interesting materials in the shape of a history of Nana Furnavees and his times ; but I fear I must, at my time of life, consider that project at an end.

" Having recovered the Ferishta manuscripts, which had, fortunately, been preserved by Mr. Erskine and by Mr. Jenkins, though the latter was for some time in great danger at Nagpore, I took advantage of the comparative leisure I enjoyed at Sattara to return to my task of editing Ferishta, and finishing the translation. Having secured several copies written in various parts of India, I was able to collate a more complete and correct edition of this valuable work than had ever before existed. I tendered it for publication to the Government of Bombay, who caused a large edition, in two volumes folio, to be lithographed from the beautiful Persian text prepared under my supervision, and granted me the sum of 5,000 rupees for my expenses, with part of which I remunerated my learned Mussulman collaborator, who had been supported for many years at my private expense.

"Some years later, Lord Clare, then Governor of Bombay, gave me forty copies, so that I was enabled to distribute the work among the chief Royal and public libraries of Europe.

"My health rapidly improved on board ship, and I relieved the tedium of the long voyage round the Cape by working up for the press the materials I had in hand. The translation of Ferishta was ultimately produced in four thick octavo volumes. In order to cover as much as possible the cost of publication, I had succeeded in obtaining a large list of subscribers in India. On the strength of these subscriptions, which they were to receive, Messrs. Longman undertook the work, engaging to place at my disposal half the remainder of the first edition. My share of the profits, after presenting many copies to my friends and to public institutions, amounted to forty pounds.

"The work was not entirely unnoticed, nor has its value been unacknowledged. Sir Henry M. Elliot, one of the highest authorities on Oriental literature, in speaking of my translation as one of the efforts of Europeans to bring the knowledge of the Mohammedan historians before the public, observes that 'the translation of the entire work of Ferishta, by Colonel Briggs, in four vols., 8vo, has thrown all similar efforts into the shade for ever.'* At a later period I was gratified by the receipt of the following short note from my valued friend and patron, Mr. Elphinstone, on sending me his *History of India*, published in 1841 :—

"'MY DEAR BRIGGS,—I am bound to send you the accompanying production, however unworthy of your acceptance, as containing my receipts for stolen goods of yours. They will be found in every page of the early Mohammedan history, but particularly in vol. i, p. 527.

"'Yours most sincerely,

"'M. ELPHINSTONE.

"'I wish I had seen your supplement on the Land Revenue before I wrote on that subject. It cost me a vast deal of trouble to attain to nearly the same conclusion.   'M. E.'"

"The reference in the *History of India* is as follows :—

"'From this time forward my principal dependence will be on Ferishta, a Persian historian who long resided in India, and wrote, in the end of the sixteenth century, a history of all the Mohammedan dynasties in that country, down to his own time. I think myself fortunate in having the guidance of an author so much

* *Bibliographical Index to Mohammedan History* (Calcutta, 1849), p. 318; see also *History of India told by its own Historians*, Posthumous Papers of Sir H. M. Elliot, edited by Professor Dowson (London, Trübner, 1875), vol. vi, p. 213.

superior to most of his class in Asia.   Where the nature of my narrative admitted of it, I have often used the very expressions of Ferishta, which, in Colonel Briggs's translation, it would be difficult to improve.'*

"The edition of Ferishta contained genealogical tables of every dynasty at the head of each chapter, and an index of the names of all towns mentioned in the work, in the Persian and English character, with the longitude and latitude of each."

The Persian edition and English translation of Ferishta were reviewed by Von Hammer in the Vienna *Jahrbücher* (No. LI, pp. 36 to 58), and in the *Journal des Savants* (1850, pp. 212-226, 354-372, 392-403), in a series of articles replete with information on the general subject, by Jules Mohl.

"During the voyage I also completed a paper on the life of Ferishta, and the translation from the Mahrattee of the autobiography of Nana Furnavees, with a series of original letters of the Peishwa, Madhoo Rao the Great, all of which were read before the Royal Asiatic Society, and are published in its Transactions.

"We reached England in the middle of June, in fine summer weather.   It would be impossible for me to describe my feelings on touching the English shore after an absence of more than twenty-six years.   I remember well that what struck me most was what seemed to me to be the general beauty of the inhabitants of both sexes, especially of the children, just as on landing in India I had been impressed—as I believe all Europeans are—with the general and, as it appears, almost uniform strangeness, I do not say ugliness, of the Natives.   By degrees, as one becomes better acquainted with the dark races, one learns to distinguish difference of features and expression, and so, after a few days in England, the impression of universal beauty began to wear off.

"Nor was it the faces and forms of my countrymen alone that gratified me.   I was equally struck with the activity of the country population at that busy time of the year, and with the verdure and evident fertility of the soil.   As we travelled through the country between Weymouth and Bath, on the first day after our landing, I saw nothing but smiling flowers covering the walls of the most insignificant, but still neat, dwellings ; and instead of barren and burnt-up wastes of many miles in extent, such as we should have often come across in India, I could not perceive a sterile spot throughout the whole journey.   We were very hospitably received at Bath by my brother, Captain Arthur Lysaght, R.N.,†

* Elphinstone's *History of India*, vol. i, p. 527.
† *Ante*, p. 7.

and on the following day I found myself in the arms of my father, who awaited our arrival at Cheltenham. He had been always in the habit of wearing powder till I left England, so that his grey hairs did not give to him in my eyes the appearance of the age which he had attained since we parted at Portsmouth twenty-six years before. He enjoyed apparently excellent health, and I could hardly realise the fact that he was in his seventieth year. He was, however, suffering from a lingering disease, which proved fatal to him about three years later. As a young man he was remarkable for his easy temper and the grace of his manners, and obtained the designation of Sir Charles Grandison. He was a favourite in society wherever he became known, and possessed great influence with many friends of distinction. Among others was Lord Hobart, afterwards Earl of Buckinghamshire, who had been Governor of Madras, as well as others whom he had known in India, and who had become from time to time Directors of the East India Company. Through their friendly patronage, he contrived to secure appointments in India for every one of his large family of eleven sons. He was a man of strong good sense, and throughout maintained a high character for integrity. Considerate kindness to all was equally remarkable in him with firmness and resolution under all circumstances.

"My youngest child, a girl, was born at Cheltenham a month after my arrival, and as soon as we could move we came to London, and shortly afterwards took a partly furnished house in the parish of East Malling, near Maidstone, in Kent. By this time I had obtained all my baggage, the most bulky, and to me the most valuable, part of which was my library, consisting of three large cases of English works, besides one of Oriental manuscripts and printed books. I caused shelves to be constructed for them, and had rendered my new habitation comfortable, as I hoped, for two years at least. But I was not destined to enjoy my quiet country residence long. In the depth of winter I received notice to quit, in a most unpleasant shape. My landlord was a great grower of hops, for which privilege a heavy duty was levied by the Government on the quantity produced. The year had been plentiful, and the amount of duty proportionately heavy. The landlord, not having the means of paying at the moment, absconded, and the collector of the duty proceeded to distrain on the premises for all he could find. Sheriff's officers came to the spot on Saturday, the 23rd of December, after sunset, without any official notice to me, to carry into effect their purpose, and my property became liable to be seized in the first instance to satisfy the demands of the Exchequer. During my short sojourn in Kent, my mind being much occupied with my unfinished work on the Land Tax of India, I had pushed my inquiries in every direction, and by all available means, into questions of tenure, and such matters as village rights of common. And thus it came about that I had made friends with the bailiff of the estate, from whom I obtained from day to day all the peculiarities of English farming, and the laws and local customs of landed property, of which I had previously known very little. This acquaintanceship now proved of essential service. The bailiff came to me with a long face one Saturday evening after dark, and told me that the Sheriff's officers were on the spot to seize all the property found on the premises of the landlord, to satisfy the demand of Government for the hop duty, that they would be at the door in half an hour, and that it was their intention to seize all the furniture and effects found in the dwelling-house, whether belonging to the landlord or his tenant; for such, said he, was the law, though I might, perhaps, in the course of time, recover compensation or damages from some one. I asked him what was to be done. ' Why,' said he, ' I am come to put you up to the best plan. The officers cannot lawfully make a seizure after sunset, or before sunrise ; nor can they do so on Sunday. This being the case, you will have time to pack up your books and furniture, and remove them off the premises before sunrise on Monday morning.'

" The bailiff undertook to procure carts, and carpenters to pack my property. In the meantime I received the Sheriff's officers very coolly at the door, where they submitted at once to my warning against any attempt at an entry or seizure in unlawful hours. The work of removal soon began. Books, crockery, and glass were replaced in their cases, and more than half our packing done when the church clock struck twelve at midnight. The carpenters having heard it, began grumbling at being made to work on Sunday. A consultation was now held, and a discussion commenced, which was chiefly carried on by the bailiff and the workmen themselves, a few of whom had no qualms of conscience at all, and justified their views by quotations from the Holy Scriptures. They declared that our Saviour allowed of works of necessity and mercy on the Sabbath day, and that this was a work of necessity and mercy, if ever there was one. As Kentish men, they were all prejudiced against the taxes and tithes on hops. Many of the party, however, stuck to the fourth commandment, to keep holy the Sabbath day, and recalled to mind how dire calamities had fallen on their neighbours by the sudden loss of crops and cattle, and even of children, by violating that injunction. It was found at last that there was a strong majority in favour of knocking off work, but they made a solemn promise, which they kept, of returning at midnight on Sunday, and of removing all my goods before sunrise on Monday morning. This was done in due course, and all my goods were in London by Monday evening. I sent on my family very early, while I remained as a rear-guard, and settled with my Sabbatarian allies, the carpenters. We took refuge with a relative until I engaged a furnished house in Portman Street, Montagu Square."

After occupying this house for a few months, during which time the house was twice robbed—first by the footman, and, secondly, on the very day of the man's conviction and sentence at the Old Bailey, by his accomplices, who carried off two hundred pounds' worth of silver plate—Colonel Briggs decided on proceeding to Paris, and devoting all his time to the completion of his work, as he says, " on the landed tenures of India and the land tax of the ancients, as compared with our own system of revenue."

"My family now consisted of two daughters of sixteen and thirteen years of age, of two younger girls, one of five years and one of twelve months old, and of a son, nine years of age. I had letters of introduction to an old retired English officer long resident in Paris, and through him was introduced to the several Orientalists and scientific men of that capital. Among them was M. Jules Mohl, a German gentleman of Stutgard, and of noble birth, who, having taken his degrees at the University of Tübingen, became so interested in Oriental literature that he settled in Paris, where the greatest advantages and facilities for such studies were then to be found, and became subsequently a naturalised Frenchman. He was made a Member of the National Institute, than which there is no higher literary honour in France. The acquirements of Dr. Jules Mohl are such as have rendered his name familiar throughout Europe as one of its best Persian scholars, and I can never cease to be grateful for the pleasure and profit I have ever derived from my friendship with him.

"During my short stay in London I had obtained access to the meetings of the Geological Society, and began to take a great interest in that subject. In Paris I availed myself of an introduction to the celebrated Baron Cuvier, the first of Naturalists in his day, and, it may be said, the first Palæontologist. At his weekly soirées I became acquainted with many eminent men of science, and was induced to attend the lectures of Brogniat and Oudouen. Among my literary acquaintances were Baron Silvestre de Sacy, Eugène Burnouf, Rémusat, Klaproth, and others. My evenings were chiefly devoted to scientific studies, but my main object at this time, and the occupation of every morning, was the completion of my work on the Land Tax of India before the renewal of the East India Company's Charter. The Parliamentary

Committee to report on the whole subject was expected to assemble in the Session of 1830, three years before the termination of the usual term of twenty years in 1833. My friend Jules Mohl, who is a thorough and correct English scholar, was of infinite use to me, both by searching for books in the Royal Library, and by affording me his well-considered opinion on many points.

"My two elder daughters were of an age to profit by the excellent opportunities in Paris for improving their knowledge of French, Italian, music, and dancing. This last accomplishment was pursued and cultivated by them—even at this distance of time, I am almost ashamed to say it—with very little gratification to me, for I had to submit more often than pleased me, to be dragged out to balls and parties, where I was assured my presence and support were indispensable, although I thought their mother's escort would be sufficient."

The following letters to his nephew, Augustus de Morgan, for which I am indebted to the great mathematician's widow,—the accomplished authoress of her husband's Life, and editress of his immortal *Budget of Paradoxes*,*—belong to this period.

"31, Rue Vaugirard, Paris,
"27th October 1829.

"My dear Augustus,—I had just finished a letter to you when yours of the 21st arrived yesterday. How can it be so long on the road? I am sorry that my replies to the queries of your friend, Mr. Long, must necessarily be short and imperfect.

Imprimis—Hamadān is a fine town situated on the highroad between Baghdad and Teheran, an ancient capital of Persia, and undoubtedly the Ἐκβάτανα of Herodotus. We—that is, Jules Mohl and I—suppose the κ in Ἐκβάτανα to have been written by mistake for a ν. Moreover, the Greeks usually write τ for δ in Oriental names, —as Ἀρταβανησ† for Ἀρδαβαν or *Urdu-bān*, one who maintains an army or horde,—*urdu*, as they still call it in Turkish and Persian, —Ἀρταβαζησ† for *Urdu-bāsh*, the head of an army, or general. They also wrote ξ for *sh*, as in Ἀρταξερξης† for *Ardashir* or *Urdu-sher*, the lion of the army.

"Are you aware that Mirza Ibrahim, the Persian Professor at Haileybury College, is translating Beloe's *Herodotus* into Persian? It might be worth Mr. Long's while to see him, and talk to him on the subject, though I don't promise him much light in that quarter.

"I am anxious to see Godfrey Higgins's apology for Mohammed.

* Longmans, 1882 and 1872.

† Artabanes, Artabazes, and Artaxerxes.

He has lately sent to Todd, who is now here, the prospectus of his
new work, which is now in the press; but I am quite sure he will
be open to easy attack, in spite of his Hebrew learning. He has
quite neglected Arabic, without which no one can really master
Hebrew,—Hebrew being the uncultivated or undeveloped Arabic,
—and he does not know a word of Sanscrit, though he declares
he will prove it to be a dialect of Hebrew, and says that Mel-
chisedec was a Boodhist! I think with him and you, that all the
Pagan Pantheon will be found to be symbols of the planets and
constellations; but Higgins will not keep within his depth, and
will sink accordingly."

From the next two letters it will be seen that the
opus magnum was finished before Briggs left Paris, and
that its general purport, an outline of which is given in
the second letter, was not very likely to conciliate the
official world, or to recommend Colonel Briggs to the
general suffrages of the Anglo-Indian Secretariat and
Civil Service.

" 31, Rue Vaugirard,
" 10th January 1830.

" MY DEAR AUGUSTUS,—Having completed the researches among
public records, I am now engaged in studying MacCulloch, Adam
Smith, and others, preparatory to commencing my last chapter.
Meanwhile I have been turning over my project for the gradual
liquidation of the National Debt of Great Britain, and for providing
an immediate remedy for the great burden of annual interest by a
succession duty, or tax on the estates of deceased persons. I wish
you could procure for me, for love or money, an account of the
property which has passed through Doctors' Commons annually
during the last thirty or forty years."

" Paris, Rue Vaugirard,
" 22nd January 1830.

" MY DEAR AUGUSTUS,—The work is finished. It has cost me a
vast deal of labour; and the worst of it is that I have been compelled in the process of revision to throw away the product of
months of hard study as irrelevant. The book opens with an
account of the nature of landed property in all countries, and the
imposts usually levied for the Crown. In ancient times this
appears to have been in India, and everywhere the same,—one-
tenth of the crop. The Hindu institutions and laws are then
explained, under which new imposts on land were introduced, not
higher than one-sixth, except in time of war, when a fourth might
be taken. The invasion and domination of the Mussulmans raised

the tax from a quarter to a half of the crop. Some of the wisest Mohammedan kings reverted to the fourth, but it was usually found to be about one-half in the countries which we occupied.

"The Chapters II, III, and IV give a history of English revenue proceedings in Bengal, Madras, and Bombay, each of these Presidencies having, at different periods, under authority from England, adopted conflicting and irreconcilable views as to landed tenures and Sovereign rights. The leading men under all three Governments *now* agree in stating that the cultivator is the sole proprietor of his land, as long as he pays the tax, or by whatever name the impost may be called. They all agree, also, in claiming the unoccupied lands for the Sovereign, and are unanimous in asserting that the present rates of land-tax are ruinous to the people, and ought to be reduced.

"From the reports of all three Presidencies it is established by authentic proofs that one uniform system of government formerly prevailed throughout India, and neither Mussulman oppression nor our own blundering arrangements have been able to effect its destruction. This system consists in the existence of village communities or corporations, each with its Mayor, or Mayor and Aldermen, originally elected by the inhabitants, who are repre-sentatives of the village, and administer all its affairs. The Mohammedans, without troubling themselves about Hindoo customs, allowed these corporations to continue unchanged, provided they paid their assessment. We have done all we can to break them up, and have endeavoured to take the interior management of the people's concerns into our hands,—to place our paid servants everywhere, and to cry down the power and influence of the popular village magnates. By these measures we have unhinged the whole frame of society, and have done infinitely more harm, and given more offence, than the Mohammedans ever did. Our claim to the whole of the landlord's profits has left no source of national wealth, and the inhabitants, though wealthy under the native Governments, are poor under ours. This is the reason why the free trade has not been successful. With the exception of cotton cloths it has entirely failed. Two steam engines for manufacturing Indian cloths on the spot have already gone to India. Four at each of the Presidencies would ruin the Glasgow and Manchester weavers, and you and I may live to see England purchasing Bengal muslins again as of old.

"I have proved that a tax such as the Company raises in India direct from the land, which it spends in great measure out of the country, and in the pay of its English officers and soldiers, is not only the most detrimental tax to the people, but is the least profitable of all taxes to Government. My remedy is to give up all the waste lands to those who are now so heavily taxed,—to allow the weight of the present tax to diminish by fixing its amount as it is, while the present landholders are permitted to take up the unoccupied tracts in their neighbourhood gratis. Landlords will thus be created ; wealth will accumulate, and with it will arise the desire and the capacity of purchasing our manufactures. If great Britain could now send a thousand shiploads of goods instead of a hundred, the poverty of the people would prevent their being sold at a profit."

" My work on the Land Tax of India", says Briggs, " was published in London in the spring of 1830 ; and as the time for my return to India was approaching, I prepared to quit Paris in the summer. In the month of June I was elected an Honorary Member of the Asiatic Society of Paris, and of the Society of Universal Statistics. We started for England on the 10th of July 1830, thus escaping by little more than a fortnight the detention, and possibly danger, that would have attended our presence in Paris during the 'three glorious days' of July. I was quite prepared to hear of the Revolution. During the last six months at least of my residence in the French capital, it seemed to be the settled opinion of all the most distinguished men with whom I was in the habit of meeting,—many of whom took no active interest in politics,—that the reign of Charles X would not last much longer."

CHAPTER VII.

The greater part of Briggs's *Land Tax of India* is of too technical a character to be commended to the notice of the general reader; and that portion of the book which refers to our land-settlements in Bengal, Madras, and Bombay has now little more than a historical value. Although Colonel Briggs perceived the ruinous errors that had been committed, and gave very plain warning of their evil effects, his observations and experience were at too early a date to enable him to discern fully in what their pauperising and exhausting conditions consisted. There has been much tinkering with the land revenue since his time, and a vast outlay in settlement and survey operations in all the Presidencies, but, with the incessant growth of debt and expenditure, there has been no respite or relief given to the agricultural population.

The first part of the book is, however, of permanent importance, and remains, in fact, unshaken and unsuperseded by any subsequent publication, whether of official origin or not. No statesman or systematic student of British rule in India can afford to disregard or to overlook it. The work is divided into three parts, the first dealing with the "Land Tax of the Ancients" in Greece and other parts of Europe, and with the "Land Tax of India" in Hindoo and Mohammedan times; the second with the changes introduced by English rule and administration; and the third, with the effects of those changes on the condition of the people and the country. In the three chapters of which the first part consists, the author proves beyond all dispute, by citations from a large number of original authorities, Hindoo and Mussulman, the universal existence of private property in land in India from the earliest ages. He shows that this right of property was never questioned by either Hindoo or

Moslem rulers, and that the assessments levied by them
upon the landed classes were distinctly a tax, and in no
sense an appropriation or demand of the rent, either in
whole or in part, or an assertion of proprietorship in the
soil.   In his second part he shows how this important
fact was everywhere and invariably ignored by the
British authorities, who, unlike their predecessors, asserted that "the State", *i.e.*, the East India Company,
was the actual proprietor of all the land in British India,
and entitled, as such, to levy an assessment upon it,
equivalent to the entire rental, precisely as an English
landlord is, by law, entitled to receive the full rent of
his estates.   In the third and last part, he shows what
dire distress and poverty this monstrous and exorbitant
claim has wrought throughout British India.

The book is written throughout in a style studiously
calm and dispassionate ; ample extracts from official
documents are given in support of every fact stated and
every inference drawn ; and at the close of the long and
laborious examination, the writer thus expresses himself:—
" I conscientiously believe that under no Government
whatever, either Hindoo or Mohammedan, professing to
be actuated by law, has there ever been any system so
subversive of the prosperity of the people at large as
that which has marked our administration."*

I have said that the second and third parts do not
now possess the value attaching to the first portion, which
establishes incontrovertibly the existence of private property in land ; but this must not be taken as implying
a lack of industry or insight on the part of the author.
Colonel Briggs saw with clearness the gross and rapacious
pretension on which the land administration of the East
India Company was based ; but, living, as it were, in the
midst of the policy which he describes, he could not see
so clearly as we can the causes which brought about the
error, or the full extent of the mischief which it was
destined to occasion.

That the East India Company was originally only a
company of merchants engaged in the trade with India,

* *Land Tax*, p. 410.

is a fact known to all, but the appalling consequences of this fact to the people of India after the Company had acquired territorial sovereignty and full administrative powers, have never been clearly perceived, or, at any rate, have been almost wholly ignored. And yet it is not too much to say that, until the extinction of the Company in 1858, this fact of its commercial origin and interests constituted the great guiding principle of all our Indian policy—our wars, our annexations, our barbarous monopolies and systems of taxation, and, above all things, our ruinous assessments on the produce of the land. The rapid decay of the ancient wealth and prosperity of India is distinctly traceable to this one fact; and until its supreme importance has been seen and acknowledged, no truthful account of British Rule in India can ever be written.

The Directors of the East India Company, in its character of a trading corporation, had, of course, to pay half-yearly dividends to the Proprietors of East India Stock. But the capital which had been subscribed for purposes of trade was, as a matter of fact, expended down to the last farthing in the struggle with the French. When Lord Clive obtained from the Mogul Emperor the decree empowering the East India Company, as Dewan, to collect the revenues of Bengal, Behar, and Orissa, he not only established the nucleus of our present Indian Empire, but he did what the Directors deemed then to be of far greater importance,—he preserved them from going into liquidation. The East India Company, at that time, did not possess one sixpence of trading capital. The capital which they had once possessed was now represented by a debt of £700,000. But they regarded Bengal, Behar, and Orissa as a large freehold estate, in the purchase of which their capital had been sunk, and proposed to carry on their East India and China trade by means of the "territorial rents" to be derived from these three provinces. This "rent"—i.e., all the surplus revenue of Bengal, Behar, and Orissa—was annually devoted to the purchase of such Indian and Chinese commodities as there was a demand for in England, and in this form sent to London to pay

I

the dividends on East India Stock. This it was which
became known as the Company's "Investment", and the
following incident will show how absolutely the existence
of the Company depended upon it. In the year 1769,
the Government of India proposed to cut down "the
Investment" by one-half for a few years, in order to provide a Reserve Fund to defray the expenses of the constantly recurring wars. The anger and consternation of
the Court of Directors upon the receipt of this intelligence are thus described in the Report of the Parliamentary Committee of Secrecy.

" That however salutary it may be to have a view to remote
events, and to provide for future contingencies, after these investments shall have been carried to the extent requisite for the
Company's immediate occasions, yet in how unfavourable a light
must appear the intentions of their servants to guard against
remote and uncertain evils abroad by *leaving the Company to sink
under absolute and present distresses at home.*"

They then go on to state the many demands they have
on hand at home, and express the utmost astonishment
at seeing their servants entertain the idea of reducing
"the Investment" without absolute necessity, and thereby
depriving them of the only means they have to answer
such demands. They then express their hopes that upon
more mature deliberation their servants will lay aside so
destructive a design ; yet they say the view of it is so
alarming as to make it necessary for them to declare their
peremptory prohibition of such a measure. They tell
them that *"every other consideration is to give place to the
essential and primary object of their investments"* . . . . .
and they conclude with positive injunctions that " their
servants do not at any time engage in plans of so important a nature without their knowledge and concurrence,
as it behoved their servants to concert with them only
such systems as materially affect the very being of the
Company".*

It would take up far too much space to indicate even
in outline how this "Investment" occasioned wars, con-

---

* Letter from Court of Directors, 23rd March 1770.

trolled taxation, and entailed upon the people of British India burdens very largely in excess of the nominal amount of "the Investment" itself. The Salt Monopoly, the opium trade, and our Inland Customs Revenue, the most ruinous and extortionate that the mind can conceive, were created exclusively for the benefit of "the Investment", and the collateral expenses which grew out of it. But it pressed most heavily upon the land. In its management of the land the one object which the Government of the East India Company consistently held to was that of obtaining the largest possible amount of money from it. For this purpose, they let it out to farmers at public auction; and then, in order to get their money punctually, left the farmers at liberty to deal with the agricultural population precisely as they pleased. Under the merciless exactions of these farmers, supported whenever necessary by the troops of the Company, all the ancient proprietary rights in the soil were lost, and obliterated in general ruin. And then the officers of the Company declared that the chaos which they had themselves created was the normal condition of agricultural India—that the State was the universal landlord, and all other so-called proprietary rights depended upon its sufferance and toleration. To this theory, the successors of those early officials have obstinately clung to this day, and the wide-spread pauperism of British India, which Colonel Briggs, in 1832, viewed with such profound sorrow and apprehension, and which has certainly not lessened since his day, is the result of the official doctrine. Assertions of this kind are so distasteful to the self-love of the English character, that they generally excite nothing but incredulity, and it is, unfortunately, impossible to put within a small compass the abundant evidence on which they rest. Except where a Permanent Settlement has saved the agricultural classes from the rapacity of English administration, the process by which they have been reduced to indigence has differed in almost every Indian province, and it would require a volume to take each region separately, and follow "the road to ruin" in each. Merely as an illustration, therefore, I take that portion of the Madras

Presidency in which Sir Thomas Munro's *Ryotwar* settlement prevails. This settlement and its effects are described as follows in a Report of the Madras Board of Revenue, dated 5th Jan. 1818.

"However beneficial in other respects our administration may have proved to the people, it is greatly to be feared that the almost immediate introduction into these districts of the Ryotwar system . . . . tended to complete the destruction of the property which it was so much our interest and our duty to support. *While the Ryotwar survey assessment professed to fix an equal and moderate tax in money on each field, we find it, in almost every instance, greatly increasing the Government demand on the country.* . . . . It has been stated by Colonel Munro that under the Ryotwar system, 'the ryot knew, before he set his oxen to the plough, and dropped his seed into the ground, the utmost limit of rent that he could be called on to pay; and that the advantage of additional labour employed on his fields would be all his own, as well as the advantage of additional produce in an abundant season, and that he also knew in an unfavourable season an abatement of the demand would be made in his favour, if his diminished means rendered him unable to satisfy it'. But where the utmost limit of rent was raised so much above the means of the ryot, and where the ability of the people was to be the limit of the collection, it is obvious that the ryot's knowledge of it was of little consequence. . . . . The Ryotwar settlement was, in fact, made annually. *If the crop was good, the demand was raised as high within the survey rates as the means of the ryot would admit; if the crop was bad, the last farthing was, notwithstanding, demanded, and no remission was allowed unless the ryot was totally unable to pay the rent.* On this point the most severe scrutiny was instituted; for not only was the whole of the Collector's establishment employed in the investigation of his means, but his neighbours were converted into inquisitors, by being themselves made liable for his failure, unless they could show that he was possessed of property. . . . . *The little profit accruing to the industrious ryot was thus taken by the State to remunerate it for the losses it sustained from the failure of the less fortunate or more extravagant.*

"Moreover, to use the words of Mr. Chaplin, the Collector in Bellary, one of the most able of Colonel Munro's assistants, it 'was the custom to exert, in a great degree, the authority of *compelling* the inhabitants to cultivate a quantity of ground proportionate to their circumstances'. This he explains to have been done by ' the power to confine and punish' them, exercised by the Collector and his Native revenue servants; and he expressly adds that if the ryot was driven by these oppressions from the fields which he tilled, it was the established practice 'to follow the fugitive wherever he went, and by assessing him at discretion, to deprive him of all advantage that he might expect to derive from a change of residence'. *Reviewing the . . . . Ryotwar system as it thus existed in practice, nothing can well be more revolting to justice, and to all sound principles of government.*"

Notwithstanding this outspoken condemnation, this system, so "revolting to justice", continued to flourish without one harsh feature in it being removed or even mitigated until the outbreak of the great insurrection in 1857. Nor must it be forgotten that while thus appropriating to itself the entire rental of the soil of British India, the East India Company, for the first sixty years of its supremacy, did absolutely nothing for the land which it professed to own. Not merely did it construct no public works of its own, but the magnificent works with which its Hindoo and Moslem predecessors had covered the country were allowed to fall into ruin. In the Gangetic Provinces, the Moslem rulers had constructed and maintained, in good repair, a splendid network of raised roads, linking the great towns together. During the first thirty years of the Company's rule, so entirely was this function of government neglected, that these roads entirely disappeared; and in Madras the tanks for irrigation were allowed, in like manner, to become useless to the inhabitants. The Company was, in fact, an absentee landlord of the worst possible description, and on the largest scale. Nominally, its rent collectors were the English magistrates of each division ; but actually, these rent collectors were a vast swarm of underpaid, irresponsible, and unscrupulous Native underlings, who, without control or supervision of any kind, were let loose like an army of locusts, to eat the wretched people out of house and home. "It is", says Colonel Briggs, " hardly credible that no fewer than *one hundred thousand* Native civil servants form the train of our European agency." What with the rapacity of the East India Company itself, the greed and unlimited power of these hundred thousand Native civil servants, doing the work, on bad pay, of our highly paid English officers, the inefficiency, procrastination, venality, and corruption of our Courts of Justice, it is not possible to exaggerate the sufferings which we have inflicted upon the agricultural classes in India, and continue to inflict to this day, under a more erudite and symmetrical, but not more genial, system.

Colonel Briggs sums up, in the following passage, the results of his examination in the year 1832 :

" My whole life has been devoted to the study of the history, the manners, the customs, and the institutions of the country. It is from these sources I have borrowed materials to show that our measures have been founded on false assumptions ; that the hundred and fifty millions of freemen in India were once ruled by judicious laws which we have overlooked ; that their institutions are founded on wisdom, and have withstood the shock of eight centuries of conquest in a manner that no other institutions with which I am acquainted ever have or could have done ; that these people peculiarly claim our protection in their ancient rights and privileges ; and that until they are restored to them they must gradually sink lower and lower in the scale of humanity : but I believe that they will never sink into a condition so abject as to render our dominion over them secure from subversion.

" On the contrary, every thought which I have ever given to the subject convinces me that our own safety will be rendered more permanent by the adoption of a system that may raise the Natives to that scale in the State to which they have a right to aspire, and for which they are fitted ; and that, by affording them advantages equal, if not superior, to those they would enjoy under the Native Governments, we shall supply them with motives of attachment and fidelity. The connection is, however, an unnatural one, and will probably, in the end, be dissolved. Let us prepare ourselves and them for that separation, by rendering them fit to govern and to defend themselves, and leave them disposed to continue a friendly connection with us. To act otherwise,—to retain them in forcible subjection, to withhold from them those natural rights to which they are entitled,—will be to hasten that disunion which may be protracted, and to lay the seeds of that revolution which may end fatally to our dominion in India."*

The introduction of European education has intervened to thwart, in some measure, and among certain classes, the fulfilment of this prediction as to the degradation of the Indian people " in the scale of humanity";

* Pp. 461, 465.

but our administration of the land remains to-day, in all its essential features, the same as described by Colonel Briggs. Always excepting the area of the Permanent Settlement, it is a system in the highest degree destructive of that sense of security whereby alone intelligence and capital can be attracted to the cultivation of the land. The English Collector and the Native money-lender follow the agriculturist wherever he goes, and share between them all that is not needed for a scanty and insufficient subsistence. We could not realise our extortionate assessments without the aid of the money-lender, and we could not obtain his co-operation unless we kept the agricultural population wholly at his mercy by our judicial system. Unlike the indigenous Punchayut, which Briggs endeavoured to regulate and modify so as to form the central pivot of cheap and serviceable courts,* our elaborate and imposing judicature, absolutely divorced from local and popular opinion, has become a fearful instrument of oppression in the hands of the usurer and the rich litigant.

Another distinctive peculiarity of British administration, the tribute extracted from India in the form of Home Charges, and its exhausting effects, did not escape Colonel Briggs's observation.

" Above all, the landholders must be allowed to retain a portion of the surplus of their crop, instead of paying the whole. Were this tax even expended in India, the evil would be less: but how is it disposed of? About one-fifth of the gross taxation, that is to say, four millions annually, is withdrawn from it, either in produce or in specie, to be expended in England, not one sixpence of which ever returns to benefit the country from which the tribute is derived. The nature of our rule, and the interest of England, seem to demand that India should support the Home Charges; and I fear it is too much to hope for the adoption of any measures which might alleviate the burthen that India now sustains from our injustice."†

The Home Charges, amounting to four millions annually in 1830, and then characterised by Briggs as an unjust burthen, have now grown to between seventeen

* *Ante*, pp. 83 to 85. † P. 459.

and eighteen millions, a tribute to Great Britain of about one-third of the true revenue of India.

" I have limited my subject to the land-tax, the principal source of our revenue. I have shown, I believe, how we have erred, not from intention, but out of ignorance. Our resources are now beginning to fail us ; we endeavour to meet the contingency by reduction of expense, but we must avoid inefficiency. The great engine of the Government is its army; it cannot be tampered with without danger. I have already witnessed two or three commotions that threatened our empire with ruin : twice from the disaffection of the Natives; once from the discontent of the Europeans. In times of peace and order the machine is sufficiently manageable, and works well : it is in times of commotion that superior minds are requisite to regulate it."*

In subsequent parts of this book it will be seen that this early recognition of the danger to our rule from any maladministration, or inequitable measure that might touch the hearts or the homes of our Sepoys, was not a casual or passing notion, or a mere piece of ornamental rhetoric, but represented a logical train of thought, and a rooted conviction arising from it. Our Native army, Briggs repeatedly urged, was a part of the population, and shared in all its feelings and interests. Here is another significant passage taken from the concluding pages of the " Land Tax" :—

" We are too apt to ascribe to the inhabitants of India a character for timidity and pusillanimity. They are neither timid nor pusillanimous : they are bold and enterprising. He who has read their history cannot deny it. The deeds of our armies in India verify the assertion ; and the false estimate we have of them may lead to our ruin. When we recollect the scene at Vellore in 1806, and the state of the Madras army at that period; when we see a population of a hundred thousand inhabitants quitting their houses and their property, and encamping for whole weeks in the open fields, rather than pay a house-tax imposed without their consent, as did the inhabitants of Benares, we. may judge whether they will tamely submit to injuries affecting whole communities. So far from their being supine, they are most tenacious of their wonted privileges. The hold we have on them is already too loose : it should be our object to bind them more strongly to our Government. We have, fortunately, in the Hindoo institutions themselves, a broad basis on which to build. Each village is

* P. 457.

entire within itself: its elders form a body of senators at home, and representatives of the people abroad. A number of such villages constitute a district, which has its chief, who represents each of these little States at the Court of his Sovereign. These individuals enjoy their family estates absolutely independent of the favour of their Prince. They hold their representative offices hereditarily, as he holds his crown; and cannot be dispossessed, but for treason, without violence and injustice."*

No greater impediment exists to the removal of even acknowledged evils and deficiencies in our administration of India than the false and fantastic notions which are prevalent concerning the condition of the country under its Native Princes. The English rulers of India conceive of that condition as one of such extreme misery and oppression that any change could hardly fail to be a change for the better, while a change which substituted British rule for what they summarily describe as "Oriental despotism" must be equivalent to a transition from darkness into light. This condition of wretchedness is never demonstrated; it is assumed to be like a mathematical axiom, which requires only to be stated in order to command acquiescence. And yet even upon the surface of things there is much which would seem to render this assertion, so confidently and constantly made, a highly questionable one. It was not the wretchedness and poverty of India which first attracted European adventurers thither. It was, on the contrary, as they say and as they describe, its wealth, the magnificence of its Princes, and the high level of civilisation and prosperity to which its people had attained. And in these days it is impossible for the least observant traveller to journey through India without meeting, in all parts of the country, the indications of a grandeur and an opulence that have only recently decayed. The most convincing proof of the general order and security prevailing in India under her Native Princes is to be seen in the irrigation tanks, the mango-groves, the wells, caravanserais, mosques, and temples—now too often in ruins—which meet the eye so frequently in almost every province. These—and they must formerly have been much

* Pp. 454, 455.

more numerous—were nearly all the creation of private liberality. They demonstrate alike the wealth and the public spirit of the people, and what is not less important in passing judgment upon a Government, the safety with which the evidences of wealth could be openly displayed. In 1829 Colonel Sleeman caused an estimate to be made of the public works of ornament and utility which in the single district of Jubbulpore—now included in the Central Provinces—were due to the munificence of private persons in days anterior to British rule. The population of the district amounted to about half a million; and there were, in various parts of town and country, erected by individuals for the public good, and with no view to personal return in profits, 2,286 tanks; 209 large wells, with flights of steps extending from the top down to the water in its lowest stage; 1,560 wells lined with masonry, but without stairs; 362 Hindoo temples, and 22 mosques. The estimated cost of these works amounted to £866,640. In addition to these, two-thirds of the towns and villages were embedded in groves of mango and tamarind trees, mixed with the banyan and the peepul, all planted at the cost of private citizens, at an estimated cost of £120,000.

Here is a picture of the wealth and prosperity of Bengal, drawn by Mr. Verelst, one of our early Governors :—

" Though our provinces (Bengal, Behar, and part of Orissa) afford no gold, silver, or precious stones, yet the vast variety and abundance of the produce of the land, and the excellence of the manufactures of the inhabitants, leave them no great occasion for imported commodities; and at the same time invite foreign merchants to purchase and export these goods and manufactures from their superior cheapness and quality. . . . . The extent of this traffic was prodigious; and besides the large investments of the different European nations, the Bengal silk, cloths, etc., were dispersed, to a vast amount, to the west and north inland, as far as Guzerat, Lahore, and even Ispahan.

" Here, then, we trace the grand and true fountain of the wealth of the Soubahs, and the splendour of their Nazims. But, besides this, there were also several collateral streams, which served in their turn to feed and swell the principal one. The advantages accruing from so beneficial a commerce, enabled the farmer and the manufacturer to discharge their stipulated revenue to their Prince; and these revenues, again, did not centre or sink in his coffers, but returned through various channels into the general circulation.* Large jaghires were granted to men of noble families, or particular favourites; while districts were allotted to other branches of the reigning family at a rate vastly below their real value. Large armies of horse were maintained, either for show or security, at an enormous expense; and even the luxury and pomp, customary among the potentates of the East, contributed in some degree, by encouraging a spirit of expense, and dissipating large sums among the people in general, which if they had remained shut up in the treasury, would have been a loss to the currency, and no present advantage to the proprietor. By these means, therefore, and the advantage of trade already mentioned, an extensive and brisk circulation of specie was kept up everywhere; the farmer was easy, the artisan encouraged, the merchant enriched, the Prince satisfied. It would not be easy to ascertain the precise era in which all these began to decline, but so much is certain, that the decline was neither sensibly felt by the country, nor perceptible to us, till after the revolution in favour of Meer Jaffier."

It was as the consequence of this revolution that the English began to govern the country, or rather to plunder it.

Extracts of a similar purport might be multiplied indefinitely, and show, beyond all possibility of dispute, that India, under her Native Princes, was possessed of wealth and abundance of goods, that her upper classes were remarkable for their liberality and public spirit, and that the industrial and lower classes were in a thriving condition. What is the explanation of all this—so contrary to the common legend, officially propagated, of disorder and misery from which we were divinely commissioned to rescue the wretched Hindoos? It would be absurd to ascribe the prosperity of India to the character of her Kings and Princes, whether reigning at Delhi or elsewhere. Great Kings, it is true, are to be found among them, but extremely bad ones in far greater numbers. And after all,

" Of all the ills that human hearts endure,
How small the part that Kings can cause or cure."

It is not in the character of the Kings or Princes of

* No "Home Charges" in those days.

India, but in that of the constitutional order at the head of which they were placed, that we must look for the explanation. As far as India is concerned, we must get rid of the popular conception of an Oriental despot, and recognise the Emperors of Delhi, as they truly were, monarchs despotic in theory, but hedged round by conditions which limited their power, certainly beyond the circle of their own Court, as effectually as if they had been devised for that end.

For the collection of the revenue, the Empire was divided into Soubas, or provinces, and these again were sub-divided into Pergunnas, or fiscal divisions. The connecting link between the Soubadar or Governor of a province, and the central authority, was the annual revenue, which he was expected to remit to the Imperial Treasury. In other respects the Provincial Governor might be regarded as a ruler with full powers, practically uncontrolled. The troops within his limits looked for pay, promotion, and reward, not to the Emperor, but to their own Soubadar. If the reigning Emperor was a strong man, the Soubadars were held in due subordination; but when the central authority became weak or unpopular, the Imperial commands became inoperative. It was thus that the Mogul Empire fell to pieces, affording the opportunities and the means for the rise of British influence, in the midst of a Hindoo revolution excited by the bigotry of Aurungzeb, who reversed the tolerant policy of his ancestors, and endeavoured to intensify Mussulman supremacy into an absolute and exclusive domination. Here, then, was the first efficient check upon the arbitrary desires of the Imperial head. The Emperors could not afford to quarrel with their own Soubadars. But the Soubadar, in his turn, was surrounded by checks as effectual as those which limited the autocracy of the Emperor. In the province which he ruled there existed both a Hindoo and a Moslem aristocracy—Zemindars, Jaghiredars, and Talookdars; and the measure of his ability to hold his own against any extraordinary mandates of the Imperial Court depended upon the warmth of attachment and fidelity which he had kindled among his more powerful vassals. On the whole, a fair field was open to merit without regard to race, colour, or religious distinction. When we came into possession of the Gangetic provinces, the wealthiest merchants, the richest bankers, the most powerful landowners were all Hindoos—a truly remarkable illustration of the liberal and tolerant spirit of the Mussulman Government.

The provincial nobility, in its turn, depended for its power and credit on the loyalty and content of the village communities, from whose labour its own wealth was derived. By the constitution of a village community it was specially adapted for migration from one part of the country to another. And communities which found the exactions of a Talookdar, Jaghiredar, or Zemindar intolerable, simply migrated *en masse* within the jurisdiction of another, from whom they were certain to receive welcome and protection. This contingency of migration, there being everywhere plenty of waste land to be settled, acted as an effectual check upon oppressive landlords. For while it impoverished the oppressor, it added to the wealth and power of a rival. Thus the political and social order in India, in the time of our Tudors and Stuarts, was so far consolidated that each grade in the Imperial fabric derived strength and support from the grade next below it, the mass of the people being thus effectually protected from oppression and extortion.

In desire and in intention the Imperial authority might be, and probably often was, as rapacious as the proverbial Oriental despot; but it had limits prescribed to its autocracy which, practically, it was impossible to overpass. The entire financial machinery, the assessment and collection of the taxes, was confided to those whose strongest interest it was to keep the burden of taxation as low as possible. From the Nawab Soubadar, or the Rajah ruling the Province or the Talook, down to the humblest ryot, there was no one who did not lose by every rupee which was abstracted from the Souba to swell the magnificence of the Imperial Court. And being

the men in possession, they were, with a fair share of
prudence and deference, and within the limits of custom
and precedent, masters of the situation. Another early
Governor of Bengal, Mr. Holwell, in a strain of moral
indignation foreshadowing our unsympathetic and in-
flexible rule, thus explains to the Court of Directors how
the fiscal exactions of the Imperial Court were checked
and limited by that chain of local and mutual interests
to which I have briefly adverted.

"The Rajahs and Zemindars by private contract with the Soubah's
officers, who are charged with the management of this department,
obtain more lands than by their *sunnuds* appear, and consequently
pay no rent to the King for the surplus land. The same artifice
is practised between the Dewans of the Rajahs and Zemindars,
and the farmers, and the tenants or leaseholders under them, by
bribing the officers of the Jummabundi, and those entrusted with
the measurements of the lands, that they may enjoy among them
the benefit of the surplus land; and I may justly aver that there
is not a tenant in Hindostan but possesses and occupies a greater
quantity of land than his *pottah* expresses, or than he pays rent
for. Consequently it is the tenant that ultimately enjoys the
benefit of the surplus land, thus gained by corruption, while the
King suffers in his rents. It extremely well answers the tenant's
purpose to possess, if he could by a small bribe, more land than he
pays for, because himself and his heirs enjoy the profit of it in
perpetuity; since by a fundamental law of the Empire, these
pottahs are irrevocable so long as they pay the rent rated to them
respectively, and so tender and indulgent are the courts of Hindostan in this particular that no tenant forfeits his land before he
has failed in his payments for twelve months; though the land-
tax by the same laws is to be paid every three months."*

With a slight deduction for a few dyslogistic terms, it
will be seen that Mr. Holwell's hostile description of the
tenure and taxation of land under the Imperial system,
is in substance just as, in accordance with the views of
Colonel Briggs, it has been represented in the preceding
pages.

The chief source of revenue then, as now, was a portion of the produce of the soil. Anterior to our rule,
though money payments were the rule in Bengal Proper,
the more general practice was to take a proportion of the

* Letter to Chairman of Court of Directors, December 1765.

standing crop in satisfaction of the State dues. This practice was stigmatised as barbarous by our English administrators, and, by degrees, we everywhere substituted assessments in cash. Lord Cornwallis's Permanent Settlement was an exception to the general rule, so far as the permanence of its demand was concerned, but it affects only a small part of British India. Barbarous as the practice of levying a tax in kind may appear, it was a practice exactly suited to the condition of the agricultural classes in India. Grain was, in fact, the currency of the village, the chief medium of exchange. The practice of levy in kind, also, preserved the State from entanglement in the labyrinth of the infinite variety of tenures which prevail in an Indian village. From the immemorial usage of village self-government, and the sacred arbitration of the Punchayut, these tenures could never become a subject of dispute in any superior courts; the Government, moreover, looked upon the village as embodied, for all official purposes, in its harvest for the year. So long as the State got its proportion of the produce, it left the allotment of each man's contribution to the village authorities, and had no occasion or desire to interfere. When we came into possession these things were a great mystery to us; and with the best intentions in the world, we introduced at one bound new methods of assessing and collecting the land revenue, which have converted a once flourishing population into a huge horde of paupers. Our first act in a newly acquired district was to decree that the land revenue should henceforth be paid in coin, without having previously ascertained if there was sufficient coin in circulation to allow of such a sudden and drastic change. There was not, and the consequence of our ill-judged and precipitate action was a ruinous derangement of values. A pressing demand for specie glutted the markets with an immense quantity of produce, which had to be sold for whatever it would bring. The first effect of British rule in an Indian province, owing to this violent change in the method of collection, was, in many recognisable instances, to reduce the incomes of the agricultural

classes by 50 per cent. Again, the assessment being
levied in money, in the event of the revenue falling into
arrears—a thing impossible under the old practice of
taking a share of the produce—it became necessary to
proceed against the defaulters by distraint or civil
process. This at once entangled the State in the intri-
cate labyrinth of land tenures, and the individual allotment of village contributions. It became necessary that
there should be a record in which the names of all occupants, together with the number of their fields and
particulars as to their tenures and rights, should be
specified. This was officially described as conferring an
important privilege upon the ryots by giving them a
transferable and saleable right in their holdings. Actually,
it transferred the guardianship of their rights from the
village community of which they were members, to their
own servant, the keeper of the village records, now
insidiously and almost imperceptibly converted into a
servant of Government. Obviously the English officer
ostensibly at the head of revenue affairs in a district
does not, and cannot, possess the minute local knowledge
required to prove or preserve the accuracy of these
village records. Those chiefly interested, the ryots, are
as helpless, for the records have been kept, from generation to generation, by their own hereditary servant, a
Brahmin, in a language they cannot read. These all
important records are now laid open, through their
Brahmin record-keeper, now free from their control, to
the tender mercies of those very Native underlings of
office, to emancipate the ryots from whose corruption
and oppression the change had been professedly introduced. These men were underpaid, without effective
supervision, and, therefore, specially liable to succumb to
bribery, and under their manipulation the records became,
in the course of a few years, a mass of confusion and
imposture. Among the many causes which combined to
produce the insurrection of 1857, none were more potent
than the fraudulent sales of land that had been effected
by means of these falsified records, by which ancient
landholders were converted by hundreds into the rack-

rented tenants of some grasping and unscrupulous usurer.

The inhabitants of an Indian village, under their own Princes, formed a sort of petty republic, the affairs of which were managed by hereditary officers, any unfit person being set aside by popular judgment in favour of a more acceptable member of his family. The village contained, in miniature, all the elements of a State, and was well nigh sufficient to protect its members from all oppression but that of armed or military violence, when all other protection was withdrawn.

By destroying the popular authority of the headman, the responsibility of the village accountant and record-keeper, and the judicial powers of the Punchayut, British administration of the land revenue subverted the entire organisation of the village communities, and may almost be said to have torn up by the roots the entire social, economical, and political fabric of India. Local self-government and local arbitration have been swept away, and a costly and mechanical centralisation substituted.

The vigorous corporate life of the village communities was not peculiar to the agricultural classes. It knit together, with hardly less strength, the trading, manu-facturing, and banking classes. It created in each class a force of social opinion which was a far more efficient restraint upon personal selfishness and dishonesty than those courts of law which seem rather to afford facilities for wealthy greed, and for fraud in every form. Formerly, when there was practically no judicial appeal beyond the class Punchayut or the patriarchs of the guild, there was, by all accounts, a spirit of trust and of honour in the carrying out of commercial engagements which have never been surpassed in any country of the world. This corporate life, as it existed without the aid of officials, and beyond their cognizance, continued to discharge its functions in a healthy and orderly manner, when both government and laws were, during a revolutionary period, replaced by anarchy, rebellion and invasion. And so it was that as one province after another came into our possession, our English officials were surprised

K

to discover behind the turbulence and disorder consequent upon the breaking up of the once magnificent
Mogul Empire, an inner social order hardly affected by
the tumult and struggle around it, but busy, active, and
prosperous.

The difference, in short, between our land revenue
system and that of our predecessors, as very clearly
exposed and explained by Colonel Briggs, was this.
They were content to levy the State demand by a simple
process which had superficially what may be called, if
you like, a barbarous appearance, but which had adjusted
itself with nicety to the social and climatic conditions of
the country, out of which it had, in truth, grown.   We
grasped at too much in every sense of the word, and in
all directions.   We aimed at an impossible perfection of
record and mastery of detail by our officials, and realised
our conception so imperfectly that we achieved nothing
but the general ruin of the people.   Since then we have
continually but impotently striven by various inconsistent
measures of reconstruction and palliation to protect the
ryots from the destructive effects of our revenue operations.   And in this year of grace, 1885, Lord Dufferin,
succeeding to the well-intended plans and labours of Lord
Ripon, is busy in attempts to solve the distressing
problems of uncertain tenures and assessments, and to
resuscitate local self-government with extremely limited
functions.

Brief and necessarily superficial as has been the foregoing sketch of the changes produced by English administration in India, it will suffice to remind us of the
historical fact that the laws and customs which we found
regulating the lives of her inhabitants were not laws and
customs which had been arbitrarily imposed upon them
by the fiat of a conqueror.   They were the natural and
genuine product of the character and faith of the native
races, and because they were so they possessed that flexi-
bility and adaptive quality which are characteristic of
all natural growths.   This or that military adventurer
might establish his supremacy in this or that portion of
the continent, but he had not the means, even had he

felt the desire, to interfere with the working of those institutions already in existence among the people. But he was conscious of no such desire. He was himself a native of the country in which he had risen to power. He had grown from infancy to manhood under the shelter and influence of these immemorial institutions. He knew of no other way of carrying on the business of the country; and he would never have entertained so wild a project—for so it would have presented itself to him—as that of devising a new system and forcing it upon his subjects. The dynastic revolutions in India, anterior to our period of power, did not aim at the subversion of political order, or at any change in the constitution of society. And the wealth-producing classes—thanks to their admirable capacity for self-government, and the strong corporate life that knit them together—were but little affected by them. But all this was changed when we appeared upon the scene. We were the products of a civilisation differing in every possible way from that which had wrought with such grand and beneficent results in India, and we regarded what we did not under-stand with the scepticism and the contempt which are usually the concomitants of ignorance. Unhappily, too, for the people of India, we differed from our governing predecessors in another all-important particular. We did not, like them, depend for the preservation of our power upon the loyalty of our subjects, but upon the might of a great nation at the other side of the globe. This con-sciousness of an independent reserve of strength has operated to make the English officials far less tender and considerate of popular feelings, affections and pre-judices than their predecessors had been. Strong in the conviction of their own intellectual and moral superiority, strong, also, in the knowledge of an irresistible material force behind them—they fell into the error of supposing that whatever they did, or attempted to do, must be, as a matter of course, a vast improvement upon anything which the people had experienced before.

There is nothing in my experience more painfully enlightening for the student of political science, as exem-

plified in our Indian Empire, than to peruse with care
the official and historical records that disclose the progress of an Indian province during the first half century
of British domination.   The same story is repeated in
province after province with heart-breaking uniformity.
A number of English officers, charged to overflowing
with self-complacent philanthropy and national confidence, are let loose upon the devoted region.   They set
to work under the impression, excited and slightly justified by recent revolution or war, that the material to be
operated on is a population quite without social or
political form, and void of anything like order, and upon
which, consequently, they can impress any shape that is
most pleasing to themselves. They are the potter, and the
people are to be as clay in their hands.   Actually, they
have before them, not only a very complex social organisation, but one of extraordinary toughness and endurance.   A desperate conflict, carried on in the dark, at once
begins between this social order and the judicial and
administrative system which obstinately ignores its
existence.   In this conflict the prosperity of the country,
both agricultural and manufacturing, is rapidly and
completely destroyed. The heaven-sent English administrators are much at a loss to account for this grievous
result.   It cannot be from any lack of wisdom in themselves, for are they not the apostles and the evangelists
of a higher civilisation?   And they set it down—most of
them, for there are always a few, like Briggs, who have
some insight into the truth—to the perversity of "the
Indian character", to the inborn depravity of "the
Oriental mind", which drive the Natives to refuse to be
happy and prosperous, although provided with all the
appliances requisite for achieving such a condition of
life. But at last, the upper classes having been destroyed,
and the lower sunk in indebtedness, the revenue begins
to fall off.   This is serious, and investigations are then
set on foot to discover the cause of this most appalling
phenomenon.   Then, but not till then, it is perceived,
but seldom confessed, that our own precipitate ignorance
has been the cause ; and an attempt is made to recon-

struct the things that we, in our blindness, have destroyed. Of course the old order cannot be, and never has been, restored in its integrity, but as in the case of Mr. Robert Mertens Bird's village settlement in the North West Provinces, a superficial semblance of it is laboriously patched together, and this lame and impotent conclusion is trumpeted abroad as an evidence of the superior wisdom and beneficence of our rule. In many cases of our administrative reforms and removal of abuses, we made the giants first, and then we killed them.

In a " Joint Report of the Survey and Assessment of the Bombay Presidency", printed in 1850, there is a whole string of half-conscious confessions, exactly confirmatory of what has been said in commenting on Colonel Briggs's *Land Tax*, and remarkably summed up in the following passage :—

> " We fully coincide in the justice of the principle of limiting the Government demand to a portion of the true rent, and believe 50 or 80 per cent. thereof, as laid down by the Board, would form a liberal assessment, and that *this principle, if capable of being carried into practice, would prove an invaluable blessing to the agricultural classes of India, and introduce a new era in their history. And we further ascribe to the fact of a portion of the rent having been seldom, if ever, left to the proprietor or cultivator in India, the characteristic wretchedness of its agricultural population, rather than to any peculiarities marking its different systems of revenue management.*"

But that "principle" has never, under the ever-growing demands of our expenditure, been found "capable of being carried into practice", and " the new era" for the agricultural classes of India has, consequently, not yet been " introduced".

The principle of gradual evolution cannot be ignored with impunity in India, any more than in any other quarter of the globe, and our work in India, so far, has been almost wholly destructive, socially, religiously, and politically. The effect of our presence in India has been to throw down the ancient land-marks, and to leave the lives and the minds of the people without a guide or a goal. There are but few traces yet apparent of a new order arising from the ruins of the past, and those are

not entirely reassuring for the stability of our rule. Our
English representatives in the East, with their faces
ever more and more set towards home, seem to be more
evidently than ever "losing touch" of the people; so that
our administration, while it perpetually grows in costliness and indebtedness, tends to become a deaf and blind
mechanism, revolving in obedience, not to popular wants
or wishes, but to the heartless routine of departments
and the narrow interests of the Anglo-Indian Services.

I shall not offer here to estimate, or to discuss, the
countervailing advantages to the Indian Empire of the
Western enlightenment, and a higher culture acquired
by certain classes of the population in consequence of
British supremacy. India has paid, and pays, for all she
receives in this, as in every other department of the
public service. Nor shall I examine the real extent and
benefit of what has been called the Pax Britannica,
broken as it has been, since 1820, by many calls to arms
within the continent ; by wars in China, Burmah, Persia,
and Abyssinia, entirely due to Imperial demands ; by
the terrible convulsion of 1857 ; and by two aggressive
wars in Afghanistan, which, between them, have cost
India more than fifty millions sterling.*

I am not discussing at present on which side the

---

* Twenty millions is a very moderate calculation for the first Afghan
war, 1839 to 1842, without including its cruel sequel, the conquest of
Scinde in 1843. The second war, 1879 to 1882, is proved clearly in
the London *Statesman* for September 1881,—the article being attributed
to about the most competent financial auditor living, General Sir George
Balfour, M.P.—to have cost quite thirty millions. A summary but very
fair demonstration of the fact can be seen in a comparison of the gross
military charges in India in Lord Northbrook's time with what they
were in Lord Lytton's.

Under Lord Northbrook.	Under Lord Lytton.
1872-73......£14,596,802	1878-79......£17,092,488
1873-74......£14,217,390	1879-80......£23,383,982
1874-75......£14,386,321	1880-81......£30,583,684
1875-76 .....£14,262,848	1881-82......£19,618,100
Total...£57,463,361	Total...£90,678,434

There is nothing whatever to account for the difference of thirty-three
millions between the two periods except the Afghan war.

balance of advantage lies from the connection of Great Britain and India. Nor do I deny that some profit may be reaped on both sides. The only question before us now is British administration of the Indian Land Tax, with that economic and social result in the impoverishment of the people of which Colonel Briggs was one of the first to warn us, and which since his time has perceptibly advanced to the stage of periodical famine.

Official apologists have lately become accustomed to deny, with an air of triumphant eulogy, that the Indian Land Tax is a tax at all, and to declare it to be a rent. It is, I am afraid, too true that in a great many provinces the Land Tax does swallow up all, or nearly all, the rent. But those who have taken to eulogising Anglo-Indian fiscal institutions on these extraordinary grounds, appear to have forgotten—they omit, at least, to remind their audience—that the Imperial State landlord of India is an alien and absentee landlord, who has half the rent and nearly half of all additional assessments remitted to him in his foreign place of residence ; while he disburses nearly one-third of the same revenues for the remuneration of the Civil and Military services, his own relatives and fellow-countrymen, who have no abiding-place on the soil, and no stake in the fortunes of India. It is not easy to see how our scientific frontier, the competitive erudition of our Collectors and Judges, or the higher culture disseminated by our Educational Department, can satisfy or pacify the tax-paying masses who are insufficiently fed and clothed.

CHAPTER VIII.

WHILE the *Land Tax* was going through the press, Briggs paid one short visit to London in May 1830, and was advised by one of his old friends at the India House to pay his respects to Lord Ellenborough at the Board of Control. He was very graciously received, and was encouraged by the President of the Board to give his views frankly and fully on every branch of Indian administration. From what soon followed, as well as from the note, shortly to be quoted, in Lord Ellenborough's diary, it would appear that on this occasion Colonel Briggs must have impressed the President of the Board of Control with a high opinion of his intelligence and talents.

" In the midst of my preparations to go back to India, an event occurred which led me to believe that my lot would be cast for some time in another Eastern country. This was the sudden death of my esteemed friend and companion, Sir John McDonald Kinneir, Envoy at the Court of Persia. Lord Ellenborough, then President of the Board of Control, offered the place first to the Honourable Mountstuart Elphinstone, and, on his declining it, to Sir Richard Jenkins, who had distinguished himself as Resident at Nagpore. Jenkins was then canvassing for the seat in the Court of Directors which he filled for many years, and he, also, declined to go to Persia. At the suggestion of the old and influential friend who had given me the benefit of his introduction and recommendation to Lord Ellenborough, I furnished his Lordship with a very comprehensive letter on the actual condition of the Persian Kingdom, the relations of the King's sons with each other, and with the chief provincial governors, one or two of whom had long entertained designs of asserting their practical independence at the demise of the reigning King.

" Foremost among these was Hussain Ali Mirza, who had been Governor of the Province of Shiraz for a very long period, and had resided there from his childhood. He, I was informed, had made up his mind to establish himself as a hereditary Governor, with the humble title of *Wakil-i-aalum*, or representative of the people. Though twenty years had passed since I was in Persia there had been little change in the politics, and very little in the personal elements of power. I had been attentive to passing events in that country, and had kept up an occasional correspondence with one person of great intelligence and talent. It was clear to me that on the demise of the reigning Shah there would be a contest for the throne, and that a decisive step in such a crisis by the British Government might make or mar our influence at Teheran, where Russia had been making way steadily during the whole of the present century.

" I may mention that at the death of the Shah in 1834 a struggle for the succession, combined with an uprising of several ambitious chieftains, took place very much as I had predicted, and tranquillity was restored mainly by the energy and ability of Captain Lindsay, of the Madras Artillery, who afterwards assumed the name of Bethune. In his capacity of a General in the Persian Army, he defeated the forces raised by Hussain Ali Mirza, the Prince of Shiraz, and took him prisoner, by which means Mohammed Ali Mirza, son of Prince Abbas, was firmly seated on the throne, and English influence for the time became dominant. For this service Captain Lindsay Bethune obtained the local rank of an English Major-General. I have somewhat anticipated matters, and gone a little out of my own course, in order to show that my views, as events proved, were not unworthy of Lord Ellenborough's attention ; and, in truth, he was greatly struck by them, and was not only pleased to say that I had given him more insight into Persian affairs than anyone with whom he had yet come in contact, but at a subsequent interview told me that he should recommend me to the Court of Directors for the post of Envoy to Persia. The East India Company then bore half the expense of the Embassy, and the Government of India, by right or by courtesy, had some voice in the appointment. Lord Ellenborough invited me to his house at Roehampton, to meet at dinner the Duke of Wellington, Sir Robert Peel, and the Chairman and Deputy Chairman of the Court of Directors."

In his *Political Diary*, Lord Ellenborough briefly mentions the favourable impression that Briggs appears to have made upon him at the first interview, where Indian affairs were discussed. " 1830—May 14. Colonel Briggs called. He is a clever man. He will prepare for me a memorandum on the Native Army. He seems equally conversant with revenue, judicial, and military matters."*

* Lord Ellenborough's *Political Diary*, edited by Lord Colchester (Bentley, 1881), p. 246.

In the sole reminiscence he gives of the little dinner at Roehampton, the Colonel gives us reason to regret that he did not record or remember a little more.

"I was much interested, after the cloth was removed, at hearing the Duke of Wellington, *apropos* of the recent occurrences in Paris, explain to Sir Robert Peel how a town might be taken and occupied, though the streets were barricaded and guns placed so as to command them. The Duke said: 'It is a tedious and dangerous operation all the same. You recollect the French were at work more than six months in taking the open town of Saragossa.' Sir Robert Peel asked how that was at last effected. The Duke replied, 'By taking house after house, breaking through the party walls on each side, till the troops got past the barricades, and took them in reverse'.

"My appointment somehow or other seemed to hang fire, though Lord Ellenborough, in order to keep me at home, arranged with Sir ·Francis Burdett that I should be called as a witness before the Parliamentary Committee then sitting on Indian affairs.* I learned afterwards that a majority of the Court of Directors were desirous of having Major John Campbell, the *locum tenens*, confirmed as Envoy, and had suggested, therefore, that the office should be filled up by the Governor-General in India, to whom a letter was addressed stating that the Court would approve of Major Campbell's appointment. I left England with my wife and two eldest daughters under the full impression that I was to be Envoy to Persia.

"On my arrival at Madras I, therefore, addressed the Governor-General, applying for employment in the diplomatic line in which I had so long served both in Persia and India, and adding that I was authorised by Lord Ellenborough to advert to the fact that he considered me the best qualified and most eligible person for the post of Envoy to the Court of Persia. I received very soon a very gracious autograph reply from Lord William Bentinck, stating that the correspondence between Lord Ellenborough and the Court of Directors on the subject had been communicated to him, but that before seeing that correspondence, anticipating that the choice might be left to him, he had written to the Court of Directors nominating the present Resident at Hyderabad, Colonel Josiah Stewart, my old comrade in Persia,† for the office, and that the selection could not now be altered. He was pleased to add that he regretted that Lord Ellenborough had not 'directed' him to appoint me, for, said his Lordship, 'While I should have had the

* "May 18th, 1830.—Examined Colonel Briggs, who gave very good evidence indeed."—Lord Ellenborough's *Political Diary*, vol. ii, p. 102.
    † *Ante*, p. 32.

fullest confidence in you, I can ill afford to spare the services of the present Resident at Hyderabad'."

The Governor-General, also, intimated to Colonel Briggs that it was not improbable his services might within a few months be required for the purpose of applying some remedy to the disordered affairs of Mysore, and invited him to offer an opinion as to, the condition of that country, and as to the measures that might be taken for its relief. The views of Colonel Briggs are given very clearly in the following extracts from his reply, dated "Madras, 22nd May 1831".

"If the accounts which have reached me are correct, we are lending our aid to enable the Rajah of Mysore to force oppressive contributions from a people accustomed to a considerable degree of freedom, already borne down by the weight of taxation, and now full of resentment and determined to resist. Our people have been repulsed three times in the field, and although our power must be asserted and submission enforced, I must be pardoned, my Lord, for saying that this is not an occasion for relentless operations. It is not a war against a pretender, or a tribe of freebooters, but against a distressed people. The Resident in the first instance, and latterly the Madras Government, have identified themselves with the Rajah and his acts. And yet, my Lord, to tell you the plain truth, the authorities here are no friends to the Rajah. People here anticipate with pleasure, quite undisguisedly, our deposing him and taking his country: they have already begun to calculate on the number of new civil appointments in the pleasant climate of Bangalore to which this will give rise.

"It seems clear that the Rajah has brought himself into a scrape. He has ceased to pay his subsidy;* his treasury is empty, and he has no credit. There is a sufficient plea for our assuming the management of his concerns when he drives his subjects into rebellion, and is unable to fulfil his engagements to us. The next question to consider is, what is the most politic mode of effecting this assumption of power?

"In the case of a minor there is not usually much difficulty, as we have seen in the cases of Travancore and Nagpore. Hyderabad presents us with the instance of an imbecile in the person of the late Nizam.† Sattara affords the example of an emancipated state prisoner. In all these cases the Resident acted the part of

---

* This was a mistake, as will be seen shortly, into which Briggs was led by the Madras authorities.

† Secunder Jah, who died in 1829.

Regent, and exercised more or less authority, more or less openly, according to circumstances. The Rajah of Mysore is neither a minor nor an imbecile, and was too young when we released him from a state prison to recollect the wretchedness of his infancy. He is a young man of about thirty-five years age, said to be active and intelligent, and though self-indulgent and grievously misled, to be by no means of an evil disposition, or insensible to the dictates of humanity and honour. He has for the last twenty years exercised unlimited power. The surrender of that power without a struggle or a pang, or the being reconciled to such a surrender afterwards, for however short a period, cannot be contemplated as possible. He is followed by a long train of courtiers and rapacious functionaries, whom it would be equally unsafe to employ, or to allow to remain idle and discontented, and, lastly, by a host of priests who have received grants of land and charges in money from his hands, all of whom would become most influential instruments in rendering our rule unpopular, and in impeding every reform. If it be not intended to depose the Rajah altogether, which I fear is the predominant wish here, it occurs to me that the situation of the Rajah of Sattara, under my predecessor in office, Captain James Grant Duff, is well suited to the present crisis in Mysore. Captain Grant Duff, under Mr. Elphinstone's instructions, established for the Rajah a complete Native Government with all its institutions, nearly as efficient as they were then capable of being rendered, and I am free to confess that such a Government presents, to my mind, the most perfect model of a monarchy in which a system of elective representation forms no part. The Rajah of Sattara's administration has, like most others in which we have interfered, the grinding evil of an annual assessment on the land, while many legitimate sources of revenue are neglected and overlooked. It is upon the whole, however, a cheaper and better administration than our own, and more calculated for the happiness of the people. Captain Grant Duff, with two English assistants, conducted all the affairs of the State, all orders being issued in the Rajah's name, and the Rajah's seal being affixed to all public documents. The Rajah sat in the Kutcherry, or Durbar, alongside of Captain Grant Duff, to see how business was conducted. His Civil List was fixed from the first, and had not, at the time of my departure from Sattara, ever been augmented.

"During Captain Grant Duff's administration the Rajah was always told that he would have the sole management of his affairs whenever he proved himself fit for it, and in April 1822, after four years' probation, the Rajah was placed in full possession of his authority. I went to Sattara just one year afterwards, and remained there till January 1827, when I returned to England. During that time I had never occasion to remonstrate against his abandonment of any of Captain Grant Duff's rules, which the Rajah seems very fortunately to respect as much as the Spartans and Athenians did those of Solon and Lycurgus.

"The Treaty of Sattara in 1818 was drawn up on the model of the Treaty of Mysore in 1799, and it seems to me that the institutions of Sattara, framed under the immediate eye of Mr. Elphinstone, might with great propriety be rendered applicable to the present circumstances of Mysore. To whomsoever the office of Resident and Regent is entrusted, he must possess the entire confidence of Government, for his task will be arduous, odious at first, and full of difficulty. He ought, moreover, to be a man fully convinced of the policy and wisdom of supporting a Native Government, well acquainted with the frame of administration capable of being worked by Natives, and accustomed himself to work with them. As he will have to travel about the country frequently, his allowances should be on the footing of the first-class Residencies, to be charged, of course, to the Mysore State.

"In Captain Grant Duff's case, he came armed with absolute power, and relinquished it gradually as he found others born and bred in the country fit to exercise it. In the present case the Resident would have to take that power in the first instance out of the hands of those who have long enjoyed its sweets. The Rajah of Sattara is a man of strong mind, free from prejudices, and of irreproachable private character. The Rajah of Mysore is represented as being in many respects the very reverse of this.

"After a trial of some years, if the new system is found to produce the good results that I should anticipate, the Rajah might be reinstated in power, and become bound (by an additional article of the Treaty if requisite) to refrain from departing from the laws and regulations which have been established, and from engagements that have been made during this period of probation, without permission having been first obtained from the protecting State."

Being given to understand that there would be no occasion for him to enter upon any administrative work for several months, Briggs now carried out a long-deferred project of travelling through the British provinces and Native States of Malwa, the North West, and Rajpootana, chiefly with a view to further investigations into the Land Tax and its assessment. He visited Delhi, Ajmere, Jeypoor, and the States governed by Scindia and Holkar, and made copious notes on many interesting topics. But a serious crisis occurred in Mysore sooner than had been expected, and on the 10th of October 1831, Briggs received at Delhi a private letter from the Governor-General, which caused him to retrace his steps as rapidly as possible to Madras. He was appointed Senior Commissioner for the government of Mysore.

CHAPTER IX.

LORD WILLIAM BENTINCK had announced his intention to the Maharaja of Mysore of assuming charge of his Highness's dominions, under the provisions of the Treaty of 1799, in a letter dated the 7th of September 1831. In this letter the Maharaja's maladministration was unsparingly denounced. After complaining that the ryots of Mysore had been handed over to the tender mercies of "needy and greedy adventurers", the Governor-General proceeds as follows :

"This mismanagement, and the tyranny and oppression that resulted, came at length to such a pass as to be no longer bearable by the inhabitants of the territory of your Highness ; and for the past year the half of your Highness's entire dominions have been in insurrection in consequence. The troops of your Highness were first sent to bring the insurgents to subjection ; the greatest excesses were committed and unparalleled cruelties were inflicted by your Highness's officers ; but the insurrection was not quelled. It became necessary to detach a part of the armies of the British Government to restore tranquillity, and take part against the insurgents. Tranquillity has for the present been restored, but the British Government cannot permit its name or its power to be identified with these acts of your Highness's misrule."

Truly a terrible indictment, which has been frequently recapitulated, and made the most of ever since, to justify the long-continued sequestration of the Mysore territories.

We shall see whether all the blame for the insurrection ought to have been thrown on the Maharaja, who were the "needy and greedy adventurers" who misgoverned the country, and what persons were properly responsible for the "unparalleled cruelties" that took place. Relying for facts partly on the Report of the Special Committee of 1833—consisting of Colonel Sir W. Morrison, Colonel (afterwards Sir Mark) Cubbon, General Hawker, and Mr. (afterwards Sir John) Macleod,—which has never yet been published, and partly on the papers of General Briggs, I shall endeavour to answer those questions. The document from which I shall quote most largely will be a long Memorandum drawn up by Briggs in 1833 as an apology for the course he had taken, and sent in the first instance to his old master, the Honble. Mountstuart Elphinstone, then living at home in the retirement from which he never afterwards emerged. Occasionally I shall quote the Colonel's Diary.

MEMORANDUM.

"In 1811 Poorniah quitted public life, and left to the Rajah of Mysore a treasury containing 21,900,000 rupees, or more than two millions sterling. The Rajah took the reins in his hands at the age of sixteen, without a check or a remonstrance on the part of our Government. His nature is gentle and mild, his propensities and tastes are what might be expected from his early emancipation from control. No wonder that he became the dupe of his favourites of both sexes. In a few years he lavished away all his treasure, and was left without the means of meeting the usual demands of the parasites by whom he was surrounded. Recourse was now had to bankers and merchants; and loans and purchases were provided for by either bills drawn on the districts, or by promissory notes payable, with heavy interest, in five or six years. The Rajah became deeply involved, and the public establishments were unpaid. All the better class of offices were sold to the highest bidder, or a certain share of the emoluments of each place was paid to the ministers and favourites at Court, the chief of whom was a fiddler.

"During the first three years of the Rajah's assumption of power, the Resident, the Honble. Arthur Cole, was not inactive. He constantly urged reform upon the Rajah. Fair promises were made from time to time; but at last, tired of the importunity of his Mentor, the Rajah deputed a secret envoy to Madras to complain of Mr. Cole's constant interference, and in 1814, the Rajah being then nineteen years of age, the Resident was forbidden by the Government of Madras to interfere in the internal management of the country. The Resident and the Rajah continued, however, to be good friends even after this, and it is notorious that the former never made a special request, public or private, that was not instantly complied with by the latter. The Rajah has, in fact, been all along, when properly managed, a mere pageant, quite at the Resident's disposal. So long as Cole remained, matters went on tolerably well. He did his own work; and his noble and generous conduct established a name for him which will never be forgotten in Mysore."

I may here interrupt Colonel Briggs's narrative, to explain that the Honourable Arthur Cole, born in 1780, was fourth son of the first Earl of Enniskillen. He entered the Madras Civil Service in 1800, and retired on a pension in 1824. He sat in Parliament, as Member for the family borough of Enniskillen, from 1830 until his death in 1854. He was never married. And as an illustration of the good old times, I may mention that when Mr. Cole gave his last shake to the pagoda-tree, a rich windfall dropped into the lap of a very humble person, his butler, who, by all accounts, had been very useful and influential in the Residency.

Just before Mr. Arthur Cole's retirement from the public service, his butler, Ramasawmy Moodelly,—called " Janopakara-kurta" Ramasawmy, the meaning of which Tamul nickname I do not know,—was made by the Maharaja Jaghiredar of Sevasamoodrum, a place about twenty-five miles from Mysore. The Mootta, or jaghire, consists of three villages, and is supposed to be worth nearly 30,000 Rs., or £3,000, a year. The principal village, Sevasamoodrum, being near the picturesque Falls of the Cauvery, and game abounding in the neighbourhood, is a favourite place of resort for English visitors,—shooting excursions for the men, and picnics for the ladies, having their respective attractions, and being easily combined. Here, therefore, old Ramasawmy, who put not his entire trust in Princes,—with strong feelings of gratitude for the favours he had gained by the goodwill of one English gentleman, and not, perhaps, without a lively sense of security for those favours in all time to come from the goodwill of English gentlemen in general,—built and furnished a spacious bungalow, kept it stocked with the best supplies, and manned with a small staff of servants ; and here all members of the official hierarchy and their families, or parties introduced by them, were always wel-

L

comed and entertained at his expense.   For some years
after Cole's retirement, Ramasawmy Moodelly, as Briggs
mentions further on, continued to be an influential person
at the Mysore Court.

A grandson of the original grantee, also named Ramasawmy Moodelly, now enjoys the jaghire, and the same
hospitality for English gentlemen visiting the Falls of the
Cauvery is still kept up at the Sevasamoodrum bungalow,
though, it is said, on a scale of expenditure somewhat
less liberal than it used to be.

We now return to the Memorandum prepared by
Briggs for Mountstuart Elphinstone, previously mentioning that the successor of Cole was Mr. James Casamajor,
of the Madras Civil Service.

" No sooner did Arthur Cole go than a new order of things was
introduced.   The power of the Residency continued, but it was no
longer exercised by the Resident.   The Resident's head man, a
Brahmin named Chowrappa, having many connections in several
districts of the country, became the organ of all communications,
the indispensable factotum of his master, and the terror of the
Rajah.   The Resident, under the semblance of non-interference,
in conformity with the instructions of the Madras Government in
1814, suffered his agent to meddle and dictate in everything, and
to accumulate vast wealth by becoming the patron or proprietor
of all the Foujdars and their deputies, who were, in 1831, without
exception, besides between thirty and forty of the Amils, all men
appointed at the instance of this low creature.

"The superior offices were purchased at the rate of 5,000 rupees
for a Foujdarree, and 1,000 rupees for each Mamlut.   The remainder of the offices were sold either by the Rajah's favourite
fiddler, or by another influential person about the Residency, one
Ramasawmy Moodelly, who had been successively butler to the
late Colonel Wilks and to Mr. Cole, who holds at this moment
from ten to twelve Talookdarees, and also has a hereditary jaghire,
recently granted by the Rajah.

" You will not be surprised at bad government following such a
system.   The ryots were awed by the British force at Bangalore,
and by the knowledge, industriously propagated among them, that
the Residency influence was paramount, and they endured the
most grievous extortions for several years.   At length, in 1830,
the oppression became more than they could bear, and a general
rising took place in nearly every district, the most serious occurring
in Bednore and Bullum, where the people invited their old chiefs,

the Polygars, to place themselves at their head, and to take the lead in throwing off the yoke of the corrupt officials. Matters went so far that, in the latter part of 1830, the inhabitants sent round proclamations calling on everyone to cease cultivating the land, keeping markets, paying taxes, or suffering the customs to be levied, and inviting all to repair to the capital, there to lay their grievances before the Rajah. It is to be remarked that, except in the Nuggur districts of Bednore and Bullum, these assemblages were mostly unarmed, and that they did not plunder on the road, but paid for what they required, most of them carrying with them flour and other provisions. In some, but rare, instances, they seized the public officers, and made them refund part of what they had unjustly exacted, but the whole extent of their violence was limited to a few slaps with a slipper.

" These commotions had become very general in November 1830, so much so that the Rajah was roused—entirely by his own sense of what was right, for his favourites tried to restrain him,— into quitting his capital, and proceeding into the districts for the avowed purpose of inquiring for himself, and granting redress. In three or four places he made some investigation, and punished the Mamlutdars. This led to the selling of places being talked about in the Rajah's camp, leading up towards a complete exposure of abuses, in which the favourites of the Rajah and the hangers-on of the Residency were deeply implicated. Their great object now was to put a stop to the Rajah's inquiries.

" At Chinroypatam, a place about fifty miles north of Mysore, and the chief town of a district farmed by the Resident's factotum, Chowrappa himself, all the shops were closed, and the people came out in crowds, unarmed, but accompanied by the ordinary noisy music used on festive occasions. The Rajah was now getting much too close upon the scent. The danger of the truth coming out becoming imminent, this was construed as open insurrection, and the Rajah was exhorted to order the cavalry to charge and disperse them. The Rajah himself, however, saw that the people were at once alarmed at the appearance of his troops, and sent forward the commandant, Bheem Rao Bukhshee, to remonstrate with them. The Bukhshee spoke to the people in a conciliatory manner, and one party came in to the camp on his guaranteeing their safety. Three of the most respectable men in Mysore, one of whom was Meer Mahmood, brother of Meer Kummer-ood-deen,—Tippoo's celebrated Cavalry General, who was settled as a jaghiredar in the Nizam's country,—were ordered to investigate their complaints. They gave it as their opinion that the ryots then assembled could prove that the public servants at Chinroypatam and in the neigh-bourhood had, within the past year, extorted from them a lakh of pagodas on their private account, and that the offenders ought to be made to refund this amount. The Amil was a near relative of Chowrappa, the Resident's man of business, who not only trembled for his relation and for others, in whose fate he was equally interested, but also for the disclosures that might be made of his own malpractices and corruption. He, therefore, worked on the Resident, who had accompanied the Rajah on this occasion, and persuaded him that the rebellion, as he called it, could only be put down by severe measures. The nominal Minister and the fiddler, in concert with the evil genius of the Residency, had been incessantly plying the Rajah with similar arguments, so that he was well prepared for the advice given him by the Resident, that the ringleaders of these assemblages should be summarily hanged as an example and a warning. The Rajah and two or three of his familiars, unconnected with the Residency party, for some time resisted this proposition; but the influence and authority of the Resident were irresistible in urging immediate action, and on that very evening of the 21st December 1830, after the report just mentioned by three impartial persons, two of the Potails (headmen) of villages, who had presented themselves in the morning on the faith of Bheem Rao Bukhshee (who protested against their execution), were hanged without even the form of a trial. In the same way fifteen Potails were summarily executed in the following four or five days, and the unarmed multitudes were everywhere attacked, and several hundreds put to death. The Rajah, feeling himself superseded, and hating the cruelties in which he had been made to acquiesce, went back to Mysore. The Resident wrote to Calcutta that peace and order had been restored. On the 5th of January 1831 the Resident thus reported these proceedings to the Government of Madras :—'His Highness, who is always averse to spill the blood of his subjects, was prevailed on to exercise his legitimate authority, and to make examples of the principal leaders, and the insurrection has thus been put an end to.' He adds that 'the ryots are paying their taxes willingly and quietly'.

"From the date of that despatch a civil war raged throughout the country. Part of a European Regiment and three Native Battalions were called out in aid of the Rajah's troops. In Nuggur the Polygars headed the people, occupied strong posts, and expelled the Rajah's officers, but committed no acts of murder or pillage. Wherever the Rajah's officials could get the upper hand they ruthlessly hanged all the leading men they could catch, often on mere suspicion; and on the 16th of March 1831 no fewer than ninety-seven prisoners were hung up on trees in one spot by torchlight, under the direct orders of a British officer* who had been lately in charge of the Resident's escort, and who had been selected by the

* Lieutenant (afterwards Colonel) Gustavus Cowper Rochfort, who died in 1875.

Resident to command the Rajah's troops. In the public correspondence there are several letters from the Rajah protesting against
such proceedings. The Polygars, who had hitherto spared the
officers of Government, now carried off twenty Brahmins, and
hanged them all, in retaliation for the slaughter of their relatives
and followers."

In a demi-official letter to Lord William Bentinck,
dated 1st April 1832, Colonel Briggs gives a similar
account of the severities by which it was attempted to
crush the first symptoms of discontent, and refers to
public records as containing positive proof of their true
source. Urging on the Governor-General the necessity
of making great changes in the list of public functionaries, he says :—

"Your Lordship will be shocked to learn that numbers of the
Mamlutdars, who forced the people into revolt, were appointments
from the Residency, and that the cruel execution of several Potails,
invited into camp on the faith of the Rajah, was a step suggested
by the interested Mamlutdars, and the Residency Moonshee, and
urgently pressed on the Rajah by the Resident himself. The Rajah
was utterly opposed to the measure, but was compelled to yield
his assent; and in issuing his orders the very next day he qualified his own share in them by inserting in his own hand-writing,
'These are the positive orders of the Resident', an assertion which
is borne out by documents signed by Mr. Casamajor.* The cold-
blooded execution of ninety-seven prisoners at Honelly, on the day

* Here is an extract from the Report of the Special Committee of
1833 :—
"105.—On the 21st December a circular notice or proclamation
was issued, directing that all persons who should thenceforward be
found carrying bones and margosa leaves,—the usual symbols of insurrection in Mysore,—should be seized, tried on the spot, and, if convicted, hanged; and on the following day printed instructions were
addressed to the Foujdar of Bangalore to cause some of the leaders of
the insurrectionary assemblages to be caught, and one or two of them
hanged in each talook; to fire upon those assemblages without hesitation if any resistance should be offered by them; and, generally,
to take rigorous measures against the evil-disposed; 'shooting such as
deserve to be shot, and hanging such as deserve to be hanged'. This
letter of instructions, which bears date the 22nd December, is concluded with a sentence in his Highness's own handwriting, to this effect:
'The gentleman' (meaning the Resident) 'strongly recommends the
adoption of these measures for putting down the insurrection, and has
given the same orders.'"

after they were taken, is reported to the Rajah on the 16th of
March 1831 as being carried into effect by order of the British
officer placed in command of the Rajah's troops by the Resident;
and against this measure the Rajah himself entered a strong and
feeling remonstrance."

The most characteristic feature in the case was that
these acts of "firmness" and wholesome severity, perpetrated in pursuance of the Resident's authoritative
counsel, and against the Rajah's will, had already been
demi-officially, that is to say secretly, reported by the
Governor of Madras to Lord William Bantinck, before the
unwelcome appointment of Colonel Briggs to be Commissioner, as horrors and acts of atrocity for which the
Rajah was to be held responsible, and for which he was to
be deprived of power.

"The Polygar, Rungapa Naik, at once retaliated by seizing and
putting to death twenty Brahmins, the first officers of Government
who suffered at the hands of the insurgents. No less than 164
persons, many of them heads of villages, were hanged without trial,
and on the most frivolous charges, besides a great number of
unarmed people killed by musketry. This information does not
come to me from private sources; it is entered on the face of
official journals kept for the use of the Mysore Government, in
some cases containing entries in the Rajah's own hand-writing,
and always bearing the signet of the late Dewan. The system of
Indian records forbids the possibility of concealing these things,
if we have access to them, but an exposure of them must ruin one
party. The full truth can never be placed officially before your
Lordship so long as the Resident, supported by the Governor of
Madras, precludes access to the Rajah and his records by the
Senior Commissioner."

We now return to the Memorandum which was sent
to Mr. Elphinstone :—

"On the 12th of April 1831, the Governor of Madras in Council
wrote to the Governor-General that he was then about to proceed
to Mysore to investigate the state of affairs, and report on them.
In this letter, among other charges, mostly very vague, against the
Rajah, the Governor of Madras—with perfect inaccuracy, as was
afterwards proved,—stated that 'the payments of the subsidy had
been delayed beyond the appointed period', and that consequently
'the troops and establishments are ready to mutiny for want of
subsistence'. On the 8th of June the Governor-General writes
that he shall wait for the promised report before issuing final

instructions, but that his present views lead him to anticipate the necessity of taking the management of the Rajah's country into our own hands, and that he should propose to govern it by a Commission of British officers. On the 4th of July the Governor sent the Governor-General, not the promised report in official form from the Government of Madras, but an informal letter and minute from himself, containing very meagre, and, as afterwards turned out, very erroneous, information. The Governor-General, however, having waited in vain till the end of August for something more explanatory, acted on this letter.

"The Governor of Madras had recommended a recurrence to the system prevailing in Poorniah's time, of a Minister, appointed by us, and having our confidence, exercising full authority in concert with the Resident. To this plan the Governor-General was strongly opposed, and on the 6th of September 1831 he wrote to the Madras Government expressing his complete dissent from the Resident-and-Dewan-system, and his resolution to vest the Government in the hands of two British Commissioners, of whom his Lordship was pleased to nominate me the senior, leaving it to the Madras Government to appoint the junior, and to supply the necessary establishments, the new Government of Mysore being made directly subordinate to the Madras Government. On the 27th of September the Governor of Madras again recorded a long Minute urging the same scheme that he had advocated on the 4th of July."

The plan on which Lord William Bentinck insisted was a grievous disappointment to the Governor, and he made hardly any secret of his dislike to it, even, as will be seen, in his personal communications with Briggs. The Governor of Madras had assumed that the conduct of Mysore affairs, the patronage, and the credit of any success, would fall into his own hands, as directly as in the case of any district in the Presidency. As an old Madras Civilian, with an elder brother in the Court of Directors, and a younger brother, under his own wing, in the Madras Civil Service, to whom he had allotted, without fear of any obstacle, the sole administration of Mysore, he took a determined aversion to what he considered the intrusion of a military officer into the best and highest place in that very country. He wanted Mysore as a new province (a very agreeable one in climate) added to Madras, open to frequent visits from the Governor, or available as a usual place of residence.

The appointment of Colonel Briggs, furthermore, was, in his view, and in that of the whole Civil Service, an encroachment on the good things properly reserved for that select and superior body.

"On the 10th of October", writes Briggs, "when I received the notification of my appointment to Mysore, I was at Delhi; on the 16th of December I was at Madras."

The Governor of Madras at this time was the Right Honourable Stephen Rumbold Lushington, a man who had shown great capacity in many situations, and whose actual position in 1831, as it was the crowning triumph, was certainly the most remarkable incident in a not uneventful career. For, placed at the head of the Government of Fort St. George, Mr. Lushington had as his colleagues in Council some of the comrades of his early public life. Several high officials at the Presidency had been senior to him in the Civil Service, and one of them had even sat in secret judgment on his conduct when he left Madras under a cloud in 1804. When young Stephen Lushington, born in 1774, came out as a Writer to Madras in 1791, the Honourable Company still retained its commercial character, and a certain speculative element still entered into the legitimate expectations of all who served in India. No one in civil employ depended entirely on his mere salary, or could, indeed, subsist upon it. In all ranks of the army, moreover, above that of Lieutenant, the chief emoluments and provision for retirement were drawn from the right of holding certain Government contracts for stores, tents, and carriage, and certain petty monopolies for the supply of necessaries to the troops. The Commandant of a corps was even allowed to levy an octroi in the regimental bazar for his own private profit. The incredible officers' mutiny of 1809 in the Madras Army arose out of measures adopted by the Government of Sir George Barlow for abolishing some of these unseemly perquisites.

The opportunities of making a fortune by recognised gains incidental to office, and by private trade, were much more numerous and extensive in the Indian Civil

Service than in the Army, while the salaries were proportionately much smaller, in fact, merely nominal. The
commercial privileges of the Company's servants were
gradually withdrawn, and, finally, private trade was
forbidden altogether under the Government of Lord
Cornwallis, between 1793 and 1797, while civil salaries
were raised on a liberal scale, and pensions introduced.
But, very naturally, some vestiges of the old system
lingered for a while, and the line between authorised and
prohibited emoluments and pursuits was not clearly
defined or strictly drawn for some years, after many
alleged infractions of the rule, and many disputes.
Stephen Lushington thus began to be a member of the
Madras Civil Service in this transition period, his first
two years of service having been passed before the
reforms of Lord Cornwallis had been instituted. From
1795 to 1799 he was Private Secretary to his father-in-
law, Lord Harris, the Commander-in-Chief,* and was
present in that capacity at the siege and capture of
Seringapatam.

Subsequently Mr. Lushington was placed in what was
considered a very good appointment, Collector of the
Peishcush, or tribute of the Southern Polygars, chieftains
in the South of India, who, under the Nawab of the
Carnatic—converted, in 1800, into a virtual pensioner—
had exercised almost independent jurisdiction in their
own estates, and whose tribute was payable in kind, as
to some extent was then also the land revenue of ordinary
districts, now everywhere commuted into cash. It had
been the privilege, an unbroken custom, as Mr. Lushington pleaded, until he took up the office, for the Collector to trade in the grain paid as tribute, in the interval
between its delivery in many instalments, and its final
sale and the appropriation of the proceeds as public
revenue. The Government of Madras, however, held
that this privilege had been abolished by the new regulations consequent on Lord Cornwallis's reforms, and the
new scale of civil salaries. The Collector of the Polygars'

* Whose biography he wrote,—*Life and Services of General Lord
Harris*, London, 1840.

Peishcush was charged with having engaged in speculations in grain belonging to the Government, and in having profited by them. An inquiry followed; Lushington left Madras under suspension from office in 1804, and having been unable to convince the Court of Directors on appeal that his interpretation of the new rules was the correct one—for he never admitted that his course had been in any way irregular—he ceased to belong to the Madras Civil Service in 1806. In 1807 he became M.P. for Rye, and in the general election of the next year obtained a seat for Yarmouth. He must at once have been recognised as a noticeable person, for in 1809 he was chosen to second the Address in answer to the King's speech. In 1824 he became Chairman of Committees of the House of Commons. In 1825 he was granted a pension on the Civil List of £1,500 a year. In 1827 he was made a Privy Councillor and Joint Secretary of the Treasury.

There are prophecies that tend to fulfil themselves. There are prophecies that may be shrewdly suspected of an origin later than their supposed fulfilment. Whether we have to do with one of either sort of prediction, with a real tradition or with a contemporary invention, I cannot say, but the story was current in 1832 that Stephen Lushington had declared in 1806 that he would never return to Madras except as Governor, and that as Governor he was determined to return. Certain it is that in 1827 the Right Honourable Stephen Rumbold Lushington was appointed Governor and Commander-in-Chief of Fort St. George and its dependencies, and arrived at Madras in November of that year.

It may as well be added here that Mr. Lushington, at the expiration of his five years' term as Governor of Madras, returned home at the end of 1832, and became once more a Member of Parliament in 1835. He afforded one more instance of longevity among the old Indian contemporaries of General Briggs. He died in 1868 at the age of 94, having married for the second time in 1856, when 82 years old.

When he entered on the Government of Madras in

1827, his elder brother, General Sir James Law Lushington, was a Member of the Court of Directors ; and a younger brother, Charles May Lushington, was in the Madras Civil Service.

We shall obtain a more clear, full, and connected view of the situation, and of the difficulties under which Briggs entered on his new office, if we again quit the Memorandum which he sent to Mr. Elphinstone, and make some extracts from the autobiographical papers, and from his unofficial correspondence.

" While at Delhi I received a private letter from the Governor-General, dated the 4th of September 1831, reciting the substance of the despatch about to be sent to the Government of Madras on the affairs of Mysore, and offering me in the most flattering terms the appointment of Senior Commissioner for the administration of that country. I felt at once the dangers before me, but I could not refuse the post. The rude means of conveyance, and the distance I had to travel, nearly two thousand miles, chiefly through tracts where British authority did not prevail, protracted my journey through Rajputana and the Deccan till the middle of December. On the 16th, immediately on my arrival at Madras, I waited on the Governor, the Right Honourable Stephen Rumbold Lushington, who received me with that courtesy and grace of manner for which he was distinguished. After kindly referring to the letter of recommendation I had brought him some months previously, on my return to India, from the President of the Board of Control, the department to which he had been himself attached, he entered on business, and made me at once to understand that he dissented altogether from the system of Government laid down by Lord William Bentinck for Mysore ; but without entering into details, he said he would send me for perusal all the recent correspondence on Mysore affairs, saying that he should be glad to see me again when I had got through the papers.

" A careful examination of these documents showed me the startling fact that the management of Mysore had been assumed on the erroneous grounds, informally laid before the Governor-General by the Governor of Madras, that the subsidy had fallen into arrears, but that as soon as the Madras Government happened to make an application on the subject to the Accountant-General, the return made by that officer had proved that no failure in the regular monthly payments of the subsidy had ever occurred.

" As the Governor of Madras was necessarily aware of the truth by this time, from the Accountant-General's report, and probably not very comfortable in his mind on the subject, and as I knew the Governor-General could not long be kept in ignorance regarding it, I did not conceive that it was my duty to press this fact on the attention of either of them, more particularly as it could have no practical bearing, in the present condition of Mysore, on the policy of our Government."

And here we will interrupt Colonel Briggs's narrative, in order to indicate, as clearly as may be, the nature and extent of the error and irregularity, under the terms of the Treaty, into which Lord William Bentinck had been misled. The following Article is that by virtue of which the Governor-General assumed the right of bringing the Mysore territories " under the direct management of the Company's servants" :—

" Article 4. And whereas it is indispensably necessary that effectual and lasting security should be provided against any failure in the fund destined to defray either the expenses of the permanent military force in time of peace, or the extraordinary expenses described in the 3rd Article of the present Treaty, it is hereby stipulated and agreed between the contracting parties, that whenever the Governor-General in Council at Fort William in Bengal shall have reason to apprehend such failure in the funds so destined, the said Governor-General in Council shall be at liberty, and shall have full power and right, either to introduce such regulations and ordinances as he shall deem expedient for the internal management and collection of the revenues, or for the better ordering of any other branch and department of the Government of Mysore, or to assume and bring under the direct management of the Servants of the said Company Bahadoor, such part or parts of the territorial possessions of His Highness Maharaja Mysore Kistna Rajah Oodiaver Bahadoor as shall appear to him, the said Governor-General in Council, necessary to render the said funds efficient and available in time of peace or war."

By Article V, which fixes the share of the revenue to be allotted for the Rajah's household and privy purse, it was provided, " that whenever and so long as any part or parts of His said Highness's Territories shall be placed and shall remain under the exclusive authority and control of the East India Company, the Governor-General in Council shall render to His Highness a true and faithfull account of the revenues and produce of the Territories so assumed".*

* *Aitchison's Treaties*, vol. v, pp. 159, 160.

Thus, according to the letter of the Treaty (Article IV), neither defects in the Rajah's domestic policy, nor the occurrence of a revolt in his Dominions, afforded sufficient grounds for even his temporary supersession, unless the payment of our Subsidy were endangered. All defects could easily be cured by enforcing Article XIV, or by "ordinances". Reasonable anxiety for the instalments of annual tribute was the only cause that could sanction the attachment of districts.

And it must be further remarked that, according to the Treaty (Articles IV and V), when it should be thought necessary to have recourse to this extreme measure, we had no right to attach the whole of Mysore, but only "such part or parts" as should be required to render the funds of the State "efficient and available". It is also clear from Article V that the management was to be temporary.

Nor did these difficulties long escape the observation of Lord William Bentinck. In a despatch to the Secret Committee of the Court of Directors, proposing the Rajah's reinstatement under conditions, dated 14th of April 1834, he writes as follows :—

" By the adoption of the arrangement which I advocate, certain doubts will be removed which I cannot help entertaining, both as to the legality and the justice, according to a strict interpretation, of the course that has been pursued. The Treaty warrants an assumption of the country with a view to secure the payment of our Subsidy. The assumption was actually made on account of the Rajah's misgovernment. The Subsidy does not appear to have been in any immediate jeopardy. Again, the Treaty authorises us to assume such *part* or *parts* of the country as may be necessary to render the funds which we claim efficient and available. The whole has been assumed, although a part would unquestionably have sufficed for the purpose specified in the Treaty."

Lord William might have added that, under Articles IV and XIV, "regulations", or "ordinances" of reform might at any time have been "introduced", without sweeping away the whole fabric of the Rajah's Government.

We now return to Colonel Briggs's narrative.

" On my second visit to the Governor he was equally gracious
as at the first, but in the course of conversation which he gradually led up to that point, and incidently referring to a despatch
from the Honourable Court thirty years old, which *happened* to be
lying on the table before him, he remarked that the Directors had
always objected to the employment of Military officers in purely
civil situations.   I was, in short, made to feel that my selection by
the Governor-General, was considered a deviation from an established and salutary rule, and was distasteful to the Right Honourable gentleman under whose immediate orders I was placed.   This
was not very promising; but the Governor went on to say, courteously enough, I must confess, and with great appearance of good
humour and frankness, that he did not understand how two Commissioners, on an equal footing, were likely to conduct affairs in
Mysore to a good end, except by dividing the country between
them, and each taking one half under his charge.   ' When you
get there, however', said he, ' I have no doubt that you and my
relative will hit on some plan, and will manage everything to my
satisfaction.'   I said we should, of course, be guided by his instructions, which, I hoped, we should soon receive.   ' Oh, as to that',
replied he, ' I shall have no instructions to give you.   You are
aware that I do not entirely agree with Lord William Bentinck's
views, but they are plain enough, and they must, of course, be
carried out.'   On this I took my leave."

Two or three days after this interview with the
Governor of Madras, Colonel Briggs took his departure
for Mysore, and his first impressions and experiences of
the work before him, and of the irreconcileable conflict
of jurisdiction and of duty in which he was soon to be
involved, can best be seen in a few extracts from the
autobiographical papers.

" On Christmas Day, 1831, I arrived at Bangalore, where I had
been informed by the Governor it was intended I should remain,
and where I was to meet my colleague, the Junior Commissioner,
Mr. C. M. Lushington.   I found him suffering from the gout,
aggravated by the fatigue of his journey from the Rajah's capital
of Mysore, where he had been living for three months with the
Resident, his old and intimate friend.   He had brought away from
Mysore all the Native establishments he considered necessary,
and had already appointed, with the approval of the Governor of
Madras, a Brahmin, named Vencatarāmāniah, recommended by the
Resident, to be Dewan, or Minister.   Mr. Lushington only remained
a fortnight at Bangalore, and then returned to Madras.   Immediately before his departure he publicly recorded his opinion—

upholding his brother's views, in defiance of the Governor-General's decision,—that the Commissioners were to act the part of the Resident, with the new Dewan, as the actual executive head of the administration. And the new Dewan was told that he was to have full powers, such as Poorniah had exercised, subject to the supervision of the Commissioners. The Governor-General's views, as conveyed to us in his instructions, appeared to me to be from first to last opposed to those of the Governor of Madras. My conscience forbade me to interpret the Governor-General's instructions according to the wishes of Mr. Lushington. I was called on to express my sentiments, which I did in two Minutes of the 6th and 12th of January 1832, wherein I declared my belief that the Commission was intended to represent the Prince, and was to be at once a deliberate and an executive body, possessing complete authority, and bearing the sole responsibility, the Dewan being, with respect to the Commissioners, a subordinate and ministerial officer."

We now return to the Memorandum sent to Mr. Elphinstone.

"During his three months of sole administration, in concert with the Resident, Mr. Lushington had made no progress in tranquillising the people, but he had certainly got through some work. He had abolished the only Court of Justice in the country, —and, I may add, that the Government of Madras forbade me to establish another. He had discharged a whole Regiment of Cavalry, maintained under the terms of the Treaty, and made over the horses, 500 in number, to the Rajah to support. The Rajah, the question of whose income was quite unsettled, gave the horses away. My colleague had also repudiated all the pensions to Tippoo's relations, and to the old servants of the Sultan's and of Poorniah's administration; and, as a master-stroke of economy—for that was the plea—he had suspended the payment of all charitable and religious grants, and had sequestrated all the *jaghires* and *inam* lands throughout the country, until their title-deeds could be examined. About 9,000 influential families were thus reduced to great straits, and threatened with ruin.

"At this time the hilly western districts of Bednore or Nuggur were still in a state of revolt, while the Mysore soldiery, long in arrears of pay, were levying contributions on the people to keep themselves alive, but refusing to act against the insurgents. More than a year's pay was due to all the establishments, military and civil. Complaints and petitions were coming in every day against the corrupt and cruel Amils, appointed or maintained by the new Dewan, under the influence and with the support of the Residency. There were more than two thousand untried prisoners in the jails."

Colonel Briggs recommended that three measures should be adopted without delay,—a loan, in order that the unruly troops and public servants might be relieved and brought to order; a general amnesty and act of oblivion; and a careful scrutiny and revision of the administrative *personnel*, without which he was convinced that every plan of redress and reform would be made fruitless and of no effect.

But nothing that Colonel Briggs proposed met with support or approval from the Government of Madras. The Governor, who had, in fact, originated them, upheld all the views of his brother, and to question or criticise them was treated as if it were presumptuous insubordination. Not recognising the provocation given, and the irritation kept up by the corrupt creatures in office throughout Mysore, the Governor and his brother considered that instead of conciliation and amnesty, some more severe examples were wanted before order could be restored. With the same blind reliance on the Residency party, the Governor could see no necessity for expurgating the public service, or infusing new blood into it. Colonel Briggs was expressly forbidden to interfere with the Dewan's administration, or with any of his appointments. Although left, after the departure of his colleague, as sole Commissioner for more than a month, he was not allowed to do anything, and he could get nothing done.

Every plan proposed by Colonel Briggs for organising a reformed administration in Mysore was rejected by the Government of Madras, in acrimonious and contemptuous terms, of which the following extracts from a despatch, dated the 17th of February 1832, may form a fair sample.

"The Right Honourable the Governor in Council has read with dissatisfaction and disappointment the foregoing papers. Lieutenant-Colonel Briggs has not only thought fit to re-assert that his information respecting a Court for the administration of Civil and Criminal Justice at the capital is 'essentially correct', but he has presumed to complain of the delay of this Board in replying to his voluminous minutes, although they have been answered with an expedition that would have been incompatible with their due consideration, had not a strong sense of public duty induced the

Board to apply their immediate and undivided attention to the prevention of the mischief likely to result from Colonel Briggs's erroneous opinions.

"The Right Honourable the Governor sees with regret the extreme pertinacity with which Lieutenant-Colonel Briggs adheres to his hastily formed opinion that the statement he made is 'essentially correct'. Upon the records of this Presidency no trace has yet been discovered of this institution at any period, and looking at the nature of its composition as described by Colonel Briggs, the Right Honourable the Governor in Council would deem its revival in a Hindoo State—even if it had ever existed— neither politic nor advisable.

"The Right Honourable the Governor in Council therefore desires that no measure may be adopted without his sanction for the revival of this or any other Court which was not in operation in 1804. Whatever changes may have been subsequently made must be regarded as excrescences not originating with, or known to, Sir Barry Close or Mr. Webbe, whose united wisdom founded upon the Hindoo institutions of the country that system of government of which they made Poorniah the ostensible instrument.

"Under the practice which has obtained since Lieutenant-Colonel Briggs reached Bangalore, the Dewan cannot know what is going on, and his mind must be kept in a continued state of irritation and alarm."

"The Right Honourable the Governor in Council willingly gave to Lieutenant-Colonel Briggs all the credit he obtained under the Bombay Government for his general zeal and activity. These qualities, if duly restrained in him, may be made useful to the public service, but if allowed to continue in the direction they have taken, would be extremely detrimental. His activity, as it has yet been exhibited, is not that which promotes the attainment of any useful end, but that which, without any fit cause, sets everything in stir and commotion, puts the public functionaries, European and Native, out of their places, and disgusts them all. There must be but one executive authority in the country, as in the time of Poorniah and Sir Barry Close. Authority to be efficient must be single, and the Commissioners will best uphold their own by maintaining that of the Dewan, so long as he is recognised in that character by the British Government."

Colonel Briggs having reported that he could place no reliance on either the capacity or the integrity of the Dewan, and having given strong reasons for desiring a change in that office, the Governor still more warmly took up the cause of his brother's nominee. In a despatch dated the 28th of February 1832, he praised "the manly

M

"independence" with which the Dewan "denies the sinister motives imputed to him by Lieutenant-Colonel Briggs", and declared that, having now "before him conflicting statements from public functionaries, each in his own sphere exercising a high office, and entitled to the confidence of Government", he must wait for the opinion of the newly appointed Junior Commissioner, then on his way to Bangalore, before deciding between the views of the Dewan and those of the Senior Commissioner.

In pursuance of the same course, the new Commissioner, Mr. Drury, having in the meantime joined Colonel Briggs, another despatch, dated the 19th of March 1832, directed that "in the event of a difference of opinion between the Commissioners, they are to record their sentiments separately, for the consideration of Government; but in any matter requiring to be immediately decided upon and carried into effect, the views of the Dewan and those of the Commissioner agreeing with him should be adopted."

Thus the Dewan was left master of the situation, the initiative and the executive of administration being concentrated in his hands, while he was made, virtually, a Member of the Commission, with a casting vote whenever he chose to demand it.

" In a private letter to Lord William Bentinck at this time", says Briggs, " I ventured to contrast my situation under the present Governor of Madras with that which I had occupied in Khandesh, or with that of Mr. Jenkins at Nagpore during the minority of the Rajah. I pointed out what seemed to me the impossibility of my fulfilling the duties imposed on me to his or to my own satisfaction, and I begged his Lordship to relieve me, and to place me in any position, however inferior, under his own direct authority."

The position of Colonel Briggs had become quite intolerable. The Junior Commissioner, as might be expected from one specially chosen and instructed by the Madras authorities, was merely an inseparable opponent. It was enough for the Senior Commissioner to propose a measure, to ensure the lively dissent of the Junior, supported by the local experience of the Dewan, and in due course by the Governor's veto.

Before the arrival of his irreconcileable colleague, in a letter addressed on the 23rd of February 1832 to the Chief Secretary to the Government of India, Briggs had again tendered his resignation, with a full defence of his own proceedings and a protest against his persecution ; and in reporting to the Government of Madras the step he had taken, he remarked that it would now be for his Lordship the Governor-General " to judge how far it may be expedient for the public service to continue at the head of the Mysore Commission an individual who has so completely lost the confidence of the Government under whose direct orders the Commission has been placed."

After defending in detail the measures he had proposed, he thus described the state of affairs at the official head-quarters of Mysore.

" I cannot conclude this despatch without adverting to the novel scene which Bangalore now exhibits. The people see the head of the Government in a manner cut off from all communication with the capital and the Rajah. They see the senior, and apparently the sole, Commissioner prohibited from interference with the measures of a Dewan whom they know to be ignorant and corrupt. They see him deprived of the means of doing them justice, left without any fixed establishment, and publicly spoken of in the bazar as the object of the displeasure and disapprobation of the authority under which he is placed. They see him here alone and unaided, unknown to the whole people, and without a single public functionary with whom he has any acquaintance, over whom he has any claim, or to whom he can venture to hold out any promise or hope of reward. In spite of these obstacles, such are the general contempt and dislike entertained for the Dewan, and so strong the conviction abroad as to the impossibility of the present system lasting, that I have—strange to say—met with the fullest support from a number of public servants here who are now out of employ. Knowing, as they do, the nature of the Dewan's proceedings and the character of the British Government, they have been induced to volunteer their aid gratuitously ; and although not one of them has opened his lips for remuneration, or has stipulated for pay, I am at this moment literally encumbered with help, and have been able, through their means, to collect a mass of authentic documents which will enable me, whenever it may be required, to exhibit, in an entirely new point of view, the history of the late insurrection and the present state of Mysore."

M 2

He thus described the extraordinary relations between himself and the Dewan.

"In the enjoyment of the confidence of the Madras Government and of the Resident, in the full exercise of a power with which I am forbidden to interfere, with all the public servants of the State —from the Foujdar of a district to the messenger of an office,— looking up to him for subsistence and promotion, the Dewan keeps up an active system of espionage, and maintains an extensive secret correspondence. Instead of my being able to transact public business with composure, my whole time has been taken up in endeavouring to counteract the plots of the Dewan to keep me in the dark."

And, in fact, the Governor-General had already, as he afterwards admitted, obtained clearer notions as to the nature of the disturbances in Mysore, and as to the actual condition of the country, from the correspondence of Colonel Briggs than from all the reports, official and private, coming from Madras. It did not at all suit the Dewan or his patrons that Colonel Briggs should be able to collect information through any channels but those which they could control, and the Government of Madras, prompted by the Residency at Mysore, manifested excessive irritation at the Senior Commissioner's volunteer establishment. The Governor was pleased to notice the subject in the following language.

"The revival of that mode of conducting public business by private servants not in the public employ, which has long been exploded in every part of the Company's territories, as tending to the worst corruption, would be as odious to the people as it would be disgraceful to Government. Except for the knowledge the Right Honourable the Governor in Council has recently obtained of Lieutenant-Colonel Briggs's proceedings, he would have considered a hint upon this matter quite sufficient to put an end to it.'

In another passage of the same letter, dated 17th February 1832, Briggs is accused of having " brought with him a band of hungry expectants", who are also characterised as " greedy foreigners".

From these assertions a conclusion would naturally have been drawn that Colonel Briggs had brought with

him, or called round him, from distant provinces, a number
of personal followers. The truth was that, although fully
convinced before his arrival that a considerable purifica-
tion of the public service would be required, he had not
sent for anyone who had ever been employed under himself, and he had held out no encouragement or hope to
any candidate who was not a native of Mysore. The
only person whom he had summoned by name to his
assistance was a Brahmin named Krishna Rao, the hereditary record-keeper of Ouscotta, a town near Bangalore,
where he was born and brought up, but who, following
the example of his father, had served with great credit
under the Government of Bombay, until, on the abolition
of his office, he retired on a pension of 400 rupees a month
—£480 a year. He was no " hungry expectant", but
in easy circumstances, as, in addition to his pension,
he enjoyed a jaghire of 5,000 rupees (£500) per annum,
which had been conferred on his father as a recognition
of long and faithful service in troublous times. Before
his arrival at Bangalore, Krishna Rao was really almost
a stranger to Colonel Briggs, who only knew him by
character as the chief revenue officer under his old master,
Mountstuart Elphinstone, when the latter was Commissioner of the Deccan, and afterwards as head of the
Deccan Department at Bombay. This was the man
whom rumour pointed out, quite incorrectly, as intended
by Briggs for the office of Dewan, and as such he became
the principal mark for the calumnies and intrigues of the
Residency party, and for the subsequent proscription of
the Madras Government.

Another person, from whom Colonel Briggs had obtained some useful and trustworthy information, and
whom he intended to restore to office on the first opportunity, was a young Mussulman of distinction, named
Gholam Mohammed Khan, otherwise Mamoo Meean,*

* These house-names, or pet-names, are very common in Southern
and Western India, both in Hindoo and Mohammedan families. Among
the Mahrattas, of all castes, some such appellation as Nana, Dada,
Bhow, Abba, Bapoo, Dajee, Tantia, or Baba, is almost invariably fixed
on a person in childhood, so that the true name is quite dropped in
after-life. The use of the real name is considered unlucky.

who had been Bukhshee, or General, of the Mysore In
fantry, a place in which he had succeeded his father,
Khan Jehan Khan, one of the celebrities of Tippoo's
army.   Secure, as he supposed, in the Rajah's favour, he
had never truckled to the Residency Moonshee, and was
one of the few men of character and position who had
tried to open their master's eyes to the corruption around
him, and who had, as plainly as they could venture to do,
deprecated the reign of terror by which it was sought to
silence the general outburst of remonstrance.   His own
men were, of course, greatly in arrears, and when forced
to take the field in all directions, to quell the insurrection, became importunate for their pay.   With rumours
abroad of his impending supersession, and even of the
annexation of his country, the Rajah's credit was very
low ; and when it was at the very lowest ebb, the young
Bukhshee had borrowed a lakh of rupees (£10,000) on
his own personal security from the local bankers, in order
to get some of his battalions to march.   But he was an
object of hatred and fear to the Residency party, and
they endeavoured to make him harmless by disgrace and
removal from office.   As soon as the Rajah's authority was
suspended, on Mr. C. M. Lushington's arrival at Mysore,
that gentleman, in concert, and of one accord, with his
old friend the Resident, whose guest he was, dismissed
Gholam Mohammed Khan from the place of Bukhshee
without any pension, and attached his jaghire.   Having
sought redress from the Senior Commissioner, he also
became a marked man.

On the 23rd of February 1832 Briggs sent in his
appeal to the Supreme Government against the harsh
and humiliating treatment he had received from the
Governor of Madras, who, doubtless, about the same
time submitted his own account and advice on the
matters of difference that had arisen.   But communications were not very rapid in 1832 ; six weeks had to
pass away before an answer could come from Simla,
where Lord William Bentinck was then residing. Allowing one week only for deliberation, and the preparation

of a despatch, the Governor-General's decision could not be expected much before the first week in April. Some days at least of this interval, Briggs, whose nervous system was completely upset by the continuous worry to which he had been exposed, determined to pass, under medical advice, with some friends at Oossoor, a place about twenty miles from Bangalore. He was detained, however, for several days by unexpected and alarming events.

One visible consequence of the rash measures of retrenchment adopted by Mr. C. M. Lushington in his three months of undivided power, was, that a concourse of soldiers, discharged without their arrears being paid, of pensioners, whose allowances were stopped, and of *jaghiredars* and *inamdars*, whose lands were sequestrated, used daily to assemble either outside the board-room of the Commission, or at the Senior Commissioner's gate, and to beset him on his arrival and departure, with outcries for relief and redress. They singled out Colonel Briggs as the special object of their clamorous appeals, not merely because he was designated as the head of the new administration, but because on one point his personal adherents, and the hostile party of the Dewan, were quite agreed in opinion, that the great cause of delay in the settlement of Mysore affairs lay in the antagonism between the Senior Commissioner on the one side, and the Governor of Madras on the other, and that all would go smooth enough if Colonel Briggs would only submit to be guided by the Governor, and to co-operate with the Resident. This he could not do, and therefore could get no sanction to his repeated suggestions of a loan, or to any of his proposals of reorganisation.

Many of the pensioners and landholders, whose incomes were suspended, and who were in constant fear of total disendowment, were doctors of the law, teachers and preachers of religion, having great influence among the discharged soldiery and the most fanatical and turbulent classes in general throughout the country, both of the Hindoo and of the Mussulman faith.   The impolicy of keeping these people for so long a time in a state of anxiety and positive distress had forcibly presented itself to the mind of Colonel Briggs, but all his warnings and remonstrances could make no impression at Madras. At last an explosion took place.

On the 3rd of March 1832 the Senior Commissioner received information that the Mysore Infantry on duty in the Fort of Bangalore, for the most part Mohammedans, were prepared, in pursuance of a plot in which a great number of the Rajah's army as well as of the Company's troops were engaged, to seize on the Fort during the night, and to murder all the European officers, including the Commandant of the Division, who were within their reach.   Colonel Briggs took steps without a moment's delay, in concert with the General Commanding at Bangalore, to relieve all the guards in the Fort with European soldiers, and to secure the alleged ringleaders in the conspiracy.   Further inquiries proved the truth of the information ; several of the persons implicated betrayed a consciousness of their guilt by flight, but were subsequently apprehended and convicted.

Incidents of a still more alarming character immediately followed the detection of this plot.   The 5th of March 1832 was a day of great solemnity among the Mohammedans, one of their chief religious anniversaries. On the morning of that day the principal mosque of Bangalore, to which the Mussulman sepoys were accustomed to resort, was found to be polluted by the worst of all conceivable abominations, the head of a pig, transfixed on a rude wooden cross, being placed in the most conspicuous part of the front of the building, while the walls of the interior were smeared with crosses in blood. A vast crowd of Mohammedans, excited to the highest pitch of horror and fury by this desecration of their place of worship, soon assembled, and commenced the work of vengeance by sacking and pulling down a small Roman Catholic Chapel which stood in the bazar, not far from the mosque.   Arms were being brought out of the houses, and the infuriated mob would undoubtedly have proceeded to more serious acts of violence, when they were dispersed by the prompt arrival of the 13th Light Dragoons and a detachment of the 62nd Foot. Every possible precaution was taken in good time. The best means were adopted for explaining to the most intelligent and influential Mohammedans in the place the absurdity of supposing that Christians could have taken part in an outrage which involved a monstrous insult to the emblem of their own faith. The clue found by Colonel Briggs was taken up, and in the inquiry which followed it was clearly proved that the pig had been purchased from a low-caste man, who had also been paid to kill it, to display its head in the mosque, and to make crosses of blood on the walls under their directions, by two Mussulman sepoys, one belonging to the Mysore troops and the other to the Company's Army. The conspirators were tried by Court-martial at Bangalore, and of those who were found guilty, four were blown from guns, and two shot. Several non-commissioned officers and sepoys, also, were transported. Altogether 130 arrests were made, but the greater number were released without trial.

The European troops at Bangalore in 1832 consisted of the 13th Light Dragoons, the 62nd Foot, and a Company of Madras Artillery, altogether about 1,200 men ; while the Natives, including a Regiment of Light Cavalry and a troop of Horse Artillery, amounted to more than 4,000 ; and there were, also, close at hand, 2,000 of the Mysore Silladar Horse, nearly all of them Mohammedans, and 2,000 of the Mysore "Barr" or Line Infantry.

The obvious aim of this dangerous combination was to rouse Mohammedan fanaticism against the Christian faith, and the European rulers of the country. But Colonel Briggs was of opinion, and certainly not without good grounds, that the origin of the movement was to be sought in the sudden loss of subsistence and of an honourable position, that had inflicted great misery upon a much respected class, spreading far and wide those rumours of general discontent, and those words of bitter

hate, which encourage fanaticism and breed insurrection.
These notions, however, met with no favour at Madras;
and the Senior Commissioner got no credit, and received
no thanks, for the share he had taken in averting a great
calamity.   On his report reaching the Madras Government, he was briefly ordered to leave all future proceedings in the hands of the military authorities.

CHAPTER X.

ON the 14th of March 1832, all immediate danger from the Mussulman plot having apparently ceased, — the military authorities being in possession of the facts, and being quite competent to deal with them, — Colonel Briggs left Bangalore for a few days' comparative recreation at Oossoor. During his brief absence, the opposite party made the best use of their time. On the 20th of March the Junior Commissioner, now alone at the Board, sent the Madras Government a general report on the Dewan's proceedings, highly eulogistic of his conduct and capacity. Within two or three days after the receipt of this despatch, the Right Honble. the Governor came in person to Bangalore, accompanied by his brother, the late Junior Commissioner, and was there joined by the Resident, Mr. Casamajor, the new Junior Commissioner, and the Dewan, — terrible odds against one poor Lieutenant-Colonel. The first attack was made on Gholam Mohammed Khan, called Mamoo Meean, the ex-Bukhshee of Infantry, one of the Dewan's opponents and victims, and a leading remonstrant against the corrupt and secret rule of the Residency Moonshee. He was accused, on information furnished by the Dewan, of having been implicated in the Mussulman conspiracy. On the very day after Colonel Briggs's rather sudden return to Bangalore—his visit to Oossoor having been somewhat cut short by the news of the Governor's arrival, and by an important despatch from the Governor-General,—the young ex-Bukhshee appeared before the Board to answer this charge. There was not an atom of evidence, or even a plausible case of suspicion, brought against him ; but before he could reply to his accusers, the Governor had already condemned him, as we shall

see, to banishment, without trial or allegation of offence.
Colonel Briggs gives his opinion on the case of Gholam
Mohammed Khan in the following extract from a Minute
which he recorded when the inquiry was over.

"On the first day of taking my seat after my return from
Oossoor (the 4th April 1832), I found that the Board had formed
itself into a Court of Investigation on the conduct of a nobleman
of high rank and family, the eldest son of one of the most distinguished officers of Tippoo Sultan's army.   Gholam Mohammed
Khan, familiarly called Mamoo Meean, is the son of the late Khan
Jehan Khan, who was selected by Poorniah, on the first creation
of the present Principality of Mysore, to the command of all the
Regular Infantry.   Khan Jehan Khan maintained a high character
throughout his life, and handed an unspotted name down to his
son, who, although I have seen little of him, I can pronounce to
be the most accomplished Native gentleman, and the most elegant
scholar I have met with in this part of India.   Brought up from
infancy among his father's battalions, he commanded one of them
while a mere stripling, and on his father's death succeeded to the
command of the whole force, under the title of Bukhshee, which
he held till within the last year.   It is due to this young nobleman
to record the opinion entertained of him by the Honble. Mr. Cole,
the late Resident at Mysore, and expressed after an acquaintance
with father and son of fourteen years.   The following letter, now
in Gholam Mohammed Khan's possession, was presented to my
colleague, and read by him in this room.   It is addressed

"'To James A. Casamajor, Esq.,
"'favoured by my particular friend,
"'A. H. Cole.   "'Gholam Mohammed Khan.

"'MY DEAREST JAMES,—Whenever after my departure for the
Mauritius this shall be given to you by Mamoo Meean, son of
Khan Jehan, I beg you to receive him as one of the most confidential friends we have at this Durbar.   He is quite a gentleman,
mild, unassuming, and withal an efficient soldier, and ready to
uphold his family name with honour.   The boy—or rather when
he was one—was left to my own care by his father, whom I visited
on his death-bed; and I have seen no man about this Durbar whom,
on the whole, I like and respect half so much.   He wants from
you ābroo,* nothing more.   I give little Khan Jehan this in time,

* Treatment consistent with his honour.   Abroo is honour or reputation.

as I may be hurried on the eve of my departure,—that is, if I am to get away at all. God bless you.

> "'Yours most affectionately,

> "'A. Hy. Cole.

"'Mysore Residency, 16th January 1824.'

"I have considered it necessary, after the treatment he has received, to put this document on record.

"Before the examination of Gholam Mohammed Khan commenced on the 4th instant, he had been subjected, I was sorry to find, to the indignity of being sent for by common peons, instead of receiving a written notice or summons, and was even threatened to be brought before the Board by a military guard. Orders of this kind under similar circumstances in other parts of India have cost the lives of those entrusted with them, as well as those of the persons needlessly insulted.

"The most minute and private scrutiny of witnesses confined in separate apartments has been entrusted to those who are known to be the Bukhshee's inveterate enemies. The written results of this inquisition did not appear to me to contain sufficient grounds for any charge; but as I found them on the table, proceedings in progress, and the Bukhshee in attendance below, I did not feel myself authorised to interfere, or to record my sentiments at that time of a measure I could not approve. Moreover, such was my confidence in the character of Gholam Mohammed Khan, and in the opinion of the honourable gentleman whose letter has been read, that I thought it better the investigation should go on without a word of dissent from me.

"The Bukhshee was required to exculpate himself from the several imputations cast upon him, by submitting to a sort of cross-examination.

"It is due to every prisoner—and he was brought here as one—that he should see and hear his accusers give their evidence. He has had no such opportunity. He has never been confronted with them. He was subjected to a close and rigid examination, from which he has come out quite clear. I never saw less appearance of guilty consciousness in any countenance. On the third day he was sent off from Bangalore to Mysore under charge of a common peon. He has lost his *ābroo*. He was not allowed to choose his place of residence, but was sent back to those *sahoucars*,* his creditors, from whose importunity he had withdrawn himself. But they are not his private creditors. He stood forth when his battalions were in arrears by a whole year's pay, and their services were wanted in the field to save the Government from ruin. At such a time, when neither his Sovereign nor the Ministers had

* Hindoo bankers.

credit to raise the money, he became security for a lakh of rupees.
How was he rewarded ? By removal from office ! His pension
has also been stopped, in common with all others in Mysore, and
his family estate has been placed under sequestration. Gholam
Mohammed Khan came to the Commissioners at Bangalore to
obtain redress ; but instead of getting any, his name has been
mixed up with infamy.

"Under these circumstances I should ill perform my duty were
I not to record my deliberate opinion that Gholam Mohammed
Khan, late Bukhshee of the Infantry, has passed through the
ordeal to which he has been subjected without a stain or a shadow
of guilt, and that, instead of being deserving of punishment, he is
entitled to the protection of Government."

In these animadversions on the treatment of Gholam
Mohammed Khan, Colonel Briggs was not merely com-
bating his colleague—he was now deeply engaged in a
personal conflict with the Governor of Madras, who had
taken the matter out of the hands of the Commissioners.
The ex-Bukhshee was "sent off from Bangalore to Mysore
under charge of a common peon", and under summary
sentence of banishment, by an order from the Governor,
which was aimed as a blow at the Senior Commissioner.
It was a bold stroke, and struck at a critical moment, for
a despatch had just arrived from Lord William Bentinck,
proving his general agreement with Colonel Briggs, and
his determination to support him.

Several days before the urgent appeal from Colonel
Briggs of the 23rd of February 1832 can have arrived
at his Lordship's camp, the Governor-General, after
balancing the conflicting statements of Madras and Bangalore, had already sent off a short despatch, dated the
27th of February, accepting, on every important point of
controversy, the views of the Senior Commissioner, and
rejecting those of the Governor. In a private letter of
the same date, Lord William Bentinck addressed Colonel
Briggs in these encouraging terms :—

"Go on, and be of good cheer. You will know that you have
my support ; and I may assure you that at my age, and with my
experience, I do not easily abandon a position deliberately taken.
I confess from what you state, as well as from the tone of the
orders and communications addressed to you from Fort St. George,

there seems too much ground for your belief that you have not the goodwill of the Governor. There is all the appearance, certainly, of a desire to counteract your measures. But in proportion as this may be true, so I would impress upon you the necessity of exercising the greater degree of temper and firmness. You have an ingenious enemy to combat with, if Mr. Lushington be really your enemy; and, as you have seen, any lapses on your part, such as imputing deficiency to the Dewan on the ground of his historical and geographical ignorance, will be eagerly laid hold of. I therefore recommend to you the prudence which it is equally necessary for me to observe. You urge that Mysore should be withdrawn from the constraint of the Madras Government, and that you should be appointed sole Commissioner. The first of these arrangements may become necessary eventually, but I am exceedingly desirous of avoiding what might be termed a *coup-d'état*, until circumstances should, to the perfect satisfaction of those who are to be ultimately the judges, bear out an act that would be so offensive to the local Government. With respect to your appointment as sole Commissioner, I will fairly acknowledge my decided objection to it. I am strongly opposed to individual agency, except in cases of great emergency, in times of trouble and danger, when the executive authority cannot be armed with too much power. But in the government of Kingdoms, such as Mysore may be considered, equally with Bengal and Bombay, where the duties are mainly deliberative, and where the acts of the agency require to be vigilantly controlled, there is no system so safe as that which the Legislature has wisely established for Indian government.

"You will see by the despatch to Fort St. George, of which a copy has been sent to you, that your interpretation of my instructions, and your general views of the course to be followed, have been approved and confirmed. Another despatch, conveying a similar approval of your sentiments on the question of military authority, will shortly follow.

"I need not add more, I hope, to convince you of the necessity of pursuing a steady, temperate and conciliatory course. Let me advise you against the adoption of innovations. Adhere as closely as you can to the institutions of Poorniah, which appear to be generally approved. He was a very able man, and knew, better than we can do, the means of promoting the prosperity and happiness of the country. Above all, avoid the introduction of any plans of English manufacture, and, as far as possible, the employment of any but natives of Mysore as public servants, especially of European officers.

"I remain, dear Sir,
"With truth, yours very sincerely,
"WM. BENTINCK."

In the official communication of the same date (27th
February 1832), referring to his original despatch, Lord
William Bentinck declares its main principle to have
been that the Commission should, "during the suspension of the Rajah's rule, exercise all the functions of a
Regency", thus preserving "that unity of action which,
while we hold the country in trust for the Rajah, he is
at least entitled to expect at our hands".   Inviting the
Governor to "a reperusal" of that despatch, he urges
that " its whole tenor is opposed to the plan of working
out the desired reforms through a Dewan".

" It never could have occurred to his Lordship to appoint two
highly paid British functionaries for the mere purpose of aiding an
officer of that description; nor can it be for an instant allowed
that the appointment of a Dewan, even though it has been approved by the Madras Government, relieves the Commissioners
from any part of the responsibility which, as the supreme authority
in Mysore, exercising full powers in all departments, they have
incurred to Government for the proper execution of its designs and
purposes.

" As observed by Lieut.-Col. Briggs, a Dewan is a Ministerial
officer, whose relative position to the Head of the State is as
that of a Secretary or other officer who may be the medium for
submitting questions, and for taking and issuing the necessary
orders."

After pointing out that the position of Poorniah, who
had, in fact, been Regent as well as Dewan during the
Rajah's minority, was not at all analogous to that of the
present Dewan, the Governor-General declared that " it
would be a deviation from the principle of administration
to be now introduced, were the Dewan to be converted
into an authority for originating plans of reform upon
his own responsibility, or were he allowed further weight
than must necessarily attach to the person who conducts
the executive correspondence with local officers" :—

" Consistently with the same view, his Lordship cannot agree
with the Right Honble. the Governor in Council, in the restrictions imposed upon the Commissioners in respect to the appointment and dismissal of Native officers.   A reform in this department is more urgently required than in any other.   The abuses
which existed through the nomination of needy favourites, or
through the sale of appointments to extortioners, having been

among the primary causes of the insurrection which led to the intervention of the Supreme Government. Unless the Commissioners exercise a searching control in this department, matters will probably remain in the same condition as before; and to enable them to do so, it is his Lordship's decided opinion that instead of leaving appointments and removals to the Dewan, with a prohibition against interference except upon cause shown, the responsibility for proper officers being employed should rest with the Commissioners, who must, therefore, have the power of nomination and dismissal, they referring to the Dewan for information only so far as they may deem expedient."

It might have been supposed that, after so signal a defeat, the Governor of Madras would have made a virtue of necessity, and giving the Senior Commissioner of Mysore, as graciously as might be, due credit for having accurately divined the views of the Supreme Government, would have left him to carry those views into execution without much let or hindrance. But Mr. Lushington was, indeed, "an ingenious enemy", and more especially after his long consultations on the spot with the Resident, the Dewan and the Junior Commissioner, he was too deeply engaged and too closely committed to be willing so easily to retire from the contest. This will more clearly appear in the following extract from Colonel Briggs's diary, and also from the extraordinary step taken by the Governor immediately after the interview therein described.

The Governor-General's private letter to Colonel Briggs, dated 27th February, was delivered at Bangalore on the 25th of March; and on the same day the official despatch of the former date must have reached the Governor's hands. The copy of the official despatch for the Commissioners' information did not, somehow or other, arrive at their office till the 30th. Briggs was still in the country, but returned to Bangalore on the 2nd of April, and the next morning went to pay his respects to the Right Honble. the Governor.

"At noon I waited on the Governor. On entering the room I was met by Mr. Drury, who greeted me very cordially, and told me he would tell the Governor I was there. I was immediately sent for, and saw the Governor alone. He rose from his chair

N

with his usual politeness, asked how I was, and made me sit close
to him.   He spoke of the climate and my health, and then
addressed me thus :—

"'Pray, Colonel Briggs, did you hear anything, or have any
warning, of this Mohammedan conspiracy before the day when
General Hawker marched the Europeans into the Fort?'

"'Nothing at all', I said; 'it came upon us all like a clap of
thunder.'   I remarked that its suppression reflected great credit
on the military authorities at Bangalore.

"'It was providential', said he.

"I observed that if the European soldiers had not been effectually separated from the Sepoys, and the latter properly managed
for two or three days after the pig affair, the consequences might
have been dreadful.   He asked me in what I thought it originated.
I said that I now believed there was no deep-rooted plot, though
it looked like it at first.   I thought it was principally caused by
distress and discontent arising among the unpaid and discharged
soldiery.

"'Well', said the Governor, 'you can get to work and settle all
those matters now.   We have given you Mr. Drury, a very efficient
man, as a colleague.'

"I said, 'Yes, certainly, Mr. Drury is not only a man of great
talent, but of great assiduity.'

"'There ought to be no difficulty', he said, 'in paying up all
arrears.   To what do they amount?'

"I explained that besides what was due to the troops, to the
Hoozoor and district establishments, the bonded debts of the
Rajah were said to amount to twelve lakhs of pagodas.

"'But', said he, 'we are not bound to pay all the Rajah's debts,
and thus to recognise and approve his profligate extravagance.'

"I said that 'we' were not going to pay the Rajah's debts.   All
such demands were against the revenues of Mysore ; and I added
that I knew not how to distinguish between the Rajah's debts and
the debts of the State.

"'Oh, yes', said the Governor, 'it is simple enough.   The Rajah
had no right to incur debts for mere wanton luxury.   We must
meet all arrears due to public establishments, and debts that can
be referred to public purposes; but those that arise from the
private caprice and vice of the Rajah, he must pay, or may pay if
he thinks fit, from his stipend.   The people who trusted him knew
very well that our Government would never sanction such transactions.'

"I replied that the people who trusted him had no reason to
think of our Government in those days.   They lent their money,
or sold their goods, on the credit of a despotic Prince.   The Rajah,
in his Sovereign capacity, had surely a right to make what pur-

chases, and incur what debts, he chose, to be paid out of the revenues, of which he was the absolute master.

"'Not at all', said the Governor, who seemed to be getting nettled at my disputation, feeling his inability to maintain his position against me, 'not at all, Colonel Briggs,—the Rajah had no right to take more than a fair share for the support of his household and dignity. He had no right to spend other people's money.'

"'Undoubtedly', I replied, 'he had no moral right to squander the revenue; but there was, before our intervention, no legal right or power above his. For the future, so long as the country is in our charge, the Rajah must rely on his stipend and share of the revenue, and no one ought to look to any other source if they choose to give him credit.'

"'These debts', said the Governor, 'must be rigidly examined.'*

"To this, of course, I acceded; and I added that I believed a large proportion of the sums claimed were for jewels, shawls, and other costly goods purchased at four times their value, and that bonds or bills at five or six years after date were given for them, and that, therefore, these debts did not call for immediate attention, and could probably be settled for much less than their nominal amount; but that the arrears to the troops, and other establishments, ought to be at once taken in hand.

"'Certainly, certainly, Colonel Briggs', said the Governor, 'and then, there is Nuggur. The state of that district is a disgrace to our Government. You should immediately settle Nuggur.'

"As I had already fully assented to that view, or rather enforced it on the Government of Madras with no effect, I said nothing more, and a pause of some time ensued; after which the Governor said, 'Well, Colonel Briggs, you now perfectly understand the footing on which you stand with Mr. Drury,—that you are to act conjointly, and not separately.'

"I said, 'Surely, sir,—I never thought otherwise.'

"'You are not', he continued, 'to take the whole Revenue Department into your hands, as you proposed;—because, you know, that is the particular branch of the administration we should most unwillingly confide to you.'

"I said I was aware of the views of the Council, and had never arrogated to myself the sole management of the Revenue or any other Department; although I suggested that, as a matter of convenience, each Commissioner should superintend the current busi-

---

* It was eventually settled that all the debts incurred by the Rajah before the administration was assumed by the British Government should be regarded as debts of the State, and that his Highness's stipend and fifth share of the revenue under the Treaty should not be charged with them.

ness of certain Departments,—just as I understood was done at Madras, where Members of Council were Presidents of the Revenue and Judicial Boards,—but that all matters of general concern and great importance should be disposed of by the Commissioners conjointly, after consultation.

" 'You certainly did not express yourself clearly to that effect before', said the Governor.

" I regretted very much that I had failed to make myself understood.

" 'Now, at any rate, Colonel Briggs, you understand your position. You have been all along in error. We are all liable to err. You can atone for it by acting cordially with your new colleague ; and you may rely on the fullest support from me. You, above all other persons, were the very man to whom I was disposed to show every kindness and attention. Did I not evince this in the letter I wrote to you at Hyderabad ?'

" I bowed, and said I was much indebted for his kindness and condescension.

" 'Why, I had resolved', he continued, 'to make you Military Auditor-General. You applied for the appointment, and you should have had it, only you were out of the way when it fell vacant.'

" I then rose, bowed again, and said I was quite sensible how much I was indebted to him for his goodwill.

" 'I have always been well disposed towards you, and anxious to advance your interests.'

" 'You have been good enough ever to express yourself so', I said, 'and I can only tender my acknowledgments for all the kindness and courtesy I have received at your hands.' I must confess that I was rather too stiff; but there was a strain on us both from first to last.

" 'Well, then', said the Governor, 'have you anything more to discuss ? If so, say it at once.'

" I said that I would rather decline discussion altogether; that I should endeavour to do my duty, and hoped to give satisfaction to my superiors.

" 'You may rely on my cordial support, if you get on well with your colleague, who is an admirable man of business.'

" I said there was no question about that, and that I should do my best in every way. During the conversation the Governor adverted several times to the Dewan, and he detained me to revert to the subject again. He said my first opinion of him seemed to be the true one,—that he was a plain, simple, and unpresuming man.

" I said that certainly such was the impression he gave one by his manner and address.

" 'Having been raised to the Office by the Government, it would be disgraceful for us to degrade him without sufficient and manifest cause. If, however', continued the Governor, 'you and Mr. Drury should hereafter think him unfit, we shall not be disposed to uphold him.'

"I said that I had made no objection to the Dewan as a person to receive and execute orders, but that he was not, in my opinion, fit to govern a Kingdom, as Poorniah did.

"'There is a great mistake about Poorniah', said the Governor. 'Poorniah was never a Regent, nor was he a Secretary; he was merely a Dewan, set up by our Government; and Mr. Webbe and Colonel Close managed the affairs of Mysore through his agency.'

"I knew this was quite wrong, for Poorniah was, after the first two or three years, almost entirely left to his own devices, but I said nothing; indeed he hardly gave me time to make any remark, but abruptly inquired, 'Who is this Krishna Rao that you have got about you?'

"I answered that he was the son of Hunamunt Rao, a very distinguished public servant, much trusted by Sir Thomas Munro and Mr. Chaplin, and who had been rewarded by a jaghire of 5,000 rupees a year. Krishna Rao was born and bred at Ooscotta in the Bangalore district, of which town he and his father were the hereditary Goomashtas. He was trained from his youth in the Revenue Department under his father, and succeeded him as Head Dufturdar at Poona, and subsequently as Head of the Dewan Duftur at Bombay, where his salary was 800 rupees a month. 'I had no acquaintance with him', I added, 'of an agreeable nature; indeed, I had only seen him once for five minutes casually in the Poona Office, but I knew he was employed some years ago, when I was in Khandesh, to make a tour through the country, and that he sent in a report to which I had to reply.'

"'Do you mean', said the Governor, 'that he was employed to scrutinise your administration?'

"'Yes, indeed', I answered, 'I knew very well what was going on then, and he acknowledges it now, and has told me exactly what his instructions were.'

"'Then how came he to think of coming here?'

"'I sent for him. I knew him to be a man of high character and ability. He was out of employ, and wrote to me at Hyderabad. I did not answer his letter till I reached Bangalore, when conceiving that the Government intended the Commissioners to remodel the administration of Mysore with men brought up in our own school, I wrote to my friend Mr. Nisbet, the Principal Collector of Dharwar, to send me Krishna Rao, who was residing in that district, and a few good Mamlutdars of the borders, who might be natives of Tippoo's Kingdom of Mysore.'

"'Aye, aye', said the Governor, 'and when he arrived, every-body gave out that he was to be your Dewan, and that the other was to be displaced.'

"'I never gave sanction to such a report; nor do I believe did Krishna Rao. If reports were to render people ineligible for office, I ought to have been incapacitated long ago, for scarcely a week has passed since I came here that I have not heard of my intended removal next Council day.'

"'Ah, I dare say', said the Governor. 'I believe Bangalore is rather famous for originating reports and scandals.'

"I said it was like all other large stations, where there were many people who had little to do but gad about and gossip.

"'Well, Colonel Briggs, you now see the footing on which you stand. The Governor-General's instructions are plain enough, and though you have been in error, we are all, as I said before, liable to error, and I trust you will not misunderstand me for the future, and that you will agree well with Mr. Drury. I have been very candid with you, and have explained all that I expect; and if you act in the spirit I recommend, you may rely on my support.'

"I bowed and left the room."

This interview took place on the 3rd of April. Not many days passed before Colonel Briggs had a specimen of the "support" he had to expect from the Right Honble. Stephen Lushington. On the 4th the Commissioners met for business, which chiefly consisted of the investigation into the conduct of Gholam Mohammed Khan. The despatch from the Governor-General of the 27th of February was formally read, and a resolution passed that, "in obedience to the orders contained in its concluding paragraph, measures be taken for giving immediate effect to the views and instructions of the Supreme Government." The Junior Commissioner did not positively object to this resolution being recorded, but he was of opinion that it was quite unnecessary and super-fluous, as the letter afforded no new instructions, and its application must be left to the Madras Government, under whose immediate orders the Commission was placed. This was a slight hint to Colonel Briggs of the Governor's intentions, but he little thought of what was coming.

The Governor of Madras still remained at Bangalore.

The two Commissioners met almost every day at their board-room for the despatch of business. The Governor and his brother, the Resident, the Junior Commissioner and the Dewan, had their meetings almost every day to compass the defeat and downfall of the Senior Commissioner. On the 5th of April the Governor gave a grand ball, at which Colonel Briggs was present. The very next day a heavy blow was struck at the Senior Commissioner, well calculated either to crush him at once, by rendering him powerless and contemptible, or to provoke him to some rash and intemperate course destructive of his interest with the Governor-General, and necessitating his removal.

The Governor-General, in the despatch of the 27th of February, had disapproved "the restrictions imposed upon the Commissioners in respect to the appointment of Native officers", and had ruled that "the responsibility for proper officers being employed should rest with the Commissioners, who must have the power of nomination and dismissal".* The Governor of Madras was determined that, even if the Commissioners must have the power of nominating and appointing Native officers, those Native officers whom the Senior Commissioner would wish to nominate and appoint should be put out of his way.

On the 6th of April, when the Commissioners met at the Board, a despatch from the Governor, dated on the previous day, sent from a few hundred yards distance, was laid before them, stating that "idle rumours" had been "propagated through the agency of intriguing and interested individuals", "calculated to produce serious mischief, by encouraging the pernicious designs of abandoned characters", to the effect that "a general change was contemplated of the Native officers under the orders of the Commission, whose places were to be supplied from amongst strangers who have been assembled in expectation of employment at this place." It was, therefore, ordered that six persons, "named in the margin", who were "suspected of being most particularly interested

* *Ante*, p. 177.

in the diffusion of these reports", should be expelled under police escort from Bangalore, " the seat of the Commission", within twenty-four hours. " If any of them" were " Natives of the country", they should be directed "to repair to their respective villages"; if "residents of Bangalore", they " must choose some other place of abode"; if not Natives of Mysore, they must " proceed beyond the frontiers of the territory".

Not one of those proscribed in this despatch was a " stranger"; they were all Natives of Mysore. Colonel Briggs was known to take a strong personal interest in two of them,—Krishna Rao, who was avowedly his right-hand man, and Gholam Mohammed Khan, the ex-Bukhshee. At his interview with the Governor, on the 3rd of April, he had been questioned as to Krishna Rao, and had expressed a high opinion of his capabilities and character. On the 5th of April the Governor ordered Krishna Rao to be turned out of the place. There could be no doubt or question for whom the blow was intended.

Not one of these persons had been convicted, or even accused, of any crime or misdemeanour. Their sole offence was that they bowed not, nor did reverence, before the Dewan, and that they sat in the gate of the Senior Commissioner. The despatch itself admits of no other meaning.

Briggs at once recorded a Minute protesting against this extraordinary measure, and appealing to the Governor for its modification, so far at least as Krishna Rao was concerned.

" It is not for me", he said, " to oppose the execution of any orders of the Right Honble. the Governor, but it is a duty I owe to the station I fill at this Board to record my dissent from a measure like this. No proofs are brought before us of its necessity ; and I can hardly believe that an act so prompt, not originating with the Board, can have the effect of giving strength to the local Government established by the Governor-General."

In this Minute he declared, as he had explained clearly enough to the Governor on previous occasions, that he

wanted the services of Krishna Rao for his own personal
assistance, and that he desired on the first opportunity,
—as soon, in fact, as the Governor would sanction the
formation of permanent establishments,—to place him in
one of the highest offices in Mysore.   He referred to
Krishna Rao's distinguished official career and un-
blemished character, quoted the flattering testimonials
he had received from the English officers under whom
he had served, and from the Bombay Government, and
concluded by trusting that on reconsideration the Right
Honble. the Governor would not " degrade" this exem-
plary public servant, or "deprive" Colonel Briggs "of
his aid".

Though it was necessary to go through the form of
making this reference, Briggs knew perfectly well that
his request would be refused.   It was very promptly
refused.   Moreover, the Colonel having unfortunately
mentioned that Krishna Rao was no "stranger", but
was born and brought up at Ooscotta, a town about
sixteen miles from Bangalore, of which he was the
hereditary record-keeper, the Governor directed that he
should not be considered as a Native of Mysore, and
allowed " to repair to his own village", as ordered in the
original despatch.   The Governor strongly objected to
Colonel Briggs employing "a confidential agent not in
the public service",—as if it was Colonel Briggs's fault
that he was not in the public service,—declaring that
this would be merely "bringing back a repetition of
those days of *dubash* influence which in former times"
had been " the fruitful source of discord, corruption, and
failure".

" The Right Honble. the Governor has learnt", the
despatch continued, " that Krishna Rao has not resided
in the Mysore country for thirty years, that his *jaghire*
is in the Dharwar district, and that his pension is payable there also.   It is not, therefore, expedient that he
should be permitted to remain at Ooscotta, upon the
pretext of his being a Native of that village; and the
Right Honble. the Governor desires that no time may
be lost in sending Krishna Rao beyond the frontiers of
the Mysore country."

This despatch was dated the 9th of April 1832.   The Colonel's diary of the 10th contains the following entries :—

"Every Native of rank and respectability who has entered my doors since my return to Bangalore has now been expelled from the Mysore country, with the exception of one, a grain-contractor, whose removal at this time would injuriously affect the supply of the troops.

"Krishna Rao came in the evening, sealed up all his papers, and left them with me, with a catalogue.   He is to call to-morrow morning early to enable me to translate some papers for my use before he goes.   He has been permitted to go to Koryconda, Zilla Bellary, seventy-two miles from hence, where his family reside, instead of Dharwar, as originally ordered.

"11th April.   Krishna Rao called at 11 a.m. with his relations, and took leave.   He said it was industriously circulated by the Dewan's party that the Governor had written to Bombay and Bengal to deprive him of his jaghire.   He did not believe it, but he felt the insult acutely, and was greatly dejected and afflicted, poor man, as well he might be.   I endeavoured to comfort him with assurances that the Governor-General would not support such persecution; and I told him plainly that I was confident that the Governor-General had long since decided the question as to my remaining here or not.   I told Krishna Rao to take example by me, and to bend before the raging of a storm which must be of short duration in proportion to its violence."

Proof that the Governor-General had long since decided in favour of Colonel Briggs, and against his persecutors, was very soon forthcoming.   On the 12th of April, the very day after the entry last quoted from the diary, it was reported that the Governor had received an express from Madras, "which came in the incredibly short space of thirty-one hours, very little less than seven miles an hour",*—that orders had been immediately given for moving with the utmost possible haste, that the tents were all struck and packed, and that the camp would be off the ground in another hour or two. The Governor left Bangalore for the Neilgherry Hills on the morning of the 13th, and before noon on that day the Commissioners received a despatch from him direct-

* It must be remembered that the mails were in those days carried by men who ran with them on foot.

ing them to suspend the operation of any orders that might arrive from the Governor-General until they had got the Governor's own instructions upon them. Evidently something very unpleasant had arrived from the Supreme Government, and the Governor of Madras had assumed a dispensing power until he could circumvent it. The breeze that had so suddenly broken up the Governor's camp was Lord William Bentinck's reply to Briggs's urgent appeal of the 23rd of February, in the form of a Minute dated the 24th of March. The Governor's copy arrived by express on the 12th of April, and that for the Commissioners on the morning of the 15th. After observing that he has received from Lieutenant-Colonel Briggs an appeal against "the harshness evinced towards him by the Madras Government", the Governor-General proceeds as follows :—

"I feel myself on the present occasion placed in a distressing predicament, but I also feel that I should ill perform my duty were I to be restrained by motives of delicacy from a declaration of my sentiments. Impressed with this conviction, I must reluctantly, but deliberately, declare that it would have better consisted with what is due to the station of the Senior Commissioner in Mysore, as well as to the dignity of the Madras Government, had a different tone been adopted in the instructions furnished to that officer.

"4. I am far from wishing to screen any public functionary, still less one of my own selection, from a fair and candid exposure of his errors; but at the same time I must not shrink from extending to him my protection when I feel satisfied that his conduct has been actuated by correct and honourable motives.

"5. Under feelings of irritation produced by reproof which he considered to be unmerited, Colonel Briggs has suffered himself to be betrayed into a warmth of expression for which he is justly censurable, and I entreat the Right Honble. the Governor in Council to reflect how materially the interests of the public service have already been injured by the course of proceeding which has been pursued.

"6. I have seen nothing in the proceedings of Colonel Briggs to alter the favourable opinion which his public reputation alone, and his selection by His Majesty's late Ministry to fill the important office of Envoy in Persia, had led me to form; and I yet indulge the hope that the same degree of confidence may be reposed in him by the Governor of Madras, and that in conducting the momentous duties confided to his charge, he may be encouraged by the support of the authorities to whom he is subordinate.

"7. But it behoves me to omit no precaution by which failure can be obviated; and I deem it indispensable to issue distinct instructions on three points, without which it would be vain to expect a successful administration of the affairs of Mysore. These three points are the following :—

"8. First, the character and past occupations of the individual now filling the office of Dewan are not such as to justify the belief that he is capable of fulfilling the duties of that eminent situation with impartiality and efficiency. The Senior Commissioner is convinced of his incapacity, and with this conviction, even were it not well founded, it is quite impossible that the affairs of the country could be creditably managed. I have, therefore, to request that the Right Honourable the Governor in Council will be pleased to give authority to the Commissioners for the immediate removal of the person in question from the office of Dewan.

"Secondly, the whole of the patronage, from the highest office in the State, including that of Dewan, down to the lowest, must rest in the Commissioners, and it is absolutely necessary that no appeal should be allowed to the Madras Government regarding removal from, and appointment to, such offices. The Commissioners being responsible for the public conduct of affairs, the choice of their subordinate instruments should (as stated in my instructions of the 27th ultimo) be left entirely to them. Any interference in this department would only embarrass their administration, and convert the officers of State from useful instruments into factious opponents, by teaching them to look to other authority besides the Commission for promotion and support. In fact it would be impossible to hold the Commission responsible for the Government of Mysore, if their subordinates in any degree were to be supported in office against their authority.

"Thirdly, with a view to secure a prompt decision of all questions that may come before them, it is important to define accurately the relative powers of the two Commissioners. It should be understood, therefore, that in all matters (including questions of patronage, of appointment, or removal from office), the Senior Commissioner for the time being is to have the casting voice, and his opinion must be considered as representing the will of the Commission."

The Government of Madras had sharply reprimanded Colonel Briggs for giving some direct instructions to Major James, an officer in charge of a detachment in one of the disturbed districts, instead of applying to the superior military authorities. "With reference to the censure passed on the conduct of Colonel Briggs on that occasion, I cannot help", said Lord William Bentinck, "recording my opinion that it was unnecessarily severe, even admitting (which is to me by no means clear) that he had erred in the exercise of a discretion to which he could have resorted with no other purpose in view than the benefit of the public service."

The Governor-General observed that the Senior Commissioner, Colonel Briggs, had proposed, in his letter of appeal, "to furnish a history of the late insurrection, and of the present state of Mysore, and as nothing has yet appeared on this very important subject in a detailed and connected form, I consider", said his Lordship, "that this design should be fulfilled." Major-General Hawker, commanding the Mysore Division, was to be associated with the two Commissioners in a Committee "for the special purpose of framing a report on the origin, progress, and suppression of the recent disturbances".

"The proclamation of a general amnesty", the Governor-General went on to say, "and the establishment of a Court of Justice, are measures of such paramount importance that they will doubtless have already been carried into effect."

These were two of the measures which Briggs had unceasingly pressed on the attention of the Madras Government, but which had hitherto met with nothing but supercilious and vexatious obstruction.

———

CHAPTER XI.

It might now have been supposed that Colonel Briggs, being fairly and firmly seated as head of the local government of Mysore, relieved from the incubus of the Dewan, and authorised, if necessary, to overrule the opposition of his colleague, would at last be able to work freely. It was not quite so easy. The Governor, under whose immediate command the Commission was placed, chose to exercise a dispensing power over the Governor-General's orders, and forbade their execution pending the issue of his own definite instructions. The Dewan could not be removed from office, and the Senior Commissioner could not make use of his casting vote, until the Governor-General's decrees were ratified, and, perhaps, qualified, by the Governor of Madras.

With the Province of Nuggur still in a state of disturbance and anarchy, the collection or loss of its revenue dependent entirely on the speedy restoration of quiet and confidence, and the rainy season approaching, every day of delay was dangerous, and might be disastrous. Briggs gave expression to his impatience and perplexity at this time, in a letter dated the 26th of April, to his friend, Colonel W. Morison, then Resident at Travancore.*

"Was ever human being placed in such a situation? His Lordship assures me of his support, but while I am subjected to the authority of my determined opponents, and bound to be obedient and respectful to them, how is it possible for me to do my duty and avoid blame? Seeing all this before me as clearly as I did at first, I ought not, perhaps, to have accepted the office. Nobly supported as I have been, I have nearly sunk under the struggle, and I hardly hope to get through it now. The Governor-General

* He succeeded Briggs as Commissioner of Mysore, and was afterwards Member of the Supreme Council of India.

can hardly overlook the fact of the Governor coming here, and acting in open and personal opposition to me, after the receipt of the despatch of the 27th February, and continuing to interfere and to obstruct business after the Minute of the 24th March. The Governor-General's orders are clear and positive, but Mr. Lushington has suspended their execution in so artful a manner that I am at a loss to know whether responsibility may not attach to me for suffering all our affairs to be thus brought to a standstill. It is so difficult to trim between forbearance and action. If I were a mere soldier I could see my way well enough; in military matters the chain of subordination almost always proves where the responsibility rests. But in ruling a kingdom it is different; the machine of government cannot be idle without danger. During the whole of my stay here my task has been that of preventing an explosion by persuading all classes that matters would soon be settled. My word will not be taken much longer, and my position is becoming contemptible. Their patience is exhausted. The arbitrary banishment of men of distinction and high character for the sole crime of helping me in public matters,—the treatment of Gholam Mohammed Khan and others of rank, have excited a feeling of hatred and disgust that cannot be described. I am cut off from every source of intelligence. The first men in the State, whose co-operation I require, write that they are now afraid to approach me from fear of losing their *ábroo*. I could act boldly at once, but I dread incurring censure for disrespect towards the Governor; and yet I shall probably be driven to do something in a few days, for matters cannot remain as they are."

In a few days he was driven to do something. The most pressing things to be done were the displacement of the Dewan Vencatarāmāniah, and the installation of his successor, which could only be carried out at Bangalore; and, secondly, the pacification of Nuggur, which required a tour to be taken through the disturbed districts by one or other of the Commissioners. But the Governor was in no hurry to give the word for the Dewan's removal, and on the subject of the disturbances in Nuggur, delay was caused by a difference of opinion. Colonel Briggs, besides being bent on a sweeping dismissal of the corrupt and oppressive officials in that Province, was in favour of publishing a general amnesty for all insurgents who would come in by a certain date,— a few leading offenders excepted, who had been personally engaged in acts of atrocity,—so that the chiefs and their

followers might return to their homes as soon as possible,
and cultivation and commerce be resumed. The Governor,
on the contrary, preferring the Resident's views, the
Junior Commissioner heartily concurring, would not
admit the misdeeds of the relatives and creatures of the
Dewan and the Residency Moonshee, but directed a proclamation to be issued denouncing the Polygar chiefs
who were " out" in the jungle as common robbers, whom
everyone ought to resist and endeavour to apprehend,
calling on the population, as " the best guardians of their
own property", "to make use of fire-arms and other offensive weapons to secure themselves, their houses, and their
property against the incursion of such depredators", and
offering large rewards for their capture. Colonel Briggs,
knowing that the natives of these districts were always
ready enough to take up arms in their own quarrels
without that " earnest encouragement" from the British
Commissioners which the Governor of Madras recommended, considered that this invitation to them to take
up the neglected or mismanaged work of the troops and
police was a confession of weakness and a dereliction of
duty on our part, and would probably operate as a public
authorisation of blood-feuds and faction fights. He, therefore, expressed his disagreement with this policy, but, as
the orders of the Madras Government were imperative,
proposed their being carried out forthwith by the Junior
Commissioner, who should proceed in person to the scene
of action. He urged, with much reason, that " no
measures could be so likely to succeed in the settlement
of the disturbed district as those wherein the views of
the person actually employed were in complete union
with those of the Right Honble. the Governor". In the
meantime he would remain at Bangalore, and give his
attention to remodelling the public service at head-
quarters and in the provinces, to forming a code of
regulations for the judicial department, and to the all-
important question of the finances.

The Junior Commissioner having warmly objected to
go on the expedition to Nuggur, Colonel Briggs at once
offered to undertake it, and to hold himself in readiness

to march at the earliest practicable moment.   But he was determined not to go until the change had been completed in the important place of Dewan.   For this two transactions were necessary, the resignation or removal of the Dewan, and the acceptance of office by a suitable successor.   The Dewan would certainly not resign without the express orders of his patron, the Governor of Madras.   So long as a desire to serve under the Senior Commissioner seemed productive of insult and exile, no one of eminence and character would venture to accept his nomination.

On the 28th of April permission was received from the Governor to act on the Governor-General's instructions by calling on the Dewan for his resignation.   But it was useless to take advantage of this permission until some one was ready to take up the duties of the office.   This no eligible person would do as long as the proscriptions remained in force.   The person on whom Colonel Briggs had fixed to fill the expected vacancy—Baboo Rao, an old Brahmin of rank residing at Mysore, who had previously occupied the place of Dewan for three years with great credit—refused even to pay him a visit at Bangalore without a written assurance that he should incur no penalty, and be exposed to no affront.   "Those who have before come on your invitation", he wrote, "and others who came of their own accord, men of the highest respectability, have been turned out of the place, and even directed to quit the Mysore territory, without any crime.   Persons, therefore, who have acquired reputation by their services under the Nawabs Hyder and Tippoo Sultan, and have served with honour ever since, are now apprehensive of coming."

Why was the Senior Commissioner of Mysore, Briggs argued with himself, to hesitate any longer in using the powers with which the Governor-General had invested him ?   The Minute of the 24th of March was sent expressly to the Commissioners, and was intended as much for their guidance as for the Governor's.   The Governor was bound to obey the Governor-General's orders, and so were they.   Those orders were that "the whole of the patronage, from the highest office in the State, including that of Dewan, down to the lowest, must rest in the Commissioners"; that "no appeal should be allowed to the Madras Government regarding removals or appointments"; that "the Commissioners being responsible for the public conduct of affairs, the choice of their subordinate instruments" was to "be left entirely to them", and that "any interference in this department would only embarrass their administration".*

It was impossible that the Governor's arbitrary banishment of candidates for office favoured by the Senior Commissioner should hold good in the face of these orders. The Commissioners could not, it was clear, have "the choice of their subordinate instruments", if those whom they had chosen, or were likely to choose, were placed beyond their reach. When the Governor of Madras resorted to that extraordinary measure, it was in pursuance of his avowed policy of leaving the patronage in the hands of the Dewan, and of upholding that functionary's authority on a level with that of the Commissioners. That policy had now been condemned and annulled by the Supreme Government. The Dewan was to have no voice in the patronage, but was, in common with all the officers of state, to be in strict subordination to the Commissioners, and to look to no "other authority for promotion or support". In the total disallowance of the Governor's policy, and the prohibition of his interference with the Commissioners' patronage, all restrictions on their patronage were necessarily disallowed. Whether the Governor of Madras formally withdrew those restrictions or not, they were null and void, and the orders which the Commissioners had passed in consequence of them could no longer remain in force. No order on the subject had been published by the Governor of Madras; none, therefore, would have to be publicly withdrawn or noticed.

At the meeting of the Commissioners on the 5th of May, Briggs accordingly proposed, and carried by his casting vote, a resolution that the persons exiled in pur-

* *Ante*, p. 188.

suance of the instructions received from the Governor of
Madras should be informed that the orders given to them
by the Commissioners of Mysore on the 9th of April
"being now deemed unnecessary", they were "permitted to proceed and reside wherever they pleased".
Briggs writes in his diary,—

"I never acted with more deliberation than I have done in this
business. I could not start for Nuggur without constituting the
reformed establishments. My endeavours to call around me the
first men in the State had failed, and I was assured that till these
proscriptions were removed, no one unconnected with the present
Dewan and the Residency gang would trust himself near me. To
have applied again to the Governor of Madras to reconsider the
question involved a great loss of time, when there was no more
time to be lost, if I wanted to secure a week or two of fine weather
in Nuggur before the rain set in. Besides, if a reconsideration had
been applied for and refused,—as it certainly would have been,
with Mr. Casamajor's vote at the Council,—I could not have taken
off the proscriptions, in defiance of a renewed prohibition, though
I might venture to do it on the assumption that they were incompatible with the Governor-General's orders, and consequently of
no effect. I knew that I was risking a reprimand, but without
running that risk, I could not reform a single office. I throw
myself on the Governor-General's protection. With my own
agents about me, I shall soon be able to prove that I am worthy
of the high trust confided in me, and that I can exercise the power
with which I am armed without abusing it.

"I sent a special messenger to Mysore, and Baboo Rao was
persuaded with some difficulty to come to Bangalore, where he
arrived on the 13th. Even after his interview with me he was
in great apprehension as to the influence of the present Dewan
with the Governor, the Resident, and the Junior Commissioner.
His first anxiety was to satisfy himself that I could protect him
from similar disgrace to that imposed on others against whom
there was no charge. He told me that had I not removed the
proscriptions, he would not have come to Bangalore, even to pay
me a visit."

Everything at this time tended to strengthen the
influence adverse to Colonel Briggs at Madras, and to
reassure the party connected with the Residency as to
continued help and support from that quarter. On the
very day, the 13th of May, a Sunday, that Baboo Rao
arrived at Colonel Briggs's house, and consented to accept

the place of Dewan, Mr. Casamajor, the Resident, also
arrived at Bangalore, on his way to Madras, where he
was to take his seat as Acting Member of Council,
received the Dewan in office, his own nominee, with
marked graciousness and some degree of publicity, and
was understood to have spoken to him in the most encouraging terms, and to have given him renewed promises of protection on the part of the Madras Government. The Dewan Vencatarāmāniah boasted without
disguise that he could not be removed unless he sent in
his resignation, and avowed his determination not to do
so.   And in truth the despatch from the Governor appears to have been worded as if to confine the Commissioners to receiving the Dewan's resignation, if he chose
to repeat an offer to that effect, which he was said to
have recently made to the Governor of Madras in person.
Any reference to the Government of Madras, or to the
Supreme Government, would have delayed matters for a
period which might be a fortnight, and might be six
weeks ; and as Briggs had now secured a competent
successor for the Dewan, and had no doubt as to the
Governor-General's intentions, he was determined that
there should be no more delay.

At the Board meeting of the next day, Monday, 14th
May, Briggs accordingly moved that the Dewan Vencatarāmāniah should be sent for, that his immediate resignation should be required, and that Baboo Rao should be
appointed in his place.   The Junior Commissioner protested against so high a functionary being treated in such
an unceremonious manner, and proposed that a letter
should be addressed to him, and a fair time allowed for
him to send in his reply.   This being overruled, he
brought forward several dilatory motions—as that the
Dewan's resignation should not be accepted until his
accounts were audited and passed; that Baboo Rao should
not be appointed until a full report on his antecedents
had been obtained from the Residency—to none of which
the Senior Commissioner would accede.

The Dewan was called in, and the substance of the
Governor-General's Minute and of the Governor's de-

spatch relating to himself having been explained to him, he was requested to resign his office. This, with all the grave dignity and humble self-possession of a courtly Brahmin, he positively declined to do, adding that if the Governor-General desired his removal, his resignation was quite unnecessary, and that he had no objection to being dismissed. He denied, also, having tendered his resignation to the Governor ; and said that he had merely expressed his willingness to resign, if the Governor was dissatisfied with his conduct. " And if that be the case now", he said, " I am quite ready to resign, but not otherwise."

Briggs firmly set aside every suggestion of a misunderstanding as a plea for adjourning the question. In reply to his colleague's repeated proposals of a postponement, he declared at last that he would not quit his chair that day until the Dewan had been removed, and his successor installed in office. When all the necessary documents for this change of ministry had been drawn up, signed and sealed, the Senior Commissioner laid upon the table the finished results of his labours in the closet during the previous three months,—complete plans for the reorganisation of every department, in method as well as in men, and circulars ready for immediate issue, restoring the judicial functions of the Potails and Amils in the villages and districts, and supplying forms for keeping and forwarding periodical registers, and also proclamations pointing out where the people ought to go, and how they ought to proceed, in order to obtain redress of their grievances, or a settlement of their disputes.

Most of the removals and appointments to office were opposed by the Junior Commissioner,—in two instances on account of persons being nominated who had been proscribed by the Governor,—but Briggs was now determined on losing no more time, and within five days of the installation of the new Dewan, all these arrangements were carried out, and the Senior Commissioner started from Bangalore for the disturbed districts of Nuggur.

During Briggs's absence from Bangalore, his irreconcilable colleague contrived to revive the hopes of the Resi-

dency faction, and to renew a general feeling of instability
and insecurity among those who had recently been placed
in office, by the very simple process of stopping their pay.
Having been left, by his own desire, at head-quarters, to
carry on the routine business of the Commission, he refused to countersign the monthly bills, on the plea that
neither the salaries nor the appointments had been confirmed by the Governor of Madras, although the new
establishments were less costly than those already sanc-
tioned, and although the Supreme Government had ruled
that "the whole of the patronage must rest in the Commissioners"; that "the choice of their subordinates
should be left entirely to them"; that there should be "no
appeal to Madras regarding appointments to office", and
that "any interference in this department would only
embarrass their administration".

After a hard day's work in camp, Briggs had his evening
enlivened by his confidential Native Secretary reading
him extracts of a letter just received from Bangalore.

"The refusal to countersign the pay-abstracts has thrown all the
public servants into dismay. Some of them have been waiting
many months in the hope of employment; they have borrowed
money, or lived on credit, but now the shop-keepers have taken
alarm, and will trust them no longer. The ex-Dewan Vencatarāmāniah exultingly said, 'Well, how is it with your fine courts of
justice and new departments? You see matters have taken another
turn. You are all a set of simpletons. Only wait fifteen or twenty
days, and you will see a pretty sight.' This measure has infused
such joy into the minds of the ex-Dewan's party, that an express
was instantly despatched to Chowrappa, the Resident's Sheristadar,
at Mysore, with the glad tidings. On the ex-Dewan being asked
lately why he still remained at Bangalore, he said 'he had made
all preparations for going to his own village, when he was desired
by the Junior Commissioner to stay a short time, and see what
would take place'."

Whether these assertions were true or false, they were
generally believed, and had a most injurious effect on
the progress of affairs. From the first, it had been the
great object of the Dewan and his patrons at the Residency to prevent Colonel Briggs from settling the disturbed districts by amnesty and conciliation. Knowing

such measures to bring with them the certainty of inquiries and explanations that would expose their extortions and iniquities, their plan was to foment the general confusion until refractory remonstrants were trans-
formed into contumacious rebels, when all old scores
would be wiped out or clouded over, and totally new
issues raised, amid the din and smoke of military coercion.
Within the last week of the Dewan's administration
Briggs received nine proposals of surrender from leading
chieftains who were "out" in the jungle, but the Dewan
was at the same time sending secret orders that they
should be followed up and attacked. The object of Colonel
Briggs was to reassure and conciliate the Polygars. The
object of the Dewan and his partisans, the district officers,
was to drive the Polygars to despair. As long as the
Dewan and his creatures remained in office it was in vain
for the Senior Commissioner to hope for the success of
his policy. Two days before the Dewan's removal, just
as Briggs had obtained permission, with some difficulty,
from the Governor of Madras to accept the unconditional
submission of the Polygars of Terrykerry, the Foujdar
of Nuggur, acting on a hint from his relative the Dewan,
tried to surprise their encampment with a body of 300
Horse, and to effect their capture. He failed completely
in this attempt, but he burned their houses, destroyed
some of their property, and, by this appearance of double
dealing, nearly frustrated the Senior Commissioner's endeavours to calm excitement and to bring the fugitives to
reason. Other instances of delay and neglect in execut-
ing orders were attributable to the same counteracting
cause. Impatient and indignant at these petty obstruc-
tions to the good work in which he felt himself to be
engaged, and, perhaps, a little too much elated by what
seemed a complete and final assurance of the Governor-
General's sympathy and support, Briggs now took a step
which exercised a most injurious and durable influence
over his professional interests and prospects. And yet
the step that he took will, I think, appear to most people
to have been perfectly natural and logical under the
circumstances of the time—to have been the step best

calculated to make him, as the Governor-General seemed
to intend him to be, master of the situation. In the
midst of the exasperating perplexities that harassed his
solitary hours in camp, he received on the 10th of July a
letter from the Secretary to the Government of India
telling him that Lord William Bentinck had resolved that
" the Mysore Commission should be placed in immediate
subordination to the Supreme Government", and that
" Mr. G. E. Drury will consider himself relieved from his
duties as Junior Commissioner on your receipt of this
communication", and forwarding extracts from a Minute
by the Governor-General having reference to the subject,
dated " Simla, 26th May 1832." The extract commenced
with paragraph 32, the preceding part having doubtless
contained some strong language regarding the Madras
Government, which it was considered unadvisable to show
to Colonel Briggs. The purport of the new rules was
that the Commissioners were henceforth to correspond
directly with the Governor-General, and that the
Governor of Madras was to have no authority whatever
over the Mysore Commission ; nor was it " considered
requisite that duplicates of the Commissioners' correspondence with the Supreme Government should be
furnished to the Madras Government". The vacant
place of Mr. Drury was filled up by the Governor-
General with the name of Mr. John Macpherson Macleod, of the Madras Civil Service ;* but in the event of
any circumstances preventing, or postponing for some
time, that gentleman's assumption of his duties, none of
the full powers of the Mysore Commission were to be held
in abeyance. " Colonel Briggs", said Lord William Bentinck, in his Minute, " from the time of his receiving these
orders, may exercise solely the full powers of the Commission until I shall have an opportunity of providing
him with a colleague."

All perplexity now ceased ; all hesitation was now at
an end. Feeling himself left to his own judgment, and
invested with the authority for which he had asked, and

* Afterwards Member of the Indian Law Commission and K.C.S.I.,
—died in 1882, at the age of 90.

believing himself assured of the firm support of the Governor-General, the Senior Commissioner at once proceeded to act. He recorded a Minute on the proceedings of the Commission, directing the immediate issue of a proclamation " calculated to ensure the future obedience of all public functionaries, and to put an end at once to the intrigues which have so long embarrassed the administration." The proclamation ran as follows :—

"It is hereby proclaimed for general information, that the Right Honble. the Governor-General of India has been pleased to place the Commission under his own direct authority, and has conferred on the Commissioners full powers to nominate and appoint all the subordinate officers, and to conduct the duties of the Government on their own responsibility. It is now accordingly notified that all persons giving currency to rumours affecting the permanency or validity of any measures of removal or appointment to offices, which may embarrass the proceedings of those filling them, and which may distract or delay the public business of the State, such persons will be considered as enemies to the Government and disturbers of the public peace of the country, and will, on due conviction, be punished, and, if it be found necessary, be even liable to be banished from Mysore. Every Mamlutdar in Mysore is desired to give publicity to this proclamation, and after having done so, to paste it on some conspicuous place in the town in which he resides, and to report to the Commission that he has done so."

It certainly may be objected to this proclamation,— the objection was made officially from Calcutta,—that it threatened certain persons with the same summary and arbitrary penalty of exile from Mysore which Colonel Briggs had considered so unjust when enforced against his own adherents by the Governor of Madras. But the Senior Commissioner only menaced the disaffected intriguers with punishment " on due conviction". The Governor of Madras had, on the contrary, banished and proscribed a number of respectable persons without either trial or accusation.

Exception was particularly taken at Calcutta to the form and style of a proclamation, as being a procedure at once disrespectful to the Government of Madras, and calculated, by encouraging familiarity with the higher official mysteries, to breed contempt of authority. Colonel Briggs, however, had chosen the form of a proclamation because publicity was essential for his purpose.   In those days there were no vernacular newspapers, and it was necessary to prevent by authentic information the confusing and contradictory rumours that would soon have been spread abroad regarding the change that had taken place in the relations of the Mysore Commissioners with the Governor of Madras.   At the same time Colonel Briggs had the good taste and tact to avoid, in the papers which he circulated, any direct mention of the Madras Government, as he had also carefully done when recalling the exiles from banishment.

It is a remarkable fact, and confirmatory to some extent of the decision at which Colonel Briggs arrived, that when a somewhat similar crisis arose in Mysore at a much later period, the Commissioner at once thought of adopting the same plan of a general proclamation. From 1864 to 1867 rumours were prevalent—not without some foundation, for the Secretary of State had at one time resolved on restoration, but was overruled by the Cabinet—that the Maharajah was to be replaced at the head of the Mysore Government, only two or three English officers being retained to exercise control over financial and judicial affairs.   Mr. Bowring, then Chief Commissioner of Mysore, refers to this subject in a letter to the Government of India, dated 18th February 1864, from which the following passage is an extract :—

" As the Province of Mysore has for nearly three years been kept in a state of agitation and uncertainty respecting the Rajah's claim to recover the administration of the territory, and as the wildest and most improbable reports have been circulated regarding its final issue, I originally proposed to put forth a proclamation announcing to the people generally the fact that the Government had decided that his Highness would not be allowed to reassume the reins of power.   To some extent this course was desirable also in the case of the Native officials, many of whom, and especially the elder men and a few influential persons whom I need not name, held a divided allegiance, which is scarcely to be wondered at, and had shared in the intrigues which have been going on for some time past.

" As, however", he continues, " I understand it to be the desire of Government to spare his Highness any mortification which might without detriment be avoided, I have contented myself with forwarding to the Superintendents copies of the orders received, which will thus become gradually known publicly, though in a manner which cannot be offensive to the Maharajah's feelings."*

Mr. Bowring does not seem to have felt—he certainly does not express—any doubt as to his full power to issue such a proclamation, or as to the complete regularity and propriety of publishing such a document, had he considered the occasion to be urgent. Had he decided on doing so, his proceedings would have been almost exactly parallel, in object as in form, with those proceedings which brought down on Colonel Briggs the displeasure of the Supreme Government in the manner thus described in his own words.

" In the midst of my difficulties in the Nuggur district, I received a letter from the Secretary to the Supreme Government, dated the 4th of June, which reached my hands only on the 26th of July, censuring severely as an act of ' unjustifiable presumption', and of great disrespect to the Government of Madras, my resolution and order of the 5th of May for permitting Krishna Rao and the other proscribed persons to return from exile. I considered, and still do consider, my justification to have been complete. I had avowed the heavy responsibility I was incurring, but I pleaded absolute necessity. If, after receiving what seemed to me full authority from the Governor-General, I had maintained the expulsion of those blameless persons, I should have been effectually prevented from forming an establishment of my own selection; and the directions of the Governor-General, which authorised me to use my casting vote in order to secure the necessary instruments of administration, would have been frustrated. These explanations, however, did not satisfy his Lordship. The Secretary was directed to convey the expression of the Governor-General's disapproval in the most unqualified manner, and to add that had it not been that the public service might have suffered, his Lordship would have thought it necessary to have suspended me from office until I could afford a satisfactory explanation. This reproof was, in fact, intended as an apology and consolation to the Government of Madras for the several mortifications arising out of their determined attacks on me. I have good reason, also, to believe now, though I had no suspicion of it at the time, that Lord William was beginning to see how difficult it would be to save Casamajor, if I had time to carry out my declared intention of getting at the records in the Residency and in the Rajah's Palace, and giving a full and true account of the origin of the insurrection, and the worst secrets of the Rajah's

* *Mysore Papers*, 112 of 1866, p. 38.

misgovernment. Every Civilian in Bengal was as desirous as those in Madras of getting rid of me, and the Governor-General was beginning to feel me as a thorn in the flesh.

"No sooner was the despatch containing this reprimand in the possession of the Madras Government than it was communicated to the Resident, and by him to the ex-Dewan. Reports were immediately circulated that my removal would take place in a very short time, that the new Dewan would be disgraced, all the new establishments broken up, and the ex-Dewan and his partisans restored to power. This was exultingly stated by the Resident in open durbar to the Rajah. Such was the extraordinary situation produced just at the moment the Governor-General had assumed the direct command over Mysore, and placed, for a time, all the authority of the Commission solely in my hands. The wide publicity given by the Madras Government and the Resident to the reproof and the reserved threat of suspension with which I was visited, neutralised the powers conferred on me, and effaced almost entirely the salutary effect of my recent proclamation. But blow followed blow. No sooner did my letter enclosing a copy of that same proclamation reach the Governor-General's camp than an adverse reply was drafted, disapproving and condemning the issue of such a document, which was also construed into a disrespectful demonstration aimed at the Right Honble. Stephen Lushington and his Councillors. From the hour I received that despatch I felt pretty sure that the tide had finally turned against me, and that I could not much longer hold my own against the whole force of the Madras and Bengal Civil Service.

"On my return to Bangalore, at the end of August 1832, I soon found that my new colleague, Mr. Macleod, had undisguisedly joined the faction of the ex-Dewan, at the head of which was placed, in fact, the Resident, Mr. Casamajor. The Governor and Councillors of Madras, Mr. C. M. Lushington, Mr. Drury, Mr. Casamajor, were all intimate personal friends of Mr. Macleod, who arrived at Bangalore prejudiced and pledged on their side, and sworn to wage war to the knife against the military interloper. He began the war at once, and his mode of attack at once revealed to me, what I had learned already from every quarter, that his base of operations, whether he knew it or not, was in the conclave of spies and intriguers directed by the ex-Dewan, and prompted by Mr. Casamajor, from whom Mr. Macleod received what he vainly imagined to be valuable and exclusive information. From the first he held aloof from the close and confidential intercourse to which I invited him. He so utterly misinterpreted my policy and mode of procedure, that he charged me—always under Mr. Casamajor's guidance—with seeking by underhand means the very object which I had, from the first, urged openly on my two successive colleagues, and on the Governor-General, as essential to the thorough rectification of Mysore affairs. I had repeatedly and continuously pointed out that to clear up the errors of the past, and to provide for the future restoration of Native government, the Commissioners ought to have personal access to the Rajah, as well as to the records of the Palace and the Residency. There was no secret, also, for the matter had been several times mentioned in conversation with my colleagues and assistants, and in my private correspondence with the Governor-General, that the Rajah had taken means to intimate to me his desire for an interview, and that I had responded in courteous and conciliatory terms, through a respectable and trustworthy person in my confidence, related to Baboo Rao, the Minister. There could have been no possible use in making any secret about it, for the object was now attainable, and, had I remained in office, close at hand. That was what was driving the conclave at the Residency to desperation, and they took the best means in their power, as it turned out, to get rid of me just in time. In express compliance with my request, the Governor-General, in his instructions of the 26th May, when taking the Commission and the Residency under his own direct orders, had made a new rule, quite sufficient for my purpose, providing for the Commissioners having interviews with the Rajah, 'to communicate personally on any important matters'. My colleague, Mr. Macleod, immediately on my arrival at Bangalore, forestalled my intention of at once arranging for personal communication with the Rajah, by recording a Minute, a mere mare's-nest as to facts, but most offensive in its tone, attacking me for having held secret correspondence with his Highness the Rajah, which had been discovered in a wonderful manner by the Resident. Now Mr. Macleod was a very different person from Mr. Drury. He was a man of very great ability, and, from various causes and connections, of considerable weight and influence. I was determined not to enter on a new period of controversy and recrimination, which might be long, and must be useless. I wanted to work, not to waste any more time. After briefly pointing out in a Minute recorded on our proceedings, the futile nature of the personal imputations against myself, I wrote on the 10th of September to the Governor-General, protesting against being hampered with another hostile colleague, earnestly recommending once more that the plan of a Board of two Commissioners might be altered so as to ensure unity of purpose and authority, and respectfully tendering my resignation of the place of Senior Commissioner."

The feelings and the proposals of Colonel Briggs at this time will be more clearly understood by some extracts from his private letter of the 10th of September 1832 to Lord William Bentinck.

"Previously to my reaching Bangalore, Mr. Casamajor, whose object is to prevent my going to Mysore, and to remove me, if possible, from the country by any means, came here and poisoned the mind of my colleague. The whole extent of my communications with the Rajah was fully and undisguisedly laid open in my Minute of the 4th instant. Mr. Macleod has had abundant time to make a specific charge, if there were any to be made, or to refute what I have said. I refer your Lordship to his Minute of the 6th, to mine of the 8th, and, lastly, to his of yesterday, as a sample of the mode in which he chooses to attack me. Human frailty can no longer bear the severe trials to which I have been subjected. Mr. Macleod was brought up in a Secretary's office, and transferred to the Board of Revenue without ever having been out of Madras for a day, or conducted business with a Native in his life. For the last fifteen years he has been a mere regulation-machine, looking out for mistakes in subordinates, and is notorious for the acrimony of his reproofs to all whom he can catch tripping in matters of routine and form. Such a man, my Lord, is not fit to conduct a Native government with Native agents. It is utterly impossible for such a man, so tutored and so prejudiced, to work harmoniously with me.

"I hope it will not be deemed presumptuous in me entreating your Lordship to look back on Sicily. Only fancy a Junior Commissioner taking you to task, and thwarting every measure you proposed, in concert with a Resident at the Court intriguing against you.

"Your Lordship could not have anticipated all this opposition. It is for you now to remove it, and I see but two possible remedies. There must either be a regular government according to our system in the three Presidencies, or a simple and economical Native administration under a sole Commissioner.

"If your Lordship should determine on having a sole Commissioner, make your selection among all the able men you have in India, and arm him with the fullest authority and confidence, as on other occasions. Let him act at his peril and on his own responsibility, keeping a diary of all his proceedings, as at present. There are many men well fitted for the office. For myself, I am sick at heart. I am able, I hope, at least to command a regiment or a brigade, and it would be a relief indeed to go back to military duty out of this fiery ordeal and purgatory."

The final decision of the Supreme Government, although not endorsing any of the offensive imputations against him, was adverse to Colonel Briggs on every point. In a despatch dated the 13th of November 1832, his resignation was accepted in the following terms :—

"Having performed the painful duty of accepting the resignation of Lieut.-Colonel Briggs, his Lordship deems it no more than justice to that officer to record his sense of the energy, activity, and zeal which he has displayed in the duties of Senior Commissioner. As far as his Lordship is able to judge, the exertions of Lieut.-Colonel Briggs have been judiciously directed in his successful efforts in restoring tranquillity to the Province of Nuggur.

"Lieut.-Colonel Briggs, on relinquishing the duties of Senior Commissioner in Mysore, will be pleased to proceed at his earliest convenience to assume charge of the Residency at Nagpore.

"With regard to the subjects discussed in the Minutes which accompanied your Acting-Secretary's letter, his Lordship feels compelled to observe that it was indiscreet in Lieut.-Colonel Briggs to hold any unofficial communication with the Rajah of Mysore, though in the transaction his Lordship can perceive nothing to detract from the character of honour and probity which Lieut.-Colonel Briggs has so long and so honourably borne.

"With respect to the recall of the individuals banished by the Government of Fort St. George, and the proclamation issued by Colonel Briggs, his Lordship directs me to state that the explanation lately afforded has not removed the impression which he originally entertained that the proclamation in question was exceedingly injudicious ; while the explanation contained in Lieut.-Colonel Briggs's letter of the 18th July, though it certainly shows that officer to have been placed in an embarrassing situation, yet it does not acquit him of the blame that has already been imputed to him. Having accepted the resignation of Colonel Briggs, his Lordship deems it superfluous to enter on any further comment with reference to these transactions."

The same express brought the following private letter from Lord William Bentinck :—

> " Camp, Allygurh,
> " *Nov.* 13*th*, 1832.

"Dear Sir,—I have to acknowledge the receipt of your letter of the 10th September, expressing a desire to be relieved from your present appointment, and it is impossible for me not to come to the conclusion that neither your own comfort, nor the good of the public service, could be promoted by your continuance in the Commission. I cannot alter its constitution. I believe it to be the form the best adapted to the Government of Mysore, with reference to the many considerations to be held in view ; and its failure must be attributed to the combination of a multitude of circumstances the most unfortunate, the most extraordinary, which, if purposely arranged by design, instead of being the result of accident, could not have more effectually damned the success of the measure. The whole transaction, from the beginning to the end, has been a series of the greatest embarrassments and the deepest mortifications to me. I lament the result, but it would only be adding to the pain I have already suffered to comment upon the causes of it. I have not been mistaken in the opinion I had formed of your possession of many of those high qualifications, ability, integrity, and experience, which peculiarly fitted you for the office. But you have been wanting in that degree of temper, prudence, and discretion requisite to encounter the opposition and violence which were opposed to you. I am happy to have it in my power to show to the world that your honour and character stand unimpeached in my opinion, by nominating you to the Residency of Nagpore on the departure of Mr. Grœme.

"Lieut.-Colonel Morrison has been appointed to succeed you, and in him you will find an honourable and independent protector against any intrigues that falsehood or revenge may attempt to raise up against you. "With respect, dear Sir,

"Your faithful servant,

"WM. BENTINCK."

The Governor-General, considers that Briggs had shown himself "wanting in temper and discretion", —the very points in which the Court of Directors, using those identical words, finally declared him to have had an "advantage" over the Madras Government ; —yet Lord William Bentinck admits that the Senior Commissioner had been opposed with "violence", and would probably be assailed with revengeful "intrigues" and "falsehood" after his departure. The truth is that he had, "from the beginning to the end", been on the defensive. If the Court of Directors had been in closer and more frequent communication with Calcutta, Briggs would have been more firmly supported, and his views as to unity of command and responsibility would have been imperatively pressed on the Government of India. But it must be remembered that in those days from nine to twelve months had to pass away before the answer to a despatch could come from the Home Government.

Colonel Briggs left Bangalore soon after the receipt of the Governor-General's orders, and before Christmas, 1832, was installed in the Residency at Nagpore.

CHAPTER XII.

IN a letter written from Nagpore on the 3rd of October 1833 to Augustus De Morgan, in London, Briggs throws some light on the changes that took place in the administration of Mysore in the first year after his departure.

" My successor, Colonel W. Morrison, a most able and honourable man, the late Commissary-General of the Madras Army, cannot read or write any Native language, and can speak very little Hindustani, so that he will be very dependent on interpreters, strangers to Mysore. Nearly all his time so far has been occupied on the Committee for inquiring into the origin and circumstances of the insurrection of 1830. My late colleague, Mr. Macleod is, I hear, heartily sick of the Mysore Commission. Not very proud, perhaps, of the part he acted when I was there, he tendered his resignation conditionally, but it was greedily laid hold on by the Governor-General, who instantly accepted it. No Junior Commissioner had been, or will be, nominated in his place. The very path I pointed out in vain to Lord William is now to be pursued, in obedience to the strict injunctions of the Home authorities, namely, the appointment of one supreme functionary, under whatever title his Lordship may please to give him, with sole responsibility, and subordinate only to the Governor-General. The plan will not be complete, nor will the machine work smoothly, if the Resident is left there, in close connection with the Rajah, and independent of the actual ruler of Mysore, the British Commissioner. The cause of all the troubles throughout my tenure of the Senior Commissionership was an unfortunate want of singleness of purpose in several quarters. It may seem boastful to say so, but no one but myself was thinking of nothing but the public work before us. Mr. Lushington wanted Mysore for his brother, and never forgave me for standing in his way. The Governor-General, as I did not understand till lately, was excessively anxious from the first, and all through the business, to screen the Resident, Mr. Casamajor, an old *protégé* and favourite of his own, so that while his despatches demonstrated that gentleman's incapacity to the perceptions of the Court of Directors, he still supported him both publicly and pri-

P

vately, and was glad to get me out of the way because I frankly avowed my aversion to the Residency party, and my conviction that they were answerable for the misrule of Mysore."

In a succession of letters from the India House in Leadenhall Street to the Government of Calcutta, the Court of Directors, from first to last, adopt and confirm all the forebodings and objections of the Senior Commissioner as to the scheme of dual control, and acknowledge, moreover, the manifest fact that all the good work in Mysore had been done by Colonel Briggs alone, impeded by his colleagues, and persecuted by the authorities at Madras. In a despatch, dated 6th March 1833, the Directors say :—

"We must observe that this unfortunate difference might have been anticipated. Two Commissioners with equal powers, appointed by two different Governments, the one a Military, the other a Civil Servant, could hardly be expected to act harmoniously together; and an officer appointed by one Government, and accountable to another, was not very likely to give satisfaction. It was, we think, unfortunate that two officers were appointed, when one, if properly selected, and allowed the number of Assistants necessary to relieve him from the burden of details, would not only have been sufficient, but preferable. When all the necessary qualities can be found in one man, unity in the directing head has numerous advantages."

After setting forth those advantages, almost in the words of Briggs himself, the despatch continues as follows :—

"We do not, however, observe in the letter from Mr. Prinsep to the Madras Government"—this is one of the letters finding fault with their treatment of Colonel Briggs—"any indication that you have become sensible of the inherent and incurable defect of the present plan, the absence of unity in the presiding head. Until this error is corrected, we are convinced that the machine will continue to work ill; and we therefore direct that instead of a Commission of two Members, a single functionary, properly qualified, and aided by the requisite number of European Assistants, be appointed to the charge of the Mysore country, and that he be superintended by the Government by which he is appointed."

In their letter of the 23rd April 1834, the Court regrets to find that " all their anticipations have been more than realised". Disunion between the Senior Commissioner and the Government of Madras has continued, and has become aggravated to such a degree, that "it would have been impossible for them to act together" any longer :—

"The advantage of temper and discretion does not, we are concerned to say, rest on the side of the Madras Government, whose strictures upon the conduct of Lieut.-Colonel Briggs were so manifestly the result of an unfortunate prepossession, and so entirely failed of being substantiated, that it was impossible for you on such grounds to remove Colonel Briggs. You had, therefore, no alternative short of that which you adopted, namely, to assume to yourselves the direct superintendence of Mysore, leaving the immediate agency in the hands of Lieut.-Colonel Briggs, and a colleague, selected, indeed, from the Madras establishment, but nominated by yourselves. In appointing Mr. Macleod you made a most unexceptionable choice.

"This was a considerable improvement, and it was attended with salutary effects.

"The Commission ceased to be a nullity, or worse than a nullity, for all purposes of good government ; and measures were taken with considerable promptitude for the reform of abuses and the pacification of the country. They were taken, however, mostly on the authority of the Senior Commissioner. Mr. Macleod found* the same difficulty as his predecessors had done in acting with Lieut.-Colonel Briggs. The latter officer ultimately tendered his resignation, which you accepted ; and the Commission now consists of Lieut.-Colonel Morrison and Mr. Macleod.

"Though we admit that the Commission as now constituted is free from many of the objections to which it was liable, we shall be glad to learn that our orders for reducing it to one Member can be carried out without public inconvenience."

To one piece of work to which Briggs himself attached much importance, the pacification of Nuggur, the Court of Directors did full justice. In the despatch which has just been quoted they say :—"One part of Lieut.-Colonel Briggs's administration would appear to have been highly successful. By a personal visit to the disturbed districts he appears to have restored tranquillity, and to have made satisfactory arrangements with the malcontents without effusion of blood. He collected, at the same time, much

* Or "made".

valuable information respecting that interesting portion
of the territory of Mysore."

Within little more than a year after Briggs had left
Bangalore for Nagpore, the change in the constitution of
the Mysore Commission, to which Lord William Bentinck
was so averse, was made, in compliance with the peremptory orders of the Court of Directors.   Colonel W.
Morrison was made a Member of the Supreme Council in
June 1834, and Colonel Mark Cubbon took his place
without the encumbrance of any Board or colleague.   In
the same month Mr. Casamajor was transferred from the
Residency to the minor appointment of Resident at
Travancore; and in 1842 the office of Resident at Mysore
was abolished under the government of Lord Ellenborough, in consequence of " the complications and disputes which it occasioned".*

The doctrine and the practice of Colonel Briggs have
been in every way justified and confirmed by the course
and conduct of his immediate successors, and by the very
questionable results of our management in Mysore.   He
laid the foundation and drew the plan for all the good
work that has been done there, and every divergence
from his programme has led to pretentious failure.

We have seen how the misrule of the Maharajah of
Mysore, and the petty revolt which was the pretext for
his being put on the shelf in 1832, were attributable, in
a very great degree, to the inexcusable and very suspicious negligence of the Madras Government, and to
the incapacity of the British Resident; and how the
Maharajah was actually stigmatised with severities in the
suppression of the revolt, which were the work of British
officials, and against which he had protested.   In the
anxiety to retain this valuable field of patronage, when
it was threatened in 1866, the resources of rhetoric were
stretched very near the confines of the *suppressio veri*
and the *suggestio falsi*, both in Calcutta despatches and
in London minutes and dissents.   It was then that we
heard of " an exasperated and revolted people", of their
wrongs, and their rescue, and the certainty of their ruin
unless they were annexed.   It was then that we heard

* *Mysore Papers* (112 of 1866), p. 38.

of Mysore being "full of European settlers", who could
not exist under a Native government, the fact being that
there were sixteen English coffee-planters in two small
corners of the country. By those who joined in the
triumphal chorus of Lord Dalhousie's career of territorial
acquisition, it was always assumed, as it came to be
officially asserted when the crisis arrived, that ultimate
annexation had really been involved and implied when
the sequestration was decreed in 1832. But this is
totally untrue. When Lord William Bentinck assumed
the administration of Mysore, he not only had no intention of annexing the country, which in the course of years
became the settled object at Calcutta, but he had no intention of permanently superseding the Maharajah. That
iniquitous and most ill-advised policy arose out of the
greed and exigencies of patronage. There was not at
first any desire to multiply departments and appointments for English gentlemen. That incubus on Mysore
grew from a small beginning into the monster that it
became at last. The Madras Government, under the
Right Honble. Stephen Lushington, whose exaggerated
demi-official reports had led Lord William Bentinck to
take the steps he afterwards regretted, and Colonel
Briggs, who did so much to expose and correct those
inaccurate reports, had not many views in common; but
they were so far agreed that none of them had any
notions of either annexation, or of spreading English
officers all over the country in every place of authority
and emolument. The Madras Government, undoubtedly
hankering after Bangalore as its head-quarters, wanted
the old system kept up, with a Madras Resident as
dictator over a Dewan of our nomination. Colonel
Briggs, as both his public and private papers prove, had
constantly two objects before him,—first, stern and
thorough reform, and wholesome restriction by ordinances, of princely absolutism, especially of power over
the revenues; secondly, the restoration of the Rajah, as
soon as might be, to his proper position at the head of
the State. The antagonism of the Madras Government,
by whom he was regarded as a hostile interloper, and the
friction of working with a Board against which he had

from the first remonstrated, made Briggs's position untenable, just as he had pacified and organised the country;
but all his plans were adopted and maintained after his
departure, and were eventually approved by the Home
Government. The Secret Committee of the Court of
Directors write as follows in a letter, dated the 23rd of
April 1834 :—

"Concerning the measures which emanated from the Commission
while Lieut.-Colonel Briggs was Senior Commissioner, it is impossible for us at present to give any decided opinion. These
measures formed the subject of warm discussions, and were mostly
adopted contrary to the sentiments of the gentleman who was
Junior Commissioner at the time. We expect that the present
Senior Commissioner, Lieut.-Colonel Morrison, will have deliberately reconsidered all the measures which have given rise to
difference of opinion, and that his judgment and experience will
have led him to confirm what has been wisely done, and to rectify
whatever may be amiss."

Colonel Morrison, his immediate successor, "deliberately
reconsidered all the measures" devised by Lieut.-Colonel
Briggs, and "his judgment and experience", even with
the not too friendly counsel of Mr. Macleod, "led him
to confirm" everything that Briggs had done. Nothing
was found "amiss", there was nothing to "rectify", and
nothing to alter. Not only did Colonel Morrison and
Mr. Macleod find nothing to rectify or to alter in Briggs's
arrangements, but as much may be said of the judgment
passed on them by the single Commissioner who succeeded
them, and who—a circumstance almost unexampled in
Indian annals—retained the post for nearly thirty years.

During the brief period of Colonel Briggs possessing
real power in Mysore, while the Commission was in direct
relation with the Governor-General, and relieved from
the meddling malice of Fort St. George, the following
measures of redress and reform were carried out :—

The apprehension of a rebellion and civil war breaking
out in the Nuggur Western districts was promptly dispelled, and the imminent danger of such a misfortune
prevented, by Colonel Briggs promptly proceeding to
that quarter, and personally re-assuring the excited popu-

lation. The civil establishments were organised in every detail, from a condition of utter confusion and arbitrary inefficiency, into a practicable and manageable system. And all this was done by Briggs, single-handed, not only with no help from his colleagues, but in spite of their captious and vexatious obstruction.

An efficient High Court of Justice was established, at the head of which was placed Ram Raz, a very able Brahmin,* who had for some years previously been the interpreter and pundit, or expounder of Hindoo law, in the Supreme Court at Madras, with whose aid the code of procedure for *punchayuts* or juries was framed.

"In conformity", says Briggs, in his diary, "with ancient practice, as in force under Poorniah's administration in Mysore, under my own authority in Khandesh, and under the admirable arrangements of my friend, Captain Grant Duff, at Sattara, the successful working of which I had been able to watch and test as his first successor, this code was privately submitted by me to the Chief Justice of the Supreme Court, Sir Ralph Palmer, who visited Bangalore in 1833, and from whom I received the warmest sympathy and the kindest help."

Before Briggs went through the ceremony of laying on the table before "the Board", the simple regulations he had prepared, there had been a blank sheet in Mysore with regard to legal principles and form. Judicial powers had been exercised by anyone, and every one, who had any power at all by virtue of office, of rank, or of property, from the Prince on the throne down to the landlord of a single village. The Maharajah, in particular—really for the benefit of certain officials near his person—retained always the prerogative of reversing or altering all decisions, on appeal or on information, and of hearing and deciding, at pleasure, any cause in the first instance.

A competent High Court was established at the capital by Colonel Briggs, with an intelligible code for its guid-

---

* An accomplished mathematician, whose name became known in Europe as the author of a learned work on Hindoo architecture, published by J. W. Parker, for the Royal Asiatic Society, in 1834, and still the text-book on the subject.

ance in principle, and a simple procedure for its practice. But by the system of *punchayuts*, the advantages of speedy justice close to their own doors, in the ordinary cases of village life, were secured for the people,—a system gradually complicated and spoiled by the permission of appeals, and finally swept away by what were called judicial reforms when annexation was confidentially decreed under Mr. Bowring's Chief Commissionership. Sir Mark Cubbon adopted the scheme of *punchayuts* as arranged by Colonel Briggs, and maintained it, though not, as just explained, quite intact, throughout his long and successful administration.

Colonel Mark Cubbon had won distinction in the Commissariat Department, through every grade of which he had passed, from Deputy-Assistant in 1810, up to Commissary-General in 1831. Although, as became speedily manifest, his administrative capacity was fully equal to the task imposed on him, he was, when he assumed the government of Mysore, not well versed in either revenue or judicial matters, or in the institutions and customs of the province over which he was to rule. But he enjoyed the immense advantage, which he knew how to appreciate and appropriate, of having before him a complete scheme drawn up in English for every department from the hands of Colonel Briggs, the whole machinery being, to a great extent, in working order, and fairly started. Looking back at Mysore after the lapse of a few years, Briggs might well have quoted the poet's humorous complaint:

> " Hos ego versiculos feci, tulit alter honores,
> Sic vos non vobis fertis aratra boves."

And still more truly might he have said :—

> " Sic vos non vobis mellificatis apes."

Butter and honey did not form his official fare ; he had done the rough work, and quaffed the bitter cup in Mysore : the sweets of office fell to those who followed him.

Colonel Cubbon understood men and things ; he knew how to guide and govern. He was not one of those fussy officials who must do everything himself, and in his own way. He thoroughly accepted the general maxim Briggs laid down for administration,—that the people should have what they want, not what we think they ought to want. But he could not stem the gradual tide of super-fine establishments as he would have wished. For several years he let well alone, and altered as little as possible, but more Assistants were forced on him. He protested, in vain, against multiplying departments, and overloading them with highly-paid officers ; but as Mysore could not be made, by any economy, to contribute more than its fixed quota to the Imperial exchequer, nothing was left for the genius of Bengal Civilianism but to extend, in every direction, the list of places and salaries, and to make Mysore pay in the form of prizes and snug berths for English gentlemen of the commissioned and " covenanted" Services.

If Briggs had remained in Mysore as sole Commissioner, he would have done the work with two English Assistants, and would never have lost sight of the object which the British Government, in good faith, and according to the treaty, ought always to have kept in view—the reform and re-establishment in working order of the Mysore State.

Colonel (afterwards General Sir Mark) Cubbon, five years after taking over charge in 1834, had six Assistants. He was induced to ask for a few more ; subsequently he was encumbered with additional establishments, particularly with Lord Dalhousie's procrustean Public Works Department, against which he pleaded in vain. When he retired in 1861, there were thirty English officers in the Mysore Commission, and he left an accumulated surplus of a million sterling in the public treasury. When the old Rajah died in 1867, annexation having in the interval been confidentially decreed, though averted by Home influence, the costly structure of jobs and salaries called the Mysore Commission included no less than ninety English officers, their aggregate salaries amounting to about £100,000 a year, or one-seventh of the net revenue of Mysore, the tribute being deducted. When the young Maharajah was enthroned in March

1881, Sir Mark Cubbon's surplus of a million in hard cash had entirely disappeared, and it fell to the lot of Sir James Gordon to hand over the State to our Ward, burdened with debt to the amount of about a million sterling, with the Treaties of 1799 arbitrarily superseded by a "sanad" or "instrument", as it is called, whereby the stipulated tribute is raised by an arbitrary decree from about one-quarter to about one-third of its gross revenue,—from twenty-five to thirty-five lakhs of rupees per annum.* No justification has ever been shown for these high-handed acts. No justification, most assuredly, can be found in the mere fact of the sequestration of Mysore and its long continuance, which more justly demanded redress and reparation.

The Mysore Subsidy, which Lord William Bentinck admitted had "never been in jeopardy", having been regularly and uninterruptedly paid in monthly instalments, according to the terms of the Subsidiary Treaty, there never was any lawful cause, under the terms of that Treaty, for taking the Rajah's dominions under the " exclusive authority and control" of the British Government. That harsh measure, declared in Lord William Bentinck's Letter to the Maharajah to have been called for by a failure in the monthly payments, was, on fuller inquiry, admitted by him to have been uncalled for, no such failure having occurred. Lord William Bentinck virtually acknowledged the "illegality" and the "injustice" of this measure.† The supersession of the Rajah was the result of erroneous information from the Government of Madras. Neither the failure of subsidy nor any "reason to apprehend such failure", as defined by Article IV of the Treaty, having existed, that supersession was unwarranted, and was, in fact, a breach of the Treaty.‡ It may be doubted whether those who are now ruling India, and are conducting our relations with the State of Mysore, have more than the very haziest idea of that critical period in its history which I have endeavoured to elucidate,—whether they do not share in the mistaken belief, founded on the official legend, that our assumption of the

---

* *Mysore Papers*, (C. 3026 of 1881), pp. 126 to 135.
† *Ante*, p. 156.   ‡ *Ante*, pp. 156, 157.

management of the State was due entirely to the mis-government of the late Maharajah and in no degree to any fault or shortcoming of ours. On this legend is based the conclusion that, in taking the government out of his hands, we were obeying a stern necessity, and performing a simple duty ; and it is not difficult for men with official instincts and inclinations to proceed to the further con-clusion that, having once redeemed the people of Mysore from Native rule, we would have been justified in refus-ing to hand them back to another Native government. Those who hold this view regard the restoration of the State of the Native dynasty, in the person of the present youthful Maharajah, as not an act of justice, but one of re-markable generosity, and think that we were entitled to drive with him any sort of bargain that seemed good to us. I assert, on the other hand, that in founding on our own mismanagement and straining of the Treaty the right to do away with the Treaty, to substitute a *sanad* or grant, and to screw down the Maharajah as if he had no inherent rights—as if the State had no corporate existence—we have exercised our power in a way not only harsh, but positively iniquitous.

On the double grounds of the wrongful sequestration, and of the self-seeking and greedy extravagance of our administration of Mysore, special care ought to have been taken to avoid all appearance of any further violation of the Partition and Subsidiary Treaties of 1799. It is a rash thing to loosen the sanctions of our Indian Treaties. We cannot justly or safely attempt to tamper with a treaty of eighty years standing, on the plea that it was originally a *bad* bargain. It was, in this case, a bargain with the Nizam as well as with the Rajah, and ought to have been scrupulously adhered to. Our only title to the greater part of our possessions in India is a title by treaty. We do not hold many Provinces directly by conquest. Our only title to possession, our only moral claim to the allegiance and subordination of the Princes of India, and, as I believe, all our future power of perma-nent influence for the education and civilisation of India, depend on the preservation and development of our exist-ing system of treaties.

CHAPTER XIII.

BEFORE proceeding to take up his new appointment at Nagpore, Colonel Briggs paid a short visit to Madras, where he was a guest of the new Governor, Sir Frederick Adam, and where he fitted himself out with camp equipage and other necessaries for a journey of upwards of six hundred miles over very bad roads. "I left the Presidency in November 1832, and proceeded to my destination by the route of Hyderabad. At Secunderabad, the military cantonment near the Nizam's capital, I stayed a few days with my eldest daughter, who had been married in the previous year to Captain Westrop Watkins, one of the staff officers of the Subsidiary force, and thence I pursued my march to Nagpore."

"Maharajah Rughojee Bhonsla, to whose court I was deputed, was a grandson of the Rajah, also named Rughojee, who fought against us at the battles of Assaye and Argaum, the son of his daughter married to a chief of the Goojur family. On the defeat and deposition of Appah Sahib, who had put his cousin, Pursojee, to death, usurped the throne, and joined the Peishwa Bajee Rao, in the second Mahratta war against us, this young Prince was, in 1819, adopted into the house of Bhonsla by the widow of his murdered predecessor. Appah Sahib was dethroned and exiled by the power of our Government, and the young Rughojee was chosen as heir with its approval, but all was done in consultation with the relatives and ministers of the reigning family, and with the common voice of the people in its favour. When installed in 1819, the Rajah was only ten years of age, and Sir Richard Jenkins, who had been Resident at Nagpore all through the time of trouble and war that preceded his accession, was made guardian of the youthful Prince and Regent of the country, employing one English officer only in each of the four great divisions to superintend the administration, which was conducted entirely by Native civil officers. Sir Richard Jenkins had transferred the government of about half the Nagpore country, the districts most nearly connected with the capital, into the young Rajah's hands in 1825, and the remainder of his dominions had been handed over by Mr. Wilder in 1829, after negotiating a new treaty with his Highness by which a tribute of eight lakhs of rupees a year was to be paid to the Honourable Company. Thus, when I arrived at Nagpore, the Rajah had been his own master for about seven years.

"The Nagpore territories covered an area of about 70,000 square miles, and included the greater part of the ancient province of Gondwanna, a tract very interesting to me, both from so large a proportion of its inhabitants belonging to the great aboriginal race of Gonds, and from its having been found exempt, on its acquisition by the Mahrattas, from the system of village municipalities which prevails through the greater part of India. This is an additional proof of the village system being a Hindoo, indeed an Aryan, institution, as it can be traced throughout the whole of Europe, and in every part of the British Islands. The aboriginal tribes of India, whether in the plains or the hills, know nothing of it. Until the conquest of Gondwanna by the first Rughojee Bhonsla, under a commission from the Rajah of Sattara, in the beginning of the eighteenth century, the country had been governed from time immemorial by Princes of the aboriginal race of Gonds, without the slightest interference from the potentates around, excepting for a short period when a portion of Gondwanna was tributary to the Mohammedan Kings of Khandesh. During this period the principal Gond chieftain, who occupied the city now called Nagpore, was compelled to visit the provincial capital, Boorhanpoor, and was there made a convert to the Mussulman religion. There can be no doubt that the conversion arose from a wish to gain the favour of a powerful neighbour, and from some notion of superior dignity being thereby acquired, for the Gond Rajahs have always been utterly illiterate, and the members of the family know no more of the doctrines and precepts of their religion than are contained in the brief creed, ' There is no God but Allah, and Mohammed is his Prophet.' The Gond Rajah is treated ceremonially by the Bhonsla as the lord of the soil, and a sort of partner in the Government, though not left in possession of any power beyond the walls of his own house. This was a piece of characteristic Mahratta policy at first, in order to avoid acknowledging that Gondwanna was held in subordination to the Rajah of Sattara or the Peishwa, but it was always a mere outward form. The Gond Rajah, however, has his own officers in every district of his original Rāj, who collect his share, one-sixteenth, of the land revenue.

"I found the country had not suffered from the transfer of the Government to the young Rajah. Like most of the Mahratta Princes, he was very little influenced by Brahmins, and had for his Prime Minister an extremely sensible Mohammedan, Gholam Ali Khan. The Rajah had few troops, not more than 4,000 altogether, and those principally Cavalry, a mixture of all classes, Mussulman, Rajpoots, and Mahrattas. On the whole, I found the Nagpore territories, as I proceeded in the course of a year through the greater part of them, well cultivated, the inhabitants prosperous and decently clothed, and the Rajah popular.

" As I have already stated, the Hindoo municipalities nowhere prevailed in the Nagpore country. Each village had a head-man and an accountant, remunerated by rent-free land ; but these offices were held at the pleasure of Government, and there were no hereditary proprietors, or proprietary tribes, as among the Hindoo communities. There were not many jaghiredars of any importance, except members of the Rajah's family and a few great people about the Court ; but in one large district, Chutteesgurh, there were some semi-independent chieftains of ancient origin, whose territories were almost unexplored. Under its subsidiary alliance with the Company's Government, the State was protected by a British Force of all arms, consisting of about five thousand effective soldiers, one-third of them Europeans. Lord William Bentinck was averse to placing too much power in the hands of his Agents at the Native Courts. He required that a weekly report should be made to the Political Department at Head-quarters in the shape of a Diary, recording the official communications, personal or in writing, that had taken place between the Residency and the Court. But above all he desired that no open or direct interference should on any pretence take place in the conduct of the Rajah's administration. Here, I have no doubt, Lord William Bentinck, rightly convinced of the great mischief that had been wrought by the excessive pressure of the Resident's influence at Hyderabad and Lucknow, went a little too far in the other direction. Had it not been for the firm and honest discharge of his duty by the Mussulman Minister, the young Prince might have been led into the same course of extravagance and negligence that had so lately brought ruin on the Rajah of Mysore. This very argument was urged upon me very soon after my arrival by the Minister, who had begged me to remonstrate with the Rajah regarding an act of personal aggression on one of the families closely allied with the Court, when I told him that to do so would be contrary to my instructions. I quite agreed with the Minister that it could hardly fail to end in some disaster, if the young Rajah were left to suppose that there was no check whatever on his personal inclinations, his desires, and his dislikes. The Minister said that after the late events in Mysore, people were beginning to say that our Government had no objection to have opportunities of destroying the independence of allied States given to it by the faults or errors of Native Rulers. I said that our Government was incapable of any such motive. I recommended him to announce to the Rajah that I had heard the current story to his disadvantage, and had observed to my visitor that it would be as well if he would ask his Highness whether the version that had come to me was the correct one, as I felt very averse to enter it in its present form, evidently incomplete and unsettled, in my Diary for the Governor-General's information. This hint had the effect I desired and expected. In two or three days I learned through the same channel that reparation had been made, and a reconciliation arranged. My report was made to the Governor-General as usual, but was not calculated to prejudice the Rajah in his eyes."

A very full and lucid account of his views as to the Imperial right and duty of interfering in the government of the allied and protected States, as to their capacity for administrative reform, and as to their true place in our political system, will be found in the following important demi-official letter from Colonel Briggs, written in reply to one that he had received from the Earl of Clare, then Governor of Bombay. The letter, in conformity, I presume, with that from Lord Clare, which called it forth, is marked "Private".

" MY LORD,—1. I sit down to reply to your Lordship's question regarding our interference in the internal management of Native States closely allied to us.

" 2. The policy of inducing the Native Princes who have been compelled to seek our protection from foreign aggression to purchase it by subsidising troops, was coupled with conditions that virtually deprived those Princes of every vestige of independence, and paralysed their strength in every sense of the phrase.

" 3. This policy arose, not merely out of the exigencies of the time when the French, Tippoo Sultan, and their well-wishers, were making desperate efforts to subvert our power, but has been more generally forced on us by the rude and uncivilised character of the Native States which border on our own territory.

" 4. These alliances at once relieve the Sovereigns who have embraced them from all apprehension of foreign enemies and of domestic insurrection. They exchange political power and ambition for the security and ease which belong to Princes tributary to a mild though potent Superior.

" 5. These treaties did not, at first, confer in direct terms the right of interference in the internal affairs of the several States with which they were formed. This right, however, inevitably followed wherever the condition of the alliance was coupled with a stipulation for the regular payment of a subsidy; for misrule in India being sure to bring down its own punishment,—a failure of revenue,—the control of the public resources, and the management of the country, were necessarily demanded by us as the only effectual security, and the territories eventually passed into our hands. This was the case with the dominions of the Nawab of Arcot, the Rajah of Tanjore, and other Principalities of less importance. In these cases we appropriated the entire administration to ourselves, reserving for the deposed Princes a certain share of the net revenue.

" 6. This may, perhaps, be the end of some more of these alliances at some future period, but I would earnestly deprecate the notion of accelerating or facilitating such a crisis in any single instance that I can foresee or conceive. We should always endeavour to guard against it and avoid it. Every extension of our territory henceforward, now that we have made ample provision for our establishments, and for securing general control, can only increase our burdens, and enfeeble our authority. But, on the other hand, we must not hesitate or procrastinate in exerting our influence, naturally and fairly acquired and maintained, and upheld for the general good as well as for our own interests, on behalf of orderly and regular government.

" 7. In the instance of our subsidiary alliance with Bajee Rao at Poona, we suffered misrule to continue too long. At length the Southern jaghiredars threatened a coalition against him, which, if permitted to run its course, might have ended in a change of dynasty. The Peishwa was precluded by treaty from calling on his former vassals and confederates for aid, and he consequently demanded that assistance from us which we were bound to afford. Our interference becoming requisite, we assumed the position of Umpire, and averted a Civil War. On this occasion we guaranteed to the jaghiredars the integrity of their estates, and to the Peishwa the fulfilment on their part of their feudatory duties.* The perfidious character of Bajee Rao brought about the Mahratta war of 1817, otherwise his reign of misrule, corrected only by our mediation in favour of the jaghiredars, might have continued during his life-time. The people would have been still groaning under the weight of his injustice and oppression,† while his claim to our support against internal revolt must have effectually checked or crushed every effort, however justifiable, of the insurrectionary spirit. Such is the actual condition of our relations with the Nizam. On the one hand, we do not consider

---

* This was in 1812,—see *Collection of Treaties*, Calcutta, 1863 (London : Longmans and Co.), vol. iii, pp. 85 and 88.

† Bajee Rao, the ex-Peishwa, died at Bithoor on the 28th of January 1851, aged seventy-seven, eighteen years after this letter was written.

ourselves warranted by Treaty to interfere in preventing misrule ; we are compelled, on the other, by giving military support, to assist in perpetuating bad government.

" 8. I cannot persuade myself that we are any more bound by natural justice as between State and State, or by the want of specific stipulations in a Treaty, to abstain from promoting reformed administration, when we have good reason to fear the evil consequences of disorder, than we are justified by our abhorrence of the misrule that has done the mischief in refusing to restore peace and order, when an actual revolt has broken out. In either case these are questions of prudence and equity as to the extent of our action that we must solve for ourselves.

" 9. If we decline to support a Prince against revolt, and look on supinely at the contest between him and his subjects, one of two consequences must ensue. Either the Native Government, without our aid, will be strong enough to put down all resistance with its own army, adding, perhaps, cruel and sanguinary punishments to its former oppression ; or else the people, getting the mastery, will dethrone, or even put to death, their hated Sovereign. In either of these cases anarchy and civil war are brought to our own doors, and all who are oppressed, and all who suffered, blame us, because they know our power could have worked a cure.

" 10. A more striking example of the impossibility of adhering to the non-interference principle could not be adduced than is presented by a review of the late events in Mysore. Our connection with that State warranted our regulating its affairs from the first, at all times, and in any shape we pleased ; but we tried the effects of non-interference. The result was a long period of mal-administration, ending in a revolt, which the Rajah was unable to suppress. In order to save the Government, it became necessary to employ our own troops, and eventually to assume the direct management of the Rajah's dominions.

" 11. If after a period of reform and organisation the reins of government are to be ultimately replaced in the Rajah's hands, under certain restrictions and limitations, we shall then be just where we ought to have been at the time when the Rajah's minority ended. The conduct and character of the Prince must determine how long our direct control should be exercised, and at what time, and how far, it should be relinquished. At no period, however, can the British Government, I conceive, withdraw its supervision, with credit or advantage to itself, from any State connected with us as is that of Mysore. The disadvantage of its having done so in this case has been sufficiently manifest.

" 12. Our treaties with Mysore, Sattara, and Nagpore are on the same model ; and it is to this middle condition between independence and incorporation that I conceive it should be our policy

Q

to reduce all the Native States,—a condition upon the whole the most favourable to all classes within them, the least dangerous and the least burdensome to us, and the most conducive to civilisation and general prosperity.

"13. I have before remarked upon the influence on · public affairs of the personal character of Native Princes, even of those who are bound by Treaty to adopt our advice in their administration. In order to render this influence harmless, without diminishing its efficacy for good, our main principle should be the formation of a regular system,—I should be inclined to call it a constitution, —which should be binding on the head of the Government, and which ought not to be essentially altered or departed from without the sanction of the Protecting Power. Such is the course, in fact, which has been followed at Sattara and Nagpore, and such, I should hope, will be the policy pursued towards the Rajah of Mysore.

"14. I have studied the Indian fiscal institutions with much assiduity and care ; I have also studied theoretically and examined practically, in the various localities, those of our own country and of several other States of Europe, and I know of no monarchical government, of which an elective representation forms no part, more adapted to promote the happiness and welfare of the people in the present form of society in India, or which could be administered more cheaply or more efficiently, than that of the little Principality of Sattara. The constitution and frame of this Government were first sketched out, with the advice and approval of Mr. Elphinstone, by Captain Grant Duff, and afterwards modelled and built up by his agency.

"15. In all States that are brought under our supervision the Civil List, that is to say the sum allotted for the annual expenditure of the Rajah and his family, ought to be fixed, as it was in Sattara, at a certain proportionate share of the net revenue, after deducting all the charges of collection. A budget exhibiting estimates for the ensuing year, both of expenses and receipts, together with full accounts of the income and disbursements of the ·past year, should be delivered to the Resident annually, and no essential changes in financial matters should be permitted to take place without the sanction of the British Government.

"16. It need hardly be added that 'the Residents to whom is entrusted the supervision of the protected States, should be men of the very highest class of public servants, carefully trained, selected, and instructed for this difficult duty ; for on their reports the British Government must, in a great measure, rely for the information by which its control will be regulated. While we have Princes on the musnud like the Rajahs of Nagpore and Sattara, who have personally witnessed the effects, and who acknowledge the advantage of European organisation and system, and who are desirous of maintaining the same, our Residents at those Courts will have little more to do than to make their weekly reports, and to watch the progress of affairs, refraining, as much as possible, from interference, and making their current counsel as palatable and unobtrusive as they can. But when Princes or Ministers feel that the eye of the British Government, or of its representative, is no longer on them, or regards their movements with indifference, or when the musnud receives a new occupant, who may be imbecile, vicious, wrong-headed, or an infant, very rapid changes for the worse may take place in States that were once well regulated, and our interference may be imperatively required. In some cases direct and open management by British officers may be unavoidable, as in the present instance of the Rajah of Mysore.

" 17. Thus, my Lord, you have my humble sentiments on this important subject. I think I have shown that we deceive ourselves in supposing that our non-interference will tend to enable the people to correct the misrule of their Princes. Even if it were so, we are pledged against non-interference. We are bound by solemn engagements in the case of all the subsidiary States to step in and check the natural corrective process of insurrection as soon as it displays itself; and when we choose, as in the case of Mysore, to refrain from interference till the last moment, we only permit the agonies of the people to be protracted without giving them a fair chance of effecting their own relief.

" 18. So far am I from advocating the principle of non-interference, that I conceive we are bound in duty to the Princes themselves and their subjects, and in the interest of our own territories, to watch carefully the administration of all Native States, and to interfere promptly whenever the infancy or incapacity of a Sovereign demands temporary guidance, relaxing our control, or withdrawing our superintendence, in the precise ratio that we recognise in Prince or Minister the faculties for directing a good Government. The policy that I contemplate is that while we are endeavouring to govern our own Provinces through the instrumentality of a more extensive Native agency, we should at the same time be preparing the protected States by constant supervision for the establishment of our institutions ; and by the conjunction of this double movement, the time may very much be hastened for the construction of that political system which must, I think, before our work is complete, overspread the whole of India.

" I have the honour, etc., etc.,

" JOHN BRIGGS.

" Nagpore Residency, 12th June 1833."

Q 2

On the 24th of January 1834, he writes as follows to Augustus De Morgan, in London.

" MY DEAR AUGUSTUS,—I really do not know how I am to repay you for your two long and interesting letters of the 28th June and 17th August last, both of which have come to hand within these few days. You ask about the state of the land question in Nagpore. This is a mildly governed Mahratta Kingdom, and presents a very fair example of what the revenue principles accepted by our Government would introduce everywhere, with the aggravation of our costly system, and without the many alleviations of Native rule. The odious system of taxing the farmer to the full extent of his profits, and of putting up these taxes to farm for two or three years at a time, flourishes here ; and the country remains half barren, the people continue for the most part paupers, and little but a bare subsistence is left to the common run of cultivators. James Mill and Holt Mackenzie, the supporters and advocates of this system, say this is not taxation, that it is merely the payment of rent to the Government as universal Landlord, a position utterly false and untenable. But even if it were not so, what would be the consequence if all the occupants of land in America or New South Wales, not to say of Great Britain, were compelled to surrender all their profits (by which alone they are at present induced to till the soil) to the State ? These two oracles, one at the India House, the other at the Board of Control, are to direct the destinies of this unhappy region of the world under the new Charter."

The Revenue settlements of the Nagpore country, after the dethronement of Appah Sahib in 1819, and during the minority of his successor, were made by English officers under the supervision of the Resident, Sir Richard Jenkins. The notice in Colonel Briggs's preceding letter of the heavy assessments on the land—while he admits " the alleviations of Native rule"—is, perhaps, one of the first hints on record of the bad example in that direction set by our administrators, and the bad precedents afforded by them, to the Native States under their management or influence.

An extract from another letter to Augustus De Morgan, dated 30th September 1834, contains an indication of the prevalent Russophobia, of which, in after years, a very small trace remained in the mature counsels to which General Briggs gave utterance.

"Our last accounts from England of June 6th exhibit the Grey administration falling to pieces, and the probability of a war with Russia. The Board of Control ought to think seriously of Persia. That country is on the eve of a great political change, on which will probably depend the ultimate fate of India. Unaided by Persia, Russia will never attempt even to threaten our Eastern possessions, and would assuredly not succeed in any aggressive movement against them. But backed by Persia, either as an ambitious and hopeful ally, or as a subdued and subordinate follower, Russia may take up a position on our North-Western frontier, and exhaust our resources without firing a shot, whenever she feels so disposed."

In consequence of bad health Colonel Briggs was relieved from his duties of Resident at Nagpore in 1835, by the Honble. Richard Cavendish of the Bengal Civil Service, a son of the second Lord Waterpark. Mr. Cavendish came from Gwalior, where he had been Resident at the Court of the Maharajah Scindia. I may add that he retired from the Bengal Civil Service on a pension in 1840; the year after his retirement he married an heiress, and died at what must have been a very advanced age in 1876, leaving a large family of children and grand-children. Mr. Cavendish never had the reputation of being a very able man, and the letter now to be cited seems to show that his erudition, even in the department of English grammar and phraseology, was hardly up to the standard of our competitive examinations. The opinions on any subject expressed by the successor of Colonel Briggs at Nagpore could not properly be noticed in these pages, but for the fact that Lord Dalhousie, at a critical period in his policy of annexation, when there was one opponent in his own Council, cited Mr. Cavendish as a competent judge in a matter of Indian history and politics. Colonel Briggs heartily sympathised with his old colleague and comrade, General Sir John Low, and took his part at home in the ineffectual struggle against the extinction of Native States.

Mr. Cavendish's letter, written a very short time after the departure of his predecessor from Nagpore, did not refer to any very weighty affair, but only to a point of ceremonial etiquette in visiting and receiving an Indian

Prince. If his despatches were usually written in the peculiar slipshod style that characterises this letter, they ought hardly to have impressed the Government of India with a very deep respect for his capacity or judgment. Yet a blundering assertion of his was quoted in 1854 in support of the iniquitous annexation of Nagpore, against which General Briggs lived to protest in the Court of East India Proprietors. " In the year 1837", said Lord Dalhousie, " Mr. Cavendish, then Resident at Nagpore, asked for the instructions of the Government of India, in the event of the Rajah dying without a male heir. Mr. Cavendish gave it as his opinion that 'adoption' should not be allowed, for the British Government conquered ' this country, and gave it to his Highness and his sons, and on his death, without an heir-apparent or posthumous child, it should escheat or lapse to our Government'."* The treaty was, in truth, made with the Rajah, *" his heirs and successors"*, not *" his sons"*, as Mr. Cavendish represented. But any stick will do to beat a dog, and so Mr. Richard Cavendish was exalted into an authority. The strain of plaintive sentiment and "regard for the feelings of others" in the letter of 1835 is not easily reconcilable with the disregard for the rights of others in that of 1837. In all probability the confiscating doctrine that dropped from the Resident's pen, and which met with no approval or response from the Government of the day, though eagerly appropriated by Lord Dalhousie, was due to no worse cause than sheer, honest ignorance, and carelessness as to the terms of the Treaty. The following letter is of some use and interest, partly as a measure of Mr. Cavendish's literary and logical capabilities, partly as an instance of the aspect assumed by the " Shoe and Chair" question when applied to the more important Princes of India in the transition period of 1835, when Sir Charles Metcalfe was acting as Governor-General, between the departure of Lord William Bentinck and the arrival of Lord Auckland.

* *Papers, Rajah of Berar* (416 of 1854), p. 29.

"To W. H. Macnaghten, Esq., Secretary to the Government of India, in the Political Department, Fort William.

"SIR,—The Maharajah according to custom returned my visit on the 21st instant; and when a few hundred yards from the Residency, I heard for the first time that it had been the custom for his Highness to sit on a guddee,* and the British and Native functionaries on the ground on his Highness's right hand, until Mr. Graeme substituted a throne or couch for the Maharajah and himself, and chairs for all the other British and Native attendants of rank, and such had ever since been the rule and practice.

"2. I determined for several reasons not to sit on the same couch or throne with his Highness, and took one of the chairs on his Highness's right hand; and have since ascertained it to be his Highness's wish to revert to the old-established custom previous to Mr. Graeme's arrival of sitting on a guddee and on the ground without shoes; but I do not like to undo what has been done without knowing the pleasure of the British Government. My opinion is in favour of compliance with the old-established custom and his Highness's wish, for the British Government under Providence is all-powerful, and the greater humility and attention shown to the weak, the more gratifying it must be to our own feelings, and must in some degree soothe the pain and anguish of the Prince and his nobles under their reverses. No one knows what to-morrow may happen to him, and it is therefore wise to be prepared, through humility and regard for the feelings of others, for the greatest reverses Providence may be pleased to visit him.

"I have, etc.,
"R. CAVENDISH,
"Resident.

"Nagpore Residency, 28th March 1835."

Perhaps an additional assurance is needed that the last two sentences, in which the climax is reached of pure benevolence and confused grammar, are given *verbatim et literatim*, as in the original. Here is the answer from the Government of India :—

"To the Resident at Nagpore.

"No. 31.   "13th April 1835.

"SIR,—I am directed to acknowledge the receipt of a letter from you, dated the 28th ultimo, reporting the Maharajah's visit to the Residency, and describing the former and late modes of reception.

"2. In reply I am directed to acquaint you that the Honble.

* Or musnud, simply a large cushion.

the Governor-General of India in Council entirely approves the partial change of ceremony adopted by you on the occasion, but he is of opinion that it would not be expedient to revert to the · custom of sitting on the ground in the Residency after the establishment of the English fashion of using chairs. At the Rajah's Durbar the Native custom, it is presumed, prevails.

"I have, etc.,

" W. H. MACNAGHTEN,

"Secretary to the Government of India."

Colonel Briggs left Nagpore early in March 1835, and arrived at Madras in April. He was very courteously and even cordially received by the Governor, Sir Frederick Adam, then on the eve of his return to England, and without any application on his part was in a few days gazetted to the command of the troops at Bangalore, with the rank of Brigadier-General. He felt himself constrained, however, to decline the appointment.

"Besides considerations of health, and the strong recommendations of medical advisers and friends, I had strong objections to take up the military command at Bangalore, though I felt the offer was intended as a kindness and a compliment. I should have been in a false and painful position at the military head-quarters of Mysore, where I had so recently been at the head of the Government, and where many persons of more or less importance—not to mention the Rajah, who was not ignorant of my views—looked upon me as their patron and protector, and would have erroneously imagined my presence in the country to be favourable to their interests or their ambition. Here were sufficient reasons for my refusing to return to Mysore, but in fact my health was much impaired. I was urged, on the highest medical authority, to proceed to sea at once, with provisional permission to go on to Europe, and this advice I felt bound to adopt.

"While at Madras in 1835, I was the guest of an old Eton schoolfellow, high in the Civil Service, Mr. John Sullivan, whose father was then a Right Honble. Member of the Board of Control. It was from him I first learned the gratifying fact, which was afterwards more formally confirmed, that in the last sentence of the Governor-General's despatch to the Court of Directors on Mysore affairs, written after having received the Report of the Special Committee, he said that he 'felt bound to record his sentiments on the conduct of Colonel Briggs, the late Senior Commissioner, during the time he held that office', and he concluded, ' I have no hesitation in saying that with the exception of the single instance of indiscretion for which he justly incurred blame, the whole of his conduct throughout that period met with my unqualified approbation.'

" I obtained leave to proceed to sea and to any British dependency within the limits of the Company's Charter, between the Cape of Good Hope and Cape Horn, and eventually to Europe. I embarked from Madras, with several old civil and military friends, for the Mauritius, where I remained for two months, enjoying a delicious climate, and the kindness of the Governor, with whom I had become connected by the marriage of my second daughter with one of his near relatives. I also experienced much friendly attention from the Judge, a connection of my own, with whom I had passed many happy days in his own family in early life at home.

" The negro freedmen, so recently slaves, seemed to me to be for the most part kindly treated, but the social revolution had not as yet settled down, and labour for wages was unwillingly and irregularly given. This had already led to the introduction of Indian coolies, chiefly from the Madras Presidency, and chiefly through the medium of Madras Native merchants and shopkeepers who had settled in the island. I was much interested in conversing both with the labouring and the commercial class of Madrassees, and I found that they had a grievance. There was an old law regarding the slaves, that they were liable to punishment for quitting their master's estate without a passport. This was made applicable to the negroes after emancipation. The Legislature also proposed that the same law should be extended to the Indian coolies. Some of the Indian merchants remonstrated, and drew up a petition against the measure to the Secretary of State for the Colonies, which they entreated me to present when I went home, and which I actually did present to Lord Glenelg. Their prayer was, I think, granted.

" From the Mauritius I took my passage in a sugar ship for the Cape of Good Hope. The state of my health had not much improved, and after a very short stay at the Cape I availed myself of the leave conditionally granted to me, and preceeded to England. I landed at Dover in the month of January 1836, after thirty-five years of Indian service, during which time I had made twenty-one sea voyages of duty in different parts of the East, and had singular opportunities of observing the different systems of discipline in ships of war of the Royal and in the Indian Navy, in the Company's regular Indiamen, in vessels manned chiefly by Indians, and in an Arab barque manned by a mixed crew of Arabs and Indian lascars."

When leaving Madras in 1835, Colonel Briggs had

by no means formed any resolution or intention of settling at home and of not returning to India. He was, on the contrary, for several years desirous of employment. The number of "political" and civil places of the first class for which military officers were eligible, was very limited. The covenanted Civil Service was engrossing more and more of them, and officers of the Madras Army were greatly at a discount in comparison with those of Bengal. In 1838, on his promotion to the rank of Major-General, he applied, but unsuccessfully, for the command of a Division. As a Colonel he was in the enjoyment of the "off-reckonings"—a double share in those days, when there were two battalions to each Regiment—so that his military emoluments, while unemployed, amounting to £1,750 a year, with the income arising from his Indian economies, made him fairly independent of official patronage. He had no sons to be provided for, and only two unmarried daughters.

CHAPTER XIV.

1835 to 1853.

FROM the day that Briggs was relieved from official trammels and took up his abode in England, finally and permanently as it proved, he may be said to have "gone into opposition" against the Government of India—the Government of all others in the world the most intensely official in its personality and its processes, and the least open to popular or party influence. Of Indian administration and Indian affairs in general, it had been commonly made a subject of solemn exhortation that they ought not to be made what is called "the sport of party". With that exhortation I have never been able to sympathise. If the extreme crisis, so often predicted and dreaded, were to arrive, and India were to become the battle-field of Parliamentary parties, I am not of opinion that any bad consequences would ensue. It would at least put an end to the impatience and apathy with which Indian affairs are now usually treated, and would make them a subject of universal attention and discussion. Being the citizen of a free country, great and strong because it is free, I cannot accept that catchword of permanent officials and reputed experts, by which discussion is deprecated, inquiry evaded, and responsibility nullified. After all, it is only a baser version of Lord Beaconsfield's audacious demand. The serene supremacy in lofty international regions, undisturbed by "the harebrained chatter of irresponsible frivolity", that he claimed for "sovereigns and statesmen", is claimed in Indian affairs not only by the executive dignitaries of Calcutta, but by "the front benches" at Westminster. Viceroys and Councillors have frequently written home

to warn the Secretary of State that if some particular
decision of their conclave should be disallowed, the very
foundations of British power in India would be upset.
And there has been too much inclination on the part of
the men actually and recently in power to accept such
warnings as legitimate.   Not party, but Parliament, is to
be silenced. For more than a century, a growing tendency
has been manifested by Ministers, without distinction of
party, to prevent Parliament from acting as a court of
revision and censure·over executive proceedings. Official
voices have warned the profane vulgar .off the Indian
field with even more of unanimity and rigour than they
have off the Continent of Europe. Terrible consequences
are always predicted, if "the spirit of party" should
permit an appeal from India to be judged on its merits
in either House of Parliament.   Unless all pretensions of
this nature are sternly set aside by representatives and
constituencies, and a just measure of real responsibility
to Parliament exacted, constitutional supervision will
never be more than an empty name and a deceptive
nullity.

  Constitutional Government is nothing if it does not
include a system of checks on autocracy, mystery, and
unadvised undertakings ; and the official hierarchy instinctively struggles against it from a dislike to the previous debate that may disclose dubious plans, and the
subsequent debate that may expose undeniable failures,
and malpractices. Close observation, and real supervision
by Parliament and the nation, are far more urgently
required for Indian than for foreign affairs.   If diplomacy
were to be let alone for a year or two by its practitioners
and by its detractors, the Empire might survive, and
not even suffer ; but the Indian question is vital, and
ever before us—national as well as international.   The
conventional cry that India must not be the sport of
party, really means that every important Indian question
must be kept out of Parliament, must be exempt from
unofficial strictures.   It really asserts that the two hundred and fifty millions of Indians in the British provinces
and the protected States, may be righteously and safely

confided, without Parliamentary or national control, to the covenanted and uncovenanted mercies of alien officials. It means that statesmen are not to decide on the merits of an Indian question, but only to take into respectful consideration the high merits of the Bengal Civil Service. It leads to Indian affairs being debated on no principle and to no purpose. Authority is supported, and the powers that be are upheld, but not morally strengthened.

Although General Briggs, as I have said, was generally to be found in opposition to the Government of India, his attachment and allegiance to his old masters, the Honble. East India Company, never wavered. On this particular point he differed from the majority of those closely allied with him in conference, most of whom held that the open and unequivocal transfer of power, patronage, and responsibility to the Crown, was essential to any large reform of Indian administration. The Indian Reform Association, of which the late Mr. John Dickinson was the founder and animating spirit, which numbered in its ranks several peers and nearly forty members of Parliament, including Mr. Bright, Mr. W. M. Torrens, and Lord Goderich, now Marquis of Ripon,* had "made up their minds", as Sir Charles Wood complained in his five hours' speech of June 3rd, 1853, "to oppose any plan not founded on the basis of what was called the single government". Briggs, on the contrary, though generally in accord with the Association, was always of opinion, in common with John Stuart Mill, and others of high repute, that the Court of Directors formed an almost ideal body of local experience and intermediate authority, usually taking the initiative, and retaining to the last the right of remonstrance and protest, as a check on the hasty and inconsiderate action into which a Minister or a Cabinet might easily be misled.

* It will be seen, therefore, that when Lord Ripon went out as Viceroy in 1880, having, moreover, been successively Under Secretary and Secretary of State for India, he was not exactly a novice in Indian affairs, and had sought for information and instruction beyond official sources.

One thing at least is certain, that there was greater publicity, and a wider field for debate, both in and out of
Parliament, under the Company's Government than there
is under that of the Crown.

General Briggs had a vote, as a holder of India stock,
in the Court of Proprietors of the East India Company,
and frequently attended its meetings. That singular
assembly, though almost deprived of direct power over
its nominal delegates, the Court of Directors, afforded a
field for openly discussing their proceedings, and for
invoking and informing public opinion. The same Act of
1858 which shut up the Court of Proprietors, also put
an end to the accidental and imperfect representation of
India in Parliament by a few of the Directors, unofficially
chosen in both capacities. Their successors, the Councillors of the Secretary of State, being mere nominees,
and excluded from the House of Commons, the media-
tisation of the East India Company did but strengthen
the secrecy and irresponsibility of Indian administration,
and confirm the supremacy of permanent officialism.

From the first day of his return home General Briggs
associated himself with the Liberal party in every possible way. He joined the Anti-Corn Law League at a
very early date after its formation, and was in the chair
at one of its great meetings in Covent Garden Theatre
on the 22nd of May 1844. In the same year he was a
candidate for the representation of Exeter as a Liberal
and a Freetrader against the Attorney-General of Sir
Robert Peel's Government, Sir William Follett, but was
unsuccessful, and never again endeavoured to become a
member of Parliament. He frequently read papers before
the Royal Asiatic Society, which were subsequently published in the Journal. He became a Fellow of the Royal
Society, and of several other learned Societies.

He was intimately associated with the little band of
Indian reformers, and assiduous in his attention to the
proceedings of the Court of Proprietors. General Briggs
fully appreciated the great principles involved in the two
Sattara cases, frequently confounded and denounced as
if there had only been one, and that one equally vexatious

and wearisome. In the numerous debates in the Court of Proprietors on the deposition in 1839 of Rajah Pertaub Singh, and on the refusal to admit the succession of the adopted son of his brother and successor, Rajah Shahjee, in 1848, Briggs voted invariably on the side of the minority, which included the names of Henry St. George Tucker, General Archibald Robertson, who had been Resident at Sattara, W. H. C. Plowden, John Shepherd, Sir Robert Campbell, Colonel Sykes, William Leslie Melville, John Forbes, and John Cotton, among the Directors, and of the Right Honble. Holt Mackenzie, General Lodwick, formerly Resident at Sattara, Joseph Hume, John Sullivan, George Thompson, Captain W. J. Eastwick (afterwards a Director and a member of the Indian Council), General Delamotte, and Alderman Salomons, in the general body of Proprietors, and which was known to have the sympathy of those who were confessedly the two best living authorities, the Honble. Mountstuart Elphinstone, who had made the Treaty and placed the Rajah on the throne, and Mr. Grant Duff, who had been the first Resident at Sattara, the Rajah's political tutor, and the organiser of the State.[*]

It is very remarkable that the principal opponents of Lord Dalhousie's destructive policy almost unanimously indicated the demoralisation and disaffection of our Native Army as a very probable and most dangerous consequence of annexing the allied States. The first warning of this description that I have observed is in a speech by Mr. John Sullivan, formerly Member of Council at Madras, in the Court of Proprietors on the 25th of April 1849, protesting against the annexation of Sattara :—

" If then you are to have no increase of military strength, no increase of political strength, who is to benefit by this measure? I will tell you—the Bombay Civil Service will get a little promotion. On one side of the account will be a few lakhs of rupees, a few writerships; and on the other all the misery and distress which Mr. Frere has pointed out, and the irretrievable loss of your character for good faith, and in losing that you will lose the only solid element of your strength. You may think that you have the strength of the sword, but never forget that the sword is in the

[*] *Ante*, pp. 56, 86, 90, 91.

hands of the Native Army. You cannot rouse disaffection among the Native Chiefs without endangering the disposition of your Native Army."

In another debate on the same subject in the Court of Proprietors, General Briggs, after lamenting the indisposition of his friend, Mr. Sullivan, in whose absence he rose to second a resolution in favour of maintaining the Sattara State, and after explaining that among the Hindus it was only through the form of adoption that any collateral heir could succeed, said :—

" An assertion on the part of the British Government that the throne of Sattara is vacant for want of an heir is a most dangerous missive to send forth through the world of India, simply because it is false. It would be better in every way, more honest and more politic, to recognise the fact that there is nothing but two solemn Treaties to prevent the British Government from annexing the Sattara territory, and to say plainly, ' It is no longer convenient for us to abide by these Treaties, and as there is no one strong enough to dispute our power, we shall take possession of Sattara.' The princes and people of India will not be deceived by your declaration as to the want of heirs. They know there are heirs, and can point to them. Those in Western India have seen the successive steps by which, as it appears to them, the Government of Bombay has broken down the Sattara Raj. First of all some estates belonging to the Rajah's feudatory jaghiredars were claimed as within British jurisdiction. The Court of Directors eventually disapproved of these encroachments, and ordered them to be given up. But this was never done. Then came the blundering cruelty of the Rajah's deposition, a matter which I shall not think of reopening now. When the new Treaty was imposed on the Rajah's brother all the feudatories were placed under the Bombay Government, which has now recommended the annexation of the State, on the plea that there is no legitimate successor, while all India knows that there is an heir. This is a momentous occasion. This is your first open declaration of a disregard for Treaty obligations and for the Hindu law of inheritance by adoption. These precedents will sap the foundation of our Indian Empire. Governments, in the plenitude of what seems irresistible power, are too apt to overlook the probable effects of their measures in the future.

" Aurungzebe in the middle of the seventeenth century had his governors in Afghanistan, and his Viceroys in Southern India as far as the Carnatic. When he had conquered the Kings of the Deccan, he thought his Empire supreme and invincible. Drunk with

the vastness of his power, he ventured to encroach on Hindu institutions and long-established immunities. He imposed the jázeea
or poll tax on all non-Moslems throughout his dominions. The
immediate consequence was that the ancestor of this very boy
whom you reject, the great Sivajee, roused his countrymen about
two hundred years ago, raised the Hindu standard against the
mighty power of the Mogul, and in twenty years imposed tribute
on all Mussulman territories; while in less than a century his
descendants held the Emperor a captive in Delhi, and spread
Mahratta supremacy from Tanjore to the entrances of the Northern
desert. We have now had our day; our first century is not yet
completed; we have conquered and annexed till very few of the
Mahratta States are left. We have prevailed hitherto, and secured
alliance and obedience, from observing good faith and from respecting constitutional rights. We have an army on our side of
250,000 Native soldiers, capable of defeating any enemy we can
expect to encounter in India, even if it be the Russian and the
Cossack from the Don or the Volga. But, Sir, our soldiers are
derived from the yeomanry and the peasantry of India. There is
no one who ought to know better than yourself with what caution
we must deal with those classes of the population. If I mistake
not, you were honourably distinguished in suppressing and punishing the terrible mutiny of Vellore in 1806,—a mutiny caused by
injudicious measures which impressed the Sepoys with a belief
that the Government intended to abolish distinctions of caste.
Those injudicious measures were rescinded, and the Court of
Directors recalled from Madras both the Governor and the Commander-in-Chief. But without occupying time with recapitulat-
ing cases that are familiar to many of us, I may remind you that
there are many Indian mutinies on record the manifest result of
a real or fancied breach of privileges or prejudices to which the
Sepoys attached importance, and which they considered to be connected with their honour and their religion. These instances of
serious disaffection among our Native troops have occurred, and
will for ever be liable and likely to recur, so long and so often as
the troops believe that there is any want of faith on the part of
the British Government towards those whom they respect, and
regarding rights in which they feel an interest. Do not let us
imagine, like Aurungzebe, that we are strong enough to defy public
opinion, or to infringe on national institutions with impunity.
The attachment of the people of India to their native dynasties is,
I fear, very much overlooked or very much despised. It is even
more dangerous to overlook their attachment to their ancient
customs of inheritance, which if rejected by us in the case of a
Prince, they will believe to be altogether disregarded by us and
threatened with subversion. It is less than a century since Great

R

Britain drove America to contend for its independence. Whenever the people of India feel that they can no longer rely on our good faith, and that their dearest rights and privileges are trampled on, I promise you that the destruction of our power will not occupy as long a time as the American war of independence.

"I will not doubt the fidelity of the Sepoys as long as they are fairly paid and dealt with fairly, but armies cannot combat national opposition; and when we recollect that those soldiers who have won India to our rule are derived from the body of the people—that their fathers and their brethren are not always subjects of the British Government, but are often born and resident in the allied States, can it be supposed that they are devoid of sympathy for their Princes, for their brethren, and their fellow countrymen—that they have no inclination and no energy to resist what seems to them oppression and treachery? They are men, with hearts, with feelings, with affections as warm as ours, and do you suppose that when the voice of the people is opposed to us that they will not join in that opposition? It is not necessary they should fight against us. It is sufficient that they should desert us, and then there will be an end of our boasted dominion of India.

"If you are not too far gone in the intoxication of your military successes, and in the contemplation of your vast establishments, I have said enough to warn you against the consequences of permitting the tide of public opinion in India to turn against you—when you refuse to recognise the validity of adoption among the Hindus, you infringe on a sacred ordinance of their religion. The Government does, in regard to sovereign Princes, what its own law officers would not venture to do in a court of justice. The Government may think itself safe in violating the most solemn engagements, trusting to the support of a powerful army. But, Sir, I feel as certain as that I stand in this room that whenever the tide of public opinion in India shall set in strong against the Government, not your 740 Civil Servants, nor your 30,000 European soldiers, nor your 250,000 Sepoys will avail you. The whole fabric of our Empire, which it has taken a century to construct, will be swept away in the torrent, and British domination in India will cease, and, 'like the baseless fabric of a vision, leave not a wrack behind'."

It will be readily understood that the convictions entertained at this period by General Briggs, and the uncompromising terms in which he expressed them, were not calculated to obtain the approval and patronage of the Home Government of India, or even so much of the confidence of the East India Proprietors as would have sufficed to place him by their votes in the Court of Directors, towards which at one time his views were turned. He was far ahead of the public opinion of the day. Lord Dalhousie, supported by the Ministry, and by the unhesitating partisanship in the Court and the House of Commons of Mr. R. D. Mangles, Sir James Weir Hogg and others of less note, was then infallible and irresistible.

The General never failed nor flagged in his interest in the Indian Army, more especially in the Madras troops. He always maintained that in the military service, as well as in civil administration, it was a great defect and danger in our system to have set aside so completely the claims and qualifications of Indians to a share in the higher offices and ranks of public employment. In 1842 he published a letter to the Marquis of Tweeddale,* then just appointed Governor and Commander-in-Chief at Madras, discussing the whole subject of the organisation and discipline of our Sepoy battalions. Referring to the appeal that had been " so repeatedly brought before the Home authorities as to the want of European officers with our Native Army in India", he said :—

" I maintain that it is not so much the want of European officers as of *efficient officers,* in whom the men might confide. Time was, as already shown in the early part of this Letter, when in the days of Mohammed Yusuf, Jemal Sahib and Clive, no troops could be more efficient than the Sepoys under their Native officers, directed only by European minds. Whosoever has served of late years with those bodies of Cavalry denominated Irregular Horse, whether exclusively raised for our service in time of war, or furnished by our Native allies and acting as auxiliaries, directed by one or two selected European officers, will bear testimony to the chivalrous spirit of those troops, and to their fidelity and discipline. It is not necessary that we should incur the heavy expense of filling the ranks of the Native Army with the same number of European officers as in the other armies of the world ; but that the masses should be commanded in detail by persons of a higher order than those now composing the Native commissioned ranks, who are respected neither by those above them nor by those over whom they are placed. I have no hesitation in saying that unless this

---

* Reprinted in 1856. Harrison, Pall Mall.

be effected, our Native Army will, from day to day, decline in character and lose its utility."*

He objected to the annexation policy, not only on account of its destroying our moral supremacy, but on account of its weakening our military position and resources. He was never tired of pointing out the great error committed by the iniquitous appropriation of the Punjaub. In 1849 he published a pamphlet on that subject, from which the following extracts explain his opinion as to the mistake made in advancing beyond our impregnable frontier.

" A single glance at the map of India must convince anyone who regards it with attention, that nature has protected its frontiers in every direction with singular care. As the eye passes over it from the mouths of the Brahmaputra and the Ganges towards the North-West, the broad and lofty ranges of the Himalaya are seen bidding defiance to the approach of any foe from beyond them. From the district of Sirhind, touching the mountains on the East, from whence flows the Sutlej, a belt of deep sandy desert extends Westward and Southward along the left banks of that river and of the Indus, till the latter enters the ocean. This desert, varying in breadth from 150 to 200 miles, is for the most part thinly dotted with small villages, if so they can be called, at several miles' distance from each other, having a few deep wells of brackish water, around which the inhabitants congregate, and are occupied in breeding camels for sale to the countries on their borders. When pressed by an enemy they fly to the nearest large town (say fifty miles off), and conceal their wells by covering them with boards and laying sand over them.

" Having traced the desert to the mouths of the Indus, the ocean embraces 3,000 miles of sea-coast, protected by our maritime power, and the line of circumvallation terminates where it began, at the embouchures of the two mighty streams which disembogue into the Bay of Bengal at its northernmost point.

" From the earliest times the people of India have regarded these as their natural limits; and all the great battles which have been fought for the defence of that Empire have taken place on the plain, close on the North of Delhi, in the Province of Sirhind,† a name given to indicate the ' head' or boundary entrance into the region of India. There should, therefore, be shown strong reasons for changing the frontier so defended by nature.

* *Letter to the Marquis of Tweeddale*, pp. 35, 36.
† There were several battles of Paniput, before those fought against Nadir Shah in 1746, and against Ahmed Shah Abdallee in 1762.

"Sir Charles Napier has stated that the line of the Sutlej is more difficult to defend than the line of the Indus, being 600 miles in extent, and capable of being crossed almost anywhere at certain seasons of the year. I am prepared to admit that neither the Sutlej nor the Indus, nor any other river in the world, is worth a straw as a natural boundary. Mountains like the Himalayas, and oceans, and deserts like that of India, and those of Africa and Arabia, are strong natural boundaries.

"The Province of Sirhind presents the only vulnerable point for an enemy to enter India, and contend against such an army as we can present to oppose him, with the least prospect of success. Our security is neither in the rapidity, nor breadth nor depth of the Sutlej or the Indus, but is to be found in the desert along the left bank of each of these streams, commencing near Loodiana, and exhibiting a breadth, North and South, from thence to Canoond, of about 180 miles, extending, as has been stated, to the very coast at the mouth of the latter river."*

After referring to the difficulties and dangers, and the heavy loss of forty men out of his escort of 500, experienced by Mr. Mountstuart Elphinstone in 1809, on the most favourable route from Delhi to Bhawulpoor, when 600 camels were required to carry provisions and water for the party,—after quoting the disastrous flight of the Emperor Hoomayoon in 1542, from Ajmeer by Ummerkote to the Indus, when the want of water drove the horses mad, and all his followers perished but twenty,—after mentioning the loss of the greater part of the invading army of the Emperor Mahmood of Ghuznee in 1024 in the desert, the General continues :—

"But the best proof, if any other were wanting, of its impracticability for large armies, is the fact that the British Government, with all its power and all its resources, cannot send reinforcements to Sind or Mooltan, but by the mouths of the Indus on the South or through Umballa Eastward of the desert, on the North, and then up or down the rivers. All the battles of which history affords us any account for the defence of India, have been fought within forty or fifty miles North of Delhi, after the enemy have *turned* the desert, and have crossed the Sutlej between Loodiana and the Himalaya. The distance between them is under forty miles."†

* *What are we to do with the Punjaub ?* 1849, pp. 5, 6.
† *Ibid.*, pp. 11, 12.

At every possible opportunity General Briggs endeavoured to spread his principal doctrines for the government of India as an Empire,—that the allied States should be carefully sustained, and encouraged in the path of administrative reform, and that our greatest peril in India was that of alienating the Native troops by assailing the leaders and celebrities of the country, and thus, in their eyes, threatening their faith and their institutions. In 1849, when the annexation of Sattara, the first in Lord Dalhousie's series, had just taken place, he warned the advocates of territorial aggrandisement, in the *Indian News*, a paper which he had the chief hand in starting, that if they did away with "the right of adoption, with respect to the Princes of India, they would tread on delicate ground." No one would believe that they were going to confine the process to sovereignties.

"If you are to do away with the right of individuals to adopt, you will shake the faith of the people of India ; you will influence that opinion which has hitherto maintained you in your power; and that influence will thrill through your army; and you will find some day, as Lord Metcalfe more than once said, 'we shall rise some morning, and hear of a conflagration through the whole Empire of India, such as a few Europeans amongst millions will not be able to extinguish.' Your army is derived from the peasantry of the country, who have rights, and if those rights are infringed upon, you will no longer have to depend on the fidelity of that army. You have a Native army of 250,000 men to support your power, and it is on the fidelity of that army your power rests. But you may rely on it, if you infringe the institutions of the people of India, that army will sympathise with them, for they are a part of the population; and in every infringement you make upon the rights of individuals, you infringe upon the rights of men, who are either themselves in the army, or upon their sons, their fathers, or their relatives. Let the fidelity of your army be shaken, and your power is gone."*

* It is very remarkable that so many of the opponents of the annexation policy, Sir Henry Lawrence, Sir William Sleeman, General Briggs, John Sullivan, John Dickinson, in the days immediately preceding the Great Mutiny, predicted the disaffection of our Sepoys as a sure consequence of our despoiling the Indian Princes.—See *Retrospects and Prospects of Indian Policy* (Trübner, 1869), pp. 230, 232.

The following letters from Mr. John Sullivan will be seen to refer to the same journal, to which that gentleman also occasionally contributed.

"Brighton, 22nd Nov. 1850.

"MY DEAR BRIGGS,—Two or three trifling inaccuracies have crept into your last interesting article, which you may as well correct to prevent carping. You club Malabar and Canara together, and say that they were ceded to us in 1792. It was only Malabar that was ceded by Tippoo in 1792. Canara was not taken till 1799. Munro was never in Malabar before 1817, and then only for a few months as Commissioner, but he was the first Collector of Canara after the downfall of Tippoo in 1799. The Nairs are in Malabar; there are no Nairs in Canara. The strangest proof that could be afforded of the inflammable materials of which our Empire is composed, was the rebellion which broke out in Canara in 1837, and which, but for the prompt arrival of a Regiment by a steamer from Bombay, would have spread over all the Peninsula. It took more troops than fought at Assaye to put it down, and the heads of villages were its most active abettors. Lewin was principal Collector. He and the Judge, and all Europeans, shipped themselves off from Mangalore, and could only regain their position under cover of the troops. Private property in land has existed in Canara for two thousand years in a most perfect form. All the land is saleable at a high price; the assessment is fixed and moderate. The people had no grievance but an abominable tobacco monopoly, and yet they broke out, risking the loss of all they possessed, and even of their lives, at the instigation of a few conspirators from Coorg.

"I am glad to see that you are at work again. If you should collect these Essays and print them separately, I think the one contained in the last *Indian News* should form the first in the series. Pray don't give the enemy an advantage by speaking in unqualified terms of the bad government of our predecessors. Considering the incessant wars and revolutions in which they had been engaged for a full century after the Mogul Empire broke up, it is quite a wonder that there was any government at all. Yet in the midst of incessant fighting, the civil institutions were undisturbed, and almost everywhere the country was flourishing. Since our last good piece of work, when we put down the Pindarry ravages in 1818, we have held India with such an iron grasp that hardly a shot has been fired in our territory; but what have we made of this quiet interval? The Government is more in debt, and I doubt if the people are so rich. Pray draw largely on your biographical stores as you go on. Give us Nana Furnavees and such like. What poor pigmies we are, as Indian administrators, when compared with Natives of that stamp! I am glad you have shown up Mr. Thornton. What a misfortune—what a crime—that the jobbing patronage given to his trumpery History should have deprived us of Elphinstone's sequel!

> "Ever yours sincerely,
> "J. SULLIVAN."

———

> "Brighton, 14th Feb. 1851.

"MY DEAR BRIGGS,—I heartily concur in all that you say regarding Sir John Hobhouse's most impudent announcement. If Ministers should determine not to make any change in the existing system, then Parliament and the country are to be excluded from all knowledge of what has been going on in India for the last twenty years, the mere events of war excepted. Never was anything more audacious. There was an excellent article on the subject in yesterday's *Daily News*. Do pray write a letter to that paper. I mean to do the same to Lord Jocelyn, though I don't know him. We must be up and doing.

> "Ever yours,
> "J. SULLIVAN."

———

> "Brighton, 12th April 1851.

"MY DEAR BRIGGS,—I have this moment received your note of the 9th, from Westbourne Terrace. It is unhappily true that Lord Jocelyn will not present the petition. This is entirely from his connection with, and feelings towards, Lord Dalhousie. He heartily concurs in our opinions, and will support them. Sir Edward Colebrooke is equally favourable to them, and will aid us with his vote and voice, though he too would rather not present the petition. We have no resource, therefore, but in Mr. Hume. It would have been better, considering his untiring advocacy of the Sattara question, if we could have placed it in other hands; but the poor Princes of India may count their friends in Parliament upon finger and thumb, and out of Parliament by digits. I can't help hoping, however, that the antagonistic opinions of the Governors-General, and the sanction of the Home authorities to *both*, may attract attention. I shall be in town on Wednesday, and could meet you at two o'clock at the Asiatic Society's rooms. Will this suit you?

> "Yours sincerely,
> "J. SULLIVAN."

The next letter was written five years later, on the very eve of the terrible convulsion of 1857, which they may both be said to have foreseen, although they certainly did not anticipate that it would come so soon, and that it would follow so closely the annexation of Oude, so lightly and so confidently undertaken.

"Brighton, 5th Nov. 1856.

"MY DEAR BRIGGS,—I was very glad to see your interesting article No. 2, in the *News* of yesterday, and I hope you will go into the whole subject in future numbers. I am particularly glad that you have given the '*Friend of India*' a rap,—the *mis*-leading paper of the East, most anti-native, and therefore most mischievous, though generally very clever."

Here is a letter in a lighter tone, and on a less irritating subject, from his old friend and comrade, Grant Duff, evidently called forth by some inquiries bearing on the biography of Nana Furnavees, the last of the great Mahratta statesmen, which Briggs had so long meditated, and for which he had collected ample materials.

"Eden by Banff, Feb. 28th, 1854.

"MY DEAR BRIGGS,—It gives me pleasure to see the handwriting of an old friend, especially when I see it, like yours, strong and vigorous; and your letter is none the less welcome because it is full of a subject pertaining to our younger days, in which I seldom see anyone who takes the slightest interest.

"I could not now lay my hand on the notes of evidence as to the matter you mention, nor do I know where I may have deposited them, but I perfectly recollect the universal opinion of the well-informed about the Poona and Sattara Courts, and that no doubt was entertained among them as to the legitimacy of Madhoo Rao Narrain. That the Ministers had several pregnant women carried up, to make sure of a successor somehow, was also generally believed, and that Nana Furnavees was afterwards much too intimate with Narrain Rao's widow; but nevertheless no one of any consequence expressed any suspicion as to the legitimacy of the child born at Poorundhur. Ballajee Punt Nathoo, Abba Joshee (Bajee Rao's private secretary), Abbajee Gonedeo, all of whom you knew, had no doubt of it; and I also recollect asking Madhoo Rao Rastia if he had ever heard it doubted, and his reply was a decided negative.

"I also rather think Rughonath Rao himself believed in the legitimacy of the child, and would have been quite content to have been recognised as Regent. So general was the belief, that however influential Rughoba may have been, and numerous as may have been the adherents of his cause, the English could never have done more than place him temporarily in the Regency.

"Mr. Mostyn's evidence at that time was not so good as yours or mine in the *impartial* period of our inquiries. I knew the widow of Nana, and remember being surprised at her very youthful appearance the first time I had the pleasure of being introduced to her,*—I think by Ballajee Punt,—but my impressions do not lead me to recollect her as particularly intelligent. The most *ladylike* Brahmin ladies I ever had occason to converse with were the wives of the last Peishwa and of the Pritee Needhee. The celebrated Warunassee Bye I was obliged to send from Waee, and she behaved *so* well when I told her how disagreeable it was for me to be obliged to tell her that the Sirkar required that she should proceed to join *Sree Munt.*† But so long as one is not obliged to depart from terms of personal respect, it is surprising how the better classes in India manifest a refinement and polish only known among Europeans of the highest rank, and in an advanced state of culture.

"Pray how do you mean to publish, and how do you mean to make your book go down with the public? The only advice I can offer must be in the style of that given me by the late John Murray, when I called upon him about my *History of the Mahrattas*,—'Can't you put something of the present day into it?' Try to connect the life of Nana Furnavees with the Golden Horn, St. Sophia and the Sultan, mix up the Peishwa's Durbar with a particular account of the receptions of Messrs. Pease and Sturge by the Emperor of All the Russias.‡ As an amusement to yourself, and a pleasure to those old friends who care about the most uninteresting history in the world, it is all very well, but I would not venture on publishing unless some bookseller would take the whole risk. If you will allow it to be published by subscription, I should be very happy to put down my name for six copies; and if I could clear up any points that may appear *muddy*, I would do my utmost to assist; but you would be astonished, though not more than I am myself, at the total forgetfulness which comes over me about India, until some person or incident recalls the

---

* Major-General Sir Arthur Wellesley, on 18th May 1804, writes to Colonel Barry Close:—"I took the opportunity, on my arrival at Panwell, to see Nana's widow, in consequence of the receipt of your letter of the 7th instant. I had a very long conversation with her. She had a Moorish woman interpreter.

"She is very fair and handsome, and well deserving to be the object of a treaty."—Vol. ii, enlarged Edition of the Duke's Despatches, pp. 1,186, 1,187.

† One of the Peishwa's titles,—equivalent to "His Majesty".

‡ This letter was written in the early stage of the Crimean War.

subject, when it returns very vividly. Ten years ago, on one occasion in London, I was pleased to find how well Hindustani came back to me; but when I last saw you, or about that time, I was obliged to try again, and found myself positively *stuck*. It is thirty-one years since the days of my pilgrimage in the East ceased. In London one has every now and then opportunities and interests that revive many things that are lost in such obscurity as mine has been. When are you likely to be in town? About the end of May? I should not have been here this winter but for circumstances I could not foresee, or get over but by standing fast and watching events. I do not think I shall get away before the end of May. Where are you then likely to be? Do you know anything of Mr. Elphinstone? I trust he is well; happy he always is, as such a mind must be. I reverence Mr. Elphinstone as the most perfect of philosophers. Whatever some of us, confident in his great powers, might have wished to see him undertake in public affairs, I think he was profoundly wise in never coming into an arena where arts must be practised so foreign to his nature and his habits that he must have died from sheer vexation and disgust, and would probably never have been known as we knew him.

"I see our friend Pottinger is about to be relieved by Lord Harris.* Pottinger has been a good deal thwarted in the good he wished to have accomplished; and by being tied down instead of being allowed to do as his experience prompted, the benefits he might have conferred on Madras were marred, and as a Governor he does not return to receive a triumph.

"Why will you call me 'Captain'? In 1827 I was by right regimentally a Major; but when Cleiland, who saw the mistake, went to the Adjutant-General (Leighton), the latter told him that he knew it, but that as Grant would never return, more good would be done to his old brother-officers if he would not insist on its being rectified, and so he meant to let it stand. When I heard this, as I intended to give up all military rank, and could not get Major's half-pay without going back to India, and as it was to be of use to old friends, I made no inquiry about my promotion, and became henceforth Mr., as a far more respectable appellation than that of the fifty Militia Captains who *captained* me until I would not answer to the name. I afterwards learned that by not being a Major I lost being a C.B.,—a matter of no consequence to one who had retired from public life.

"Believe me, my dear Briggs,
"Yours most sincerely,
"J. C. GRANT DUFF."

* Right Honble. Sir Henry Pottinger, Bart., G.C.B., was Governor of Madras from 1847 to 1852.

In the last quarter of 1856 (although, as is often the case, there is 1857 in the title-page), General Briggs published a little book, *India and Europe Compared.** In this work he set forth once more, reduced to a very small compass, his views as to the Land Tax, the Native Army, and the more extended employment of educated Indians in the higher branches of the public service. In discussing the probabilities and possibilities of a Russian invasion, he glanced once more on our deplorable abandonment of India's true frontier by the annexation of the Punjaub. He reminded us that, "though India has suffered frequent invasions during the last three thousand years, her territorial ramparts have never changed."

" Greeks, Mohammedans, and Scythian or Tartar hordes, have one and all had to pass the gorges of the Sulimany range, before crossing the Indus at Attock, whence they entered the Punjaub. There they had to encounter the hardy mountaineers of Cashmere and the Himalaya, and passing over the fertile district of Jullundhur, found before them a desert, impassable for an army capable of protecting itself. Hence they were compelled to keep close to the Himalaya range, for the sake of water and forage, along a narrow slip of from thirty to forty miles wide ; till, after a march of more than a hundred miles, they came to the plain of Paniput, where they had to encounter the army of India."†

And he once more gave expression to the anxieties, very real and decided, though vague as to imminence and urgency, caused by the destructive and provocative policy of Lord Dalhousie.

" The present peaceful disposition of the Natives ought not to lull us into a conviction of our security.

" The several modes by which the Natives have corrected abuses, or have got rid of tyrannical masters, are familiar to them. None is more common or so effectual as to withdraw from Government altogether by the process of the 'Wulsa', or gathering, as practised in Mysore, as before described. We have seen the inhabitants of the populous city of Benares, resisting an infringement of their local privileges by the imposition of a house-tax without consulting them, quit their homes, and live for several weeks in the open fields, stopping all intercourse with the town, and obtaining universal sympathy throughout the district. We have witnessed a

---

* W. H. Allen & Co., Waterloo Place.
† *India and Europe Compared*, p. 255.

similar insurrection in Bareilly on a like occasion, which cost much bloodshed. We have witnessed a general disaffection pervading the whole of our Native Army of Madras, which commenced by the massacre of the European portion of the garrison of Vellore; and we have seen partial plots of a similar nature in other parts. It was often said by one of the wisest of our Indian statesmen (the late Lord Metcalfe), that we sit on a volcano, not knowing when it may burst forth and overwhelm us. We have more to apprehend from revolutions commencing with peaceful withdrawal from our Government, than from the outbreaks of Native Princes, who, for the most part, are not sufficiently popular with their subjects, and have no adequate resources to combat successfully against our gigantic power."[*]

"The question for consideration, as regards the Native Princes of India, is, whether it be our true interest to hasten the time when the rest of India may be subjected to our immediate rule, with the feeling of the whole of the upper classes opposed to us, or to retain and foster as long as it be possible the existent Native Princes, and gradually raise the character of their Government to an approximation with ours, and thus secure their aid in more ways than one, in case of future wars. We ought not to forget the assistance which both the Mysore and the Hyderabad Governments rendered us in the last two Mahratta wars, by bodies of efficient troops, furnished at the moment of exigency, and kept up in time of peace, nor the pecuniary aid which Oude has supplied, when our coffers were exhausted, and our credit at a low ebb, in similar emergencies. It is the tendency of our auxiliary alliances to increase the wealth of the subsidised States, and to place at our disposal their military, and in many cases their pecuniary resources.

"My own conviction is, that by insuring good government to the Native States, judiciously introduced, we shall add more to our moral and political strength than by their extinction,—a conviction which has forced itself upon my mind after a long and deliberate consideration of the subject, and after having passed a great part of my life in official intercourse with the Ministers of several Native Courts,—a conviction which it is my satisfaction to know accords with that of some of the wisest statesmen that India has produced."[†]

"Let us beware lest by injudicious measures and too hasty encroachments on prejudices held sacred among her subjects, our Government drive to desperation her teeming and brave population. Let us not calculate on keeping down insurrection by means

* *India and Europe Compared*, pp. 233, 234.
† *Ibid.*, pp. 248 to 253.

of our European troops, in case our Native Army becomes exten-
sively disaffected; for at such a season we may find that those
gallant soldiers who have gained for us an Empire (the largest, with
the exception of China, of any in the world) may be induced to
sympathise with their suffering countrymen, and either withhold
their services, or, even worse, turn those arms against us which
they have so faithfully wielded in our favour."*

In the very next year after these words were penned,
the Sepoys did "turn their arms against us". The experiences of the great Mutiny and Rebellion of 1857,
which was only suppressed by operations extending over
more than two years, at a cost of forty millions sterling
and more than a hundred thousand human lives, brought
to the minds of English statesmen of both parties a very
general conviction as to the inexpediency of the policy
of annexation. That conviction has never come home
with the same force to the Civil and Military Services of
India. Eager as ever for distinction, for promotion and
for special employment,—confident as ever in their own
special capabilities,—they have never been thoroughly
cured of the official craving for centralisation and for
uniformity, or of the Anglo-Indian contempt for the inconvenient rights and impertinent claims of "Natives".
The covenanted Civil Service and the Staff Corps are
almost as unanimously moved by the spirit of national
domination and professional monopoly as they ever
were.

With very natural predilections for his old masters and
associates, and with much reasonable justification based
on recent proofs as to the absolute action of the Cabinet
in the wars of Afghanistan and Scinde, General Briggs
could never be brought to admit that the East India
Company in any form or aspect was exclusively or even
principally to blame for the disasters of 1857, or for the
iniquities and malpractices which, as he had foreseen and
always maintained, had led up to them. Under the
system of double-government, which gave the ultimate
authority and the secret initiative at will to the Cabinet,
he held, surely with good grounds, that the Ministry was

* *India and Europe Compared*, p. 261.

far more responsible than the Court of Directors. He claimed more independence for the Court as the best cure for the defects in British control. In the following letter Mr. Grant Duff alludes to some speeches of that purport made in the Court of Proprietors during the last agony of the East India Company.

> " Campagne Livingstone, Pau, Basses Pyrénées,
> "January 18th, 1858.

"MY DEAR BRIGGS,—I have just read your speech, and also Sykes's, in the Court of Proprietors. Both have spoken well and wisely. I, however, agree with you in thinking that this terrible rebellion has been for some considerable time hatching. Many stimulants towards it have been applied, but fear—fear of compulsive conversion by *hikmut**—has been the great lever by which the ordinary Sepoy mind has been perverted. Twelve years' regimental duty,—during which time I was only absent from one muster,—nine years Linguist, and seven years Adjutant, when I was in constant contact with the men of my own regiment and of many other corps, made me as well acquainted with the Sepoy mind of the Bombay Army as it was possible for any European ever to become. I loved the Sepoys,—and well I might, for in more than one instance they proved their regard by sacrificing their lives for me; and I need not bring to your recollection that my knowledge of the Sepoys was of some use when they were sorely tried in 1817. It may also be borne in mind that the Bombay Army did, and still does, represent the whole Army of India, as, excepting your Coromandel men, we have Sepoys of all castes: and in my day, I should say we had a much larger proportion of Christians than you now state. I observe Lord Shaftesbury quotes you as having told him that Clive's Sepoys in Bengal were all low-caste men. Are you sure of that? We know, indeed, that Sepoys, as well as subsidiary alliances, originated with Dupleix. The first Topasses were the sweepings of Pondicherry, and ours were much the same from Madras. How they ran away, and how they fought, Orme's pages have well recorded. But I have always understood that Mohammed Yoosoof got the *topee* or cap changed—in name at all events—into the *puggree*, a distinction which at once admitted a · better description of men, and that such was the mixture embarked on Clive's expedition to Bengal. I have been at no pains to verify the fact, but it is of some importance at this moment; and as I see you quoted as an authority (than whom, where is there a better?), I wish to call your attention to the quotation, that you may not be accounted among the number of those who would recommend

* Trick or subtlety.

corps of entirely low-caste men. I am convinced that under the same temptation as the Bengal Sepoys they would prove even more atrocious and abominable, if that be possible, than those madmen have been.

"In matters of caste, I have had infinitely more trouble with low-caste than with high-caste men, inasmuch as pretension without foundation is always more pertinacious than when there is any solid reason for assuming forms or privileges, and therefore I would have you warn the authorities to beware of corps composed solely of low-caste, or indeed of any one caste, of Natives of India. I say of any one caste, as in fact there is no safety except in a wisely poised admixture. Goorkhas, I suppose, must be kept by themselves, but Punjaubees can mix with others.

"You may recollect I was always against too many Poorbeeas. The first time I ever met Mr. Elphinstone, in 1812, I had a very keen argument with a certain Sir Robert Colquhoun, of the Bengal Army, when I quoted the prophecy of poor Thomas Grant, of the 15th Bengal,—murdered, as you recollect, in Persia,—who said, that unless they adopted our Bombay plan of mixing all, and allowing no caste exemptions from soldiers' duties, or from pick and spade, discipline must come to an end in the Bengal Army; at which, and at many Bhurtpore anecdotes, detailed by Cleiland, Sir Robert became very wroth, and Mr. Elphinstone, though he took the Bengalees' part, laughed heartily at our respective prejudices and *esprit de corps.*

"But as late as 1832, when replying to queries from the Board of Control, I repeated the warning I gave more than forty years ago in India, as to the danger of having more than a fourth of Poorbeeas in any Bombay corps.

"But it is not the Army system alone which has led to this awful catastrophe,—the emancipation of the Native press; the Mohammedan massacre in Afghanistan, and our final evacuation of that country; our unjust and rapid annexations; the unheard-of mistake of always making the paramount authority a person new to India, appointed also by a Home authority, which overrides all Indian knowledge and experience, have all contributed. And now we are about to plunge deeper into misgovernment and crime through that irresistible popular clamour which Lord Palmerston has managed, and good, well-meaning, ignorant men have excited, under the idea that we have discouraged Christianity, and have pandered to paganism. I am sure I do most sincerely wish the Native mind were in such a state of enlightenment as to receive the great truths of Christianity; but to suppose that we can force knowledge on them, or even appear to be conveying knowledge to them with a view to proselytism,—why, it is simply *burking* the only chance of progress. We can only convert India, as we have conquered and as we must keep it, through the Natives themselves, but if we go too fast, all we have seen is nothing to the horrors we shall see.

" Of Christian Sepoys you and I have known many. I have had among them several very good non-commissioned officers. In other regiments, I have seen here and there a Christian Native officer ; but I was never able to promote one. Native Christianity is too often merely a licence to eat and drink whatever comes in the way ; and at the very time one may be anxious to promote one of these men, he may get drunk, even on duty ; and in short, until they can respect themselves, it would be unjust, and very much against Christianity, to place them in a position from which their speedy degradation would be a sort of disgrace to their creed. All I can say is, such motives as are alleged against Indian authorities never influenced me. I am writing as if I had commanded the Regiment, but the truth is that an old Adjutant must be the chief person in regulating promotions; and every officer in the Regiment always consulted me before he recommended a Naig. On duty no Brahmin, with us, ever thought of making objections to standing shoulder to shoulder with a Purwaree. We had, however, few Brahmins *proper* among our Hindustani Sepoys.

" After you succeeded me at Sattara, or just at that time, there was a most rascally trick played by a Christian writer,—a very respectable-looking fellow,—and a man whom I had always treated with only too much consideration. He was also remarkably well paid. The Bengal Government, in the midst of my terrible over-work, imposed on me the duty of selling their lottery tickets. I entrusted them to this Christian. He sold the tickets ; collected the money ; and spent it in riot and debauchery. I think it was your old friend, Yessoba, who warned me. I seized the gentleman, and finding it was all true, I kept a constant watch over him, but did not send him to jail, at the earnest entreaty of the other clerks, he protesting that he would repay the money, which he borrowed from them to make up the deficiency. I warned them of what would happen if the surveillance were removed, and for their security had him carefully watched; but a Brahmin, whom you probably recollect, as he was a Madras writer, named Butcha Rao, came forward, paid all the other Purvoes,* and begged that I would not discharge 'his friend' from my employment. I acceded to his request. The villain was always afraid to bolt while he knew the horse-dawk might overtake him, but no sooner was my back turned than he went off, and years afterwards I heard that poor Butcha Rao was thus ruined. So much for the difference in this instance between a Christian and a Brahmin. Unless I thought you recollected the circumstance, I would not bring this case

* Clerks.

S

forward; but how many more could we adduce of a moral tendency exactly opposite to what is alleged ?

"Next to fear of contrived conversion, nothing can excite and alarm the minds of our Indian subjects so much as meddling with the land tenures, for which this is a bad time. They seem to have been proceeding on a mode of settlement for Oude as hasty and imprudent as well could be; and I fear that there the *casus belli* may be our greatest difficulty, because there is a cause there, while elsewhere there may have been none,—but I must call a halt. I only meant to write three lines about Topasses, and here I am in my third sheet.

"It is too distressing to Mr. Elphinstone to read any writing, much more my horrid hand,* and I therefore refrain from writing much to him; and I would not tax your eyes, had it not been that I am sure you are not one of those who would like to be quoted as an authority for enlisting whole corps of low-caste men.

"My wife joins me in kind regards, and I am always, my dear Briggs,

"Yours most sincerely,

"J. C. GRANT DUFF."

* Mr. Grant Duff does great injustice to his handwriting, which is small and peculiarly elegant, and, for a man above seventy years of age, very firm and legible.

CHAPTER XV.

My personal acquaintance with General Briggs began in 1865, when he was in his eightieth year, and living, it may be said, in strict retirement, only leaving the pretty little house in Sussex—Bridge Lodge, Burgess Hill, his residence for the last twenty years of his life—for occasional, and gradually less frequent, visits to London. For a long period he had occupied chambers in Tenterden Street, Hanover Square, just opposite to the Oriental Club, where he was a well-known and always a welcome figure. He was at this time a man of extraordinary energy and activity, both mental and bodily, for his age. A great improvement had, by his own account, quite recently taken place in his health, which he attributed to his adoption of the dietary popularly known as "Banting", from the name of the author of a pamphlet which attracted much attention to the subject. It seems only right to give the testimony of General Briggs, from a memorandum in his own handwriting, to the efficacy of that system of diet.

" In the year 1836, after a residence of upwards of thirty-three years in India, I returned to England in impaired health, and weighed at the age of fifty-one—my height being 5 ft. 9 in.—12 stone 12, or 180 lb. I was very well in 1843, and enjoyed health until in 1858 I contracted rheumatic fever, and during the following six years I suffered severely from rheumatism and occasional attacks of gout, and for three winters was confined to the house for two or three months together on account of bronchitis, for which disease I visited annually the various thermal springs of Germany and England recommended by professional men. In 1864, at the age of seventy-nine, I read the third edition of Banting's pamphlet on Obesity, in which he proved that by a system of diet he had not only reduced his inconvenient bulk, but had relieved himself from several diseases with which he had been afflicted. I then weighed fifteen stone four pounds, or 214 lb., and was a burden to myself. I commenced Banting's dietetic system in May 1864, and continued

s 2

it strictly and regularly for twelve months, during which time I gradually lost 46 lb. in weight and ten inches in girth, nor have I found more than one or two pounds difference of weight for the last two years. I still continue it without any sensible alteration, and have lost all symptoms of any disease whatsoever.

DIET.

		Solid.	Fluid.
Breakfast .	Dry toast	2 oz.	
	One egg	$\frac{1}{2}$ oz.	
	Tea with yolk of egg . .		6 oz.
Lunch . .	Dry toast	2 oz.	
	Broth		6 oz.
	Sherry		4 oz.
Dinner . .	Fish and meat with dry toast	10 oz.	
	Claret		6 oz.
	Total .	. 14$\frac{1}{2}$ oz.	. 1lb. 6 oz.

August 1867."

The immediate cause of the introduction to General Briggs, which led to our subsequent intimacy and close association in several matters connected with Indian politics, was the effort promoted by the old Rajah of Mysore to save his kingdom from extinction at his death, and to obtain his personal restoration as reigning and ruling sovereign. So far as the more important point went,—the rescue of the State from annexation, for which a decree was undoubtedly recorded *in petto* at the India Office,—that effort was ultimately successful.

At this time I was acting in concert with Dr. Campbell, the Rajah's accredited agent in London, and with the advice of Colonel Macqueen and Colonel Gregory Haines, who, having filled high offices in the Mysore Commission, and possessed the full confidence of Sir Mark Cubbon, were designed by the Rajah to be the chief ministers of his country during any prescribed period of probation. I drafted all the despatches in which the Rajah—quite capable of understanding and sanctioning all that was going on—combated the wonderful sophistries and pre-varications of the Calcutta Foreign Office,[*] while the

* *Mysore Papers* (112 of 1866).

destiny of Mysore as a State was trembling in the balance.

A book, *The Mysore Reversion*,* which I published, to supply what was then quite deficient, a tolerably complete and popularly intelligible statement of the Rajah's case, drew from the General a very gratifying letter of thanks and appreciation, and the proposal of a conference at his chambers in Tenterden Street, to be followed by a dinner at the Oriental Club. I remember well how much I was impressed, on this first occasion of our meeting, by the marvellous vivacity of the old man of eighty, the brightness and point of his table-talk, full of special information and anecdote, poured forth in his peculiar shrill voice, without much interruption or comment on my part. From that day our communications were never broken off for many weeks together. He was as ready and fluent in writing letters as in conversation. I visited him several times at Burgess Hill, and always when he was in town; and he astonished me more than once in the two years after our first interview by making his appearance at my house, having walked nearly half-a-mile from the Metropolitan Station.

In the vicissitudes and progress of the Mysore controversy the General took the intensest interest. In the movement set on foot for saving the Mysore State he co-operated with his old comrade, Sir John Low, and his old antagonist, Mr. Casamajor, the Resident in 1832, who could not, however, be induced to meet the *quondam* Senior Commissioner on a footing of friendly reconciliation. In 1866 General Briggs took part in a deputation introduced by Sir Henry Rawlinson, M.P., to the Secretary of State for India, Lord Cranborne, now the Marquis of Salisbury, and said a few words on the unwarrantable prolongation of management by the Mysore Commission, and the advisability of restoring the country to the Rajah.

During the Parliamentary Session of 1867, I prepared a petition to the House of Commons, presented by John Stuart Mill, then M.P. for Westminster, praying for the

* Trübner, 1865.

maintenance of Mysore as an allied and tributary State, signed by many distinguished old Indians of the Civil and Military services, some of them contemporaries and comrades of General Briggs. Among these were General James Stuart Fraser, who had been Resident at Mysore, and fifteen years Resident at Hyderabad, and General Sir John Low. When I visited the latter to obtain his signature he was only passing through London—from the Continent, if I recollect rightly—on his way to his place in Fifeshire, and a slight indisposition prevented his old friend from coming up to town to see him. Sir John Low was very particular in pointing out that he had left room for a signature above his own. " Tell Briggs", he said, " that he must sign just over my name ; we were both of us Assistants to Sir John Malcolm ; but he was my senior in the Madras Army, and my senior also in the Political line."*

A little book of mine, *The Oxus and the Indus*,† induced the General to write me the following letter, the longest that I ever received from him.

" Bridge Lodge, Burgess Hill,
" 20th June 1869.

"MY DEAR EVANS BELL,—I always receive with gratitude your works which you so kindly send me, and read them with pleasure, and, I will add, with instruction. I reduce your policy set forth in *The Oxus and the Indus* to this: that in order to avoid the incessant inroads of the Hill tribes, and to promote commerce and draw closer the connection between Cabul and India, you propose to restore to Sher Ali and his successors the territory beyond the Indus, so that the Ameer of Cabul may keep the Waziris and the Afridis, *et hoc genus omne*, in order, which we cannot do, and may have reason both to fear and to trust our power on the Indus more than that of Russia on the Oxus. I am too old now to sit down and enter as fully on this great subject as I should wish. I could not do justice to it without going back to the time when the Kingdom of the Sikhs was at its zenith, when Runjeet Singh had a formidable disciplined army under Avitabile, Ventura, and others whose names I forget. But it appears to me that the greatest mistake Runjeet Singh ever made was that of turning his attention

---

* General Sir John Low, G.C.B., G.C.S.I., died 10th January 1880, aged 91.

† Trübner, 1869. Second edition, 1872.

to the conquest of Peshawur and the Derajāt, and the greatest mistake in our policy of that time was in backing him up in retaining those acquisitions against Dost Mohammed. The Sikhs never got any revenue from those Provinces without military coercion; and it is just the same in fact now: the revenue does not pay for our troops. These were, I believe, the views taken by Sir Alexander Burnes, but he was too young a man to be allowed to put them forward too prominently in 1838 and 1839. He was on his promotion, as it were, and his business was to attend to his instructions. His instructions were to demand of Dost Mohammed the relinquishment of all claim over the Afghans of Peshawur and the Derajāt, and to confirm by a treaty their conquest by Runjeet Singh. Dost Mohammed's reply was, ' We are all brothers, and I have no power over them ; nor would they at my bidding submit themselves quietly to be the subjects of a Hindu Rajah like Runjeet Singh. Even if I had now any control over them I would certainly never consent to the transfer of a Mussulman population to an idolatrous Prince.'

"These were the views of my old friend, Sir Henry Russell, formerly Resident at Hyderabad, who for many years wrote some remarkable letters to the *Times* under the signature 'Civis', which were afterwards collected in a volume. He strongly condemned the policy of extending our borders beyond the Sutlej and the Desert which embraces India properly so called : and even after the second Sikh war he advocated, as I did, the retention of Dhuleep Singh as ruler, under English tutelage, leaving the Mohammedans west of the Indus to unite, as before the time of Runjeet Singh, with their brother Afghans on and beyond the Suleimani mountains.

"I am pretty sure also that these were the views of Sir Henry Lawrence. My memory is not so good as it was, and I have no journal or correspondence to go by, but I perfectly well remember his telling me in London, before the Mooltan rebellion broke out, that he had recommended to Lord Hardinge that the heavy exactions of the Sikh Government on the Afghans of the Derajāt should be reduced to a mere nominal tribute, and that their own Chieftains should be charged with their management, on condition of peaceful submission and of their preventing all inroads into the Punjaub; but the loss of revenue, however insignificant or imaginary,—when measured against expenses,—was not to be endured by the Civilians. And I don't think I am wrong in saying that he expressed a wish for some opportunity of reconciling our Government with Dost Mohammed, and subjecting him to our influence, by having those districts restored to Afghanistan.

"There was a slight connection between Henry Lawrence and myself, from my brother James having married one of his wife's sisters, and I had many conferences and discussions with him, though we generally were of the same opinion, when he was in London. When the second Punjaub war broke out he told me that it was brought about by a breach of promise on the part of his successor, Sir Frederick Currie, at the expense of the ill-fated Moolraj of Mooltan. The promise had been made by Sir Henry Lawrence, and his *locum tenens*, who perhaps did not fully understand it, ought not to have swerved from it. Moolraj had succeeded his father as Nazim or Governor of Mooltan, over which Province they had both of them ruled like vassal Princes, paying a fixed tribute to Runjeet Singh. During the disturbances and revolutions that followed the death of the great Maharajah, Moolraj had maintained himself quite independent of the Durbar and of the military Punches, and had paid no tribute at all, on the plea that he was obliged to keep up an extra number of troops to preserve order and to protect the Province from plunder. On Henry Lawrence, as Regent for Dhuleep Singh, demanding the arrears of tribute, Moolraj declared his inability to pay such an immense demand, and was invited to come to Lahore in order that some settlement for the past and the future might be arranged. After some dispute the arrears were not insisted on, but absolute submission to the Government of Lahore was required and acknowledged, and the payment of tribute was to recommence from the date of the British occupation.

"Moolraj had at first argued very strongly for better terms, but Lawrence told him that he could only offer him the choice of three courses :—(1), to take his seat at the Council board as a member of the Regency, and appoint a Deputy for Mooltan under the Resident's terms; (2), to retire from public life; or (3), to pay up the arrears due to the existing Government from the period of its institution, and to continue as Nazim of Mooltan on the new conditions of tribute and subordination. Moolraj chose the last course.

"Lawrence's back was no sooner turned than the Durbar demanded a heavy payment in lieu of the arrears due from the date of Runjeet Singh's death. Moolraj, who was not a Sikh, but a *Banya*, was no favourite at Lahore on account of the independent character of his rule, which had been all the more independent because there were very few Sikhs in the Mooltan Province; and the members of the Regency tried to put the screw on him. Unfortunately, Sir Frederick Currie, not knowing or disregarding Sir Henry Lawrence's promise, leaned to the strict measure suggested by the Durbar. Moolraj was again summoned to Lahore, where he was urged to retire from office, with the injunction that he must produce the accounts of all his collections and expenditure, and pay up the balance due, as he understood, from the accession of the Regency presided over by the Resident, but as it appears was still intended by the Durbar, from the demise of Runjeet Singh, which would have imposed six years more of arrears of tribute upon him. The two young officers, Agnew and Anderson, proceeded to Mooltan to take charge. At their first interview with Moolraj they, however, demanded the accounts and the accumulated arrears of tribute from the death of Runjeet Singh, which Moolraj said was 'a breach of the agreement made at Lahore'. He declared that, owing to the demands made upon him by the two Commissioners, he could not pay his own troops, to whom heavy arrears were due. The troops, already disaffected from knowing that they were about to be discharged, now thought that the English Commissioners were going to discharge them without settling their arrears. They attacked the English camp, and murdered the young officers. Moolraj was thus compromised, and was probably coerced by the soldiers. He defended Mooltan as long as he could, and on the capture of the city was tried for his life, convicted, and sentenced to death, but the sentence was commuted to imprisonment for life on the recommendation of the Court, who very justly considered that he was in a great measure a victim to circumstances. Few people know what a victim he was, and how he was driven and forced into rebellion.

"In addition to these notes, I send you a pamphlet* I wrote about the same time that my old friend, Sir Henry Russell (*Civis*), was writing to the *Times* about the Punjaub. Our views did not differ, nor do I conceive they differ much from your views on the Afghan question.

"Before the disastrous retreat of our army from Cabul in 1842, I addressed a letter to the *Indian News*,—the first Anglo-Indian paper published in London, to the establishment of which I contributed with a few friends,—and I pointed out the imminent probability of an outbreak in that quarter from the hostile spirit that by all accounts began to be evinced towards us, and the probable check to our arms, if not the utter destruction of the force, if our Sepoys were compelled to march, fight, and bivouac in the height of an Afghan winter.

"Sir Henry Willock, an influential East India Director, strongly denounced the notion of trusting to our Hindustani soldiers amidst the snows of Cabul. His experience in the command of an escort of Madras Cavalry at Teheran, during two winters, convinced him that, clothe them as we might, the ordinary exercise on a fine winter's day brought on violent bowel-complaints, and that from chilblains only, the best Sepoys became perfectly useless and quite disheartened. My letter found its way into the Calcutta papers,

* *What are we to do with the Punjaub?* By Major-General Briggs, London, 1849.

and attracted considerable notice when its prognostications were so sadly fulfilled.

"These objections to campaigning in cold regions with tropical soldiery are always overlooked by those who talk of assisting the Afghans, or of conquering them, in their own country, with an Indian army.*

"On one point I do not agree with you, as to the origin of the Afghan war, and I am well acquainted with the facts. The scheme was not concocted at Calcutta, but at Teheran. Sir John McNeill, our Ambassador in Persia, was the originator of the idea. It was adopted by Lord Palmerston; and Sir John Hobhouse, afterwards Lord Broughton, admitted and indeed boasted before a Committee granted to John Bright to inquire into the origin and consequences of the Cabul disasters, that 'the Directors not only did not approve of the Afghan expedition, but they had nothing to do with it from first to last; I made it, and carried it out on my own responsibility'. Lord Auckland received his orders from the Secret Committee of the Court of Directors, *i.e.*, from the Cabinet. It is true that poor Sir William Macnaghten, who was made Envoy and bear-leader to Shah Shooja, and most of the Government House set at Calcutta, went into the project *con amore*, but they were mere executive officers, obeying the Home Government. Burnes had always taken the opposite view, and did all he could to defend and support Dost Mohammed. Sir John Hobhouse and Lord Palmerston garbled the correspondence when presented to Parliament, in order to make out that Sir Alexander Burnes had been the prime mover in the plan of restoring Shah Shooja, and that he had represented Dost Mohammed as hostile and unmanageable. But all this was disproved by the publication of duplicates of his despatches by his brother, Dr. James Burnes, and by Kaye.

"The Board of Control, in my recollection, has done an equally bad act of suppression by the denial of the existence of two strong Minutes by Sir Henry Ellis and Holt Mackenzie, both members of the Board of Control and Privy Councillors, on the validity of the Treaty of Lucknow of 1837, which was repudiated by Lord Dalhousie as never having been confirmed in England, a false pretence which was made the pivot for the deposition of the King of Oude in 1856. I know that those two Minutes, which would have dispersed Lord Dalhousie's sophistries to the four winds, were on the

---

* The General's experience did not extend to the qualifications of our Punjaubee Sepoys, nor was he aware that great numbers of Afghans were in our service, and that we could recruit them in any required number. There is no necessity now that we should march unwilling Hindustanis or other "tropical" tribes into the cold regions. All Hindustanis, however, are not unwilling or unfit for service in cold climates, nor even Madras Sepoys, with proper equipment.

records of the Department, but, with some mental reservation as to their not having been officially communicated, or some such convenient scruple or quibble, their very existence was denied.* Thus was removed the last obstacle to the annexation of Oude, a measure which, coming on the top of others of a similar character, did more than anything else to ripen the seeds of the Sepoy war, as Kaye calls it. But I have wandered from the origin of the Afghan war. As I said, this was the work of Sir John McNeill,† who had been raised to the post of Ambassador after having been Doctor to the Embassy, when he had been allowed to practise his profession among all who wished for his attendance, and to take fees wherever he could get them. This of course lowered his position in the eyes of the Court, and advantage was taken of it by the Russian Envoy to sneer at the medical capacity and antecedents of our representative. The result was that McNeill was constantly slighted, struggled in vain to uphold his proper influence, and became very unpopular and very sour. He was thus prepared and inclined to oppose the policy of Persia on the occasion of the campaign undertaken against Herat, which, according to the Treaty with the Governor-General of India in 1800, he was justified in doing. When the King of Persia marched on Herat, McNeill refused to accompany him, and encouraged the Herat Vakeel to remain behind also. He received instructions, however, from England to join the camp, and endeavour to prevent the siege. He was too late: the trenches had been opened and siege operations commenced. Soon after McNeill reached the camp, it was discovered that he was carrying on a correspondence with Eldred Pottinger, who was defending the place. One of McNeill's chuprassees, bearing a letter from Pottinger, was intercepted at the outposts and brought before the King. McNeill was furious when he heard of it, and not only demanded the release of his messenger and the delivery of any letters he might have brought, but also the severe punishment of the officer who had apprehended the chuprassee. The King, a thorough diplomatist, sent back the messenger and the letter unopened, expressing regret for what had occurred, but declined to punish the Persian officer at the outposts, who had only done his duty. When McNeill threatened to leave the camp and refer the matter to his own Government, the King remained firm, but offered to send an autograph letter of explanation to the Queen. McNeill would accept no apology, represented the case as he viewed it to our Foreign Office, and was authorised to demand his passport for England. Persia was left entirely under the influence of Russia, while Lord Palmerston and Sir John Hobhouse adopted McNeill's plan of strengthening our position in

---

* See *Punjaub Papers, East India (Annexation of Oude)*, 102 of 1858.
† Born 1795, died at Cannes in 1883.

India by seeking a quarrel with Dost Mohammed Khan, and by wantonly forcing on the unwilling Afghans a King, Shah Shooja, who had been twice expelled by his countrymen. The miserable result we know. Had our dealings with the Persians and Afghans been left from the beginning to the policy of the Governors-General of the day,—virtually nominated by the Crown, and always communicating with the Cabinet,—no invasion of Cabul would ever have been arranged at Calcutta; India would never have expended twenty millions beyond the Indus, or have plunged into the policy of annexation to retrieve the loss, or have become involved in her present predicament with the Afghans to the east of the Suleimani mountains.

I have not written such a long letter for years. Excuse erasures and corrections. Since a late attack of illness I find I am getting too old to copy my first drafts of letters, and I have no amanuensis.

"Ever yours sincerely,
"JOHN BRIGGS.

"P.S.—On speaking about our North-West frontier with a Bengal Civilian of the Punjaub school, he said that if Henry Lawrence had been allowed to have his own way, he would have squandered all the surplus revenue in conciliating the Sirdars and the Afghan tribes. How has the opposite policy turned out? Where is the surplus revenue?"

Two days later came a supplementary letter on the same subject.

"Bridge Lodge,
"22nd June 1869.

"MY DEAR E. BELL,—One word more about the Afghan war. It is fully admitted that the project was carried out by Sir John Hobhouse, who sent out his orders to Lord Auckland through the Secret Committee, without the consent or knowledge of the Court of Directors. We so far agree that the *modus operandi* and military details were left to the Indian Government, and that there was no opposition or serious objection made at Calcutta. The object was to secure protection against Persia to the Afghan rulers of Herat and Candahar. The object was a good one, and I have no doubt it could have been effected through the mediation of Alexander Burnes by means of a small subsidy to Dost Mohammed, with a supply of the munitions of war, and assurance of military aid if necessary. But instead of any effort being made to strengthen the hands of Dost Mohammed, the ruler in possession, and of whose popularity there was no doubt, or to win him over to our views, the Indian Government unfortunately became the tool of Runjeet Singh, and instructed Burnes to demand of Dost Mohammed the formal cession to the Sikhs of the districts occupied by his Afghan brethren, the liege-men of his predecessors. Failing in this negotiation, the Indian Government acquiesced in the plan of making war on Dost Mohammed, the popular Prince of Cabul, in favour of Shah Shooja, the twice-dethroned king. Shah Shooja had been for years a pensioner on the bounty of Runjeet Singh, before he took refuge in our territories, and no doubt it was a fundamental article of the first secret agreement between them, to which we afterwards became a party, that the Shah should transfer Peshawur and the Derajāt by treaty to Runjeet Singh, and should take some steps to subject the Afghan tribes to the Sikh ruler, which Dost Mohammed was unable or unwilling to take.

"Meanwhile Henry Pottinger was employed in reconciling the Ameers of Sinde to the passage of our troops into Beloochistan, and through the Bolan Pass into Afghanistan. Notwithstanding our disasters, the Ameers subsequently gave every facility for the return of our force from Candahar. They were repaid by ruin and exile. You know the whole story; and we are of one accord as to the actual state of the case. We are in a false position in the North-West, both from a political and a military point of view, and no railways will improve it. I can see no remedy but that proposed by Henry Lawrence, provided that we are quite sure of the fidelity of the Ameer, Sher Ali Khan, or that we can get a tight hold over him. Since his visit to Umballa he seems to have so fully appreciated our system of administration that he promises fairly to be a good ruler and a faithful ally. As for the Russians, they will never attempt to invade India till they have a safe *point d'appui* in Afghanistan. It will be our fault if they ever get it.

"Ever yours very sincerely,
"JOHN BRIGGS."

Before quitting the subject, I feel bound to add that with regard to the policy of drawing the Afghan State as a satellite within the Imperial system by the attraction of Peshawur, I still hold the same opinions, more strongly if possible, that I expressed in 1869. Nothing that I have heard, nothing that has occurred since then, seems to me to have had any significance or any tendency but that of strengthening and confirming that view of the question. My pamphlet was a good deal noticed at the time, and when a second enlarged edition was published in 1874; but I have never seen any intelligible argument against the policy therein recommended, except one based on strategic and military considerations, which seems to me to be so utterly unsound as to prove the very conclusion it is intended to subvert. That argument cannot be more clearly and concisely stated than in the words attributed to the noble soldier and excellent man, General Colin Mackenzie, whose counsel in 1849 had unquestionably great influence over Lord Dalhousie's decision.

"The two Military Secretaries, Colonel Stuart and Colonel Benson, now strongly advised Lord Dalhousie to secure the friendship of the Afghans by restoring the province of Peshawur, which had been wrested from them by Ranjit Singh. Sir Henry Elliot was greatly opposed to this, and wrote to Mackenzie to come immediately to camp. . . . . The Governor-General sent for him on his arrival, and asked his candid opinion. During a prolonged conversation, he proved, to Lord Dalhousie's satisfaction, that the Indus, a fordable river at times, was no boundary at all, and that our only strong and thoroughly defensible frontier was the one we already held. To give up Peshawur would be to place the Afghans inside the gate of India, instead of keeping them outside. The Governor-General acknowledged his obligations to his adviser by following his advice."[*]

Instead of keeping the Afghans "outside", exposed to outside influence, I *want* to bring them "inside the gates of India". I do not wish to enrol the Ameer as a feudatory,—which would weaken the Afghan Ruler without conferring any strength on the Queen-Empress,—but I wish to have a material guaranty for his good behaviour and co-operation in the shape of his richest and most valued Province, within the reach of the Viceroy of India.

"The Indus", exclaim certain military experts, in accord with Colin Mackenzie, "is no boundary at all",— a "fordable river" is not "a defensible frontier". Does any one really believe that we have to defend our frontier against the Afghans? It is quite true that a river is a bad frontier for a State that is always on the defensive,—for a weak State,—but it is a very good and convenient boundary for its powerful neighbour. No

[*] *Storms and Sunshine of a Soldier's Life* (Douglas, Edinburgh, 1884), vol. ii, p. 43.

one, surely, can fail to understand that Switzerland would be weaker, and more at the mercy or under the dictation of Germany or France, if she had a rich Canton in the plains.

For a full and complete explanation of the facts and arguments, I must refer to *The Oxus and the Indus.**

In carrying out the policy of engrafting Afghanistan on the Indian Empire, much would, of course, depend on the conditions, and the opportune occasion, to be determined and arranged by our Government.

If we desire to provide Afghanistan with a defensible frontier ; if we desire to keep that State under British influence ; and if we desire to prevent the otherwise inevitable and legitimate interference of Russia, we should adhere to the same strategic principles in that settlement of the frontier between Turkestan and Afghanistan that we now have in hand. Afghanistan, being a weak State, should have the strongest possible frontier on the side in contact with Russia. The territory of Herat should certainly not be advanced beyond the Paropamisus range. The Afghans should have no outlying possessions or posts, in the plains, like Punjdih, open to Russian influence, which is and must be dominant and supreme throughout the Turkoman region.

The next letter opens up another subject of growing importance, the political and constitutional aspirations of educated Indians in the great centres of our commerce and administration—a class for whom the General, referring to their adoption of our forms of address, had invented the facetious epithet of "the Esquirearchy".

> "Bridge Lodge, Burgess Hill,
> "26th June 1872.

"MY DEAR EVANS BELL,—I return with many thanks and kind regards to Mrs. Bell her entertaining work.† I seldom read novels, and have not for years read one which I have enjoyed so much. I hope she will soon give us another. I observe Mr. Disraeli, in adverting to the charges imposed on the Parent State by the Colonies, declares India to entail the most permanent and extrava-

---

* Second edition, Trübner, 1874.
† *A First Appearance*, three vols. (Hurst and Blackett, 1872).

gant drain of all. This is rather too bad, though it may be prophetically true. India has not cost us a shilling as yet, and pays for all she gets. Will Dadabhai Naoroji and the East India Association let this error pass uncorrected ? I see, also, that Lord Northbrook, in his opening address to the Natives at Calcutta, urges them by all means to study and qualify as Civil Engineers, for which duties, he says, they are especially adapted. He did not mean to mock them, of course, but any of them who knew the state of the case must have felt his advice to be a mockery. Lord Northbrook was not, I suppose, aware of the monstrous establishment at Cooper's Hill created by the Duke of Argyll for the express purpose of confining that branch of the service to our own countrymen. Dadabhai Naoroji ought not to have let a man like Lord Northbrook leave England in utter ignorance on such a subject. These legitimate grievances remain unredressed, and little notice is given to the threatened encroachments of the Esquirearchy at the three Presidency towns. Observe the last paragraph but one in the first page of the last *Allen's Indian Mail*, in which we are told that Dadabhai Naoroji's friends at Bombay—'the inhabitants of Bombay' they are called, but we know what that means—have presented a Memorial urging 'the establishment of a Corporation of at least one hundred members, and of a Town Council consisting of twenty-four Aldermen with a Mayor'; that the salaries of all executive officers of the Municipality should be fixed by the Corporation, and that the municipal funds should be at their disposal. Why, a Corporation of a hundred members would be a regular legislative assembly. Once accustom the Esquirearchy to play at Parliamentary debates, and there will soon be the *jeu de paume* in a Bombay racquet-court, or a ship-money question somewhere up country, with a Hampden-Jee at its head. The Lord Mayor and Aldermen are to fix the salaries of all executive officers, which means that they are, sooner or later, to appoint them all, and in good time to have their own Recorder and Magistrates. In a few years the Presidency towns would be a nice refuge for a Mussulman Lord George Gordon, or a Mahratta John Wilkes. I suppose I am not Liberal enough for these days. Certainly my notions of a liberal policy for India do not go in the direction of encouraging the Esquirearchy.

> "Believe me, yours very sincerely,
>   "JOHN BRIGGS."

It is not very extraordinary if General Briggs, when eighty-six years old, had not quite kept pace with the age, and had not entirely realised the changes worked in the political mind of India by half a century of English education. Still his instinct was right in the main; and those who see that the progress and propagation of Western ideas are inevitable, and should be adapted and utilised, not opposed, may yet, in a very great measure, share his misgivings. Until British statesmanship has effaced all the artificial inequalities that have been set up between the several races of the Empire by the influence of the pretentious, though petty, class of English officials, I should myself have much doubt and anxiety as to the effect of any liberal measure of self-government in India resting on an elective and representative basis. Until every British subject is a British citizen,—until the distinction of "European British subject" is no longer maintained by any Act of Parliament or of the Indian legislature,—until the Imperial Power is free, by the extinction of the covenanted Civil Service, to open a career to talent, there will be no security for peaceful progress, and the preposterous costliness of Anglo-Indian administration will remain incurable. If competitive examination is to remain as a condition of entrance to the public service, the competition must be brought within reach of every citizen's domicile. A long sea-voyage and expensive residence abroad must no longer form an almost insurmountable obstacle to the advancement of Indians in their own country. Until the true principles of Imperial rule over various nations and races are accepted and enforced by the great Council of the Empire, there may well be some hesitation as to encouraging or stimulating the constitutional aspirations of educated Indians, General Briggs's "Esquirearchy". There are many signs of India being on the verge of an epoch that might produce a Mirabeau or a Paul Louis Courier. Such personalities bring light into the liberal air; but in an atmosphere of alien prejudice and race tyranny, they scatter incendiary sparks and multiply risks of explosion.

It has been the fashion lately for the Anglo-Indian official class, and the writers inspired or instructed by them, to attribute all troublesome criticism and all presumptuous claims to one class of Indians only, whom they call

T

"Bengalee Baboos", and against whom a stereotyped form of abusive disparagement is invariably employed. But this is a very great mistake. The names of Hurris Chunder Mookerjee, of Keshub Chunder Sen, and of Kristo Dass Paul will remind those who have really looked into these matters how much has been done by Bengalees to rouse and to direct the Indian mind within this generation. The career of Lall Mohun Ghose in his own country, and the career that seems to be opening before him here, may give us an example of at least one Bengalee possessing courage, energy, and large views as well as a remarkable gift of oratory. But it is a great error to suppose that intellectual unrest and the spirit of inquiry are confined to Bengal, or that in that quarter there is the most reason to apprehend the rise of political agitation. Western India is more decided and more ready than Bengal to appropriate Liberal principles and methods, and much more likely to initiate a serious and well-organised movement against inequalities of race. There are geographical and, above all, historical conditions that place the centre of political thought and action nearer to the cities of Bombay and Poona than to Calcutta or any place in the north of India.

The last chapters of self-development and self-dependence in India belong to the Western region. The Mahratta Confederation emancipated the Hindus and extinguished Mussulman domination, destroyed the Mogul Empire, and set up religious and social tolerance. Even the battle of Paniput was a triumph and a glory for the Mahrattas. They fought in the cause of "India for the Indians", while the great Mohammedan Princes of Delhi, of Oude and the Deccan stood aside, intriguing and trimming. And though the Mahrattas were defeated, the victorious Afghans retired, and never again interfered in the affairs of India. The Mahrattas did more,—they lifted the cold shade of aristocracy and caste from the ranks of the people. They opened a career to talent, irrespective of birth and creed. High commands, the first places in council, great estates, even sovereignties, fell to men of humble origin. Moslems were welcomed to comradeship on equal terms. Brahmins were preferred for their capacity, not merely for their caste, and had to prove their capacity, in defiance of tradition and scripture, by leading armies to the field. Mahratta campaigns and conquests brought the more distant parts of the continent closer together, and made their tribes and their languages mutually known.

The Hindu revival of the seventeenth and eighteenth centuries, which paved the way for British intervention, was a movement of social and political progress, in which the Mahrattas took the lead, it may be said, unconsciously, instinctively, without premeditation or prevision. Nations never know exactly what they want, or exactly where they are going. Their struggle to keep the lead compelled the British Government to assume absolute supremacy. But, notwithstanding their subjugation, the Princes, the chieftains, and the warlike tribes of Western and Central India, have always retained a place in the popular annals and recollection as the last upholders of Indian chivalry and military honour against the arms and arts of Europe.

The closer intercourse between races and tribes,—the nationalisation of India,—begun during the Mahratta revolution, has gone on with ever-increasing rapidity under the influence of the improved means of communication, material and intellectual, with which British rule has overspread the continent. Roads and railways, sea and river steamboats, the post-office, and the electric telegraph, freedom of speech and the press, tend to efface caste distinction and privilege, provincial jealousies, and even the differences of languages. Our schools and universities have created "the Esquirearchy", well typified by Dadabhai Naoroji, and including such men as the Honble. Vishwanath Narayun Mandlik, now in the Viceroy's Legislative Council, Sir T. Madhava Rao, and many others belonging to various provinces of India. From the very fact of its comparative prosperity under the Permanent Settlement, and the large influence of its wealthy landlords, political activity in Bengal, especially in Calcutta, has hitherto been chiefly concentrated on its

local affairs and interests. General criticism of British
rule, on an extended field, and from Imperial points of
view, has occupied far more attention in Western India.
In Poona, the capital of the Peishwas, and in Bombay,
the great centre of commerce and finance for the
Deccan, Guzerat, Malwa, and the Central States, the
interrupted work of the Mahratta Confederation is carried
on by men like Dadabhai Naoroji and his disciples.   In
the proceedings of the Poona Sarvajanik Sabha, and of
several Associations in Bombay, Indians are called to
united and concerted action in politics, and strictures
are constantly published in general agreement with those
of General Briggs's work on the Land Tax, and with
Chapter VII of this book, proving to a demonstration
the inordinately expensive and exhaustive nature of
British administration.   Nor is the more delicate question of its exclusive and scornful character kept quite out
of sight. ' For my own part, like General Briggs, but
with more sympathy, perhaps, and more hope, I look
with some apprehension on the influence of " the Esquirearchy" and the much abused Bengalee Baboos.   My
apprehension is that the movement will continue to be
misunderstood and misrepresented. The educated Indians
are working in good faith and in loyalty to the British
Crown, but they have no power to enforce their instructions or their warnings.   They have not even a consulta-
tive share in the Government.   Men of this class and
calibre are at once an honour and a reproach to our
system of rule.   We have reared them, but there is
literally no place for them at our board.   They have no
hold or authority, either on the one side over the
assumed experts who direct the administration, or on
the other over the latent passions, desires, and forces of
the Indian continent.   We will not recognise them as
true interpreters ; the people will not have them as
leaders.   They are too "Native" to be acceptable to our
officials, too English to be popular.   But their work is
not without influence or without result.   With the best
intentions, with truth and right enforcing their facts and
their deductions, they are giving body and soul, senti-

ment and reason, to the general discontent. Their lessons are taken to heart by all of their countrymen who have any political interests or aspirations. They are giving, like the loyal writers and reformers in France before the Revolution, an impetus to thought and action, over which, when the fulness of time comes, they will have little or no control. Our statesmen might do well to listen to them. The secret of Empire is not to be found in Administration Reports, or in the mutual admiration of the members of an official guild.

General Briggs joined, in 1872, in another ineffectual effort to prevent the violation of an Indian treaty, and the destruction of another of our living title-deeds. A petition to Parliament and a memorial to the Secretary of State, in which he took part, could not check the scheme that had then been formed, and has now been consummated, for the degradation and spoliation of the Nawab Nazim of Bengal. On that subject he wrote as follows :—

> "Bridge Lodge, Burgess Hill,
> "8th May 1872.

"MY DEAR EVANS BELL,—Many thanks for your *Bengal Reversion*. It lets one completely behind the scenes. The mistakes of Sir Frederick Halliday and the inveterate feeling of Lord Dalhousie led us into this great wrong. But perhaps I ought not to attribute so much to the personal or free action of Lord Dalhousie, for I have good reason to believe that in Lord Auckland's time, long before the appointment of Lord Dalhousie, there was a conclave of Whig Ministers and magnates at Lord Lansdowne's place, Bowood, to discuss the policy of upholding or of absorbing the Native States, and it was decided that we should avail ourselves of all opportunities for adding to our territories and revenues at the expense of our allies and of stipendiary Princes like the Rajah of Tanjore and the Nawabs of the Carnatic and Bengal. In this direction the Bombay Government set the example by annexing the inconsiderable principality of Coluba, under the pretext that an adopted heir had no right of succession. This led the way to the more important and more impolitic cases, under Lord Dalhousie, of Jhansi and Nagpore. Lord Dalhousie only acted on the policy prescribed by the Ministers in England. The same policy led to the denial of the validity of the Treaty of 1837 with the King of Oude, duly concluded and ratified by the Governor-

General, and recognised by Lord Dalhousie's predecessor, Lord Hardinge. This denial opened the way for the annexation of Oude. It is undoubtedly true that since Pitt's India Bill of 1784, the Cabinet, and not the Court of Directors, have taken all important steps in the government of India. Soon after the deceptive effect produced by the early operations in the Afghan War, under Sir John Keane, began to clear off, there was a Special Committee of the House of Commons to ascertain the cause of the war, and I think Mr. Bright was on it. Either he or some other member asked Sir John Hobhouse, then President of the Board of Control, if the Court of Directors approved of the Afghan War, when he replied almost in these words : 'The Court of Directors had nothing to do with it. I made the Afghan War, and I believe it will lead to achievements and develop resources which the most remote fancy has not yet depicted or anticipated.' After the disastrous termination of this war, Sir John Hobhouse tried to throw the weight of it on Sir Alexander Burnes, then dead, by garbling his despatches, as proved by his brother, Dr. James Burnes, who had duplicates of the original correspondence, and published them. Sir John Hobhouse, for this and similar services to the State, was raised to the peerage.

"During the interval between 1784 and 1858, when the Crown assumed the direct government of India, the Proprietors of India Stock had the privilege, under certain rules, of calling a meeting, at which the Directors were bound to be present, and might be called to account for such measures as might be considered prejudicial to proprietary interests, Hence the Court of Proprietors became in some degree an Indian Parliament, open to the public, and where at least there was the power of exposing injustice or maladministration to the public and the press. There was, also, some little power of confirming or forbidding the grant of pensions and gratuities. The Act of 1858 has changed all this ; and though a Council, consisting for the most part of public servants long resident in India, was then instituted by way of continuing the Court of Directors, the new Councillors cannot sit in Parliament, and need not be consulted by the Secretary of State, if he chooses to act without them. I understand that they really act in small committees as the heads of the several departments at the India Office. The Secretary of State or his Under Secretary may find the Councillors useful to dictate the proper words and phrases to enable them to answer questions in either House of Parliament, as if they were thoroughly up in the subject, but they are not bound to consult the Council, except with regard to the expenditure of money, an exception which I believe they have found the means of nullifying. Sir Charles Wood said this quite plainly when asked the question in the House of Commons.

" I am shocked to perceive that the Government—whether in London or Calcutta is not quite clear—should garble a public document, as you show was done, by forming two paragraphs out of one, and suppressing that one which required of the Governor-General to pay a certain sum to the Nawab Nazim's family out of the fund reserved for their benefit.* But after the treatment of Burnes's despatches by Sir John Hobhouse, one can be surprised at nothing of this sort."

Although not properly falling within the scope of this work, I cannot refrain from here adding a letter from one of General Briggs's contemporaries—one who often co-operated with him in the Court of Proprietors—the Right Honble. Holt Mackenzie, for many years Joint Secretary of the Board of Control, in which he refers to the disin-heritance, in spite of an existing Treaty, of our earliest and most serviceable ally, the Nawab of the Carnatic. It affords another proof of the fact that Lord Dalhousie's rapacious policy was carried on in defiance, not only of every fair principle, but of all the best authority.

" 28, Wimpole Street, Cavendish Square, W.,
" 11th December, 1868.

" DEAR SIR,—I am much obliged to you for sending me your volume, of which the title,† I fear, only indicates too plainly the probable fate of any fresh appeal to the House of Commons seeking a review or reversal of the decision passed by the Indian authorities in the case of the Carnatic Nawab. I have never, indeed, had any doubt as to the hereditary title of the family, though as a Calcutta functionary and Finance Secretary in times . when the hard demands of the exchequer left little room for tenderness in maintaining the rights of the Government, I can scarcely be supposed to have taken too favourable a view of any claims adverse to those rights. But I do not wonder that opposite views should prevail when I see the strange conclusions to which so able and, in private life, so amiable a man as the late Lord Dalhousie was led by what I must regard as a kind of monomania. In truth, if the Executive of any Government is allowed to be judge in its own case, and especially if allowed to act without a full hearing of the parties opposed to it, there is no extent of injustice into which it may not fall, urged on by motives to which it gives ever to itself the false colour of zeal and public spirit. And I need not say how many circumstances must operate to make

* *The Bengal Reversion* (Trübner, 1872, pp. xv, xvi).
† *The Great Parliamentary Bore* (Trübner, 1868).

Parliament a bad tribunal to which to appeal in cases relating to India, such as you have advocated. It seems to me there is only one thing that would afford a fair prospect of justice being done. And that is a rule prescribing that whenever the Government took or withheld any property claimed by a Native Prince, otherwise than by right of warfare, the case should be referred to some tribunal acting judicially, and of course hearing counsel, and that the Government should be bound by the decision of such tribunal when formerly reported to it. We have, I believe, in the Judicial Committee of the Privy Council, such a tribunal as would well answer the purpose of securing substantial justice—certainly it would have been such when presided over by the late Lord Kingsdown. And it does not occur to me that there need be any difficulty in referring to it any case in which a Native Prince, not subject to the ordinary Courts, and consequently not protected by them, should appeal to the Crown for redress. And this could be done without any new legislative provision, though such provision is of course desirable to take the cases out of the reach of individual caprice or discretion. Had such a rule prevailed, I am persuaded we should have had no more doubt as to the right of adoption by Native Princes than there has been in the case of wealthy Natives in our provinces. And it seems to me that if your clients applied for such a rule, they would have a much better chance of success than by any perseverance in asking for a review or reversal of the decision they complain of, whether with the India Board or either of the Houses of Parliament. All, I conceive, must admit that *ex parte* decisions by persons necessarily but imperfectly informed, and without the aid of counsel, must be unsatisfactory. And every candid man must rejoice in being able by such a rule to relieve himself from the duty of being judge, without the means of forming a just judgment. But I have written much more than I intended. If the general notion be approved, all details may readily be settled. Grant Duff, I doubt not, will show himself not unworthy of the name of Mountstuart Elphinstone, and the Duke of Argyll, I should hope, has too much talent and virtue to allow any personal prepossessions to stand in the way of doing right. Of all securities for our Empire, justice, administered in a spirit of kindness and respect (I will not say toleration), is the best—the only good—foundation. God knows how soon another storm may try the strength of the Empire that looks so grandly imposing.

> "Yours faithfully,
> " HOLT MACKENZIE."

If ever the supremacy of Great Britain in India should be wrecked or grievously shaken, it will be through reliance on the illusions raised up by a self-complacent and self-interested bureaucracy. There have been some signs of late—traceable chiefly to the personal action and influence of Lord Ripon as Viceroy—of a healthy desire to court popular sympathy and co-operation in India. Every word and every measure indicating such a tendency has called forth marked disapproval and opposition from the official class, its partisans in the press, and its pensioned representatives at home. Unless our statesmen can free themselves quickly from the pretensions of experts and permanent subordinates, the immediate future of the Indian Empire will be gloomy and stormy.

The administrative directors of India, according to their own official and literary avowals, do not really believe in an Indian Empire. The word "Empire" is constantly on their lips, but they have not the smallest notion of its true meaning. Theirs has always been a policy of disbelief, distrust, and contempt. It is not in response to any invitation or encouragement from them that the leading Princes of India have recently placed their troops and their treasuries at the disposal of the Imperial Government in the prospect of war with Russia. The general judgment of the Anglo-Indian Services, as expressed on every occasion, and through every organ at their command, has always been that the armies of the Indian Princes constitute an element of danger, and must in every case be locally counterbalanced and watched by British troops.*

The rapacious policy of Lord Dalhousie's period, the realisation for a time of all their dreams and schemes of promotion and enhanced emolument, forms the sole ground for the high place that Governor-General occupies in the estimation of our Civil and Military Services. Although the condemnation of that destructive and disastrous policy by our leading statesmen of both parties, and by

---

* See, for a very fair statement of the ordinary official views, a book, full of exaggerations and blunders, *The Armies of the Native States of India* (Chapman and Hall, 1884), reprinted from articles in the *Times*, and dedicated to the Earl of Dufferin, who is advised "to imitate the policy of Lord Dalhousie".

public opinion at home, has almost reduced its admirers to silence, the practical temptation has never presented itself to the departmental mind without precept and principle at once giving way. We are told by his son, Mr. H. M. Durand, the present Foreign Secretary at Calcutta, that Sir Henry Durand, who filled that office for five years, was "decidedly opposed to the sweeping annexations of Lord Dalhousie, which, while they weakened our military position, had also unsettled the minds of our Indian feudatories, and sown fear and distrust broadcast."* Yet when two actual proposals of annexation were made, while he was at the head of the Foreign Office, those of Dhar and Mysore, both of them most iniquitous and impolitic, Sir Henry Durand was bitterly bent on absorbing both those States. His son, the present Secretary, in the book just quoted, distinctly sets forth as sound doctrine the perverse heresy as to forbidding adoptive succession by which the "sweeping annexations" of Lord Dalhousie were perpetrated and justified,—a heresy which Lord Canning and the Home Government explicitly recanted.† Mr. H. M. Durand, moreover, in that same book, wishing, as the apologist of his father, to exalt unduly a well-deserving potentate, the Begum of Bhopal, at the expense of a Prince, the Maharajah Holkar, of much higher merit and importance, says that during the mutinies and rebellion of 1857, "*State after State turned against us*". By this very erroneous assertion he betrays a curious ignorance of the annals of his own department, and suggests an unfriendly prejudice against the protected States. *Not one single State* in India "turned against us". No Prince connected by Treaty with the Imperial Government joined or favoured the rebels.‡

---

* *Life of Sir H. M. Durand* (W. H. Allen, 1883), vol. i, p. 282.

† *Ibid.* p. 286 ;—and *Letter to Mr. H. M. Durand from Major Evans Bell* (Chatto and Windus, 1884), p. 56.

‡ There were three or four instances of petty chieftains having hereditary jurisdiction, and of stipendiary Princes turning against us, but not one of them can justify Mr. Durand's misstatement. There was, for instance, the Nawab of Furruknuggur, undoubtedly a blood-thirsty traitor. The guilt of the Nawab of Banda was doubtful. The

The Bombay authorities and English functionaries, with practical unanimity, would not have hesitated, if Lord Northbrook had taken up the ordinary official parable, to have annexed the Baroda territories, when the misconduct of Mulhar Rao Gaekwar, ten years ago, seemed to afford a pretext. Let there be the smallest opening offered for creating a new salaried Commission, or for converting a Chief Commissioner into a Lieutenant-Governor, through the ruin of an allied State, and pretexts and precedents will not be wanting, or plausible proofs (as was vehemently urged while the fate of Mysore was yet undecided), that "this is quite an exceptional case".

At this very moment there is a case of annexation as bad in law and as bad in policy as any one on Lord Dalhousie's list, provisionally decided by the Bombay Government, pending the demise of the ruling Chieftain. The estate of the Vinchoorkur Chief was declared in 1819 by the Honble. Mountstuart Elphinstone, during the settlement of conquests from the Peishwa, to be held on hereditary tenure. The present Chieftain, having no son, has adopted the son of his brother, but the Bombay Government, refusing to recognise the adopted heir as the rightful successor, proposes to confiscate half the territory, and to sub-divide the remainder. The chieftainship is to be broken up, and the family degraded and impoverished, in order that lands producing about £4,000 a year—sure to be swallowed up in establishments—may be added to a Bombay collectorate. It is true that this estate is not a sovereignty, and the Vinchoorkur is not a Prince, but the principle violated is exactly the same as in the deplorable cases of Sattara, Jhansi and Nagpore; and the results in destroying a conservative centre and alienating popular feeling are identical. The Vinchoor estate has always been well managed, and the local jurisdiction well administered. The Chief may be considered to have as powerful an influence over as wide a range as

execution, after a court-martial, of the Rajah of Bullubghur near Delhi, was very like a judicial murder; that of the Nawab of Jhujjur was little better. But not one of these personages was the head of a State.

the heads of the house of Douglas or Campbell possessed
in Scotland during the sixteenth century.   The Bombay
Civilian cares for none of these things, but believes firmly
in Administration Reports, and "I have the honour
to be".

On the other hand, the Indian "Esquirearchy", typified
by Dadabhai Naoroji, whom General Briggs admired and
esteemed, though with a little old-fashioned mistrust as
to the spread of liberal and constitutional doctrines in
India, have always upheld the sacredness of treaties, and
the maintenance of Native States.   The best men in the
great Presidency cities of Calcutta, Madras, and Bombay
—those most eminent for their wealth and for their
attainments—took the deepest interest in the rescue of
Mysore, and alike in the reform and in the administrative independence of the Baroda State.   The true Imperial insight has never prevailed in the ranks of the
Anglo-Indian Services, and we shall inquire among them
in vain for the secret of reconciling order and progress on
the Indian continent.   For that secret, for clear views of
the policy of tutelary federation pointed out by the
words and work of General Briggs, our statesmen had
better turn, while there is yet time, to such men as Sir
T. Madhava Rao, and the unpretending gentleman whose
name I have unavoidably mentioned so often, Mr. Dadabhai Naoroji, who has done good work for the Empire
both as a critic of our fiscal system, and as the adviser
and Minister of Native States.   They know the fundamental truth, which has quite escaped the notice of our
Indian Secretaries, Commissioners and Councillors, both
in their acts of state and in their legislative acts, that
what the Indian Empire demands is Union, but not
Uniformity.

There is little for me to add as to the closing years
of the General's long life.   The visits to Tenterden
Street and the Oriental Club became less frequent, and
ceased entirely in 1873.   The death of Mrs. Briggs in

1870 was, of course, a great shock, and he seldom left home after that event. He was always glad to see old friends, and to talk over the topics of the day, and the subjects that had so long interested him and occupied so much of his attention. He retained full possession of all his faculties to the last. His occasional contributions to the periodical press, especially to *Allen's Indian Mail*, continued up to within two or three months of his decease. He died at Bridge Lodge, Burgess Hill, on the 27th April 1875, and would in three months more have completed his ninetieth year.

General Briggs had two sons, both of whom died in early boyhood. Three daughters survive him,—Clara, widow of Colonel Nicolay, of the Madras Army ; Julia, widow of Thomas Marsh Nelson, the eminent architect ; and Emma, wife of her cousin, Underwood French, Esq., one of the last of the learned society of Proctors. The General's grandchildren and great-grandchildren are very numerous.

PRINTED BY
WHITING AND CO., LIMITED, 30 AND 32, SARDINIA STREET, W.C.

www.ingramcontent.com/pod-product-compliance
Lightning Source LLC
Chambersburg PA
CBHW020849020726
47497CB00005B/1332